Twentieth-Century Chinese Stories

PREPARED AS ONE OF THE COMPANIONS TO
ASIAN STUDIES   *Wm. Theodore de Bary*, EDITOR

TWENTIETH-CENTURY CHINESE STORIES

EDITED BY *C. T. HSIA*

with the assistance of Joseph S. M. Lau

COLUMBIA UNIVERSITY PRESS
NEW YORK

C. T. Hsia, Professor of Chinese at Columbia University and a Fellow of the School of Letters at Indiana University, is the author of *A History of Modern Chinese Fiction* (1961) and *The Classic Chinese Novel* (1968).

Portions of this work were prepared under a contract with the U. S. Office of Education for the production of texts to be used in undergraduate education. The draft translations so produced have been used in the Columbia College Oriental Humanities program and have subsequently been revised and expanded for publication in the present form.

Copyright © 1971 Columbia University Press
Library of Congress Catalog Card Number: 72-173986
Clothbound edition ISBN: 0-231-03589-6
Paperbound edition ISBN: 0-231-03590-X
Printed in the United States of America

10 9 8 7 6 5 4 3

TO CHI-CHEN WANG

Professor Emeritus of Chinese,
Columbia University,
and Pioneering Translator of
Modern Chinese Fiction

Foreword

Twentieth-Century Chinese Stories is one of a series of Companions to Asian Studies sponsored by the Columbia University Committee on Oriental Studies. The series includes bibliographical guides, syllabi, and manuals introducing different aspects of Asian civilizations to general education and the general reader. These aids are intended to complement the basic texts and translations appearing in the series of Translations from the Oriental Classics and the Introduction to Oriental Civilizations, also sponsored by the Committee.

The early phases of this project were assisted by a grant from the Office of Education, under the National Defense Education Act, to prepare materials for use in undergraduate general education concerning Asia. It is to the credit of the responsible officials that, in pursuing this aim, they consulted with representatives of the academic community, and were prepared to support the type of program recommended to them as truly in our broadest national interest—one which emphasized the humanistic study of Asia and an appreciation of the basic values in other civilizations.

This group of representative works of short fiction by contemporary Chinese authors takes its place beside C. T. Hsia's first contribution to this series, *The Classic Chinese Novel*, and Burton Watson's *Early Chinese Literature* and *Chinese Lyricism*. Together they represent a significant advance, quantitatively and qualitatively, in the development of materials for the study of Chinese literature.

WM. THEODORE DE BARY

Preface

In preparing this volume of twentieth-century Chinese stories, I have made it a rule not to include translations from earlier anthologies nor to retranslate stories already available in English. All but one of the nine selections are newly translated, and in the case of the single exception, Miss Nieh Hua-ling's "The Several Blessings of Wang Ta-nien," I have consulted the Chinese version in revising it so that it differs considerably in wording from the earlier English version which appeared in *The Atlantic Monthly*. This principle of selection accounts for the omission of several famous names that one would normally expect in an anthology of this sort, such as Lu Hsün, Lao Shê, and Mao Tun. But while I have not aimed at comprehensiveness, it may be said that I have deliberately attempted by a new anthology to impress upon the Western reader the strength and vitality of modern Chinese fiction. I do not confidently expect success since so many anthologists before me have failed to secure his interest in that fiction, but at least, unlike some of my predecessors,[1] I have chosen all my stories for their intrinsic literary interest and their representative importance in the development of the modern Chinese short story. A number of them, I am convinced, are among the indubitable masterpieces of that genre.

The first five authors represented in this volume, from Yü Ta-fu to Eileen Chang, have received major attention in my *History of Modern Chinese Fiction* (Yale University Press, 1961). In a sense, the present

[1] Thus Mr. W. J. F. Jenner, editor of *Modern Chinese Stories* (Oxford University Press, 1970), warns the reader in his Introduction (p. vii): "In their formal and technical qualities the stories of nearly all modern Chinese writers except Lu Xun [Lu Hsün] have little to offer to those in search of literary novelty and brilliance. The main aims of this collection are to illustrate life and to see some Chinese views of the world."

anthology is a companion volume to that study and shares the conviction of its thesis that at its best modern Chinese fiction represents "a considerable achievement" despite the heavy odds with which it has to contend: "the inescapable immaturities attendant upon a literary re-orientation; the national conditions of instability and turmoil; the climate of patriotic utilitarianism; and, most important, the highhanded and eventually triumphant Communist plot to subvert literature into a mechanical form of propaganda" (p. 507). What is truly modern in modern Chinese fiction, then, surmounts these odds to achieve varying degrees of excellence even though, in the aggregate, this body of work cannot compare in subtlety and power, in magnitude and grandeur, with the best Western fiction of the twentieth century.

The modern tradition in Chinese literature has not been carried forward on the mainland since 1949, and mainly for that reason my three examples of fiction since that date are culled from Taiwan publications. I wish I had space to include some examples of the revisionist fiction subject to vehement attack by the mainland press a few years ago precisely because it is expressive of the defiant, critical temper of the earlier modern literature, but my exclusion of the standard Communist product is justified not only on artistic grounds but by reason of its easy availability in English. The Foreign Languages Press of Peking has put out translations of nearly all the acclaimed mainland novels as well as a number of short story collections of representative value. And as for the general reader without access to a large library, he should find in Mr. Jenner's aforementioned paperback anthology of *Modern Chinese Stories* enough Communist stories to satisfy his curiosity.

There has yet been no systematic survey of Taiwan fiction, and in choosing Nieh Hua-ling, Shui Ching, and Pai Hsien-yung for this volume, I am aware of my gross unfairness to several others equally deserving of inclusion. But since so little of that fiction is known in the West,[2] a few samples are better than none, and I can only hope that it

[2] A few years ago the Heritage Press of Taipei launched a series of well-printed paperback anthologies which, unfortunately, has received practically no attention in this country. The titles include: Yu Kwang-chung, tr., *New Chinese Poetry* (1960); Nancy Chang Ing, tr., *New Voices: Stories and Poems by Young Chinese Writers* (1961); Nieh Hua-ling, ed., *Eight Stories by Chinese Women* (1962);

will be possible for me or some other scholar to prepare in the near future an anthology exclusively devoted to Taiwan fiction.

The term "Taiwan literature" is in some sense a misnomer since many of the best contributors to Taiwan's literary periodicals do not live there. The three authors chosen here, as well as a number of other serious writers now in their thirties or late twenties, have been residents of the United States for some years though nearly all of them received their college education in Taiwan. Others are scattered in Hong Kong, England, Europe, and other parts of the globe. Nearly all the serious fiction writers of Taiwan and abroad are students of modern Western literature by training or personal choice, and they are thus technically and stylistically more resourceful than their predecessors in the 1930s and '40s. Unlike the latter, they avoid burning social and political issues, but they remain characteristically Chinese in their nostalgia for their lost homeland and in their intense awareness of their frustrations or lack of identity in Taiwan or abroad as a "rootless generation," in the apt phrase coined by the novelist and story writer Miss Yü Li-hua. Not accidentally, therefore, all my examples of post-1949 fiction register this sense of desperation among the Chinese—in Taiwan, in America, and in a British protectorate in the South Seas.

Joseph S. M. Lau was to be the co-editor of this volume but, regrettably, his return to Hong Kong in 1968 has made full collaboration difficult. In addition to Yü Ta-fu's "Sinking," he translated Ting Ling's famous long story "Miss Sophia's Diary." Despite my great sympathy for Ting Ling, which had prompted me to suggest that story for inclusion, it now appears to me very much dated and therefore unusable. Dr. Lau's editorial role appears even more diminished as a result, and in recompense I can only thank him for his magnanimity in not minding the story's rejection and for all the assistance he has rendered me at the initial stage of planning the book. I am also greatly indebted to my co-translators for their wholehearted cooperation. In particular, I am grateful to Professor Hou Chien for his superb rendering of Chang T'ien-i's "Spring Breeze" and to Miss Eileen Chang for undertaking

---

Lucian Wu, ed., *New Chinese Stories* (1961), and *New Chinese Writing* (1962). Chu Hsi-ning (Tsu Hsi-nin), probably the most serious writer of fiction residing in Taiwan, is represented by one story, "Molten Iron," tr. by Nancy Chang Ing, in F. Sionil Jose, ed., *Asian PEN Anthology* (New York, Taplinger, 1966).

with amazing success the arduous task of translating her own long story "The Golden Cangue."

I have edited all the translations with great care to ensure their readability and fidelity to the original and have prepared all the footnotes except those to "The Golden Cangue," which, with one exception, have been supplied by Eileen Chang herself. For several selections which I have revised extensively I feel it proper to take both responsibility and credit as cotranslator. I have not, however, altered Pai Hsien-yung's decision to make a few minor cuts in his own story "Li T'ung: A Chinese Girl in New York," nor have I completely adhered to the Chinese text of "The Several Blessings of Wang Ta-nien" in polishing its English version because the latter appeared first in print and is entitled to consideration as an independent creation. But except for these minor discrepancies and a few inconsequential emendations, all the stories parallel their originals sentence by sentence, and if any inadvertent mistranslations still remain in the book, I alone am to blame. In closing, I want to express my thanks to Miss Elisabeth Shoemaker of Columbia University Press for her expert editing, to Miss Constance Cooper and Mrs. Laura Doeringer for typing a large portion of the manuscript, and to Professors Chiang Yee, Liu Ts'un-yan, and Yao Hsin-nung for several small favors.

C.T.H.

April, 1971

Contents

A Note on Translators

Hou Chien, a veteran translator, is Associate Professor of English at National Taiwan University.

Joseph S. M. Lau (Ph.D. in Comparative Literature, Indiana University) has taught at the University of Wisconsin and Chung Chi College, the Chinese University of Hong Kong, before assuming his present post as Senior Lecturer in English at the University of Singapore in 1971. A prolific author and translator in Chinese, he has written *Ts'ao Yü*, a monograph in English on the famous Chinese playwright (University of Hong Kong Press, 1970).

Russell McLeod, a doctoral candidate in Chinese at Stanford University, is Acting Assistant Professor of Chinese at the University of Hawaii.

Wai-lim Yip (Ph.D. in Comparative Literature, Princeton University), poet and critic, is Associate Professor of English at National Taiway University, on leave from the University of California, San Diego. He is the author of *Ezra Pound's Cathay* (Princeton University Press, 1969) and translator of *Modern Chinese Poetry: Twenty Poets from the Republic of China, 1955–1965* (University of Iowa Press, 1970).

Yü Ta-fu

Like many another eminent writer of the May Fourth period, Yü Ta-fu (1896–1945) grew up in northern Chekiang and received his advanced education in Japan. While still a student there in 1921, he became a founding member of the Creation Society, a highly influential literary clique in the twenties, and published a volume of three stories called *Sinking* (*Ch'en-lun*), which immediately established his reputation as a writer of autobiographical compulsion unafraid to expose his weaknesses and fantasies. His exploration of the individual psyche as a moral theme for fiction was certainly something new, but he was not defiantly modern in the sense that he repudiated the old Chinese culture. Though far better read in Western and Japanese literature than most of his contemporaries, he shared their humanitarian and patriotic concerns, and by the early thirties, when he had exhausted his vein of fiction, a traditional sensibility reasserted itself in his essays and poems. Along with Lu Hsün, he is generally regarded as one of the finest poets in the traditional style among modern Chinese writers.

Yü Ta-fu's characteristics as a modern writer rooted in traditional sensibility are already apparent in his first volume. There his love of nature and his proud consciousness of his own worth and the world's vulgarity, while obviously showing the strong influence of Western romanticism, are also traceable to the Chinese literary tradition. But no traditional writer, of course, could have shown such strong obsession with his own sexual frustrations and equated his personal failure with the impotence of China in quite the same fashion. Though another story in the volume, "Moving South" (*Nan-ch'ien*), strikes me as a richer work of art for its ironic depiction of Sino-Japanese relations and its satiric portrayal of American Christian missionaries, "Sinking" has made a greater impact upon Chinese youth and is rightly considered a more important work of its time for its dual concern with the emotionally charged themes of sex and patriotism. The reader of the present translation, however, must bear with its narrative ineptitude and technical crudities since most Chinese short story writers of the early twenties, with the major exception of Lu Hsün, were beginners and could not yet be expected to reach competence in that Western form of fiction. The story is also very sentimental, but, as I have contended in *A History of Modern Chinese Fiction* (hereafter referred to as *History*), "precisely because of the utter discrepancy between the excessive emotion and the trivial action, 'Sinking' has generated a kind of nervous intensity which transcends its manifest sentimentalism."

SINKING

TRANSLATED BY *Joseph S. M. Lau and C. T. Hsia*

1

Lately he had felt pitifully lonesome.

His emotional precocity had placed him at constant odds with his fellow men and inevitably the wall separating him from them had gradually become thicker and thicker.

The weather had been cooling off day by day and it had been almost two weeks since his school started.

It was September 22d that day. The sky was one patch of cloudless blue; the bright sun, timeless and eternal, was still making its daily circuit on its familiar track. A gentle breeze from the south, fragrant as nectar, brushed against his face. Amidst the half-ripened rice fields or on the meandering highways of the countryside he was seen strolling with a pocket edition of Wordsworth's poems. On this great plain not a single soul was around, but then a dog's barking was heard, softened and rendered melodious by distance. He lifted his eyes from the book and, glancing in the direction of the barking, saw a cluster of trees and a few houses. The tiles on their roofs looked like fish scales and above them floated a thin layer of mist like a dancing ribbon of gossamer.

"Oh, you serene gossamer! you beautiful gossamer!" [1] he exclaimed, and for reasons unknown even to himself his eyes were suddenly filled with tears.

After watching the scene absently for a while, he caught from behind him a whiff suggestive of violets. A little herbaceous plant, rustling in the breeze, had sent forth this scent and broken his dreamy spell. He turned around: the plant was still quivering and the gentle breeze compact with the fragrance of violets blew on his pallid face. In this crisp, early autumn weather, in this bright and pellucid *ether*, his body felt soothed and languid as if under the influence of mild intoxication. He felt as if he were sleeping in the lap of a kind mother or being transported to the Peach Fount Colony in a dream or else reclining his head on the knees of his beloved for an afternoon nap on the coast of Southern Europe.

Looking around, he felt that every tree and every plant was smiling at him. Turning his gaze to the azure sky, he felt that Nature herself, timeless and eternal, was nodding to him in greeting. And after staring at the sky fixedly for a while, he seemed to see a group of little winged angels, with arrows and bows on their shoulders, dancing up in the air. He was overjoyed and could not help soliloquizing:

"This, then, is your refuge. With all those philistines envying you, sneering at you, and treating you like a fool, only Nature, only this eternally bright sun and azure sky, this late summer breeze, this early autumn air still remains your friend, still remains your mother and your beloved. With this, you have no further need to join the world of the shallow and flippant. You might as well spend the rest of your life in this simple countryside, in the bosom of Nature."

After talking in this fashion, he began to pity himself as if a thousand sorrows and grievances finding no immediate expression were weighing upon his heart. He redirected his tearful eyes to the book:

> Behold her, single in the field,
>   Yon solitary Highland Lass!
> Reaping and singing by herself;
>   Stop here, or gently pass!
> Alone she cuts and binds the grain,

[1] All italicized common words, phrases, and sentences in this translation appear in English in the original.

> And sings a melancholy strain;
> O listen! for the Vale profound
> Is overflowing with the sound.

After reading through the first stanza, for no apparent reason he turned the page and started on the third:

> Will no one tell me what she sings? —
>   Perhaps the plaintive numbers flow
> For old, unhappy, far-off things,
>   And battles long ago:
> Or is it some more humble lay,
> Familiar matter of to-day?
> Some natural sorrow, loss, or pain,
> That has been, and may be again?

It had been his recent habit to read nonconsecutively. With books over a few hundred pages it was only natural that he seldom had the patience to finish them. But even with slender volumes like Emerson's *Nature* or Thoreau's *Excursions*, he never bothered to read them from beginning to end at one sitting. Most of the time, when he picked up a book, he would be so moved by its opening lines or first two pages that he literally wanted to swallow the whole volume. But after three or four pages, he would want to savor it slowly and would say to himself: "I must not gulp down such a marvelous book as this at one sitting. Instead, I should chew it over a period of time. For my enthusiasm for the book will be gone the moment I am through with it. So will my expectations and dreams, and won't that be a crime?"

Every time he closed a book, he made up excuses for himself in this way. The real reason was that he had already grown a little tired of it. However, a few days or even a few hours later he would pick up another book and begin to read it with the same kind of enthusiasm. And naturally the one which had touched him so much a few hours or days earlier would now be forgotten.

He raised his voice and read aloud once more these two stanzas of Wordsworth. Suddenly it occurred to him that he should render "The Solitary Reaper" in Chinese.[2]

After orally translating these two stanzas in one breath, he suddenly felt that he had done something silly and started to reproach himself:

[2] Yü Ta-fu's translation of the two stanzas is omitted here.

"What kind of a translation is that? Isn't it as insipid as the hymns sung in the church? English poetry is English poetry and Chinese poetry is Chinese poetry, why bother to translate?"

After saying this, unwittingly he smiled a little. Somewhat to his surprise, as he looked around him, the sun was already on its way down. On the western horizon across the great plain floated a tall mountain wrapped in its mists which, saturated with the setting sun, showed a color neither quite purple nor quite red.

While he was standing there in a daze, a cough from behind his back signaled the arrival of a peasant. He turned around and immediately assumed a melancholy expression, as if afraid to show his smile before strangers.

II

His melancholy was getting worse with time.

To him the school textbooks were as insipid-tasting as wax, dull and lifeless. On sunny days he would take along a favorite work of literature and escape to a sequestered place in the mountain or by the sea to relish to the full the joy of solitude. When all was silent about him at a place where sky and water met, he would now regard the plants, insects, and fish around him and now gaze at the white clouds and blue sky and feel as if he were a sage or hermit who had proudly detached himself from the world. Sometimes, when he ran into a peasant in the mountain, he would imagine himself to be Zarathustra and would repeat Zarathustra's sayings in front of the peasant. His *megalomania*, in exact proportion to his *hypochondria*, was thus intensified each day. Small wonder that, in a mood like this, he didn't feel like going to school and applying himself to the mechanical work. Sometimes he would skip classes for four or five days in a row.

And when he was in school he always had the feeling that everyone was staring at him. He made every effort to dodge his fellow students, but wherever he went, he just couldn't shake off that uncomfortable suspicion that their malevolent stare was still fixed on him.

When he attended classes, even though he was in the midst of all his classmates, he always felt lonely, and the kind of solitude he felt among a press of people was far more unbearable than the kind he experienced when alone. Looking around, he always found his fellow students engrossed in the instructor's lecture; only he, despite his physical presence in the classroom, was wandering far and wide in a state of reverie.

At long last the bell rang. After the instructor had left, all his classmates were as lively and high-spirited as swallows newly returned in spring—chatting, joking, and laughing. Only he kept his brows knit and uttered not a sound as if his tongue were tethered to a thousand-ton rock. He would have liked to chat with his fellow students but, perhaps discouraged by his sorrowful countenance, they all shunned his company and went their own ways in pursuit of pleasure. For this reason, his resentment toward them intensified.

"They are all Japanese, all my enemies. I will have my revenge one day; I'll get even with them."

He would take comfort in this thought whenever he felt miserable. But when in a better mood, he would reproach himself thus: "They are Japanese and of course they don't have any sympathy for you. It's because you want their sympathy that you have grown to hate them. Isn't this your own mistake?"

Among his more sympathetic fellow students some did approach him, intending to start a conversation. But although he was very grateful and would have liked to open his heart to them, yet in the end he wouldn't say anything. As a result, even they respected his wishes and kept away from him.

Whenever his Japanese schoolmates laughed and joked in his presence, his face would redden because he thought they were laughing and joking at his expense. He would also flush if, while conversing, one of these students threw a glance at him. Thus, the distance between him and his schoolmates became greater each day. They all took him to be a loner and avoided his presence.

One day after school he was walking back to his inn, satchel in hand. Alongside him were three Japanese students heading in the same direction. Just as he was about to reach the inn, there suddenly appeared before him two girl students in red skirts. His breathing quickened, for girl students were a rare sight in this rural area. As the two girls tried to get by, the three Japanese boys accosted them, "Where are you going?"

Coquettishly the two girls answered, "Don't know, don't know."

The three students all laughed, pleased with themselves. He alone hurried back to his inn, as if he had done the accosting. Once in his room, he dropped his satchel on the tatami floor and lay down for a rest (the Japanese sit as well as sleep on the tatami). His heart was still beating wildly. Placing one hand underneath his head and another on his chest, he cursed himself:

"You coward fellow, you are too coward! If you are so shy, what's there for you to regret? If you now regret your cowardice, why didn't you summon up enough courage to talk to the girls? *Oh, coward, coward!"*

Suddenly he remembered their eyes, their bright and lively eyes. They had really seemed to register a note of happy surprise on seeing him. Some second thoughts on the matter, however, prompted him to cry out:

"Oh, you fool! Even if they appeared interested, what are they to you? Isn't it quite clear that their ogling was intended for the three Japanese? Oh, the girls must have known! They must have known that I am a Chinaman; otherwise why didn't they even look at me once? Revenge! Revenge! I must seek revenge against their insult."

At this point in his monologue, a few icy teardrops rolled down his burning cheeks. He was in the utmost agony. That night, he put down in his diary:

"Why should I have come to Japan? Why should I have come here to pursue my studies? Since you have come, is it at all surprising that you should be treated by the Japanese with contempt? China, O my China! Why don't you grow rich and strong! I cannot bear your shame in silence any longer!

"Isn't the scenery in China as beautiful? Aren't the girls in China as pretty? Then why should I have chosen to come to this island country in the eastern seas?

"And even if I accept the fact that I have already come here, there is no reason why I should have entered this cursed 'high school.' [3] Those who have returned to China after studying only five months here, aren't they now enjoying their success and prosperity? How can I bear

[3] A Japanese "high school" of the early modern period provided an education equivalent to the last two years of an American high school and the first two years of college.

the five or six years that still lie ahead of me? And how can I be sure
that, even if I managed to finish my long years of studies despite the
thousand vexations and hardships, I would be in any way better off
than those so-called returned students who came here simply for fun?

"One may live to a hundred, but his youth lasts only seven or eight
years. What a pity that I should have to spend these purest and most
beautiful seven or eight years in this unfeeling island country. And,
alas, I am already twenty-one!

"Dead as dried wood at twenty-one!

"Dead as cold ashes at twenty-one!

"It would be much better for me to turn into some kind of mineral,
for it's unlikely that I will ever bloom.

"I want neither knowledge nor fame. All I want is a 'heart' that can
understand and comfort me, a warm and passionate heart and the sympathy that it generates and the love born of that sympathy!

"What I want is love.

"If there were one beautiful woman who understood my suffering, I
would be willing to die for her.

"If there were one woman who could sincerely love me, I would
also be willing to die for her, be she beautiful or ugly.

"For what I want is love from the opposite sex.

"O ye Heavens above, I want neither knowledge nor fame nor useless lucre. I shall be perfectly satisfied if you can grant me an 'Eve'
from the Garden of Eden, allowing me to possess her body and soul."

III

His home was in a small town on the Fu-ch'un River, about eighty or
ninety li from Hangchow. The river originates in Anhwei and mean-
ders through the length of Chekiang. Because it traverses a long tract
of variegated landscape, a poet of the T'ang dynasty wrote in admiration that "the whole river looks like a painting." When he was fourteen, he had asked one of his teachers to write down this line of four
characters for him and had it pasted on the wall of his study. His study
was not a big one, but since through its small window he could view
the river in its ever-changing guises in rain and shine, morning and
evening, spring and autumn, it had been to him as good as Prince

T'eng's tall pavilion.[4] And it was in this small study that he had spent more than ten years before coming with his elder brother to Japan for study.

When he was three his father had passed away, leaving the family in dire poverty. His elder brother, however, managed to graduate from W. University in Japan, and upon his return to Peking, he earned the *chin-shih* degree and was appointed to a position in the Ministry of Justice. But in less than two years the Republican revolution started in Wuchang. He himself had by then finished grade school and was changing from one middle school to another. All his family reproved him for his restlessness and lack of perseverance. In his own view, however, he was different from other students and ought not to have studied the same prescribed courses through the same sequence of grades. Thus, in less than half a year, he transferred from the middle school in the city K. to one in the city H. where, unfortunately, he stayed less than three months owing to the outbreak of the revolution. Deprived of his schooling in the city H, he could only return to his own little study.

In the spring of the following year he was enrolled in the preparatory class for H. College on the outskirts of Hangchow. He was then seventeen. Founded by the American Presbyterian Church, the college was notorious for its despotic administration and the minimal freedom it allowed its students. On Wednesday evenings they were required to attend vespers. On Sundays they were not allowed to go out or read secular books—they could only pray, sing psalms, or read the Old and New Testaments. They were also required to attend chapel every morning from nine to nine twenty: the delinquent student would get demerits and lower grades. It was only natural that, as a lover of freedom, he chafed under such superstitious restrictions, fond as he was of the beautiful scenery around the campus. He had not yet been there half a year when a cook in the employ of the college, counting on the president's backing, went so far as to beat up students. Some of his more indignant schoolmates went to the president to complain, only to be told that they were in the wrong. Finding this and similar injustices altogether intolerable, he quit the school and returned to his own little study. It was then already early June.

[4] Celebrated in the T'ang poet Wang Po's lyrical prose composition, "T'eng Wang ko hsü."

He had been home for more than three months when the autumn winds reached the Fu-ch'un River and the leaves of the trees on its banks were about to fall. Then he took a junk down the river to go to Hangchow where, he understood, the W. Middle School at the Stone Arch was just then recruiting transfer students. He went to see the principal Mr. M. and his wife and told them of his experience at H. College. Mr. M. allowed him to enroll in the senior class.

It turned out, however, that this W. Middle School was also church-supported and that this Mr. M. was also a muddle-headed American missionary. And academically this school was not even comparable to the preparatory class at H. College. After a quarrel with the academic dean, a very contemptible character and a graduate of H. College as well, he left W. Middle School in the spring. Since there was no other school in Hangchow to his liking, he made no plans to be admitted elsewhere.

It was also at this time that his elder brother was forced to resign his position in Peking. Being an upright man of strict probity and better educated than most of his colleagues in the ministry, he had invited their fear and envy. One day a "personal friend" of a certain vice minister asked for a post and he stubbornly refused to give him one; as a result, that vice minister disagreed with him on certain matters and in a few days he resigned his post to serve in the Judicial Yuan. His second elder brother was at that time an army officer stationed in Shaohsing. He was steeped in the habits of the military and therefore loved to squander money and associate with young gallants. Because these three brothers happened at the same time to be not doing too well, the idlers in their home town began to speculate whether their misfortune was of a geomantic nature.

After he had returned home, he shut himself in his study all day and sought guidance and companionship in the library of his grandfather, father, and elder brother. The number of poems he wrote in his diary began to grow. On occasions he also wrote stories in an ornate style featuring himself as a romantic knight-errant and the two daughters of the widow next door as scions of nobility. Naturally the scenic descriptions in these stories were simply idyllic pictures of his home town. Sometimes, when the mood struck him, he would translate his own stories into some foreign language, employing the simple vocabulary at his command. In a word, he was more and more enveloped in a world of fantasy, and it was probably during this time that he sowed the seeds of his hypochondria.

He stayed at home for six months. In the middle of July, however, he got a letter from his elder brother saying: "The Judicial Yuan has recently decided to send me to Japan to study its judicial system. My acceptance has already been forwarded to the minister and a formal appointment is expected in a few days. I will, however, go home first and stay for a while before leaving for Japan. Since I don't think idling at home will do you any good, this time I shall take you with me to Japan." This letter made him long for his brother's return though he did not arrive from Peking with his wife until the latter part of September. After a month's stay, they sailed with him for Japan.

Though he was not yet awakened from his *dreams of the romantic age*, upon his arrival in Tokyo, he nevertheless managed to pass the entrance examination for Tokyo's First High School after half a year. He would be in his nineteenth year in the fall.

Just when the First High School was about to open, his elder brother received word from the minister that he should return. Thus his brother entrusted him to the care of a Japanese family and a few days later returned with his wife and newborn daughter.

The First High School had set up a preparatory program especially for Chinese students so that upon completing that program in a year they could enroll along with the Japanese students in regular courses of study in the high school of their choice. When he first got into the program, his intended major was literature. Later, however, when he was about to complete the course, he changed to medicine, mainly under pressure from his brother but also because he didn't care much either way.

After completing his preparatory studies, he requested that he be sent to the high school in N. City, partly because he heard it was the newest such school in Japan and partly because N. City was noted for its beautiful women.

IV

In the evening of August 29, in the twentieth year of his life, he took a night train all by himself from Tokyo's central station to N. City.

It was probably the third or fourth day of the seventh month in the old calendar. A sky the color of bluish-purple velvet was studded with stars. The crescent moon, hooked in the western corner of the sky, looked like the untinted eyebrow of a celestial maiden. Sitting by the window in a third-class coach, he silently counted the lights in the houses outside. As the train steadily surged ahead through the black mists of the night, the lights of the great metropolis got dimmer and dimmer until they disappeared from his ken. Suddenly his heart was overtaken by a thousand melancholy thoughts and his eyes were again moist with warm tears. *"Sentimental, too sentimental!"* he exclaimed. Then, drying his tears, he felt like mocking himself:

"You don't have a single sweetheart, brother, or close friend in Tokyo—so for whom are you shedding your tears? Perhaps grieving for your past life or feeling sad because you have lived there for the last two years? But haven't you been saying you don't care for Tokyo?

"Oh, but how can one help being attached to a place even after living there for only one year?

> The orioles know me well because I have long lived here;
> When I am getting ready to leave, they keep crying, four or five sad notes at a time." [5]

Then his rambling thoughts turned to the first Puritans embarking for America: "I imagine that those cross-bearing expatriates were no less grief-stricken than I am now when sailing off the coast of their old country."

The train had now passed Yokohama and his emotions began to quiet down. After collecting himself for a while, he placed a postcard on top of a volume of Heine's poetry and with a pencil composed a poem intended for a friend in Tokyo:

> The crescent barely rising above the willows,
> I again left home for a distant horizon,
> First pausing in a roadside tavern crowded with revelers,
> Then taking off in a carriage as the street lights receded.
> A youth inured to partings and sorrows has few tears to shed;

[5] A couplet from a quatrain by the T'ang poet Jung Yü, entitled "I-chia pieh hu-shang-t'ing" (Bidding goodbye to the pavilion on the lake on the occasion of moving my home). I am indebted to Professor Chiang Yee for this identification.

The luggage from a poor home consists only of old books.
At night the reeds find their roots stirred by autumn waters—
May you get my message at South Bank!

Then after resting for a while, he read some of Heine's poetry under a dim light bulb:

Lebet wohl, ihr glatten Säle,
Glatte Herren, glatte Frauen!
Auf die Berge will ich steigen,
Lachend auf euch niederschauen! [6]

But with the monotonous sound of the wheels pounding against his eardrums, in less than thirty minutes he was transported into a land of dreams.

At five o'clock dawn began to break. Peering through the window, he was able to discern a thread of blue making its way out of the nocturnal darkness. He then stuck his head out the window and saw a picturesque scene wrapped in haze. "So it's going to be another day of nice autumn weather," he thought. "How fortunate I am!"

An hour later the train arrived at N. City's railroad station. Alighting from the train, he saw at the station a Japanese youth wearing a cap marked by two white stripes and knew him for a student of the high school. He walked toward him and, lifting his cap slightly, asked, "How do I find the X. High School?" The student answered, "Let's go there together." So he left the station together with the student and took a trolley in front of its entrance.

The morning was still young and shops in N. City were not yet open. After passing through several desolate streets, they got off in front of the Crane Dance Park.

"Is the school still far off?" he asked.

"About two li."

The sun had risen by the time they were walking the narrow path between the rice fields after crossing the park, but the dewdrops were still on the rice stalks, bright as pearls. Across the fields in front were clusters of trees shading several scattered farmhouses. Two or three chimneys rising above these structures seemed to float in the early

[6] The author's note on the source, as well as his Chinese translation of the quatrain, which follows the German in the original text, is omitted here.

morning air, and bluish smoke emanating therefrom curled in the sky like incense. He knew that the farmers were preparing breakfast.

He inquired at an inn near by the school and was informed that the few pieces of luggage sent out the previous week had already arrived. The innkeeper, used to Chinese lodgers, gave him a hearty welcome. After unpacking, he had the feeling that the days ahead promised much joy and pleasure.

But all his hopes for the future were mocked by reality that very evening. For his home town, however small, was a busy little town, and while he had often felt lonely amid large throngs in Tokyo, nevertheless the kind of city life there was not too different from what he had been accustomed to since childhood. Now this inn, situated in the countryside of N. City, was far too isolated. To the left of its front door was a narrow path cutting across the rice fields; only a square pond to the west of the inn provided some diversity to the scene. Since school had not yet begun, students had not yet returned and thus he was the only guest in this spacious hostel. It was still not too unbearable in the day, but that evening, when he pushed open the window to look out, everywhere was pitch darkness. For the countryside of N. City was a large plain, with nothing to obstruct one's view. A few lights were visible in the distance, now bright and now dim, lending to the view a spectral quality. Up above the ceiling he could hear the scampering rats fighting for food, while outside the window several *wu-t'ung* trees would rustle whenever there was a breeze. Because his room was on the second floor, the rattle of the leaves sounded so close that he was frightened almost to the point of tears. He had never felt a stronger nostalgia than that evening.

He got to know more people after school started, and his extremely sensitive nature also became adapted to the pastoral environment. In less than three months he had become Nature's child, no longer separable from the pleasures of the countryside.

His school was located on the outskirts of N. City which, as has already been mentioned, were nothing but open fields offering broad horizons of unobstructed vision. At that time Japan was not so industrialized and populous as it is now. Hence this large area of open space around the school diversified only by clumps of trees and little knolls and mounds. Except for a few stationery shops and restaurants serving

the needs of the students, there were no other stores in the neighbor-
hood. A few inns, however, dotted the cultivated fields in this mainly
untilled wilderness. After supper he would put on his black serge man-
tle and, a favorite book in hand, take a walk in the lingering glow of
the setting sun. Most probably it was during these *idyllic wanderings*
that he developed his passion for nature.

So at a time when competition was not as keen as today and leisure
was as plentiful as in the Middle Ages he spent half a year of dreamlike
existence in a quiet retreat simple in its manners and uncontaminated
by the presence of philistines. These happy days and months seemed to
go by in a twinkling.

The weather was now getting milder and the grass was turning
green under the influence of warm breezes. The young shoots in the
wheat fields near the inn were growing taller inch by inch. With all
nature responding to the call of spring, he, too, felt more keenly the
urge implanted in him by the progenitors of the human race. Unflag-
gingly, he would sin every morning underneath his quilt.

He was ordinarily a very self-respecting and clean person, but when
evil thoughts seized hold of him, numbing his intellect and paralyzing
his conscience, he was no longer able to observe the admonition that
"one must not harm one's body under any circumstances since it is in-
herited from one's parents." Every time he sinned he felt bitter remorse
and vowed not to transgress any more. But, almost without exception,
the same visions appeared before him vividly at the same time the next
morning. All those descendants of Eve he would normally meet in the
course of the day came to seduce him in all their nakedness, and the
figure of a middle-aged *madam* appeared to him even more tempting
than that of a virgin. Inevitably, after a hard struggle, he succumbed to
temptation. Thus once, twice, and this practice became a habit. Quite
often, after abusing himself, he would go to the library to look up
medical references on the subject. They all said without exception that
this practice was most harmful to one's health. Since then his fear had
increased.

One day he learned somewhere in a book that Gogol, the founder of
modern Russian literature, also suffered from this sickness and was not
able to cure himself to the day of his death. This discovery comforted
him somewhat, if only because no less a man than the author of *Dead*

Souls was his fellow sinner. But this form of self-deception could do little to remove the worry in his heart.

Since he was very much concerned about his cleanliness and health, he now took a bath and had milk and several raw eggs every day. But he couldn't help feeling ashamed of himself when taking his bath or having his milk and eggs: all this was clear evidence of his sin.

He felt that his health was declining day by day and his memory weakening. He became shy and especially uncomfortable in the presence of women. He grew to loathe textbooks and turned increasingly to French naturalistic novels as well as a few Chinese novels noted for their pornography. These he now read and reread so many times that he could almost recite them from memory.

On the infrequent occasions when he turned out a good poem he became overjoyed, believing that his brain had not yet been damaged. He would then swear to himself: "My brain is all right, since I can still compose such a good poem. I mustn't do that sort of thing again. The past I can no longer help, but I shall control myself in the future. If I don't sin again, my brain will be in good shape." But when that critical moment came each morning, he again forgot his own words.

On every Thursday and Friday or on the twenty-sixth and twenty-seventh of every month he abandoned himself to this pleasure without qualms, for he thought that he would be able to stop by next Monday or next month. Sometimes when he happened to have a haircut or a bath on a Saturday evening or the evening of the last day of the month, he would take that as a sign of his reformation. But only a few days later he would have to resume his diet of milk and eggs.

Hardly a day passed in which he was not troubled by his own fears as well as by his sense of guilt, and his hypochondria worsened. He remained in such a condition for about two months and then the summer vacation began. However, he suffered even worse during the two-month vacation than before: for by the time school resumed, his cheekbones had become even more prominent, the bluish-gray circles around his eyes even bigger, and his once-bright pupils as expressionless as those of a dead fish.

V

Again it was fall. The big blue firmament seemed to be suspended higher and higher each day. The rice fields around his inn had now turned the color of gold. When the chilly winds of morning or evening cut into his skin like a dagger, he knew that those bright autumn days were not far behind.

The week before, he had taken along a volume of Wordsworth and strolled on the paths in the fields for a whole afternoon. From that day on he had not been able to free himself from the spell of his cyclic hypochondria. Moreover, the two girl students he had met a few days before stayed in his memory and he couldn't help blushing whenever he recalled that encounter.

Recently, wherever he went, he was unable to remain at ease. At school he had the feeling that his Japanese classmates were avoiding him. And he no longer wanted to visit his Chinese classmates simply because after each such visit his heart felt all the more empty. Those Chinese friends of his, hard as they tried, still couldn't understand his state of mind. Before each visit he expected to earn their sympathy, but it turned out that no sooner had they exchanged a few words than he began to regret his visit. There was one, however, whose conversation he enjoyed, and sometimes he told him all about his private and public life. On his way home, however, he always regretted having talked so much and ended up in a worse state of self-reproach than before. For this reason a rumor circulated among his Chinese friends that he was mentally sick. When the rumor reached him, he wanted as much to avenge himself on these few Chinese friends as on his Japanese schoolmates. He was finally so alienated from the Chinese that he wouldn't even greet them when he met them in the street or on the campus. Naturally he didn't attend any of the meetings for Chinese students, so that he and they became virtual enemies.

Among these Chinese students there was one eccentric. Probably because there was something reprehensible about his marriage, he seemed to take particular delight in malicious gossip—partly as a means of covering up his own immoral conduct. And it was none other than this eccentric who had spread the rumor that he was mentally sick.

His loneliness became most intolerable after he had cut himself off from all social contacts. Fortunately, the innkeeper's daughter held some attraction for him, for otherwise he could really have committed suicide. She was just seventeen and had an oblong face and big eyes. Whenever she smiled, she showed two dimples and one gold tooth, and quite often she put a smile on her face, confident of its charm.

Although he was very fond of her, yet when she came in to make his bed or deliver his meals, he always put on an air of aloofness. And however badly he wanted to talk to her, he never did because he could hardly breathe in front of her. To avoid this kind of insufferable agony, he had lately tried to leave his room as soon as she entered it. But the more he tried to avoid her, the more he longed for her.

One Saturday evening all the other students in the inn had gone to N. City to amuse themselves. For economic reasons he didn't go there. He returned to his room following a brief after-dinner stroll around the pond on the west side. But it was difficult for him to stay by himself on the deserted second floor and soon he got impatient and wanted to go out again. To leave the place, however, meant passing the door of the innkeeper's own room, which was situated right by the main entrance, and he remembered that the innkeeper and his daughter were just having dinner when he returned. At this thought he no longer had the desire to go out again, since seeing her would mean another torturing experience.

Instead, he took out a novel by George Gissing and started to read but, before he had finished three or four pages, he heard, in the dead silence, some splashings of water. He held his breath and listened for a while, and soon he started panting and his face turned all red. After some moments of hesitation, he pushed open the door quietly and, taking off his slippers, went down the stairs stealthily. With the same kind of caution he pushed open the door to the toilet and stood by its glass window to peep into the bathroom (the bathroom was adjacent to the toilet; through the glass window one could see the goings-on in the bathroom). At first he thought he would be content with just a glance. But what he saw in the next room kept him completely nailed down.

Those snow-white breasts! Those voluptuous thighs! And that curvaceous figure!

Holding his breath, he took another close look at the girl and a muscle in his face began to twitch. Finally he became so overwrought that his forehead hit the windowpane. The naked Eve then asked across the steam, "Who is it?" Without making a sound, he hurriedly left the toilet and rushed upstairs.

Back in his room he felt his face was burning and his mouth parched. To punish himself, he kept slapping his own face while taking out the bedding to get ready for sleep. But he could hardly fall asleep. After tossing and turning under the quilt for a while, he strained his ears and concentrated all his attention on the movements downstairs. The splashing had stopped, and he heard the bathroom door open. And judging by the sound of her footsteps, he was positive she was coming upstairs. Immediately he buried his head beneath the quilt and listened to the whisper of his inner voice, "She is already outside the door." He felt as if all his blood were rushing to his head. Certainly he was now in a state of unusual excitement, compounded of fear, shame, and joy, but if someone had asked him at this moment, he would have denied that he was filled with joy.

Holding his breath, he strained his ears and listened—it was all quiet on the other side of the door. He coughed on purpose—still no response. But just as he was getting puzzled, he heard her voice downstairs talking with her father. Hard as he tried (he was so tense that his palms were soaked in sweat), he still couldn't make out anything she was saying. Presently her father roared with laughter. Burying his head underneath the quilt, he said through clenched teeth, "So she has told him! She has told him!"

He didn't get a wink of sleep that night. Early next morning he stole downstairs to make a quick toilet and rushed out of the inn. It was not yet time for the innkeeper and his daughter to get up.

The sun was rising, but the dew-drenched dust on the road had not yet dried. Without knowing exactly where to go, he headed east and before long saw a peasant pushing a cart of vegetables coming his way. "Good morning," the peasant greeted him as their shoulders brushed. This took him by surprise, and immediately his emaciated face flushed red. He wondered, "So he also knows my secret?"

After walking hurriedly without any sense of direction for a long while, he turned his head and saw that he was already a great distance from his school. The sun had now risen. He wanted to ascertain the time but could not do so since he had forgotten to take his silver pocket watch along. Judging by the position of the sun, it was probably about nine o'clock. He was very hungry, but unwilling to go back and face the innkeeper and his daughter, though all he had on him was twelve cents, hardly enough for a decent snack. Finally he bought from a village grocery store twelve cents' worth of food, intending to eat it in a nook unseen by others.

He kept walking until he reached a crossroads. There were very few pedestrians on the side path running from north to south. As its south side sloped downward flanked by two precipices, he knew that the path had been dug out of a hill. Thus the crossroads was the tip of the hill, while the main path on which he had been walking was its ridge and the intersecting side path sloped in two directions following the contour of the hill. He paused at the crossroads for a while before choosing the southern path flanked by precipices, and at its termination he came upon a large plain which, he knew, would lead to the city.

Across the plain was a dense grove where, he thought, the A. Shinto Temple was located. When he had reached the end of the path, he saw that there stood upon its left precipice a parapet encircling a few cottages. Above the door of one of these cottages hung a tablet inscribed with three Chinese characters, *hsiang hsüeh hai* (sea of fragrant snow).[7] He walked up a few steps to the entrance of the parapet and with one push opened both leaves of the door. Stepping casually inside, he found a winding path leading uphill flanked by a great many old *mei* trees and knew for sure that this was a *mei* grove. He walked up the northern slope along this winding path until he reached the hilltop where he saw stretching before him a plateau of great scenic beauty. From the foot of the hill to the plateau, the whole grove covering the surface of the slope was most tastefully planned.

West of the plateau was the precipice, which faced another across the gulf, and down below was the narrow pathway he had just traversed. Aligned on the edge of this precipice were a two-story house and several cottages. Since all their doors and windows were tightly shut, he knew that they were restaurants and taverns, open only during the season of the *mei* blossoms. In front of the two-story house was

[7] A traditional metaphor for a grove of *mei* or Japanese apricot trees.

a lawn with a ring of white rocks at its center, and inside the ring an old *mei* tree crouched on its gnarled trunk. At the outer edge of the lawn marking the beginning of the southern slope stood a stone tablet recording the history of the grove. He sat on the grass in front of the tablet and started eating the food he had bought in the grocery store.

He sat on the lawn for a while even after he had finished breakfast. There were no human voices around; only from the trees in the farther distance came the occasional chirping of birds. Gazing at the azure sky, he felt that everything around him—the trees and houses, the lawn and birds—was being equally nourished by Nature, under the benign influence of the sun. In face of all this, his memory of last night's sin vanished like a boat sailing beyond the outer rim of the sea.

From the plateau to the end of the downhill slope there were many little winding paths. He got up and took a random walk among these until he came to a cottage situated midway on the slope surrounded by *mei* trees. Nearby on the east side was an ancient well covered with a heap of pine needles. He turned the handle of the pump several times trying to draw up some water, but the machine only creaked and no water came up. He thought, "Probably this grove is open only during the flowering season. No wonder there's no one around." Then he murmured as another thought flashed upon him, "Since the grove is unoccupied, why don't I go and ask the owner if I could lodge here for a while?"

This decided, he rushed downhill to look for the owner. As he came near the entrance, he ran into a peasant around fifty years of age coming into the grove. He apologized and then inquired, "Do you know who owns this place?"

"It's under my management."

"Where do you live?"

"Over there." The peasant pointed to a little house on the west side of the main path. Following his direction, he saw the house on the far end of the western precipice and nodded to acknowledge its existence. Then he asked, "Can you rent me that two-story house inside the grove?"

"Sure. But are you by yourself?"

"Yes."

"Then you might as well save yourself the trouble."

"Why?"

"Because I have had student tenants before and they hardly stayed more than ten days before they moved out, probably because they couldn't stand the solitude."

"I am quite different from the others. I won't mind the solitude as long as you agree to rent the place to me."

"I can't think of any reason why not. When do you want to move in?"

"How about this afternoon?"

"It's all right with me."

"Then may I trouble you to clean it up before I move in?"

"Certainly, certainly. Good-by!"

"Good-by."

VI

After he had moved to the *mei* grove, his hypochondria took a different turn.

Over some trivial matters he had started a quarrel with his elder brother, which prompted him to mail to Peking a long, long letter severing ties of kinship. But after that letter was sent, he mused for many an hour in front of his house. He thought he was the most miserable man in the world. Actually, he was the one to blame for this fraternal split, but precisely because a quarrel of this sort is usually more bitter than a quarrel among friends, he hated his brother like a viper or scorpion. When he was humiliated, he would reason thus: "If even my own brother could be so unkind to me, how can I blame others?" After reaching this conclusion, he would review all the unkind things which he imagined his brother had done to him and declare that his brother was bad and he himself was good. He would then itemize his own virtues and list all his past wrongs and sufferings in an exaggerated fashion. When he had proved to his own satisfaction that he was indeed the most miserable of all men, his tears would course down like a waterfall. A soft voice would seem to be speaking to him from the sky, "Oh, so it's you who are crying. It's really a shame that such a kindhearted person as you should be so maltreated by the world. But let it be since it has been decreed by Heaven, and you'd better stop crying since it won't do your health any good." As soon as he heard this voice, he would feel greatly relieved: there seemed to be infinite sweetness in chewing the cud of bitter sorrow.

As a means of retaliation, he gave up his study of medicine and switched to literature, intending this change of major to be a declaration of war, since it was his brother who had urged him to study medicine. Also, changing his major would delay his graduation for a year, which meant shortening his life by one year, and the sooner he died, the easier it would be for him to maintain a lifelong enmity toward his brother. For he was quite afraid that he would be reconciled with his brother in a year or two, and he changed his major to help strengthen his sense of enmity.

The weather had gradually turned colder. It had been a month since he moved up the hill. In the past few days dark clouds had hung heavily in the somber sky, and when the frosty northern winds came, the leaves on the *mei* trees would begin to fall.

Upon moving to his retreat, he had sold some old books to buy cooking utensils and had made his own meals for nearly a month. Now that it was getting chillier, he gave up cooking and ate at the grove keeper's house down the hill. Like a retired monk idling in a temple, he had nothing to do but to blame others and reproach himself.

One morning he got up very early. Pushing open the window facing the east, he saw a few curls of red cloud floating on the far horizon. The sky directly above was a patch of reddish silver-gray. Because it had drizzled the day before, he found the rising sun all the more lovely. He went down the slope and fetched water from the ancient well. After washing his face and hands with the water, he felt full of energy and ran upstairs for a volume of Huang Chung-tse's [8] poetry. He kept pacing along the winding paths in the grove as he chanted the poetry. Soon the sun was up in the sky.

Looking southward from the plateau, he could see, at the foot of the hill, a large plain checkered with rice fields. The unharvested grain, ripened to a yellowish gold, gave a most brilliant reflection of the morning sun against the background of a violet sky. The scene re-

[8] This famous Ch'ing poet (1749–83) is the hero of Yü Ta-fu's story, "Ts'ai-shih Chi."

minded him of a rural painting by Millet. Faced with this magnificence
of Nature, he felt like an early Christian of Jesus' time and could not
help laughing at his own pettiness:

"Forgive, forgive! I have forgiven you all who have wronged me.
Come ye all and make peace with me!"

Just as he was contemplating—with a book of poems in hand and
tears in eyes—the beauty of the autumnal scene and thus getting lost
in thought, all of a sudden he heard two whispering voices close by
him:

"You have to come tonight!" It was clearly a man's voice.

"I want to very much, but I'm afraid. . . ."

It was a girl's seductive voice and he felt instantly electrified, as if
his circulation had stopped. Looking around, he found himself standing
by a growth of tall reeds. He was on its right and the couple were
probably on its left, completely oblivious of his existence.

"You are so kind. Do come tonight, because so far we haven't . . .
in bed," the man continued.

". . . ."

He heard the noise made by their sucking lips, and immediately he
prostrated himself on the ground, as stealthily as a wild dog with a stolen morsel in its mouth. "Oh, shame, shame!" he cursed himself severely in his heart, "How can you be so depraved!" Nevertheless, he
was all ears listening to what they were doing and saying.

The crunching of fallen leaves on the ground.

The noise of undressing.

The man's rapid panting.

The sucking of lips.

And the woman pleading in half-audible, broken tones: "Please . . .
please . . . please hurry . . . otherwise we . . . we will be seen. . . ."

Instantly his complexion changed to ashen gray, his eyes reddened
with fire, and his upper teeth clattered against his lower. He could
hardly get up, let alone run away from the scene. He was transfixed in
agony.

He waited there until the couple had left before he went back to his
bedroom upstairs like a drenched dog and covered himself up with a
quilt.

VII

Without bothering with lunch, he slept until four o'clock—until the whole area was suffused with the late afternoon sun. In the distance a thin veil of smoke was seen floating leisurely on top of the trees across the plain. Hurriedly he ran downhill to get on the road and headed south without any apparent reason. He eventually crossed the plain to arrive at the trolley stop in front of the A. Temple. A trolley came by just then and he boarded it, without knowing why he should be taking the trolley or where he was going.

After running for fifteen or sixteen minutes, the trolley stopped and the operator asked him to change cars. So he took another trolley. Twenty or thirty minutes later it reached its last stop, and so he got off. He found himself standing by a harbor.

In front of him was the sea, lazing in the afternoon sun, smiling. Across the sea to the south was the silhouette of a mountain floating hazily in translucent air. To the west was a long dike, stretching to the middle of the bay. A lighthouse stood beyond the dike like a giant. A few tethered boats and sampans were moving slightly, while a number of buoys farther out in the bay shone red on the water. The wind carried from a distance broken snatches of a conversation, but he was unable to tell what it was about or where it came from.

After pacing aimlessly for a while on the bank, he suddenly heard something which sounded like chimes. He went over and saw that the musical signal was designed to attract customers to the ferry. Soon a steamboat came by from the opposite side. Following a middle-aged worker, he too boarded the ferry.

No sooner had he landed on the eastern bank than he found himself in front of a villa. The door was wide open, showing a courtyard neatly decorated with a lawn, flowering plants, and miniature hills made of rocks. Without ascertaining the identity of the place, he simply walked in and was immediately greeted by a very sweet feminine voice: "Please come in."

Taken by surprise, he stood there in a daze and thought, "This is probably some kind of restaurant, but I have heard a place like this cannot be without prostitutes."

At the thought of this he became invigorated, as if he had just been drenched by a bucketful of cold water. But he soon changed color because he didn't know what to do with himself, whether to advance or retreat. It was a pity that he had the lust of an ape and the timidity of a rabbit, which accounted for his present quandary.

"Come in. Please do come in." That seductive voice called from the hall again, accompanied by giggles.

"You devils! You think I am too timid to come in?" he said to himself in anger, his face burning hot. After stamping his feet lightly, he advanced, gnashing his teeth and clenching his fists, as if preparing to declare war on these young waitresses. But hard as he tried, he couldn't possibly erase the flushes of red and blue on his face nor compose its twitching muscles. So when he came near these girls, he almost cried like a child.

"Please come upstairs!"

"Please come upstairs!"

Bracing himself, he followed a waitress of around seventeen or eighteen upstairs and felt somewhat calmer. A few steps on the second floor and he came into a dark corridor; immediately his nostrils were assaulted by a strange mixture of the perfume of face powder and hair tonic and the special kind of bodily fragrance that distinguished Japanese women. He felt dizzy and sparks floated before his eyes, which made him reel. After steadying himself, he saw emerging from the darkness in front of him the oblong, powdered face of a woman who asked him with a smile:

"Would you like to have a place by the sea? Or did you have a special place in mind?"

He felt the woman's warm breath upon his face and he inhaled deeply without being aware of what he was doing. But as soon as he became conscious of his action, his face reddened. With great effort he mumbled an answer:

"I'll take a room facing the sea."

After taking him to a small room by the sea, the waitress asked what kind of food he would like, and he answered:

"Just bring a few dishes of what you have in readiness."

"Want some wine?"

"Yes."

After the waitress had left, he stood up and pushed open the paper windows to let in some fresh air, for the room was very stuffy and her perfumed presence lingered on, suffocating him.

The bay was calm. A light breeze passed by and the surface of the sea was wrinkled into a series of waves which, under the reflection of the setting sun, glinted like the scales of a golden fish.

After watching the scene from the window for a while, he was moved to whisper a line of poetry:

"The setting sun has crimsoned my seaside chamber."

Looking westward, he saw that the sun was now only about ten feet from the horizon. But however beautiful the scene, his thoughts were still with the waitress—the fragrance emanating from her mouth, hair, face, and body. After repeated attempts to engage his mind elsewhere, he resigned himself to the fact that in his present mood he was obsessed with flesh rather than poetry.

Before long the waitress brought in his food and wine. She squatted by him and served him most attentively. He wanted to take a close look at her and confide to her all his troubles. But in reality he didn't even dare to look her in the eye, much less talk to her. And so, like a mute, all he did was to look furtively at her delicate, white hands resting upon her knees and that portion of a pink petticoat not covered by her kimono.

For Japanese women wear a short petticoat instead of drawers. On the outside they wear a buttonless, long-sleeved kimono with a band about fourteen inches wide around the waist fastened into a square bundle on the back. Because of this costume, with every step they take, the kimono is flung open to reveal the pink petticoat inside and a glimpse of their plump thighs. This is the special charm of Japanese women to which he paid most attention whenever he saw them on the street. It was also on account of this habit that he called himself a beast, a sneaky dog, and a despicable coward.

Precisely it was the corner of the waitress's petticoat that was perturbing him now. The more he wanted to talk to her, the more tongue-tied he became. His embarrassment was apparently making the waitress a little impatient, for she asked, "Where are you from?"

At this, his pallid face reddened again; he stammered and stammered but couldn't give a forthright answer. He was once again standing on the guillotine. For the Japanese look down upon Chinese just as we look down upon pigs and dogs. They call us Shinajin, "Chinamen," a term more derogatory than "knave" in Chinese. And now he had to confess before this pretty young girl that he was a Shinajin.

"O China, my China, why don't you grow strong!"

His body was trembling convulsively and tears were again about to roll down.

Seeing him in such agitation, the waitress thought it would be best to leave him to drink alone, so that he could compose himself. So she said:

"You have almost finished this bottle. I'll get you another one."

In a while he heard the waitress coming upstairs. He thought she was coming back to him and so he changed his sitting position and adjusted his clothes. But he was deceived, for she was only taking some other guests to the room next to his.

Soon he heard the guests flirting with the waitress, who said coquettishly, "Please behave. We have a guest in the next room." This infuriated him, and he cursed them silently:

"Bastards! Pigs! How dare you bully me like this? Revenge! Revenge! I'll revenge myself on you! Can there be any true-hearted girl in the world? You faithless waitress, how dare you desert me like this? Oh, let it be, let it be, for from now on I shall care nothing about women, absolutely nothing. I will love nothing but my country, and let my country be my love."

He had an impulse to go home and apply himself to study. At the same time, however, he was very envious of those bastards next door, and there was still a secret corner in his heart which expected the waitress's return.

Finally, he suppressed his anger and silently downed a few cups of wine, which made him feel warm all over. He got up and opened some more windows to cool himself, and saw that the sun was now going down. Then he drank a few more cups and watched the gradual blurring of the seascape. The shadow cast by the lighthouse on the dike was getting longer and longer, and a descending fog began to blend the sky and the sea. But behind this hazy veil the setting sun lingered on the horizon, as if reluctant to say good-by. After watching this view for a while, he felt inexplicably merry and burst out laughing.

He rubbed his burning cheeks, muttering, "Yes, I'm drunk. I'm drunk."

The waitress finally came in. Seeing him getting all red and laughing idiotically in front of the windows, she asked:

"With the windows wide open, aren't you afraid of the cold?"

"I'm not cold, not cold at all. Who can afford to miss this beautiful sunset?"

"You're indeed a poet. Here is your wine."

"Poet? Yes, I am a poet. Bring me a brush and some paper and I'll write a poem for you."

After the waitress had left, he was surprised at himself and thought, "How have I become so bold all of a sudden?"

He became even merrier after emptying more cups of the newly warmed wine and broke into another round of loud laughter. In the next room those bastards were singing Japanese songs aloud, and so he also raised his voice and chanted:

> Drunk, I tap the railing and feel the chillier because of the wine;
> Rivers and lakes again turn bleak in the dead of winter.
> The mad poet with his profound pity for the parrot
> Was spared through death—his bones buried in the Central
>   Province—
> The further ignominy of another talented youth
> Exiled to Ch'ang-an with the title of grand tutor.
> It's not too hard to try to repay a life-saving meal
> With a thousand pieces of gold,
> But how many could pass through the capital
> Without heaving five long sighs?
> Looking homeward across the misted sea,
> I, too, weep for my beloved country.[9]

After repeating the poem several times, he fell asleep on the floor.

[9] Like the earlier poem intended for a friend in Tokyo, this poem is Yü Ta-fu's own composition in the eight-line, seven-character *lü-shih* style. I have expanded its second and third couplets into eight lines (ll. 3–10) because otherwise these highly allusive couplets could not have made much sense to the general reader. The "mad poet" of l. 3 is Ni Heng, a precocious and utterly proud scholar of the Later Han dynasty who once wrote a *fu* poem on the parrot, indirectly comparing himself to this bird of supernal intelligence forced to live in captivity. At the age of twenty-six he was executed by Huang Tsu, governor of Chiang-hsia (Central Province), one of the several patrons he had offended with his rude arrogance. "Another talented youth," in l. 5, refers to Chia I, a Former Han writer

VIII

When he woke up, he found himself lying underneath a red satin quilt scented with a strange perfume. The room was not big, but it was no longer the same room he had occupied in the late afternoon. A ten-watt bulb suspended from the ceiling gave a dim light. A teapot and two cups were placed beside his pillow. After helping himself to two or three cups of tea, he got up and walked unsteadily to the door. Just when he was opening it, the same waitress who had taken care of him in the afternoon came in to greet him: "Hey, there! Are you all right now?"

He nodded and answered with a smile, "Yes. Where is the toilet?"

"I'll show you."

He followed her and again passed through the corridor, but it was now lit up and from far and near came singing and laughter and the sound of the samisen. All this helped him to recall what had happened this afternoon, especially what he had said to the waitress when in a drunken state. His face flushed again.

Returning from the toilet, he asked the waitress, "Is this quilt yours?"

"Yes," she answered with a smile.

"What time is it now?"

"It's probably eight forty or eight fifty."

"Would you please give me the check?"

"Yes, sir."

After he had paid the bill, tremblingly he handed the waitress a banknote, but she said, "No, thanks. I don't need it."

---

of greater fame. His hopes for a political career were dashed when he was assigned or rather banished to the state of Ch'ang-sha to serve as its king's tutor. A few years later he died heartbroken at the age of thirty-three. Han Hsin, a prominent general under the founding emperor of the Former Han dynasty, was befriended in his youth by a washerwoman who repeatedly gave him meals when he had nothing to eat. After he had achieved fame, he sought her out and gave her "a thousand pieces of gold" (l. 8). Liang Hung, a recluse of the Later Han, once passed through the national capital and composed a "Song of Five Sighs" (*Wu-i chih ko*), each of its five lines ending with the exclamatory word *i* (alas!). Emperor Su-tsung was highly displeased, and Liang Hung had to change his name and live in hiding.

He knew she was offended by the small tip. Again red with embarrassment, he searched his pocket and found one remaining note. He gave it to her, saying, "I hope you won't scorn this paltry sum. Please take it."

His hand trembled more violently this time, and even his voice quivered. Seeing him in this state, the waitress accepted the money and said in a low voice, "Thank you." He ran straight downstairs, put on his shoes, and went outside.

The night air was very cold. It was probably the eighth or ninth of the lunar month, and the half moon hung high in the left corner of the grayish-blue sky, accompanied by a few lone stars.

He took a walk by the seashore. From afar the lights on the fishermen's boats seemed to be beckoning him, like the will-o'-the-wisp, and the waves under the silvery moonlight seemed to be winking at him, like the eyes of mountain spirits.[10] Suddenly he had the inexplicable urge to drown himself in the sea.

He felt in his pocket and found that he didn't even have money for the trolley fare. Reflecting upon what he had done today, he couldn't help cursing himself:

"How could I have gone to such a place? I really have become a most degraded person. But it's too late to regret, too late to regret. I may as well end my life here, since I'll probably never get the kind of love I want. And what would life be without love? Isn't it as dead as ashes? Ah, this dreary life, how dull and dry! Everyone in this world hates me, maltreats me—even my own brother is trying to push me off the edge of this world. How can I make a living? And why should I stay on in this world of suffering?"

This thought gave him pause, and tears began to roll down his face, which was now as pallid as a dead man's. He didn't even bother to wipe away those tears, which glistened on his moon-blanched face like the morning dew on the leaves. With anguish he turned his head to look at the elongated shadow of his thin body.

"My poor shadow! you have followed me for twenty-one years and

[10] In using the term *shan-kuei* (mountain spirits), the author must be alluding to the female deity of identical name celebrated in one of the "Nine Songs." Cf. David Hawkes, tr., *Ch'u Tz'u: The Songs of the South* (London, 1959; Boston, 1962), p. 43.

now this sea is going to bury you. Though my body has been insulted and injured, I should not have let you grow so thin and emaciated. O shadow, my shadow, please forgive me!"

He looked toward the west. The light on the lighthouse was doing its job, now beaming red and now green. When the green beam reached down, there would immediately appear on the sea an illuminated path of light blue. Again looking up, he saw a bright star trembling in the farthest reach of the western horizon.

"Underneath that shaky star lies my country, my birthplace, where I have spent eighteen years of my life. But alas, my homeland, I shall see you no more!"

He was thinking such despondent thoughts of self-pity as he walked to and fro along the shore. After a while, he paused to look again at that bright star in the western sky and tears poured down like a shower. The view around him began to blur. Drying his tears, he stood still and uttered a long sigh. Then he said, between pauses:

"O China, my China, you are the cause of my death! . . . I wish you could become rich and strong soon! . . . Many, many of your children are still suffering!"

(Author's note: revision completed on May 9, 1921.)

Shen Ts'ung-wen

A native of West Hunan, Shen Ts'ung-wen (1902–   ) was until his twentieth year a provincial youth totally unacquainted with the new culture of modern China. At that age, after being exposed to some books and magazines expressive of that culture, he decided to go to Peking and become a writer. But his new career did nothing to change his innate conservatism born of a passionate attachment to the simple, honest ways of his backward home region, and throughout his creative years he drew sustenance from his memories of that region. Neither liberal nor Marxist, Shen Ts'ung-wen was almost unique among modern Chinese writers for his loyalty to rural values.

At first the young writer dissipated his fertile imagination over a large quantity of short stories, but in time he took his talent more seriously and evolved a distinctive prose style most remarkable for its effortless rendition of landscape and its rich evocation of subtle nuances of feeling. His fiction is usually labeled pastoral, but its pastoralism is actually shot through with a profound awareness of the ills that beset China. By the middle thirties Shen Ts'ung-wen had a series of distinguished short story collections to his credit, and of all his contemporaries only Chang T'ien-i, more brilliant as a satirist, could equal him in creative fecundity.

One has to read a great deal of Shen Ts'ung-wen in order fully to appreciate his many-sided achievement. A number of his best-known works, including the novelette *The Border Town* (*Pien-ch'eng*), are available in Robert Payne and Ching Ti, trs., *The Chinese Earth* (London, 1947), but, unfortunately, the volume captures little of his charm and style. My two selections, needless to say, can hardly suggest his range, though they are among his best. In 1943 Shen Ts'ung-wen published the collection *Black Phoenix* (*Hei-feng chi*), containing several of his best pre-1937 stories in a revised form. Both "Quiet" (*Ching*) and

"Daytime" (*Pai-jih*) are translated therefrom, though the author gives no indication whether he has made any change in the latter story except for the title.

With his great love for the humble people of his home province, Shen Ts'ung-wen is especially noted for his gallery of vivacious heroines—all Hunanese girls of artless candor, either still insulated in their world of childhood gaiety or just awakened to the world of adult passion. Ling-ling, the heroine of "Daytime," is the youngest of these, a child fully invested with individuality. Though not a great psychologist, Shen Ts'ung-wen is abundantly endowed with the Keatsian negative capability that enabled him to enter the mind of a little girl with ease. "Daytime" is not a great story: it resorts too often to exposition and its final epiphany captures no true moral moment. But certainly the author has recorded Ling-ling's afternoon with truth and warmth: her encounter with Little Bolt in the back garden is nothing short of magnificent.

"Quiet" is a superb story which strikes me as almost faultless. I have said in *History* that

it seems to me to have distilled in a few pages the art of Shen Ts'ung-wen in all its complexity—impressionistic rendition of scenes and feelings as well as a pastoral regard for human dignity in the teeth of ironic awareness of the chaos and sorrow of a war-torn China. . . . What Shen Ts'ung-wen has accomplished is the feeling of quietness, a mood of poignant sadness completely objectified in the helplessness of all the characters in their automatic motions of work and play, in the small-talk which fails to dispel gloom, and especially in the contrasting views of the dingy house and the loveliness of spring outside. The precise details observed from the vantage-point of the terrace—the river and meadow, the kites and horses, the nun and the bride—become each a symbol of liberty and joy beyond the reach of the family.

QUIET

TRANSLATED BY *Wai-lim Yip* and *C. T. Hsia*

Extremely long, the spring days. The long, long bright days. In a small town, the old people either warmed themselves in the sun or dozed off; the young, having nothing else to do, would fly kites from sun terraces or open grounds. Up in the sky the white sun and clouds moved very slowly and whenever a kite had freshly broken away from its owner, here and there people would lift their heads to peer into the sky. The little children would shout the loudest, waving their hands and stamping their feet, hoping that this ownerless kite would fall into their courtyard or its thin string would get tangled on the forked laundry poles erected at the corners of their terrace.

Yo-min, a girl about fourteen with an undernourished-looking pale little face and wearing a new, knee-length blue gown, was watching such a kite from the sun terrace above the back part of her house. She saw it gliding down obliquely above her head, and the broken end of its string caught between the roof tiles of the house next door. Over there a fat woman on the sun terrace was poking at the string with a bamboo pole, hoping to get the kite. Meanwhile Yo-min heard some noise behind her: a little boy on all fours was climbing the stairs. Soon a small head rose above the top rung of the staircase. With his bright and lively eyes the boy looked furtively around without going farther up, calling out quietly to the girl:

"Little auntie, Grandma is asleep now. Can I come up for a minute?"

Yo-min, upon hearing the voice, immediately turned her head. Looking at the boy, she reproached him softly:

"Pei-sheng, you ought to be spanked. Why climb up again? Aren't you afraid of being scolded when Mommy comes back?"

"Little auntie, I only want to play a tiny bit. Please don't say anything. Grandma is sleeping." The boy repeated his request humbly, his voice weak and tender.

After knitting her brows to scare him a little, the girl walked over to help him climb up to the terrace.

This sun terrace, like all such terraces in the town, was nothing but the flat portion of the housetop sparsely fenced with a number of laths. These laths, usually old and rickety, were stuck into a wooden framework around the terrace. The two now leaned against the mildewed railing, rotting and about to collapse, and counted the kites of various sizes in the blue sky. Directly below the railing sloped the roof proper, with its loosely spaced tiles. Since there had been several days of spring rain, some patches of the roof were overgrown with green moss. The roofs of the houses on the same row were contiguous, and each terrace faced two others on its left and right. On some terraces clothes and bed sheets were hung high up on the bamboo poles to dry, and they fluttered in the breeze like flags. Facing the front of the house was a stretch of the stone wall surrounding the city; from the terrace one could see the new sprouts of the grapevines with roots in the stone crevices. Behind the terrace a limpid stream flowed softly. On the other side of the bank was a broad meadow, like a big green carpet embroidered with variegated flowers. Beyond the meadow, one could see in the distance a number of vegetable plots and a small, red-walled nunnery. The peach trees by the hedges of the plots were in luxuriant bloom, as were those in the Buddhist convent.

The sun was quite warm, and the scene extremely quiet. The two said nothing to each other, but gazed at the sky and then at the stream.

Its water was not so green as it would be in the morning and evening. Some patches looked blue and some patches directly under the sun were the color of silver. Across the stream, one section of the meadow was filled with rape, now bursting into a shimmering gold. Another section was striped with pieces of white cloth, brought here to dry by men from the dyer's shop in the town. These spread out in great lengths, the two ends of each piece weighted down with big rocks. Elsewhere, three people seated on boulders were flying kites. Among them was a young boy who, a reed pipe in his mouth, was blowing out various bridal tunes. In addition, five unattended horses, three white and two light brown, were grazing and moving about at ease.

Seeing two of the horses starting to run, Pei-sheng cried out in glee, "Little auntie, little auntie, look!" Little auntie gave him a look and pointed her finger downward. The boy understood and hurriedly put his palm over his mouth so as not to disturb the people downstairs. Looking at little auntie, he shook his small head as if to say, "Don't talk, don't talk. Don't let them know."

Both gazed at the horses, the lawn, and the other sights, the boy delirious with joy and the girl lost in thought over recent events that already seemed so remote.

They were refugees here. This place was neither their home nor the destination of their journey. With Yo-min on the trip were her mother, sister-in-law, elder sister, sister's son Pei-sheng, and the maid Ts'ui-yün—all of them women except for the five-*sui*-old boy.[1] Not at all sure of what they were doing, they had got on board a small sailboat and sailed for fourteen days. When the boat arrived here, they should have changed to a steamship, but when they inquired for news they learned that Wuchang was still under siege and that no ship or train bound for Shanghai or Nanking could proceed from there. This news proved that what they had heard up north was not true. Thus stranded, they found it impractical to return home since this would mean running into more expense, more trouble, and possibly danger. So at Mother's suggestion they moved into this house as their temporary quarters, sent back to I-ch'ang the soldiers that had escorted them, and wrote letters to Peking and Shanghai in the expectation of getting replies.

After they had settled here, Mother and Sister-in-law longed only

[1] Four years old according to the Western way of counting age.

for a messenger from I-ch'ang, and Sister for letters from Peking, but Yo-min herself centered her thoughts on Shanghai. She hoped only that the letter from Shanghai would arrive first so that she could go back to school. To go to I-ch'ang to live with her father, a military representative in the Ministry of War, and her big brother, an army officer, would not be half so good as living with her second brother, who was a teacher in Shanghai. But Wuchang had been under siege for a month and was not yet taken. Who could tell when the Yangtze River would be reopened for commercial travel? Forty days gone already. Accompanied by the maid Ts'ui-yün, she went every day to stand before the local daily's office building by the city gate and read the newspaper posted on its bulletin board and then hurried back to relay all the news to Mother and Sister. Then from these items of news they each tried to find cause for comfort or hope. Sometimes they exchanged the good dreams they had had the night before, trying self-deceptively to read into them all kinds of auspicious signs.

Mother had always been sickly. Since arriving here, for over a month she had waited in vain for any message from the people she had written to. The money she had taken along for the journey was dwindling fast. Her ill health aggravated by these worries and also by the hardships endured on the voyage, Mother had naturally worsened. Yo-min frequently thought, "If we cannot sail in another fifteen days, I will go to the Kuomintang School for Cadre Training." At that time there were indeed many girls around the age of fourteen enrolled in the Kuomintang School. So why shouldn't a colonel's daughter who doesn't have to pay one cent to get into the school? After six months I will be a graduate assigned to serve at various places and receive a monthly salary of fifty dollars. Naturally, all these were things she had learned from the newspapers and had kept in her own mind, without daring to bring them out before her mother.

While she was thus thinking of getting a copy of the school's bulletin and of her chances there, Pei-sheng heard his grandmother coughing (all along his keen ears had been listening for her movements, for if she knew upon awaking that he had surreptitiously gone up to the terrace, she might scold him again for not heeding her warning against the danger of falling into the gutter and breaking his small hands), and he pulled at Yo-min's gown and whispered:

"Little auntie, help me down. Grandma is awake!" The boy only knew how to climb and could not get down the stairs without help.

After Yo-min had accompanied the boy downstairs, she found Ts'ui-yün washing clothes in the courtyard, and so she squatted down beside the washtub and helped the maid rub some of them. But she soon found the work dull and said, "Ts'ui-yün, you are already too busy here. Let me hang these for you on the terrace." She grabbed some clothes that had been wrung out and went up on the terrace again. In no time she had them hung on the bamboo poles.

Because the section of the small river observable from the terrace was quite far from the bridge, there was a ferryboat there for public convenience. This ferryboat, however, was as narrow as a bench and usually beached on the shore, since it served few passengers besides the men from the dyer's shop going to the lawn to dry cloth and a few laborers crossing the river to carry back loads of loess. Very often the boat saw no business for half a day. Right now, the ferryman was sound asleep on a big rock in the middle of the meadow. The sunlit boat, weather-beaten and bleached to a grayish-white color, also seemed very listless as it floated on the water, moving and rocking ever so slowly with the breeze.

"Why is everything so quiet?" thought Yo-min to herself, even though a fair distance across the river some boatwrights were driving nails, *bing-bang, bing-bang,* into the sides of a boat, and the itinerant peddler of sewing goods was rattling his small drum in a nearby hamlet on the opposite bank. The unceasing banging and rattling vibrated in the air, making her feel the more keenly the quietness of the town.

After a while, from the convent with the blooming peach trees emerged a young nun in a black cowl and a gray cassock, a new bamboo basket in her hand. With brisk steps she crossed the big meadow toward the riverside and stopped at some distance to the left of the ferryboat. Squatting on a rock, she slowly rolled up her sleeves and took her time to look around and watch the kites before taking out, unhurriedly, a large bunch of green vegetables from the basket and rinsing them clean one by one in the flowing water in front of her. Thus stirred, the water flickered with sunlight. Then, a little later, from the bank along the edge of the town came a countrywoman. She called the ferryman, wanting to cross the river. It took the ferryman some effort to punt the boat over and then ferry the woman to the other side

of the river. For some reason beyond Yo-min's knowledge, the ferryman yelled at the woman as if they were in a quarrel. But the woman
said nothing in return and went away. Soon after, there appeared on
this side of the river three men, each carrying on his bamboo pole two
large empty baskets. They called the ferryman from the bank, and the
ferryman punted as slowly as the last time. On this trip a dispute broke
out among the three countrymen. The ferryman, however, said nothing, and no sooner had he reached the bank than he nailed his pole
into the sand. Soon the six baskets were seen in a line disappearing toward the edge of the big meadow.

At this point, the young nun had finished washing the vegetables
and was now pounding a garment or a piece of cloth with a pestle.
After several vigorous poundings, she shook it in the water a few times
and then started pounding it again. The sound of the pestle bounced
against the city wall, giving rise to ringing echoes. Later the nun,
probably intrigued by the echoes, stopped pounding and called out
loudly: "Ssu-lin, Ssu-lin." The other side responded: "Ssu-lin, Ssu-lin."
Not long after, from the nunnery came the loud call of another
woman, "Ssu-lin, Ssu-lin," followed by some indistinguishable words.
It must be that she was asking whether Ssu-lin (apparently the young
nun's name) had finished her errand. The latter, her work done and
now tired of playing by the waterside, picked up her basket and went
back purposely treading on the empty spaces between the pieces of
white cloth being sunned.

After Ssu-lin was gone, some vegetable leaves drifting slowly by the
ferryboat reminded Yo-min of how very happy the young nun had appeared to her a moment ago: "The young nun must have hung the
clothes on the bamboo poles by now! . . . must be massaging the ab-
bess's back by tapping it with her fists under that blooming peach tree
. . . must be intoning Buddha's name while teasing a kitten with her
hand . . ." All these things she had imagined amused her very much,
and made her smile. She even tried to mimic the young nun by calling
out softly, "Ssu-lin, Ssu-lin."

Thinking thus of the nun's happiness, of the water in the river, of
the flowers in the distance, of the clouds in the sky, and then of her
mother sick in bed, Yo-min, almost without knowing it herself, felt
somewhat lonely again.

She remembered the magpies [2] chattering for a long time on the terrace this morning, and since the mailman usually came by this time,
perhaps she might as well go down to see if there were any letters
from Shanghai. As she reached the edge of the staircase, she saw Pei-
sheng on all fours on the lowest step, trying to climb up again without
making any noise. The boy, too, must be quite lonesome.

"Pei-sheng, you bad boy. Mommy will be back in a minute. Don't
come up again."

When Yo-min got down from the terrace, Pei-sheng pulled at her,
wanting her to bend her head until her ear was close to his little
mouth. Then he whispered, "Little auntie, Grandma is spitting that
again . . ."

Yo-min went into Mother's room and found her lying still on the
bed, like a dead person, breathing calmly but weakly. Her thin and
narrow face was a mask of fatigue and anxiety. Mother had apparently
been awake for some time, and upon hearing footfalls in the room she
opened her eyes.

"Min-min, see for me how much water is left in the thermos bottle."

While Yo-min was pouring out hot water to mix with Coacose [3] for
the patient, her eyes fell upon Mother's emaciated face and small nose.

"Mother, it is an extremely nice day today. From the terrace one
can already see the peach blossoms in full bloom in the small nunnery
across the river," said Yo-min.

The patient said nothing in reply, but smiled a little. Remembering
the blood she had coughed up a while ago, she stretched out her emaciated hand to touch her own forehead and then muttered, "I don't
have fever, do I?" So saying, she looked at Yo-min and smiled
tenderly—a smile so helplessly pitiable that the girl sighed, almost inaudibly.

"Is your coughing better today?"

"Better now, it doesn't matter, and doesn't really hurt me. I was not
careful this morning and ate some fish which made my throat burn a
little bit. It doesn't matter."

[2] The Chinese traditionally regard the magpie (hsi-ch'üeh) as an auspicious bird.
Hearing its chatter in the morning has led Yo-min to think that she will receive
good news during the day.

[3] I have translated the term K'u-a-k'o-ssu as a trade name, Coacose. It is probably
a cocoa-flavored preparation like Ovaltine.

Thus exchanging remarks, the girl thought of going over to inspect the small spittoon near the pillow. The patient, knowing what she intended to do, said, "There's nothing." And then: "Min-min, stand there and don't move. Let me see. You've grown taller again this month. Almost a full-grown person now!"

Yo-min smiled bashfully. "I don't look like a bamboo, Mama, do I? I am afraid it's not pretty to grow so tall at the age of fifteen. People will laugh at a tall girl."

Then a pause during which Mother seemed to have recalled something.

"Min-min, I had a good dream. I dreamed that we were already on board ship. The third-class cabin was shamefully overcrowded. I was very uneasy, but I thought to myself that in a few days when we arrived we should be able to rest for half a month or so."

In fact she had made up the dream herself and, her memory being so poor and disorganized, she was telling it a second time.

Seeing her mother's small waxen face, Yo-min forced a smile, saying, "Last night, I really dreamed that we were in a big ship and Cousin San-mao came to meet us. But he also seemed to be the man from the Fortune Hotel whose job it was to welcome its guests at the pier. He gave each one of us a copy of the tourist guide. This morning the magpies chattered for quite a while. It seems that it should be time for the mail to arrive now."

"If not today, it should be arriving tomorrow."

"Maybe he will come himself."

"Didn't it say in the paper that the Thirteenth Division in I-ch'ang is being transferred?"

"Could it be that Papa has already set out?"

"If he is coming, he should first cable us."

Thus saying this and that in a purposely optimistic vein, each tried to beguile the other into a better mood. Contrary to their words, the girl was actually saying to herself, "Mama, what can we do now that you are so ill?" and the patient to herself, "It is really rotten to go on being ill like this."

Meanwhile, just back from the fortuneteller's place north of the town, Sister and Sister-in-law were talking in whispers in the courtyard. Yo-min moved to the door and assumed a cheerful voice as she said, "Sister and Elder Sister-in-law, a while ago there was a kite whose broken string got tangled between the roof tiles. The woman next door wanted to drag it down, waving a bamboo pole. Instead of getting the kite down, she broke many tiles. Isn't it funny?"

Sister said, "Pei-sheng, you must have gone up with Auntie to the sun terrace again. You might break your leg and get lame and become a beggar in the future."

Pei-sheng was squatting beside Ts'ui-yün and helping her wash the vegetables when he heard his mother. He didn't dare reply but looked at little auntie with a furtive smile.

Smiling back at Pei-sheng, Yo-min started walking past the courtyard and she pulled Sister toward the kitchen, telling her in a low voice, "Sister, it seems that Mama has spat blood again."

"What are we going to do?" Sister said. "There should be mail from Peking by now."

"Have you got the fortuneteller's tally with you?"

While getting out the tally slip and handing it to Yo-min, Sister beckoned the squatting Pei-sheng to come over. Pei-sheng went to his mother and embraced her with his small arms, saying, "Mommy, Grandma has again coughed up blood. She put it away under the pillow."

"Pei-sheng, I told you not to go into Grandma's room to disturb her, understand?" said Sister.

Pei-sheng, as if he really understood, said, "Yes, I know," and then: "Mommy, Mommy, the peach flowers across the river are all in bloom now. Can you let little auntie take me to the sun terrace to play for a while? I won't make trouble."

Sister put on an angry face: "No, after so much rain, it is very slippery up there," and then: "Why don't you play in your own room? If you go up to the terrace, Grandma will scold little auntie!"

The boy walked past little auntie, squeezed her hand, and obediently went into his own little bedroom.

Ts'ui-yün had by then finished rubbing and rinsing the laundry. Yo-min, helping her to wring the clothes dry, said, "Next time let's wash clothes by the river. It is much more convenient. There are scarcely any people using the ferry. It should be quite all right for me to go there." Not saying anything in reply, Ts'ui-yün bent her head and let a smile appear on her blushing face.

The patient in her room had a fit of coughing. Sister and Sister-in-law went in to see her. Ts'ui-yün had already wrung the clothes dry and was about to go up to the terrace. Yo-min looked at the shadows cast by the sun in the courtyard for a while, and then, walking over to the patient's room, she looked inside the partially open door. She saw that Sister-in-law was cutting out clothes patterns from paper while sister, seated on the edge of the bed, was trying to inspect the little spittoon. Mother wouldn't let her at first, stopping her with her hands, but eventually Sister saw its contents and repeatedly shook her head without making any comment. The three of them all wore forced smiles and tried deliberately to lighten their present burden of sorrow by changing their topic of conversation and recalling some event of the distant past. They ended up in a discussion about sending out letters and telegrams. Yo-min, without knowing why, felt the acid of sorrow seeping through her heart. Red-eyed, she stood in the courtyard, biting her lips as if angry with someone. Then, after a while, she heard Ts'ui-yün calling her from the terrace:

"Miss Min, Miss Min, come up quickly. See the bride on horseback. She is about to ferry across the river."

A minute later, Ts'ui-yün called out again:

"Come, come quick and see. A tile-shaped kite has broken loose. Come, come, it's right above my head now. Let's catch it."

Yo-min lifted her head and saw even from her limited view of the sky in the courtyard a high-flying kite reeling like a drunken patrolman. She could even vaguely see a portion of the white string waggling in the sky.

Not to watch the kite nor to see the bride, Yo-min nevertheless went up on the terrace after Ts'ui-yün had come down. Leaning, as usual, by the railing, she viewed everything both distant and near, and her heart began to calm down. She did not leave the terrace until after she had seen the men from the dyer's shop folding up the cloth into squares like bean-curd cakes and placing them neatly on the lawn, and had further watched smoke rising above the tiled roofs of the nunnery and of other houses, near and far.

Down from the terrace, she peeped into the patient's room, finding all three, Mother, Sister, and Sister-in-law, asleep. She then walked into Pei-sheng's room. He, too, had dozed off for a time, sitting on the floor beside his little velvet toy dog. She walked into the kitchen. Ts'ui-yün, sitting on the bench by the stove, was stealthily applying Peerless Brand tooth powder to her face as if it were facial powder. Probably afraid that she might startle the complacent maid, Yo-min hurried to the middle of the courtyard.

At this moment, she heard knocking at a neighbor's door, followed by a brief exchange between someone asking a question and another answering. A strange thought occurred to her: "Who is asking whom? Could it be that Papa and Big Brother have arrived, and are asking for the correct house number?" Such a thought made her heart pound with excitement, and she hurried to the door. Should there be a knocking or pulling at the string of the doorbell, it must have been the expected ones from afar.

But everything soon lapsed into silence.

Yo-min smiled aimlessly. Under the slanting sun a part of the wall and the laundry stand on the terrace cast their shadows on the floor of the courtyard just as elsewhere a paper flag cast its shadow on the tomb of the man the women here were expecting—Yo-min's father.

(Author's note: Written in memory of my elder sister's deceased son, Pei-sheng. Shanghai, March 30, 1932; revised in Kunming, May 10, 1942.)

DAYTIME

TRANSLATED BY *Wai-lim Yip* and *C. T. Hsia*

Ling-ling had black hair, black eyebrows, dark bright eyes, red lips, and equally red cheeks. She liked to skip when walking, and put her thumb in her mouth when not doing anything in particular. She was only five years and seven months old, and no matter who asked her, "Ling-ling, anyone in mind you want to get married to?", she would open her eyes wide and put on hoydenish airs, saying, "I am a man. I want to be married to nobody."

She indeed thought she was a man and tended in consequence to be a little mischievous. Precisely for this reason the adults around her loved to tease her in order to enjoy the masculine mien she assumed when making her reply. She became thus a source of joy to them. When asked a third time, however, she would realize their intent to tease, say nothing in return, and run away. Yet the next time someone asked her the same question, she would give the same answer, oblivious of his intention.

Like so many children of old-style, urban middle-class families, she was, despite her obvious intelligence, somewhat improperly cared for at home and consequently rather lonely. Her mother, a typical old-fashioned bourgeois housewife, had little to do every day and frequently whiled away her time by playing mahjong for low stakes at a relative's house. Ling-ling played at home with an amah and an elder sister around the age of twenty. Although the amah had many chores to attend to and Sister usually had needlework to do or some old books to read, Ling-ling would play by the side of either until she was bored or tired. Then she would fall asleep on any old chair. Upon waking, she would cry for a while without any apparent reason, and when Sister asked, "Why are you crying?", she would say to herself, "Indeed, why should I cry?" She would finally feel better and start playing again all by herself.

When tired of playing, she was like most children in wanting to cling to her mother, demanding to be patted, consoled, and loved. Since Mother was seldom home, Sister had to perform these functions in her place. But Sister could not be as attentive or demonstrative as a mother would be, and very often, when Ling-ling was playing with abandon, Sister would curtly dismiss her from her presence and thus intensify her sense of solitude. By the same token, because she did not play enough, she was a little more imaginative than most girls of her age in larger and busier families.

Today, Mother had again gone to Third Aunt's house. Before leaving, she told the others that she would have supper there and that if she had not returned by the time the lamps were lit, Chao Ma should bring along a lantern and fetch her. After Mother had left, Ling-ling, leaning against the small door opening on the garden, watched listlessly the expanse of dazzling sunshine in front of her. At the same time she had a hand planted inside her pocket to play with four tinkling coins. She counted them back and forth for a long time and then took them out to admire them, warm and damp with her palm's sweat as they were. If there hadn't been these few coins to remind her to behave, Ling-ling might have slipped out of the house to play and wandered as her fancy dictated.

Mother had put these four coppers in her palm before leaving. At the same time she was straightening Ling-ling's clothes and giving instructions, turning her head toward Sister:

"I will ask Sister when I return. If Ling-ling has been a good girl and hasn't cried or made trouble, I will bring back a big apple. But if Ling-ling should be bad, there shall be no apple and the coppers will have to be put into the piggy bank to punish her. What's more, she will soon be given away as a child bride. . . . Sister, can you keep all this in mind?"

Sister only smiled and didn't bother to remember these words, but Ling-ling did.

When Mother was gone, Sister went into her own room to do some work. Ling-ling, mindful of Mother's words and of the promised apple, which seemed to her such a big, round thing of rare sweetness and taste, decided not to leave her. When Sister went upstairs, she followed her upstairs, and when Sister went down to the kitchen, she followed her there, too. As usual, she followed Sister around like a kitten: her hands, her mouth, and her entire body seemed never for a moment to be still. She could not forget the apple, and she knew she had to please and obey Sister in order to get it.

Chao Ma was kneading some dough, and when Sister went over to help her, Ling-ling knew they were going to make cakes. She was intrigued by their hands whitened with flour and insisted on making a cake herself; therefore, clutching at Sister, she obtained a piece of dough and began to knead it.

Having done her share of work, Sister now reclined on a rattan chair trying to read a book. But before she could start, Ling-ling climbed on her lap and wanted her to tell stories. Sister told one, but she was not content and shook her head, demanding a second, and then a third. Full of energy, she pressed her chubby little body against Sister's, grasping, pulling, rubbing, kneading, and making incessant noises to boot. Her crop of short hair was all tangled after she had repeatedly rubbed it against Sister's body. Trying to concentrate on her reading, Sister finally got tired of this endless pestering and tried to put her down, but before her feet had touched the floor, she was up again.

Had Sister remembered Mother's words, she could have simply said, "Ling-ling, if you keep on like this, you won't have the apple this evening," and Ling-ling would have stopped. But it did not occur to Sister to use this simple warning to calm her down.

Both were now drenched in sweat, and no matter how hard Sister coaxed her, Ling-ling still stuck to her like taffy.

Usually, when Ling-ling was unhappy, Sister would put aside her work to cheer her up, but when Ling-ling was overly high-spirited, she would send her away in order to concentrate on her own task. Suddenly Sister seemed to have lost her temper, and assuming an angry expression long familiar to Ling-ling, she said:

"Ling-ling, why do you pester me like this all the time? Why don't you go and play alone in the garden?"

These words prompted Ling-ling to look imploringly at Sister, who, however, remained unappeased in her anger. Without saying a word, Ling-ling stepped out of the room and dragged her feet to the door of the garden, nursing her grievance.

The wronged girl was about to walk into the garden to see if the seeds of the four-o'clock flowers had already turned black when she heard a cackle issuing from the barn situated on one side of the garden. After laying an egg, the hen in the barn would customarily jump out of her coop and cackle loudly, very much like Chao Ma quarreling with someone. On other days Ling-ling would skip and run to the coop to see whether the new egg was brown or white, and before running back to the kitchen in the rear to tell Chao Ma the news, she would sometimes furtively touch the egg with her finger (when Chao Ma was taking the egg out in her presence, Ling-ling would at most dare touch it once since children were by custom not allowed to handle eggs when they were still warm). Now that Sister would not pay her any attention, she was somewhat peevish and unwilling to run to the rear to see Chao Ma. And she felt like throwing a stone at the cackling hen, saying to herself, "If you cackle, I'll hit you." But as she started to run, the tinkling of the coins in her pocket reminded her of Mother's words, and of the apple and the rest.

"When Mother is not home, shouldn't Ling-ling be a good girl?"

"I should, I should," Ling-ling answered her own question. "I ought to behave." But while Mother would reward her for good behavior, Sister would still ignore her even when she was a good girl in front of her. Should she go back in to sit beside Sister or should she stay here in the sun and chase chickens and catch insects by the cluster of sunflowers? She had no idea what she should do.

She didn't understand why Sister should be angry with her today. Believing this to be the case, she felt hurt though she had no desire to tell her wrong to anybody.

She stood alone at the door and looked around. From the big *wu-t'ung* tree came the insistent, deafening notes of the cicadas. The sky above was exceptionally blue. A white cloud flew by the tree and across the wall of the garden. When it disappeared behind the wall, another cloud rose and advanced in its wake. She watched the clouds in a trance, imagining that people were riding upon them for a carefree excursion all day long: far more interesting than similar excursions on the ground. She also remembered some cloud-riding gods from the stories she knew. She gazed at the clouds, spellbound.

The sun, only at her feet a while ago, was steadily advancing to cover more of her body, and yet she had no thought of leaving her post at the door. When Chao Ma came out to get the egg after the hen had cackled for some time and found Ling-ling standing dazed in the sun, she said:

"Ling-ling, why stand under the sun? Won't it be a crime to be grilled by the sun until oil comes out of your pores?"

Ling-ling retorted:

"Oil coming out of my pores? Only fat people like you would drip with oil under the sun."

"When you get darkened by the sun, nobody will marry you."

"None of your business even if I get darkened."

Chao Ma knew that this was the Ling-ling that had been hurt. Afraid that she might start to cry, Chao Ma did not dare to provoke her but proceeded immediately to the barn to get the egg. Soon after she had gone inside with the egg, Ling-ling heard Sister calling her from the house:

"Ling-ling, Ling-ling, come in and see. Here is an egg with a double yolk. Quick!"

But Ling-ling answered, almost whispering:

"Ling-ling isn't coming."

Sister tried again: "Let's play with the tangrams and act out the story of Curio Dealer Chang Selling His Wife."

Ling-ling, still in a low voice, replied:

"I'm not coming."

It seemed Ling-ling was giving herself a lot of trouble today. Having said that she wasn't going to see the double-yolked egg, she didn't know why she should still want very much to see it. But since she had given her word, she seemed to know that Sister would now be telling

Chao Ma in whispers, "Ling-ling is sulky today. Don't provoke her; otherwise she might cry," and so she kept telling herself, "I will not cry. I will not. Indeed I will not."

Ling-ling's little heart could tell the difference between the ways Sister and Mother treated her. Normally, she loved them both as the two best people in the whole world. Then there was Chao Ma, one of the best as well as worst people in the world. Mother was, after all, Mother, possessed of the peculiar maternal gift for good-natured patience. She loved to play with Ling-ling, allowing her to roll all over her body. When she felt in the mood, she would hug Ling-ling so tightly that she could hardly breathe. From this kind of indulgence in animal love and horseplay, Ling-ling derived an unspeakable joy. As long as Mother was not tied up with work, she would always encourage Ling-ling to play to her heart's content, to laugh and shriek unrestrainedly.

With Sister, however, the situation was different. She was not as demonstrative of affection as Mother. She liked to say: "Ling-ling, how could you mess up your clothes like this?" or "How could you be so unmannerly, like a wild girl?" And yet, when Ling-ling did something wrong and her infuriated mother, stern-faced and cursing, would look everywhere for the feather duster to beat her with, the crying or cowed girl found in Sister her only salvation. Before the duster could fall upon Ling-ling's body, Sister would snatch it from Mother's hand and plead at the same time, "Ling-ling is in the wrong, but please don't beat her." Dragging Ling-ling to her own room, she would then lovingly wipe with a corner of her dress the grievous tears of humiliation flowing from her eyes and comfort and reason with her to such charming effect that Ling-ling, though still sobbing, would feel considerably better and lift her head to kiss her on the mouth. In Ling-ling's mind Sister was now the most adorable person in the whole world. Even if the child, feeling herself wronged, wanted to make trouble in a perverse and obstinate fashion, by now her tears would stem as much from gratitude as from anger. Very soon the stories Sister was telling would fascinate her and hold her attention.

For instance, if Ling-ling was slightly ill, Mother would always make her cry by forcing her to take medicine, but after crying, she would submit to Sister's coaxing and take the bitter liquid with her eyes closed.

The difference between Mother and Sister was this: Mother could enhance Ling-ling's happiness by sharing it with her while Sister could make her happy when she was miserable. Ling-ling could not express in words their distinctive virtues relative to her needs, but in her mind she had a pretty good notion of what they were.

At night, when Ling-ling dreamed of being chased by a ferocious dog, the end of her dress caught between its teeth, it was usually Sister who came to her rescue. And she was always very much puzzled when she woke up and found herself lying against Mother's body. It could be said that Ling-ling's heart and mind grew under Sister's influence. Every time she heard that Sister was about to marry, she would come to her and ask softly, "Sister, is it true you are going to be married?" And Sister would say, "If you go on saying such foolish things, I will not talk to you any more. For the sake of Ling-ling, I will never get married, not even when I am old." Ling-ling believed her and thought all such gossip was a lie. But when Sister was angry with her, she would wonder, "Sister won't talk to me. She cannot act like this unless she is getting ready to be married."

As for Chao Ma, Ling-ling thought she was at once good and bad. All Ling-ling's misdeeds were usually reported to Mother by Chao Ma, which caused her to be scolded or beaten. On these occasions she hated Chao Ma and would ignore her when she saw her. Mimicking the air of a male relative, she would look askance at this bad woman and mumble, "What sort of thing are you? What sort of thing are you?" Also, she would not let Chao Ma help her at her bath and fill up her bowl of rice at dinner. But, after a while, when she found Chao Ma fixing her little red dress or embroidering her little pillow with a floral design or doing some other special favor for her, she would soften and appreciate her goodness. During the spat, no matter how much Ling-ling detested Chao Ma, when she saw Mother divide things to eat among the family and naturally leave no portion for Chao Ma, she would secretly save some for her: plums, peanuts, and hazelnuts. She wouldn't, of course, save a whole tangerine for Chao Ma when she herself received only one, but even then she would keep a few sections. Later, when she was ready to be reconciled but still too sulky to want to talk to Chao Ma, she would without fail throw in her lap whatever was saved for her and then run away at flying speed. After some time, Sister would tell the incident in front of all, and when she maintained,

"Ling-ling loves Chao Ma after all," Ling-ling would argue bashfully, "I don't love Chao Ma," and keep saying this until everybody agreed.

Unavoidably, Ling-ling would sometimes also regard Mother or Sister as a "bad person," just like Chao Ma—especially Sister when she was cross or unreasonable and made her cry. The crying child would think that Sister was no good either. But this notion seldom persisted, for soon Sister would be a different person in her eyes again.

Right at this moment, probably because the day was a bit too long or because she could not play when she wanted to, Ling-ling was still somewhat resentful of Sister, and because she herself had ignored Sister a while back, she also believed that Sister was still angry with her.

She looked up at the sky, now ablaze with sunlight, and felt that her feet were getting numb after standing for so long. So she stretched a bit and sat down on the doorsill. She thought it most inexplicable that a hen could lay such shapely eggs and wondered who could have taught it such a trick. She was thus engaged in idle speculation when behind the short hedge of altheas flashed the shadow of someone moving. With her keen eyes, Ling-ling readily identified him as Chao Ma's son Little Bolt [1] and asked quickly:

"Little Bolt, is that you?"

"It's me," was the answer.

Overjoyed, Ling-ling crawled through the althea hedge to join Little Bolt.

Little Bolt was a twelve-*sui*-old boy. There was not a thing that he had not attempted. The whole day he fooled around outside the back door with a group of dirty, ill-clad, and lowborn children. Thin and tall, he had a monkey's head, bulging eyes, and the air of a young rapscallion. But to Ling-ling he was an exceptionally capable and versatile boy who could whistle all kinds of sounds and do all sorts of tricks, ranging from fishing eels and loaches from the pond to catching flies in the air with one hand. Brave and nimble, he commanded Ling-ling's interest and admiration with all his enviable talents, even though he was only a servant's son.

Ling-ling often saw his mother chasing after him and trying to beat him with a broom or a laundry pole of bamboo. Mother forbade her to

[1] "Bolt" is used here in its primary sense of a door bolt. The boy's name is Hsiao-shuan-tzu.

play with Little Bolt, and Sister, too, said that it was not nice to play with him. She did not take their admonitions very seriously, but Little Bolt, who had often taken her out of the house to play and been beaten every time, was now wary of coming near her.

Seeing Little Bolt with a bamboo stick in one hand and a basket made of bamboo slats in another, Ling-ling asked:

"Little Bolt, how many loaches did you catch yesterday?"

Little Bolt remembered that his mother had beaten him with a broom yesterday for taking Ling-ling out to play, and so he put on airs, saying:

"Let's not talk about fishing. I shouldn't have taken you out to play yesterday. I got hit on the head seven times and wasn't I dizzy!"

"Where are you going now?"

"To the West Dike."

Ling-ling knew that by the dike there were lotuses with white blossoms, green pods, and umbrella-sized leaves, and that once she got there she could pluck a few of each of these things. She also knew that it was quite cool walking under the willows on the dike, that people played chess there or sat on stone stools blowing on the flute, and that underneath these stools were a great many crickets continually rubbing their wings to produce lutelike music.

"Isn't it hot at the West Dike?" she asked.

"Not at all. Many people cool themselves there."

"I have been there only twice."

"You want to go?"

"Let me think." Without doing any real thinking, she added, "All right, I'll go with you."

Little Bolt also pondered for a while and then shook his head.

"It's not a good idea. I don't want to take you. When my mother knows you are not here, she will beat me again."

"Your mother has gone to a party. Don't be afraid."

"You are not afraid, but I am."

"Are you afraid of being beaten? I have never seen you cry after a beating. You are a man!"

Moved by her flattery, he smiled at Ling-ling and sighed resignedly, saying:

"All right, let's go. I have a bronze head and iron brow, just like

Old Monkey,[2] and no one can fell me. May I escort Your Ladyship to the West Dike? Let's go by the back door."

Afraid that they might run into Chao Ma at the door, they walked under the pumelo trees along the rear wall. The garden was not small. On a slope, it was divided into three sections all planted with various kinds of trees, including the flowering and fruit-bearing ones. Along the rear wall it was even more densely wooded. Once summer arrived, Ling-ling did not dare to walk there alone, for fear that centipedes might bite her. But now accompanying her was Little Bolt of matchless bravery! And since it was so nice and shady by the wall, she told him not to leave in a hurry but rather to sit down and relax.

So the two sat on a stone bench to listen to the cicadas. With their keen eyes they looked among the leafy branches and could see clearly these insects, none too large in size but capable of producing very loud notes.

"You want me to catch them for you?" asked Little Bolt.

"No, Sister won't let me play with insects."

"You are afraid of your sister, aren't you? How can one be afraid of one's sister? I can never figure that out. Your sister often puts powder and rouge on her face, like an opera singer of female parts. You shouldn't be afraid of her."

"But she has never sung anything from an opera. She makes people afraid simply because she looks grand. Chao Ma obeys her. I obey her. All the men in the world ought to obey her!"

Little Bolt could hardly agree and hit the trunk of a big oak tree hard with his bamboo stick to show his manliness.

"I don't obey your sister. She has no control over me. She is not a mother tiger. She cannot eat me up."

"Yes, she can."

"Then she must be a mother tiger transformed. Only a mother tiger can eat me up."

"She is a mother tiger."

Hearing this, Little Bolt laughed. Ling-ling, in spiritedly defending Sister and trying to make even Little Bolt afraid of her, had admitted that Sister was a tigress by simply following the drift of the conversa-

[2] The mythological hero of the novel *Journey to the West,* also translated by Arthur Waley under the title *Monkey.*

tion. But when Little Bolt abruptly stopped talking, Ling-ling sensed that something was amiss and asked Little Bolt with gentle diffidence:

"A mother tiger, do you really think Sister is like that? Sister never bites people. She knows how to put one in good humor and tell stories and sing the long song of the Seven Heavenly Sisters. She is a grand person but not a tiger."

"At first I said she was not a tiger," retorted Little Bolt, "but you thought she was. I can't argue with you now; I'd better figure out a way to escape from your sister whenever I see her."

Ling-ling was about to say, "But Sister is the best person in the world," but Little Bolt had spotted dates on a date palm by the wall and was already walking over there.

The date palm at the corner of the wall was a big one. From among its sparse and slender branches and leaves hung an abundance of big, snow-white dates that had been green only a few days ago and were now fully ripe. Ling-ling jumped with joy at the sight and ran after Little Bolt. And when she reached the palm, Little Bolt had just made a spring while holding onto its trunk and suspended himself from the ground. In the twinkling of an eye, he was up like a monkey to the spot where the trunk forked, and then he sat astraddle a branch and began to shake it. Filled with joy and anxiety, Ling-ling lifted her head to look at him, crying out repeatedly, "Be careful! Don't fall down and don't you dare to fall on my head!"

Paying her no heed whatever, Little Bolt shook the branch up and down so vigorously that her face reddened with fear. Covering her head with her hands so as not to look at him, she cried out:

"Little Bolt, if you keep on shaking it like this, I'll leave."

So Little Bolt stopped shaking the branch and began picking the dates methodically. When he got hold of a very big one, he said, "Ling-ling, this is the biggest. Watch out. The magic missile is upon your head. Defend yourself."

Ling-ling held out the skirt of her dress and caught the date in time. She ate half of it in just one bite, but she was still not fast enough to catch the second one hurled from the palm. So she busied herself picking dates from the ground. Laughing, hopping around, and uttering half-suppressed cries of glee, she was in the highest spirits.

One upon the tree and the other under it—the two ate countless dates until they were finally surfeited. Sitting on the branch like a monkey exhausted from playing, Little Bolt paused for a while before slipping down the tree. He then produced another handful of the biggest dates from his pockets right in front of Ling-ling.

Ling-ling was afraid of blood, and when she saw the red stains on Little Bolt's hand accidentally cut by the prickles of the palm, she averted her gaze. But Little Bolt nonchalantly put his hand against his mouth and sucked it for a while, and then squatting down, he grasped a fistful of brown earth with the same hand and released it, as if nothing had happened.

He asked Ling-ling if she had enjoyed the dates. Ling-ling, whose hands were as full of dates as was her stomach, nodded with a smile and jumped a couple of times. She was reminded of the coins inside her pocket when they tinkled, and so she took them out, saying:

"I have four coppers. Mother gave them to me before she went out."

"Four?"

"One, two, three, four."

Just then, the beating of a bamboo clapper was heard outside the wall. Little Bolt knew it was the peddler of cold drinks prepared with the puree of dates.

"The man out there is selling date puree," he said. "Why don't we buy a bottle to drink?"

"Is date puree made of dates?"

"Yes, but it tastes better than fresh dates. It's made of red dates and not white dates. Don't you like red dates?"

"Yes, I like them very much. Let's go buy some."

Little Bolt's mind was quick. He told Ling-ling not to go outside for fear that people who knew her might catch her eating on the street. She'd better wait here while he went to buy the puree. He would be back in no time, he promised.

Ling-ling thought, "This is better," and thrust her coppers into his palm. Dashing out at flying speed, the recipient of these coins found on the peddler's stand a small roulette decorated with a movable dragon's head. From its mouth dangled a needle pointing at such prizes as candy Buddhas, pagodas, and bodhisattvas. Soon he lost three coins betting. With the remaining coin he got some date puree, but not enough to fill a bottle. So he asked the peddler to add some plain water and shook the bottle for a second. Soon Ling-ling saw her nimble and wily companion running back, a bottle of muddy-yellow liquid in his hand.

Ling-ling took one swallow when she got the bottle and felt that her mouth was sweet all over.

"Little Bolt, you want some?" she asked.

Remembering the candy pagadas and Buddhas he had tried to win, Little Bolt felt somewhat guilty and declined the offer. Sucking at the bottle, Ling-ling tilted her head to allow the liquid to gurgle down her throat. When she finally felt too full, she wiped her lips with her arm and handed the bottle to Little Bolt, who emptied it as soon as his lips touched it. He now asked:

"Ling-ling, how did you like it?"

"Real yummy."

From somewhere in the distance Chao Ma's voice was heard:

"Miss Ling-ling, where are you?"

Little Bolt was afraid to be seen by his mother. Using the pretext of returning the bottle, he disappeared like smoke.

Ling-ling hid the dates in her pockets, her heart uneasy and her stomach full. As she stepped out of the garden into the main hall, she saw on the large square table a big steamer full of piping hot little cakes. Sister was busy putting them on the plates. When she saw Ling-ling, she said:

"Little Ling-ling, come, let me give you a big one."

Although surfeited, Ling-ling could not refuse. Besides, when a child sees something freshly made, even if her overstuffed stomach is tight as a drum, she cannot help wanting one more bite. After she ate half of a hot cake, however, Ling-ling's stomach began to ache. Putting down the cake, she went out and sat by the door watching the cackling chickens raking up earth along the wall. She now remembered Mother's warning that one could die of cold or uncooked foods sold by street venders. Her aching stomach upset her, and yet she didn't dare tell Sister her trouble.

Sister came out and found Ling-ling sitting there alone with knitted brows, looking out of sorts. Thinking that she was still sulking, she walked over to cheer her up:

"Ling-ling, doesn't the cake taste good? How about having one more and saving two . . ."

When her eyes fell on Sister's face, Ling-ling remembered her silliness in having called her a mother tiger and felt somewhat ashamed. Sister continued:

"What's the matter? Still angry? I have stories. Run along and get a book. I'll tell you a good one."

Ling-ling said, almost inaudibly, "Sister, I have a tummy ache," and then burst into tears.

From the child's face, Sister could tell this was no lie. Very much worried, she took Ling-ling in her arms to carry her into the house, at the same time calling Chao Ma. When Ling-ling was lifted up, all the dates fell from her pockets onto the floor, rolling away in all directions. But they now meant nothing to the crying and groaning child, who willingly let Sister carry her into her own room.

Putting her down on the bed, Sister unbuttoned her clothes and asked what she had eaten. Ling-ling told everything, which made Sister even more worried. She ordered Chao Ma to look for Little Bolt and find out exactly what he had given her to eat. Chao Ma hurriedly left, invoking a variety of curses to shorten Little Bolt's life as she went. While her grumbling Sister was rubbing her stomach, Ling-ling lay quietly and watched a flat spider's "white nest" [3] on the canopy of her bed.

After a while Chao Ma came back. The pot of medicine she had earlier prepared was also ready. But since Ling-ling suffered only from overeating, she was already better after Sister had rubbed her rumbling stomach for some time. Chao Ma asked, "Shall I go and get T'ai-t'ai [4] back?" Ling-ling begged Sister not to do so. Seeing that her stomach ache didn't really seem to be serious, Sister agreed and sent away Chao Ma for the time being, telling her not to let Mother know, for otherwise all three of them would get a scolding from her. After Chao Ma was gone, Ling-ling hugged Sister out of gratitude and let her kiss her lips and forehead.

Sister asked, "Are you all right now?"

"I am much better."

"Why did you play with Little Bolt? You are a young lady. Behave

---

[3] *Hsi-chu,* also known in China as *pi-hsi* or *pi-ch'ien,* is a small flat-bodied spider with the scientific name *Uroctea compactilis.* The female of the species secretes white silk to make a coin-sized "nest" in which to deposit eggs.

[4] Meaning Ling-ling's mother. *T'ai-t'ai* is the honorific for a married woman.

with dignity and do not play with little rascals or eat anything you find, understand?"

"I won't do it again."

Although Sister seemed to be lecturing, her goodness and solicitude had touched a tender spot in Ling-ling, who felt like crying before her to indicate that she would never again make trouble or play with little rascals.

Sister forbade Ling-ling to get up, but afraid that the child might feel lonely, she fetched a book and sat on the edge of the bed to keep her company while reading. Ling-ling agreed to everything. While Sister was reading, she kept quiet, allowing the food in her stomach to digest slowly and at the same time gazing intently at the spider's coin-sized nest on a wooden panel supporting the canopy of her bed.

And so Ling-ling thought of her coins, of the way Little Bolt talked about Sister, and of other things and other times.

Her reading done, Sister made a mark at the place where she had stopped and closed the book. She then turned to Ling-ling and asked:

"Ling-ling, how is your tummy now?"

"Doesn't bother me any more." But she seemed still to have something on her mind, though she was too shy to speak out. Sister noticed her condition and reassured her, "Ling-ling, be a good girl. Don't worry. I'll not tell Mommy what happened."

Ling-ling shook her head and beckoned with her hand to ask Sister to bend her head so that she could whisper something strictly confidential. When Sister bent her ear to the small mouth, Ling-ling said softly:

"You may be a mother tiger, but I am not afraid. I want to be married to you."

Sister stopped to think for a second and laughed out loud, bending down to lift Ling-ling and kissing her all over. Still bashful, Ling-ling found her eyes wet and then she sobbed.

In tears, Ling-ling kept thinking: "I want to be married to you. I really want to."

Chang T'ien-i

Chang T'ien-i (1907–   ) was the most brilliant and powerful short story writer of the thirties. During a decade remarkable for the abundance of talented story writers, none could match him for the economy of his comic art, the depth and range of his satiric representation. Gentry, bourgeoisie, and proletariat alike are grist to his satiric mill, and his grasp of the essential meanness of the human soul and of the deep animosity existing between different social classes is truly astonishing. His world, therefore, is filled with snobs and malcontents, abject underlings and ambitious schemers intent on getting ahead, and every kind of oppressor abusing his power and position to inflict pain on his inferiors out of sheer malice. Though a Marxist and a member of the League of the Left-wing Writers (a Communist organization dominating the literary scene in the thirties), Chang T'ien-i was too much of a realist fascinated by the ugly social phenomena of his time to observe in his best stories the required leftist formulas of protest and rebellion.

Though his birthplace was Nanking, Chang T'ien-i is the scion of an eminent Hunanese family of scholar-officials. His mother was a noted poet and one of his sisters became in time a famous educator in support of the Kuomintang, but Chang stuck to his nonconformist path and after middle school supported himself as government clerk, army officer, reporter, and schoolteacher. His varied experience in these jobs must have given him special insights into many walks of Chinese life.

"Spring Breeze" (Ch'un-feng, 1936), one of Chang T'ien-i's assured masterpieces, must have drawn upon his personal experience as a teacher. It examines a free elementary school in the aspect of an artificial society cemented by the bonds of hatred and contempt. The main victims are the poor schoolchildren, maltreated alike by their teachers and well-to-do classmates out of sheer scorn and malice. In *History*, I have commented on the story in part as follows:

Chang T'ien-i has written many animated comic stories about student life, and in this one he exhibits, with more than his usual moral clairvoyance, the depravity and corruption among his assorted teachers and students. . . . The hero of "Spring Breeze," Teacher Ch'iu, is somewhat better than his colleagues by virtue of his deep dissatisfaction with his present lot and his ambition to quit the place and enter college. But he is equally ridiculous, equally impatient with and contemptuous of the poor children. He again is the small man who has taken on the evil quality of his environment because he hates it and is unable to leave it. The wealth of Dickensian comedy in "Spring Breeze" is rooted in the sardonic perception of how one doomed class on a slightly higher economic level may positively hate another on a lower.

Several earlier anthologies of modern Chinese fiction have featured stories by Chang T'ien-i, including Edgar Snow, ed., *Living China* (New York, 1936); Chi-chen Wang, ed., *Contemporary Chinese Stories* (New York, 1944) and *Stories of China at War* (New York, 1946); and Yeh Chun-chan, tr., *Three Seasons and Other Stories* (London, 1946). More recently, Sister Mary Gregory, S.P., translated "Mid-Autumn Festival" (*Chung-ch'iu*), a haunting study of cruelty, for No 1 (Spring, 1965) of *The Tea Leaves*, an occasional publication sponsored by the Departments of Comparative Literature and of East Asian Languages and Literatures, Indiana University.

SPRING BREEZE[1]

TRANSLATED BY *Hou Chien*

Prologue

Morning. Quite comfortable it was in the sun. Neither hot nor chilly.

Now and then, there would be a light breeze. Nobody knew where it came from or where it was going. Afterwards only the sensation of having been caressed would remain on one's face, as though a piece of velvet had been drawn across it.

At such a time, the slimy greenish rivulet would lazily wrinkle itself, and people walking along the bank would smell something unpleasant mixed with the fragrance of the flowers and grass.

Somebody spat in disgust. Upon that, one of the teachers passing by began to complain of the rivulet. It was his opinion that, since a school was here, the least people should do was fix that ditch so it would not stink.

"I myself have brought this up with Principal T'ung. He said—he said the commissioner would not want to spend money on that."

They did not pause, and their elongated shadows swept along the ocher-colored wall beside them.

One man younger than the others sneered:

[1] In its original publication in *Wen-hsüeh* (*Literature*), VI, No. 2 (Shanghai, February, 1936), the story carried an inscription, "For Shih-ch'ing."

"One shouldn't demand too much. Our children are sent here to school—without costing us a penny. What more do we want?"

Walking by the school entrance, they stared hard at the gray gate. It seemed so out of keeping with the ocher-colored wall. But the sign, inscribed in black on a white ground, could not be more out of place:

THE SPRING BREEZE PRIMARY SCHOOL

ESTABLISHED BY THE PROVINCIAL

HIGHWAY BUREAU

The gate was closed, presenting a forbidding aspect to the pedestrians. As though quite displeased by their criticism, it coldly watched them walk away.

Some ten minutes later, it opened a little way, and spewed out a boy with a scar on his eyelid, who went away skipping and jumping.

Quietness reigned inside, except for the chirping of sparrows.

The two peach trees in the yard were in vigorous bloom. They seemed too healthy to mind the frequent shedding of their petals. The few that had drifted into the corridor appeared especially gorgeous.

The corridor was named Neatness Road: gray cement dotted with black spots. To prepare for the PTA meeting held here the Saturday before, Principal T'ung had ordered the janitor to remove the black spots but a great deal of mopping had had little effect. At the end of the corridor were piled several chairs with broken legs—the victims of the meeting.

A number of dark streaks left by pencils could be seen on the wall. Evidently somebody had been too lazy to sharpen his pencils with a knife, but had made do by rubbing the points there.

It was quite clean higher up. There were posted there only the class schedules and the weekly assignment sheets for each teacher. And the characters were all finely drawn, like those in an elementary textbook.

The last poster, though, was by a poor hand. The heading itself was badly drawn. There were no wrongly inscribed characters, however. It said:

PTA MEETING ON THE FOURTH ANNIVERSARY OF THE SCHOOL

An Address by Commissioner Chi

Recorded by Jen Chia-hung, Monitor, Fifth Grade

In truth, the recorder had been Teacher Chin. All the punctuation marks were clearly placed, all the indentations clearly observed.

Parents, Teachers, Girls and Boys:

Today is the fourth anniversary of the establishment of this our Spring Breeze Primary School. So I am very happy. Now we have this meeting of parents and teachers. We have invited all you

Parents, Teachers, Girls and Boys,

and I am very happy. This school was founded by Commissioner Liu, my predecessor, on receiving the personal order of

His Excellency the Governor of the Province,

who gave instructions that a school should be established to solve the problem of education for the staff of the Provincial Highway Bureau. It therefore charges no tuition or any other fees. Instead, it provides books, pens, ink, paper, and what not, all free of charge. This school was formerly called Primary School for the Children of the Staff and Workmen of the Provincial Highway Bureau, but the name has since been changed to The Spring Breeze Primary School. "Spring breeze" means "education," for people of ancient times used to compare education to the spring breeze. Today, however, I have also a new discovery for you. I have always advocated equal treatment for everybody. The spring breeze treats everybody equally: however humble or exalted a man is, the spring breeze will make no distinction between him and others. In this our school, the children of government employees and workmen all study equally, they all equally pay nothing, and they all equally share the spring breeze. We must all be grateful to

His Excellency the Governor

for his benevolence, and be friendly to one another. Today I do not know why I am in such a good mood, but apparently being with you

Parents, Teachers, Girls and Boys

has made me very happy. I have therefore talked to you on my newly discovered meaning of "spring breeze," so that we shall make no distinctions because of our positions but be friends and love one another.

The end.

I

It was a fine day. No cloud anywhere. The rays of the sun appeared even to have bleached the blue in the sky.

Upstairs everything was as usual. Teacher Ch'iu had a book in his hand. He was not reading, however, but leaning on the railing, his bushy brows tightly knit together and his chin in his right hand. He gave the impression of one suffering from a toothache.

The children were playing noisily in the yard. The din pierced his ears like pinpricks.

A boy in a Western-style suit, however, was standing under a peach tree quietly chewing his toffee or some other kind of candy. Beside him, a scabby-headed first-grader hungrily watched the other's mouth, though he had nothing to put into his own except his dirty forefinger. The sleeve of his light-gray cotton coat had a patch on it.

Teacher Ch'iu observed to himself irritably:

"What a greedy little pig!"

Around one corner of the wall shouts and laughter suddenly burst out. Some half a dozen children all stripped to their undershirts were jostling one another trying to kick at an olive pit. Those whose undershirts had missing buttons showed their jutting ribs blackened with filth.

Then the same admonition that came every day repeated itself from upstairs:

"Don't make any noise!"

Biting his underlip with his large front teeth and knocking on the railing with his book, Teacher Ch'iu brought his foot heavily down, making the floorboards tremble, and called out:

"Don't you dare make another sound, Yü Ta-ch'ang! Get in, Yü Ta-ch'ang—no more playing outside for you. . . . You little rascal and born convict, how dare you still stand there?"

But he soon regretted his outburst. Why did he lose his temper? Hadn't he been told that he had heart disease?

Desperately, he tried to calm his breathing. He removed all expression from his face, and started pacing slowly, his hand on the right side of his breast. He remembered that was where the heart was.

The yard gained a great measure of peace. Fearfully, the children glanced up and pretended to be well-behaved. But the untamed look in their faces betrayed them.

"The school is being operated in vain, this school!" Squinting his eyes, he let his breath slowly out through his nostrils.

But it was not until the tall teacher Ting came up to the corridor to sun himself that Teacher Ch'iu began his discourse.

"Our school is hopeless," he sighed. "But you must realize that I am actually no pessimist. . . ."

After this opening remark, he rolled his book into a cylinder, to help with the gestures, and stuck his chest out as though preparing to address an audience of several thousand people.

He started with the dirty clothes of Yü Ta-ch'ang and his companions. He divided this subject into five items and he had original notions on each of them. Every time he spoke a sentence that seemed especially meaningful or brilliant, he would repeat it two or three times.

Whenever his eyes chanced to fall on the other's face, he could not help thinking to himself:

"What a vulgar nose that!"

Yet his eloquence never flagged. After all, among all the people in the school, Teacher Ting was the only one who could appreciate him.

Teacher Ting was all ears, only now and then putting in a word. But a clownish expression would appear on his face, which was his way of indicating that he was only being witty when he interrupted. According to him, that was a type of "vitamin."

So he shrugged his shoulders and protruded his underlip:

"They sure have excellent bringing up at home: all great raisers of lice!"

With his thumb on his nose, he wriggled his four fingers in the air a few times. These were always stained with various colors: iodine or mercurochrome.

If truth must out, it had to be admitted that Mr. Ting was a graduate of some school for nurses, though he preferred to be called doctor. On the strength of that he had been put in charge of health matters in addition to his teaching. Didn't Principal T'ung praise him in glowing terms, saying that nobody was Teacher Ting's match when it came to inoculations and vaccinations?

That did not keep Teacher Ch'iu from detesting his nose, however. Not even while he was talking his heart out.

When he reached the wall and was turning around, Teacher Ch'iu took the opportunity to contemplate his auditor with disdain. "How strange: his nose is really like a pug's!" he inwardly commented.

Outwardly, he was citing a statistic: two thirds of the student body consisted of young rascals. These scapegraces were so intractable there was no teaching them at all. He scowled as though he were standing in the sun during the worst of the dog days, and the small patch of hairs in between his knitted brows became especially dark.

He then pronounced his conclusion with great conviction: no amount of school education would be of any use without a good education at home. So why spend so much money on this school for such a bunch of hopeless cases?

"I have nothing else to say except that it is a waste of education."

After repeating the verdict he solemnly looked into the face of the other man.

Teacher Ting rubbed his chin and drew a deep breath. He was rather sorry for his colleague: a top graduate from a normal school— the holder of a Number One diploma, and so very young, too, and yet he was made to deal with little rascals!

He felt called upon to say something serious. He assumed a grave air—and thus looked suspiciously as though he were on the point of joking. He raised his voice to indicate that he was by no means completely discouraged. After all, there were still some good children in the school, and some who dressed cleanly and knew what personal hygiene meant, and whose fathers or brothers, respectable officials in the bureau, had afforded them a good upbringing at home. Resuming his capacity as a doctor, he then earnestly counseled Teacher Ch'iu against undue excitement, which was definitely bad for a man with a heart condition.

Finally, he even put in a little of his "vitamin":

"You say our school is a vain undertaking, don't you? Well, if it is disbanded, you know perfectly well our meal ticket will—" Spreading out his hands in the manner of a clown in a magician's act, he enunciated in a heavily nasal voice, *"van-ni-shih!"*

And he waited complacently for the laughter that should follow.

But the commotion downstairs broke out again at this moment. The children were clapping their hands and crying out "Jen Chia-hung! Jen Chia-hung!" Even the whitewashed wall and the sun seemed to be echoing the name.

Jen Chia-hung entered the gate with a basketball under his arm. He walked with long strides, his worsted spring topcoat flapping.

"Jen Chia-hung, let's play ball, let's play ball."

"Jen Chia-hung, I'll join in, okay?"

"Huh, you dirty little brat!" Jen Chia-hung shouted in the hoarse falsetto common among boys in the subteens or early teens. "All right, come, come, come. Take my topcoat to the classroom. . . . Hey, my satchel too!"

His shoulders lifted and both his hands on the railing, Teacher Ting watched them with a smirk on his face. Then he glanced at Teacher Ch'iu.

The other compressed his lips. There was one thing he could not understand. Jen Chia-hung's father was a chief engineer in the highway bureau, and earned more than three hundred dollars a month. So why should he send his son into a den of young rascals? He sighed ponderously.

Jen Chia-hung himself, however, was not aware of this grievance. As usual, he was dressed tidily, his hair well-groomed, and he was playing with spirit. After throwing his ball to a boy in a gosling-yellow woolen sweater, he rushed to where the girls were, intercepted the shuttlecock Ch'ien Su-chen was kicking, and kicked it with great vigor.

The girl twirled, and her new lined gown of rayon flashed in the sun. She exclaimed in the kind of shrill voice with which she sang her favorite song, "The Express": [2]

"You jerk, you!"

Jen Chia-hung laughed, whirled around, and in doing so slapped the first-grader Yu Fu-lin on his scabby head—*p'i!*

Yu Fu-lin staggered several steps back and, holding his head in his hands, began to cry.

So the routine downstairs repeated itself: quarrels, fights, bawling. Yu Feng-ying, a fifth-grader, pulled Yu Fu-lin to her side and, her sallow face clouded and her lips pale with rage, started bickering with Jen Chia-hung.

"Ugh," Teacher Ch'iu muttered to himself, his eyes wide open. "What a scold she is!"

[2] "The Express" (*T'e-pieh k'uai-che*), a comic song of fast tempo, was very popular in the early thirties. Its title symbolizes the extraordinarily short span of time (about two hours) within which a modern Chinese girl gets engaged and married and gives birth to twins. The words of the song are recorded in *Hsin hsi-k'ao* (A new guide to records) (Shanghai, 1937), p. 265.

But Jen Chia-hung paid her no attention whatever. Instead, he was playing ball, his face wreathed in a big smile.

Somehow, many others got embroiled in the row. Ch'ien Su-chen stopped playing with her shuttlecock and dashed over. Her arms akimbo, her lips pulled down at the corners, and her neck sticking out, she was now talking to Yu Feng-ying's face:

"Honestly, just a little shove, and you think your brother is dying, eh? Holy cow, what a great sister you are! And no wonder the teachers are saying we have a big scold in the school!"

"What—what? You bait people when they have done no harm to you, yet you—"

Jen Chia-hung threw out his ball with force. Nonchalantly, he interrupted:

"I touched a scabby head, and that brings bad luck. I am generous enough not to demand compensation."

Thereupon the little rascals started calling Jen Chia-hung names. Yü Ta-ch'ang pushed his way into the crowd and, waving his blackened arm scaly with dirt, shouted:

"Bully, bully, shameless bully! And a monitor, too!"

On his perch, Teacher Ch'iu was again furious. He stamped and smote the railing with his fist: "Yü Ta-ch'ang, Yü Ta-ch'ang! You brat! Scat!"

When he saw that the imp had actually left, Teacher Ch'iu dragged Teacher Ting into their room. He was still grinding his teeth.

"Such a life, such a life! All little ragamuffins, bad eggs, all deserve to be shot!"

II

Three beds were spread out in the room, giving it a crowded look. In the very middle there were three desks arranged in a triangle, on which were piled exercise books of the pupils.

On a wire strung at one end of the room were hung some towels, one of which was still dripping water, wetting the whitewashed wall. A sheet of letter paper pasted to the wall had changed color after repeated soaking and the red rulings had become blurred, but the neat characters written on it were legible. They appeared to stand out against the damp ground:

"Yours humbly being a victim of trachoma, it is respectfully urged that nobody use his face towel. Please forgive him for making this impertinent request.

Chin Meng-chou"

The only things remotely decorative in the room were the postcards of scenic spots which Teacher Ting had thumbtacked on the wall. The other posters were all notices in the handwriting of Teacher Chin, the dean of students. Near the spittoon, for example, could be seen a reminder: "Please spit into the spittoon for the sake of hygiene." And on the door—a couplet, too:

"No idler but the sagacious may enter.
Let not robbers but the virtuous come."

The notice beside the window was new: "Please do not make any noise after yours humbly is in bed so that his sleep is not disturbed."

Invariably, a signature would end the message, a signature in a cursive style hardly decipherable. The mark of his chop under the signature, however, was a brilliant and conspicuous red, with a ring of oozy oil around it.

On the wall near Teacher Chin's desk there was another note: "Seat of the Dean of Students." This strip of paper was relatively short: originally there had been an exclamation mark under the phrase, but when he was posting it he had for some reason cut that part off.

The desk itself sported still another notice, which seemed to ogle its host: "Hands off yours humbly's books without his consent." Below this exhortation was a fat exclamation point, followed by the ubiquitous signature, with the chop mark bringing up the rear.

Teacher Ch'iu swept his eyes over these strips of paper and snorted: "What an insufferable boor!"

At the present moment the dean of students was engaged in a hot debate with Teacher P'i, the principal's administrative assistant. His blearily reddish eyes glaring, Teacher Chin was thumping his desk and shouting. He could not believe that the school did not have two dollars on hand, and he took this as a sign that they were all trying to squeeze him out of his position. He pointed the fingers of his right hand into Teacher P'i's face and gave the desk a heavy blow with the other hand.

The horse face of the assistant contracted, and his supporting neck sagged also as he countered with a question:

"What do you mean, I am trying to squeeze you out?"

They could quarrel to their hearts' content, but Teacher Ch'iu was not going to interfere. Instead, he lit a cigarette, and leisurely opened a copy of the *English Weekly* as though nothing had happened.

"They are going to use their fists," he thought.

But Teacher Ting was officiously trying to intercede. He put on the facetious face of Oliver Hardy and whispered his advice: it was against the principle of hygiene to be angry. Then he patted Teacher Chin on the back, shrugged his own shoulders, and uttered some witticism about its being a bad proposition to be upset for a measly two dollars: it would cost much more money if one became sick from the anger.

"Therefore—this exalted doctor of yours has the right to forbid you two to show anger."

Then he hurriedly bit the tip of his tongue with his front teeth to refrain from laughing.

Teacher Chin was not impressed. Far from simmering down, he started abusing his opponent. His chest sticking out, the corners of his mouth crinkled, he spat out every word with force, and even let fall such terms as "graft" and "embezzlement." His tone was threatening: it would give him great pleasure, he said, to produce some evidence and see if some people could still go on with their corrupt practices in the school.

Everybody knew Teacher Chin got his position through Secretary Pei of the provincial government.

So his opponent flushed, saying:

"Haya, why get so excited, friend? About that money, why, of course I shall try to get it for you. Will it be all right if I give it to you tomorrow or the day after? It won't make much difference if you get it a bit late, will it?"

"Nothing doing!"

"But . . . but . . ."

The arbitrator gazed at the floor for a while. Suddenly, with eyes popping wide and mouth rounded up to let out an "Oh!", he lifted his face and asked the antagonists to have some regard for it and stop fuming. Then poking at his own nose, he added that he had a silver dollar in his pocket, which he was willing to put up for the present occasion.

Teacher Chin did not even bother to turn, merely saying:

"One dollar isn't enough."

The administrative assistant sighed, his right hand tremblingly rubbing his left.

Teacher Ting scratched his head, and said he would try to borrow the other dollar from the two women teachers. He went to their room. Walking on tiptoe and craning his neck ever so often, he recounted the quarrel and even mimicked Teacher Chin's angry expression.

The women teachers laughed shrilly. Hugging each other's waists, they rolled on the bed.

The male teacher was goaded to greater efforts and displayed the whole range of his art. On leaving them, he bowed three times; then, standing at attention, he lifted both hands to his brow, and saluted in the fashion of military officers in the movies.

But Teacher Chin retained his frosty face when he received the money. He took out a copper and tapped the silver dollar. He scrutinized the paper note against the light of the window. At last, he pushed both silver and bill into his pocket—without saying anything.

Teacher Ting shrugged.

"Well, he is still furious. Something must be the matter with his liver."

With a benevolent look, he continued to stare at Teacher Chin's reddish eyes. Occasionally he glanced in Teacher Ch'iu's direction as though he were afraid the other would disapprove of his meddlesomeness. At the same time, he held his breath in an attempt to make out what Teacher Chin was mumbling through his thick lips.

Teacher Ch'iu was shifting his eyes from the periodical to the administrative assistant, as the latter walked stealthily out of the door, not forgetting to turn his long face for a last furtive look at Teacher Chin.

"A despicable coward that," Teacher Ch'iu puckered his lips in contempt. "He must be going to the kitchen to take it out on poor Ch'ang-shou. Nauseating!"

He became aware that Teacher Ting had registered on his face a desire to talk to him, and hastily withdrew his eyes to pretend that he was deeply engrossed in his reading. At the same time, he felt the right side of his chest and listened to his own breathing.

The dean of students remained motionless except for his thick lips, which were working busily. One could gather at a glance that he was at odds with the whole world. He was especially irascible in the class-room, and would look sternly at the children, eager to find some fault with them.

"Wang Ch'ien-sheng," Teacher Chin would walk down the plat-form and address a victim, "I have told you to sew your buttons back on. Why didn't you?"

And another roar:

"When your teacher is talking to you, what do you do? Should you reply while still seated?"

The boy hastily stood up. He was sallow and emaciated, with a dried-up face. Looking at him, one could hardly believe he was a creature of flesh and blood.

Teacher Chin was exasperated by what he saw:

"Speak up, speak up! Why didn't you sew them back on? Are your family all dead? A rascal born and bred! The mold of a beggar! Speak!"

And he was pulling and tweaking the child's ear.

"I . . . I . . ." Wang Ch'ien-sheng held back his tears as much as he could, his voice quivering. "My mother doesn't have the time. . . . She has to. . . ."

"So you always have excuses, eh? You . . . you. . . ."

He slapped the child in the face, and the youngster fell back in his seat.

"You and your trashy family, you. . . ." The dean of students gnashed his teeth, his face turning pale. Suddenly, he pounded the low desk for the use of Wang Ch'ien-sheng and some other pupils, causing their pens and inkslabs to jump. "Rotten egg! You muddled rotten egg! So you want to sit down when you answer your teacher, eh? Give me your hand!"

He took up an inkslab from the desk and brought it down against the small palm with all his might. A tense, oppressive thudding noise rose up in the room, mixed with the half-suppressed sounds of tremulous weeping. At times the child couldn't help interposing his other hand, and then there would be the dull, sickening sound of the inkslab hitting against the knuckles and bones.

He flailed until his arm was too weary to go on. But his reddish eyes still bulged.

"Don't you dare cry! If you do, I'll . . ."

Pulling out his handkerchief, Teacher Chin wiped his left hand, and began pacing among the pupils. His wrath subsided only when he reached the boy in a Western-style suit.

"Sit up, Tseng Chen. You'll become humpbacked sitting like that."

He stroked Tseng Chen's cheek.

The children had become quiet now, so quiet they could hear the humming bees outside.

But his ire returned when he was back on the platform. He was indignant with the children because their arithmetic exercise books were so dirty.

"Shih Kuo-hsing, I have told you to replace your exercise book, so why don't you? When the school issued notebooks to you, it didn't mean to have you abuse them."

The boy called Shih Kuo-hsing stood up woodenly, and answered with no expression on his face:

"My father doesn't have the money. He won't let me replace it."

"What?" The teacher's eyes were again starting out of their sockets. "You don't have the money to replace it? Then you should have been careful when you used it. How dare you make it so very filthy? Look at Tseng Chen's book and see how clean his is."

The boy muttered something under his breath, as though he were afraid of being overheard. He knew very well that Tseng Chen and some of the others had changed to new books several times over. What was more, they always copied their exercises only after the teacher had corrected them.

Teacher Chin jumped.

"How dare you say anything? You don't keep your book clean, and you won't replace it. Yet you, you . . . A real rascal you! You will be trundled out the Small East Gate and shot as an example yet! Come here!"

Since he could find no other instrument, he used his fist and rained blows on the boy's head and shoulders without discrimination. He struck even harder after the boy had briefly put up a show of resistance.

All the children who had dirty exercise books were then beaten one after another. They had all refused to replace their smeared exercise books and were willing to let the teacher lose face when the inspector from the province came and looked over the school. They were all intransigent savages. According to him, their fathers and big brothers were themselves worthless beggars, scoundrels. He was sure they sent their urchins to this school only to harass the teachers, to make them suffer the criticism of the commissioner and others high up in the Bureau.

So he had to let out his rancor on their bodies.

At last, he pantingly said:

"Listen, you who just got punished, you! The police are after vagrants and rascals, so be careful, or you'll all be shot. You who are here only to create disturbances . . ."

Seeing a number of pupils peeping in at the door, he abruptly turned upon them: "Why are you not in class?"

"Teacher T'ung isn't up yet."

"Then go up to your classroom and read by yourselves. How dare you stand here gaping, you little rascals?"

III

Teacher Ch'iu was in his classroom, teaching third-grade Chinese. As the children were receiving their punishment in the next room, he could not make himself heard at all.

His left hand was resting on the book on the desk, and his right was on his chest. He did not raise his voice, for that might be harmful to his health.

Sometimes, his mind would light upon something of no immediate concern:

"How strange! Teacher Chin is addicted to beating the children."

To be sure, there was much to be desired of the second graders. But he was certain they had become worse because Teacher Chin was their arithmetic teacher and regularly beat them. He had brought this up with Teacher Ting, and advanced three arguments to support his opinion that once you start beating them, you will have to beat them all the time, or they'll be unmanageable.

So he scowled, and sighed a very deep sigh to give vent to all his bitterness against the world.

One has to admit that, when Teacher Ch'iu punished, he always strove to be fair. But fairness could be an inconvenience sometimes. He well remembered how, when he first returned after last year's summer vacation, he had once scolded a pupil named Mao Hui-liang, and how Principal T'ung had said to him, half apologetically and half apprehensively:

"Mao Hui-liang is actually a good pupil. If you are too severe with him, I am afraid of the consequences. After all, he is a boy of good upbringing. His uncle is the chief of the secretariat at the Highway Bureau, and enjoys the confidence of Commissioner Chi."

Regrettably, however, there were only eight or nine pupils in the class who might be considered to have been well brought up. These were always neat and personable, and it was true they did not require too much severity in handling.

It was the other forty-odd children who were troublesome.

"They are real menaces. They use up the best in a man and make him suffer from a heart condition. What a school!"

Suddenly he felt a fit of suffocation. He wanted to jump up and let off steam. His face, though, remained stern, presenting the aspect of an overcast sky when a storm was imminent.

And then there was always the scourge Yü Ta-ch'ang to make him feel worse.

"Yü Ta-ch'ang, what are you playing with? Come and stand over there!"

He pointed to one side of the platform, and put his hand back on his chest while he spun his face right and left, looking the children over.

"Huang Ch'ao, why are you looking at that window? Huang Ch'ao!" He rapped the desk with an eraser. "Come here!"

He fixed his eyes on the boy's face unswervingly, then turned his back, and wrote the character *chih* (intelligence) on the blackboard, producing a series of scraping sounds.

"What character is that?"

"*Chih,*" the child answered in a small voice.

He had calculated on Huang Ch'ao's failure to recognize the character, so that he would have a good pretext to punish him. Now he was honestly surprised—and very much disappointed, too.

"What?" he snarled.

The imp thought his answer had been wrong, and stretched out the palm of his hand in fear.

"What are you doing, what are you doing?" Teacher Ch'iu exclaimed. "You little slave, you abject, sniveling, born slave! Obviously, you didn't know whether your answer was right or wrong. You just bluffed. Stand over there!"

Huang Ch'ao was visibly relieved. He stood there on the platform and winked at Yü Ta-ch'ang, who, having nothing better to do, plucked at the hole in his shirt, which soon grew from an inch-long rent to one of six inches.

The teacher slowly let out his breath, and continued his lecture, lingering over the last word of each sentence.

"The young boy in this lesson—is he a good boy or a bad boy?"

"A good boy," the children answered in unison, and, like the teacher, lingered over the last word.

"Why is he a good boy?"

Different answers now came up in confusion.

"Speak one at a time." He clapped his hands. "Those who can answer raise their right hands. . . . I said right hands, not the left. Wang Shao-ch'iu, did you hear me? Right hand, I said. The other one, the other one! K'ang Chia-hsiang, I told you to raise your right hand. Can't you tell which is your right hand, which is your left? Idiot!"

To avoid another surge of temper, he picked out a more pleasing boy to answer his question.

And the answer completely conformed to the textbook:

"The boy is clean. He says 'good morning, sir' when he meets the teacher. The boy is a good boy."

A smile lurked around the corners of Teacher Ch'iu's mouth. The knitted brows began to loosen.

"And?"

"When his father gives him money, he does not spend it. The boy will not let his younger sister scold the servants. He changes his clothes every day. . . ."

"What is a servant?"

"He is an orderly."

The answer amused the teacher and elicited a genuine grin from him. He waved the boy down, and raised his voice a little to ask the other children if they ever scolded their servants or if they spent the money their fathers gave them.

The answers were again confused, but it was apparent many said that their fathers never gave them any money. One boy with a boil on his face admitted to spending money: every morning his brother gave him three coppers to buy a sesame cake and he ate it on the way to school. Most of them, however, had no idea what a servant was. They knew about orderlies, though: the uncle of Liu Chih-ch'eng, of the first grade, was one.

But a few other boys called out that they had a servant at home.

"There is one in my home, honest. He is Wang Ch'ang-fa. Wang Ch'ang-fa is a bad man. He stole twenty cents from my brother on Monday. . . ."

"Teacher Ch'iu, my daddy is putting my money into a savings account. . . ."

"Teacher Ch'iu, Teacher Ch'iu, Yü Ta-ch'ang and Huang Ch'ao are making faces at us. They are trying to make us laugh. Yü Ta-ch'ang even stuck his tongue out."

Teacher Ch'iu's face changed its color at once. He gave the offenders twenty strokes each with the blackboard eraser. Then he let his breath out slowly, and put his hand on the right side of the chest—he could feel how violently his heart was throbbing.

"How these brats persecute me! The rascals!"

He gnashed his teeth. He thought he would fall seriously ill. Perhaps he might even die. And his newly married wife would then be big with child, she would cry and tell other people how she had never had any luck. When her husband was alive, she would moan, he made only thirty-two dollars a month and did nothing whatever of importance.

A chill crept up his spine, and he shivered. He wished he could throw a bomb at the school.

After class, K'ang Chia-hsing showed him a character in his book and asked how it was pronounced. He slapped the boy on the face with all his strength and stamped his feet:

"Where were your ears in class, you idiot? You, you, you! Oh, this terrible life . . . I am sure I am going to be sick, sick. . . ."

Holding his chest, he shuffled away.

The classes after that were worse. The little rascals were unmanageable, as was to be expected. And in the next room Teacher Chin was back to his routine, beating more than half the class with his fist or inkslabs while he bellowed and the pupils wailed. Across the hall, a woman teacher was teaching singing. Her voice was so tinglingly shrill he could not stand it at all. It gave him the sensation of biting into a sour plum.

There was also Teacher Ting's high-spirited voice. He sounded joyous enough to suggest a mahjong player who has just laid down a hand that will win a huge pile of chips for him. It distracted the attention of the children in his own class. It also seemed to make them envious: what fun it was to be in Teacher Ting's class!

For laughter now and then erupted in Teacher Ting's classroom.

Teacher Ting enjoyed this, and he was striving to attain new heights. Both his brows and his eyes danced.

"Do you know the meaning of 'cleanliness'?" Holding his book aloft, Teacher Ting asked a question he had been constantly asking.

The class as usual gave the gratifying reply: " 'Cleanliness' means hygiene."

Teacher Ting nodded.

"Right you are, children. Hygiene, yes, hygiene, and that is the most important thing in the world. Such as having inoculations and vaccinations. If somebody is not vaccinated—would that be right?"

"No!"

"Ah, correct again. If one does not have vaccination one will be like Liao Wen-pin and become pock-faced. Why didn't you get vaccinated, Liao Wen-pin?"

"I don't know," Liao Wen-pin replied in a woebegone voice, and wiped his mouth on his sleeve.

Teacher Ting, pointing at Liao Wen-pin's face, started a long tirade, very much as though the brat had done something bad enough to be put down for a major demerit. He shrugged, he raised his brows, and finally he poked at his own face with both hands while his mouth constricted.

"Hi, hi, hi! Pockmarks, all pockmarks! How ugly, ugh, how ugly. Oh, my goodness!"

The pupils all laughed uproariously; some even applauded and stamped.

Liao Wen-pin burst out crying.

The one on the platform mimicked him with a loud "Wa!" Then he forced back his laughter, but the corners of his mouth were still crinkled and his eyes twinkling.

"Why do you cry? Is it anybody's fault you have pockmarks?"

Another fit of laughing went up. Teacher Ting waved his hand, but when he saw he could not stop the pupils, he just stood there, his abdomen pushed out, his face beaming.

"Yu Fu-lin," at last he exclaimed, "do you think you have the right to laugh at others? Your scabby head is as ugly as pockmarks. Ah, dirty, dirty."

He pulled out a piece of gauze to cover his mouth, and chuckled behind it. It was only when the whole class had regained order that, assuming a more serious mien, he asked another customary question: who was the cleanliest in class.

The pupils knew what Teacher Ting wanted:

"Lin Wen-hou."

All the eyes were cast upon Lin Wen-hou.

And the cleanliest boy hastened to look solemn, with his lips tightly closed. Though his eyes were rolling right and left, he sat very stiffly there; his chest was all the way out, leaving a big hollow on his back. He appeared almost like an ill-shaped stone statue.

Teacher Ting blew his nose into the gauze. Raising his brows, he was on the point of saying something when Lin Wen-hou exclaimed:

"I report to the teacher: Chiang Jih-hsin is winking at me!"

The teacher looked sternly at Chiang Jih-hsin, jutting his underlip out, and warningly shook his head.

After a while, Lin Wen-hou called out again:

"I report to the teacher: Chiang Jih-hsin rubbed his filthy clothes against mine. They are so filthy."

Many of the children looked at Chiang Jih-hsin, then turned their gaze on Teacher Ting. Several of the faces wore an expectant expression, as though they hoped something would happen. One of them loudly smacked his lips.

"Ah, Chiang Jih-hsin, you are asking to have a little warming up, aren't you?" Teacher Ting jocosely rolled up his sleeve while he made a funny face to arouse laughter.

He did not even pretend to listen to the dirty boy's plea, but went on talking:

"You set the penalty: how many strokes do you say? What, you didn't do it on purpose? What do I care if you didn't? You'll get the beating whether you meant it or not. Hurry up, say how many strokes. Two, did you say? Hi, hi, hi, isn't that a bit cheap?"

Only when he set the penalty at fifteen strokes did he begin to administer the punishment with the blackboard eraser. At the same time, he shrugged, creased his nose, and cracked: "This is a sort of vitamin for the little rascal."

IV

The fourth session. Teacher Ch'iu had no class.

He leafed over the newspapers in the hall, hoping to find the copy of the Shanghai *News* [3] that had arrived yesterday, but Principal T'ung had already mailed it to his home town. He rapped the table, a Western-style dining table, with his knuckles, sniffed, and smelled an unpleasant odor.

The hall served as both conference room and library. A cabinet stood against the wall. It was filled with publications, mostly bulletins from the provincial government and monthly journals of the highway bureau. In addition, three copies of the *Youth Magazine* lay together in a neat pile. These had been donated by Jen Chia-hung and belonged originally to his uncle. Two issues were from 1916, the other, 1919.

Teacher Ch'iu let out a deep groan. The place seemed hemmed in. The four walls around him so pressed down upon him that he could hardly breathe.

[3] The *News* (*Hsin-wen Pao*) was the largest-selling newspaper in Shanghai until the outbreak of the Sino-Japanese War in 1937.

He did not know when, but a bee had strayed into the room. It whirled in the air, flew against the glass door several times, and was always frustrated in its attempt to escape. Its humming was both monotonous and depressing.

"How dull, how dull." Teacher Ch'iu's face was furrowed.

After a while he felt the pulse on his left wrist with his right hand. He was weak all over, and as weary as though he had just had a fist fight with somebody. But he sensed his heart was beating irregularly, and this obsession turned and turned in his brain to distress him. Did he have to be buried alive like this forever, forevermore?

His colleagues—they were cut out for this kind of work. They were all fools good only for handling the little rascals. Here he again gasped, and felt sorry for the one third of the pupils who deserved a better deal.

He pushed the newspapers aside, and when one sheet fell off the table he did not bother to pick it up. Holding his chest and deliberately regulating his breathing, he persuaded himself that, from now on, he should try not to be so easily excited again. It was not worth it to sacrifice his health for a scanty thirty-two dollars a month.

But—but—wasn't it human nature to prefer the good and the beautiful to the bad and the ugly?

He opened the door leading into the yard, his eyes on the bee. At the same time, he turned over in his head the words and phrases he would use to present under three headings the problem now occupying his mind. From that he passed on to his own situation, and concluded that it would be practically impossible not to be furious with the little rascals. He was by nature contemptuous of all that was mean and low, and then, why, he was simply dead set against evil.

The humming around his ears started again. The bee had not flown out.

As though he were afraid of being stung, he walked softly out the door. Breathing deeply, he decided to talk to Teacher Ting about the matters that perplexed him.

He was destined to be thwarted, though. Teacher Ting was in his classroom.

"The imbecile!"

He found he still had thirty minutes on his hands, and he did not know what to do with them. He walked into the yard, and then came back. Finally, he decided he wanted to bask in the sun. He remembered the seven advantages to be derived from that practice: the sun emits ultraviolet rays, it kills germs, etc., etc.

He heard some stirring in the room of Teacher T'ung, the principal. He also heard him calling out in a feminine scream:

"Little Joke, Little Joke."

The teacher lounging in the sun glanced up toward the room and thought: Ha, a model principal he is, just getting up at this hour!

Little Joke went into Teacher T'ung's room with a basin of water in his hands. This was the boy with the scar on his eyelid. He helped Ch'ang-shou, his cousin, and ran errands for the school for one dollar a month. He wore an old padded coat several sizes too large for him but only summer trousers. As soon as he put down the water, he started to leave with bowed head, forgetting to take the chamber pot with him.

Teacher T'ung gave the boy two resounding knocks on the head with his knuckles as a reminder.

The noise attracted several pupils, who crowded at the door to peep in.

Teacher T'ung pulled the toothbrush out of his mouth and yelled, "What are you doing here?"

"This period for us is science, and—"

"Go study by yourselves."

Ten minutes later, Teacher T'ung sallied out with a cup of jasmine tea in his hand. It was said that he had acquired the habit in Tientsin. His father had once run a fur shop there.

He sipped, smacked his lips, and began a conversation with Teacher Ch'iu. He grumbled against Teacher Hua, who was on leave at home to get married, and who had therefore left behind him classes to be substituted for. Worse, all his classes were in the morning, so that Teacher T'ung could not sleep as much as he wanted.

"Now, you know me," he said. "I'm not in robust health. When I can't have my sleep, I'm no good at all."

He then proceeded to talk about how short of funds the school was, and ornamented his speech with many quotations. He had barely mentioned that "even a clever woman cannot cook without rice" when somehow he landed on another: "Restore the valued jade to its rightful owner."

Teacher Ch'iu watched the other's mouth, and thought, "How is it his gold teeth have turned the color of brass? They certainly make him look more like a mercenary businessman."

The talker was getting voluble. Without knowing it, he began to gesture, and spilled his tea. He had by now broached the topic of Teacher Chin. He bent his back to be close to Teacher Ch'iu, lowered his voice, and confided that, though his family had been "reduced to straitened circumstances," Teacher Chin still had the temper of a spoiled heir.

" 'A leopard cannot change his spots.' So what is there to do?"

Teacher Ch'iu looked intently at the other's face. He suddenly recalled how one night, when the principal was drunk, he had ordered Ch'ang-shou to get Commissioner Chi over. He was not obeyed, and he bawled like a baby. He wanted to "settle his accounts" with the commissioner. He said that he had taken great pains to run this school, and yet he was reprimanded when he had embezzled a measly eighty dollars!

Everybody remembered how like a madman he had behaved then. Teacher Ting had prepared some boric acid solution for him, but instead of drinking it he had grabbed at Teacher Ting to kiss his cheek. He had then mumbled indistinctly of how he once met Yü Ta-ch'ang's mother, how, though but poorly dressed, the woman struck him as quite clean, and how she made sheep's eyes at him. Women from such families could be had easily, he said. Give her one dollar, at most one dollar, and she's yours.

Teacher Ch'iu now smiled. He looked at the principal's mouth, and then his hands, and straightened to leave. He was afraid the other might spill tea on him.

"Why are you smiling?" Teacher T'ung asked. "At the bickering between Chin Meng-chou and Old P'i?"

He proceeded to give his opinion on this subject at some length. Teacher Ch'iu felt he had been putting up with the other for a long, long time, but the speaker showed no sign of letting up. He was compelled to sit down again. He massaged the right side of his chest, and groaned from time to time. He was able to relax a little only when Ch'ang-shou appeared and approached Teacher T'ung.

Teacher Ch'iu averted his face. He knew that the janitor had come to demand the sixty cents which the principal had owed him since last month when he was playing mahjong and sent Ch'ang-shou out to buy some cooked beef, without giving him the money.

As on previous days when Ch'ang-shou came to demand the money, Teacher T'ung was enraged.

"What's so great about sixty cents? You're making yourself a nuisance asking for it day after day! You think I am going to welsh?"

Ch'ang-shou walked away muttering to himself, reached for the bell in the hall, and rang it with all his strength. The noise was deafening. Then he went to move the clock ten minutes forward.

The whole building, upstairs and on the ground floor, began to rumble. The children sang and yelled. One could distinguish the earsplitting soprano of Ch'ien Su-chen singing "The Express."

Sparrows in the yard shivered and flew away.

Teacher Ting shrugged, saying, "The rats are out of their cage."

Teacher Ch'üan, who had her hair curled in a beauty parlor, parted her heavily rouged lips and guffawed. She wiggled, and, putting her hand on Ch'ien Su-chen's shoulder, started to sing with her:

"Gosh, how extraordinarily fast, *ai ai ai.* . . ."

Teacher Ch'iu knitted his brows. He wanted to blow up. Fiercely, he kicked away his chair, and stalked up the stairs with ponderous steps while stopping his ears with his hands.

The noise of iron utensils striking against one another could be heard from the kitchen. A whiff of the strong odor of cooked onion flowed over and through the windows on the upper floor.

"Dash it, onions again! This is atrocious!"

Boisterous laughter suddenly broke out downstairs.

Impatiently, he walked toward the railing of the corridor. There below he saw Teacher Ting making all kinds of funny faces and pushing Ch'ien Su-chen toward Jen Chia-hung. He was saying at the same time: "Show us how you can love, how you can love!"

Around them, a crowd of children were clapping, jumping up and down, and yelling something he could not hear.

Ch'ien Su-chen pouted. She stamped and she giggled. But she was careful in her struggle because the short slits on her gown did not permit easy movement. She hit only the dirty boys nearest her—how dared they laugh at her?

She pulled herself free and ran toward the front gate. When she saw

Jen Chia-hung was going to chase after her, she turned her neck and looked at him menacingly. "You naughty thing—taking advantage of me like that!"

Teacher T'ung heehawed with complacency. It was his opinion that this was a good instance of "calf love."

The two women teachers had laughed until they were purple in the face. They then patted Teacher Ting on the shoulder, accusing him of being a tease.

Teacher Chin was not present, however. It was his habit to go to the kitchen before a meal was served. If he saw there was meat in the pot, he would ladle out a whole bowl of broth for himself, and tell Ch'ang-shou to add more water to the pot.

Ch'ang-shou's wife had often complained to the two women teachers: "A shameless glutton, that Teacher Chin. He gulps down the broth, and lets Ch'ang-shou get a tongue-lashing from Teacher T'ung. When he gives me his drawers to wash, they are so soiled I wonder at his nerve."

"All ignorant imbeciles!" Teacher Ch'iu compressed his lips and entered his room. He would not descend the stairs until Little Joke called him to lunch.

On that day the daily routine at the lunch table again took place. Teacher T'ung, tasting the broth, frowned darkly and shook his head. Then his henchman Teacher P'i summoned Ch'ang-shou in a loud voice. Then Teacher T'ung began to call Ch'ang-shou a sneak who had secretly drunk up the stock. He fumed while casting furtive eyes in Teacher Chin's direction.

"How can you say you didn't drink the stock? You can't be innocent unless you swear an oath: whoever drank the stock is a turtle's egg, a whoreson. Say it, a turtle's egg, a whoreson! Why don't you swear?"

Teacher Ting drank one spoonful of the broth, and solemnly pronounced that its diluted taste was in strict accord with the principle of hygiene. The thief had evidently been concerned that too much oil might hurt their stomachs.

The two women teachers sank under helpless giggles. Teacher Ch'üan covered her mouth with a small handkerchief, while Teacher Lou lowered her head until her lips touched her bowl.

Only Teacher Chin remained expressionless, and continued eating, oblivious of all around him. He rattled his chopsticks and spoon defiantly, however, as though they were protesting for him:

"You people are all relatives and from the same native place. You think you can freeze me out. Well, well, well. I am not going to be pushed around."

Teacher Ch'iu paid no attention to the scene either. Instead, he was chewing his food slowly, deliberately. It was his belief that, if a man is to be energetic, he must rely on the health of his digestive organs. So he went on masticating slowly, his face leaning to one side as if he were straining his ear to listen to his elegant chewing.

V

The afternoon sessions were to begin at one forty. But many of the pupils returned to school right after lunch and the period in between was always boisterous. The teachers had had their full meal, and it was the time of the year when they did not have to take their nap. Everybody was therefore in good spirits.

Jen Chia-hung and his friends were playing with his basketball. They stood in a circle, taking up the greater part of the yard. What was left of the space was appropriated by Ch'ien Su-chen and her fellow players at shuttlecock. Some of the other children wanted to squeeze out a tiny bit of ground for marbles, and raised a ruckus. But Teacher Chin soon had the dispute settled.

"No marbles allowed. Marbles are for beggars. Give them to me."

The teachers were surrounded by children considered pleasant. They were all neat and clean, and some even had cold cream on their faces. Their parents got along well with the teachers, and would give them presents on festive occasions: moon cakes, glutinous rice dumplings, cookies in British-style tins, and preserved plums that came from stores already wrapped as gift packages.

Last week, when they had come to attend the PTA meeting, they had not neglected to bring gifts.

So the teachers took the children up on their laps, and asked them why their sisters had not come that day, whether one boy's sister had entered senior high, and who was the lady in the green dress. Sometimes they inquired after their students' mothers, female cousins, and even aunts.

Mu Yang-hao was the only boy holding a children's magazine in his hand. He was leaning on Teacher Ch'iu, who was telling him the pronunciation and meaning of certain characters as well as the general drift of the story. When the child interrupted, he would listen with a smile on his face, and answer him carefully. He believed it was his duty to do so, and it was all so interesting.

Finally, he explained to Mu Yang-hao the moral contained in the story. "Look," he said, "the boy here is diligent and frugal, and he comes into a great fortune. The other boy spends all his money like dirt, and at last he squanders all he has." At the close, he asked, "Should one be diligent and frugal?"

"Yes," the boy answered briskly. "People who don't have money —they haven't learned to be diligent and frugal. Why can't they learn, Teacher Ch'iu?"

Teacher Ch'iu lifted the boy up and lovingly nuzzled his face. He was thinking how much better off he would be if he could get to teach at some missionary school. The children there would be all as likable as this one. Or perhaps he should try to enter college. He heaved a sigh.

A few little rascals were looking at them, half curious, half afraid.

Most of the pupils stayed in the classrooms. They were clamoring, singing, or playing the fingerguessing game. Yü Ta-ch'ang was standing on the platform joking with the first-grader Chiang Jih-hsin.

"Chiang Jih-hsin eats dog's droppings every day. He did today."

"Aw, I didn't today," Chiang Jih-hsin retorted.

"You didn't today, but you did yesterday, and I saw you do it."

"No, no. I didn't do it yesterday either."

"You lie. I went to stool, and you ate it at once."

Teacher Ch'iu could not contain himself any longer.

"You brutes, you brutes!"

He went in, and dragged Yü Ta-ch'ang into the yard. The boy stumbled after him and was permitted to stand still only when they reached the wall.

The principal, having added some boiling water to his tea, sipped and shook his head. He was sure Teacher Ch'iu had been too lenient.

He then expressed his wonder: why did those in charge of the nation's education forbid the teachers to beat the pupils? Otherwise the school might order a few ferules.

"There are too many little rascals here. 'They have two thirds of the land.' What can one do but beat them?"

Teacher Ting now put in a word. He said if vivisection were to be performed upon these children, one would surely discover something called the "savage's tendon." He twitched his brows, and watched his colleagues for reaction.

But nobody laughed. The two women teachers were still in their own room.

Teacher Ch'iu gave Teacher Ting's nose a fierce glance and sat down in his seat.

"Really," he touched the right side of his chest and felt his jagged ribs. "What can the nose of another man possibly have to do with me? Yet I'm irritated!"

The sun shone obliquely in, and the windows and doors traced various parallelograms on the ground. Particles of dust flitted in the light like rolling smoke. One hardly dared to breathe.

The basketball out there repeatedly hit the cement pavement and sent up dull, heavy thuds. The small feet pattered. The children were yelling:

"One pass here. Pass me one. Hey, pass it to me!"

Teacher P'i raised his horse face, and looked at the glass panes with misgiving.

A few little rascals in the first and second grades were running along Neatness Road. For reasons hard to understand, they seemed bent on dashing through the narrow space between the two circles of children playing basketball and shuttlecock. When they succeeded, they would laugh contentedly and nod to those on the opposite side.

Opening his eyes wide, Jen Chia-hung commanded in a hoarse squawk:

"Go away, you brat. I fuck your mother!"

But Yu Fu-lin rushed through. He laughed as he ran, and did not dare let out his breath until he reached the farther side. Then, turning to face Neatness Road, he made funny faces to show his triumph. He walked a few steps more, rubbing the wall with his right hand.

They always wiped their hands on the wall. The lower part of the whitewash, from approximately two to three feet above the ground, had all turned grayish black.

The basketball had now reached Jen Chia-hung's hands.

"Hey," Jen Chia-hung whirled around toward Yu Fu-lin and abruptly hoisted up the ball.

The other boy ducked his scabby head. All laughed.

Jen Chia-hung repeated the hoisting a number of times. Yu Fu-lin became reassured, and was thinking of dashing back through the two groups of players when, at this precise moment, suddenly, the large, round thing whizzed through the air and landed square in his face.

There was a commotion. Scores of throats were making a loud clamor, which reached everywhere.

"Jen Chia-hung hits people!"

"Blood, blood . . . Yu Feng-ying!"

"Beat him, beat him!"

Some of the little rascals were shouting at the hall door, obviously trying to draw the teachers' attention.

From one window—where an iron bar had broken away—a dirty head popped out, yelled, "Jen Chia-hung should be flogged," and immediately withdrew.

Several teachers hurried out: "What is the matter?"

Yu Fu-lin was sitting on the ground bawling. Blood streamed from his nostrils and stained his chin a sickening red. It dripped down upon the front and sleeves of his coat. The dusty patch left by the basketball on his face had turned into mud after being washed by tears: his features were now hardly recognizable.

His sister had seized Jen Chia-hung's collar and was butting him in the chest with her head.

"I'll kill you, I'll kill you, I'll . . ."

Jen Chia-hung struggled to get his neck free while he grabbed the other's hair with his left hand. At the same time, he was using his right hand against the enemy like a genuine athlete, hitting her in the face or scratching her neck.

He did not even forget to give her the treatment reserved for the coeds when he was friendly: he felt the slight protrusions on her chest, pinched her in the thigh, and punched her between the thighs.

The children all milled around, yelling and waving their arms.

Ch'ien Su-chen had forgotten about her new gown of rayon. She rushed to help beat up Yu Feng-ying. Brandishing her two tightly clenched fists, she howled:

"Shameless slut . . . with a boy . . . so. . . ."

Teacher T'ung was stamping and screeching in his womanlike voice. He was so worked up his two gold teeth nearly fell out.

But nobody was listening to him.

The other teachers chased away the crowding imps, forced their way into the middle of the fracas, and with difficulty dragged Yu Feng-ling away.

The combatants were gasping for air. Jen Chia-hung's collar had been mauled out of recognition, and Ch'ien Su-chen's gown was terribly wrinkled.

Yu Feng-ying's face had turned a livid gray, with stripes of red and blue. She was trembling all over.

The principal was glowering at her, his lips ferociously contorted.

"You slut, you vixen, you beast . . . You would fight, would you?"

"We have been trampled on enough. They tread on us as if. . . ."

"Tread on you? Why don't you come to your teachers?"

The corners of Yu Feng-ying's mouth twitched. Her hands, closed in fists, were shaking. Another eruption seemed to be on the way. But she merely wheeled around, walked a couple of steps away, and mumbled between her clenched teeth:

"Come to my teachers!—that would be the day, when that could be of any use!"

Everybody winced at the remark.

A blue vein stood out on Teacher T'ung's forehead. He looked as though he were ready to explode. His fist describing arcs in the air, he stamped his feet and squealed with utter disregard for his windpipe:

"What did you say, what did you say? You are expelled. Now. Get out! Yu Fu-lin too. Teacher P'i, Teacher P'i, prepare the notice. Expel both. Right away!"

He ran forward precipitately, and then retreated. He seemed to be at a loss, his pale lips working up and down, and his nose wheezing. As some of the children continued to gape at him with eyes bulging and mouths hanging open, he shrieked:

"Get out!"

Soon afterwards he rushed back into the room. He hit the desk and exhorted Teacher P'i to hurry up with the notice.

"Oh, oh, what a slut! What a bitch! It's really—it's really—it would be good if we could send her to prison."

The other teachers did not echo his opinion. They merely shooed away the pupils packing the doorway.

Teacher Ch'iu looked at Teacher Chin, and then at Teacher Ting. His face showed no expression at all. His right hand, however, was on his chest, as usual. When he heard the principal's difficult breathing, he said to himself:

"Stupid pig—raging over such a trivial incident!"

As a matter of fact, the expulsion of pupils was nothing unusual. Indeed, it was done several times a month. It might be said that the practice had become a sort of hobby with Principal T'ung and Teacher P'i.

The whole matter was officially closed by half past one.

Teacher Ting thereupon put on a grave aspect, and said he wanted to talk something over with Principal T'ung. He hoped, he continued, the principal would never be so irked again, for, from a medical point of view, anger was something not very beneficial to health.

Teacher T'ung replied, "But one can be exasperated beyond endurance! Yu Feng-ying's elder brother is a mere porter. Think of that!"

Here Teacher T'ung raised his voice. Of all people in the world he despised porters most. He proceeded to recount his one experience with them in Hankow. Yes, they had actually besieged him demanding two dollars. He could not even find another porter for his luggage, for these rotten eggs were all "birds of a feather," all villainous vipers.

The story had been told numerous times. But the listeners were attentive, and Teacher Ch'iu even sighed in obliging sympathy.

Only Teacher Chin seemed not to hear. He was concentrating on a newspaper, and kept blinking his reddish eyes.

The storyteller glanced at Teacher Chin, and grumbled inwardly: "Could it be he is also 'hand in glove' with the porters? Look at his expression of badly concealed rancor. Ugh!" Then he exchanged a look with Teacher Ting.

Teacher Ting raised his brows once. He believed that "vitamin" was expected of him, and so he heaved his shoulders, puckered his lips, and turned toward the door. He started walking in jerky imitation of Charlie Chaplin. He twisted his feet into the shape of an obtuse angle, and was so intent upon his performance that his knees hurt. But he was shaking with mirth, though he would not let any laughter escape him.

When he reached the door, he bit the tip of his tongue to restrain his laughter and, still mimicking Chaplin's silly posture, turned to face his supposed audience.

Nobody was looking at him, however.

VI

Teacher Ch'iu took a nap that afternoon. He did not attend his class, but told the children to study by themselves.

When he woke up, school was already out. The desks and chairs were rattling. A few pupils whose turn it was to clean up were there sweeping the floor.

Many children were singing as they walked away with their satchels under their arms. Ch'ien Su-chen was again singing her favorite song, "The Express," and from her room Teacher Ch'üan accompanied her.

Teacher Ch'iu yawned.

"How strange—I can't understand it at all. Why should the Board of Education insist on making singing a part of the curriculum?"

The sun was tinting the glass windows golden; the shadows swayed and flickered.

He yawned again.

"You awake?" Teacher Ting turned to ask him.

He did not answer, but quietly listened to his own breath, to the beating of his heart. There was on the bookshelf opposite him an alarm clock supplied by the school for the common use of the roommates, and he kept his eyes on it. At the same time he was feeling the pulse in his left wrist with his right hand.

Teacher Ting had to turn back to continue his chatter with Teacher P'i.

The administrative assistant had one elbow on the desk. He was bending forward to see what Teacher Ting was writing.

The alarm clock ticked while Teacher Ting's pencil rustled on his paper.

"Do you know what this is?" Teacher Ting indicated the sheet of paper, and eagerly looked at the other's horse face.

The character on the paper looked like a "2," but the tail trailed and trailed, and a dot was placed above it.

The administrative assistant shook his head numbly.

Teacher Ting glanced apprehensively at Teacher Ch'iu, then whispered his explanation. But his words were all slurred, and some seemed to have remained in his throat. He appeared sorely afraid of being overheard.

"It stands for 'quinine.' When a doctor prescribes, he always writes the word this way. Look here—" His head leaning to one side and the tip of his tongue cleaving to one corner of his mouth, he wrote "Tab 20" followed by his signature: Dr. Johnson Ting.

"It's awful, you know." He jutted out his underlip. "People always call me 'big dog head' (ta kou t'ou) because they don't know how to say the word do c tor correctly. They can only get the nearest sounds in Chinese. I have myself to blame for this, of course. Why should I be a physician? So I have to let them call me 'big dog head' . . . Big Dog Head Ting, Ting the Big Dog Head!"

Another familiar gesture followed: the thumb on the nose, the four fingers clawing the air.

Teacher Ch'iu slid off his bed. He lit a cigarette, and thought to himself:

"All persons with long faces are idiots. Without exception."

He took up the English Weekly, leafed through it casually, and sighed. He was angry with himself for not having studied English hard. He should try to gain more education, so that he might make more contributions to society.

Teacher Ting's mumbling annoyed him grievously. He put on his slippers, and decided to seek out a sanctuary downstairs, so that he would be able to think.

Some of the pupils had not left yet. They were running around in the yard, their satchels under their arms. Some kicked at the pebbles while they scampered.

Teacher Ch'iu scowled again. He looked up at the sky, and felt his forehead.

"Must I remain buried here all my life? I should try to get more education."

He told himself not to be impatient, but to study the matter carefully, systematically. He calculated in orderly detail how he was to raise the necessary expenses. This called for a five-point plan: first, he must try to save; second, he must economize; third, he must put aside ten dollars out of the thirty-two a month he was making. . . .

His mind wandered to something else:

"How strange it is—-why are the little rascals not afraid of scoldings and beatings, but always so very bad? Yes, it must be their low nature."

And he repeated the last sentence once again.

He stood under one of the peach trees. Then he walked over to the hall.

The Shanghai *News* could not have arrived much more than ten minutes ago. Yet it had already been taken by Teacher T'ung into his own room.

"What was I thinking before this? It seemed . . ."

Scratching his head, he took up a local paper, threw it down again, and straightened with great care, as though he feared his chest might be injured if he did not. His gait was slow and steady. He seemed to be counting how many steps there were between where he was and Teacher T'ung's door.

Suddenly, he stopped.

He could hear conspiratorial murmuring in the principal's room.

"Did Teacher Chin talk to you about anything else just then?"

"No." It was the hoarse voice of Jen Chia-hung.

"That's good. I'll tell you what. Be cautious if you ever talk with Teacher Chin again. He is a sick man. So after this . . . By the way, do you know what his disease is?"

Silence.

"Well, you'll know when you look at his trachomatous eyes. Trachoma, do you know? That's because he is suffering from . . . from . . . well, an unmentionable disease. 'A secret not to be divulged.' He has 'sown his wild oats,' and when one does that one will . . . Do you understand now?"

Afterwards they spoke of Jen Chia-hung's father, their words interspersed with Teacher T'ung's laughter.

Teacher Ch'iu's chest tightened. He felt as though he had lost something. He bit his lips, and protested inwardly:

"And Jen Chia-hung *will* listen to these mountebanks, these . . . these . . ."

As though he were trying to show his displeasure with his unworthy associates, he kept silent all through supper and went upstairs straight afterwards.

He was certain those people would never climb up in life. How strange that they were willing to submit themselves to such a rut: squabbling, beating the little rascals, playing mahjong!

"Pigs, all stupid pigs."

The alarm clock on the bookshelf went on ticking, as though it were its intention to irritate him. The noise would neither quicken nor slow down. There was no variation. It held everybody's time to the same track, and dragged on and on.

It was only five minutes after eight. They had started playing mahjong in Teacher T'ung's room. Whenever Teacher Ting heard an invitation yelled to him, he would run over, happily calling out:

"Great, great. I'll raise both my hands to support the motion. And one leg too. This here game of mahjong, why, one must not look down upon it. To play a game is more healthful than a session under the sunlamp."

The next day, though, he would grumble to Teacher Ch'iu how he had lost two dollars. He was not fond of gambling, he would say, but then he was certainly not going to be a wet blanket.

"A really vulgar man. One can see that by merely looking at his nose," Teacher Ch'iu reflected.

Teacher Chin was no friend to the others, but he never refused to take up one side of the game. Only he would start muttering before he finished the first round. He knew the others were out to get him, they were banded together to squeeze him dry. But, by gosh, he was not going to knuckle under. He went on picking up the tiles.

Then there were the two women teachers. They always took part jointly. One would sit down at the table and the other would look on. Every time one got a good tile the other would shriek with joy. At other times, however, they would hum a tune through their noses while beating time with their toes. They twisted and laughed whenever Teacher Ting made a remark, and they did so as though it were part of their duty.

Teacher Ch'iu alone stayed upstairs. He did not feel in the mood to read or correct exercises. He merely lit a cigarette and propped his temple in his right hand. He thought he had a fever.

"This life is killing me! I must change. Yes, I must! I shall become vulgar just by remaining here. This is horrible."

As to his future, why, it might be considered under six headings. He took a puff of his cigarette and moved his right hand to the center of his forehead. Then his thought wandered, and he again felt feverish.

He lay down on his bed and stared absently at the ten-watt light bulb for a long time. Out of habit, he sighed again, held his chest, and knitted his brows:

"Dash it," he thought, "another day has passed. The same things will happen again tomorrow. I still have to face the little rascals, to expel bad pupils. The very same things, eternally, without end. . . ."

Wu Tsu-hsiang

Chang T'ien-i was one of the many who began to receive critical attention in 1928–29; during the early thirties, an even larger number of fiction writers emerged, and several of them, especially Ai Wu and Ou-yang Shan, continued to be productive until the Cultural Revolution of 1966. But in the three or four years before the outbreak of the Sino-Japanese War in 1937 the most brilliant of that group was Wu Tsu-hsiang (1908–   ), a native of southeastern Anhwei who began to write even while a student of the Chinese Department at Tsing Hua University. He wrote about his home region with an unobtrusive sympathy for the poor and downtrodden and a deep-seated disgust for their oppressors. But whatever his personal feelings, he records the manners and speech habits of peasants and gentry with equal accuracy and thus achieves an unsentimental realism rare among his fellow leftist writers. Unfortunately, he wrote little; except for his patriotic novel *Mountain Torrent* (*Shan-hung*, 1942), practically all his best work is contained in *The Stories and Essays of Wu Tsu-hsiang* (*Wu Tsu-hsiang hsiao-shuo san-wen chi*, Peking, 1954), which includes, in addition to four hitherto uncollected pieces, the bulk of *West Willow* (*Hsi-liu chi*, 1934) and *After-dinner Pieces* (*Fan-yü chi*, 1935). A professor of Chinese at National Peking University, he has for the past two decades specialized in literary research and criticism.

"Fan Village" (*Fan-chia p'u*, 1934) is Wu Tsu-hsiang's masterpiece. Though the conventional leftist formula of peasant revolt is followed at the end, it dilutes little the tragic force of the story's main concern with the clashes between Hsien-tzu Sao and her mother. The daughter is eventually driven to matricide, but the author has accounted for the event not only in financial terms—her desperate need for money to save her imprisoned husband—but in moral terms as well that fully establish the mother as an evil person despite her pathetic life as a domestic with a large family to support. In *History* I have described her as "the type of snobbish and mean-spirited person who through long habituation to town life has adopted her employers' attitude of contempt toward her own folk, especially those deviating from their path of honest poverty, and who, in the atrophy of her good impulses, has clung to money as her very life." Hsien-tzu Sao's hatred for her mother is thus understandable, and she further gains our sympathy by her deep love for her husband, which is given astonishing reality in the scene where she begs the yamen officer Wang Ch'i-yeh to save him. A painstaking artist, Wu Tsu-hsiang elaborates every scene with description and dialogue to establish its importance in the total design. Thus the vignettes of beggars, militiamen, and townspeople fleeing from the bandits clearly reinforce the impression of social calamity enveloping the principals. The present translation is almost entirely based on the Chinese text in *After-dinner Pieces*, though in a few minor instances it has adopted the emendations introduced by the author in *The Stories and Essays of Wu Tsu-hsiang*.

The Peking journal *Chinese Literature* has featured two of Wu Tsu-hsiang's stories in translation: "Green Bamboo Hermitage" (*Lü-chu shan-fang*, No. 1, 1964) and "Eighteen Hundred Piculs" (*I-ch'ien pa-pai tan*, No. 11, 1959). A long story rivaling "Fan Village" in fame, the latter gives a powerful account of a clan meeting involving many deftly sketched participants.

FAN VILLAGE

TRANSLATED BY *Russell McLeod*
and *C. T. Hsia*

1

On a sunny day of the eighth month the lonely fragrance of *kuei* blossoms [1] floated about the village with its single row of thatched huts.

This was Fan Village, and people from the various hamlets and small towns of the southwestern district [2] had to pass through here to get to the county seat or through the county seat to the port city. A long line of some thirty or forty huts faced on the east side a road paved with loose stones. Large cracks were visible on the low, earthen walls of most of these huts. Some walls managed to stand because they were propped up with fir logs, while large chunks of mud had already fallen

[1] "Probably the most popular autumn-blooming tree in China is the Kuei Hua, *Osmanthus fragrans*. It is a small-or-medium-sized tree, with thick, dark, shining evergreen leaves that are ornamental all year round. . . . The individual flowers, or florets, are small, yellow or white, and somewhat insignificant, but they are produced in such lavish profusion that they virtually cover the entire tree and therefore present a beautiful sight when in full bloom. They also have a pleasant perfume that pervades the air to great distances." H. L. Li, *The Garden Flowers of China* (New York, 1959), p. 151.

[2] Of Anhwei Province.

from others. Some huts even showed rotten rafters and ceilings, as if they were no longer inhabited.

Booths made of straw and logs lined the main road, one before each thatched hut. In the bright sun the straw roofs of the booths and huts alike appeared dark gray. The straw ropes binding the thatch that should have assumed the pattern of rhomboid checks were now either loosened or broken, and most of the fir logs serving as pillars no longer stood straight. Inside each booth were heaps of straw, some seeming to have fallen from the roof and some gathered from the fields to serve as mattresses for beggars fleeing from an area of famine. Several benches and tables made of thin planks, thickly covered with dust and decrepit beyond use, lay about in the straw.

A woman emerged from one of these thatched huts and leaned against a pillar of the booth in front. She had a blade of dogtail grass in hand, and was picking her teeth with it and at the same time gazing up and down the road.

The woman, probably twenty-six or twenty-seven *sui* old, looked strikingly haggard with her disheveled black hair and a square black headache plaster on one of her temples. Below her coarse, thick but plucked eyebrows was a pair of diffident and bloodshot eyes which were probably infected. They were staring hard, even though it seemed to require some effort on her part to keep them open. She wore a knee-length coat of glazed cotton, already patched in several places but freshly laundered.

Shading her forehead with one hand, she squinted her eyes in a long stare, gazing for a while at the southern stretch of the road and then turning around to gaze toward the north. In both directions the road twisted and turned to a mountain slope, with not a single traveler in sight.

All of Fan Village was dead still except that someone in a neighboring hut was continually pounding sandals into shape with a mallet, and a baby was crying now and then.

A light breeze carried the lonely fragrance of the *kuei* flowers to the woman's nostrils. Raising her head, she looked through a hole in the roof at the big, tall tree and saw its blossom-laden branches ashimmer with a pale golden light. She then looked again at the long row of tumble-down huts and at the booth floor heaped with straw until finally she threw away the blade of dogtail grass she had been holding in her mouth and breathed out a long sigh.

"Is everybody dead?" she softly mumbled to herself as she began to recall the bustling Fan Village of several years ago.

In those years each booth contained neat rows of boards and benches and a wooden table straddled the threshold of each hut. On this table were yellow bamboo chopsticks inside a bamboo container, a stack of earthenware bowls with the right amount of tea leaves inside each, packs of Player's and Capstan Navy Cut cigarettes, plates of soybeans cooked with red peppercorn, fried fresh-water fish, sautéed leeks, and other dishes. On the stove of each house were two or three steaming kettles, their lids jumping, singing like broken-voiced opera singers in the role of the flirt. As for the passing travelers, some carried loads on a pole, some were chair-bearers, some pushed wheelbarrows, and some drove animals, and still others were the owners, clerks, and managers of shops. They brought big lots of salt, sugar, kerosene, piece goods, and other foreign commodities from the port city to the various villages and small towns of the southwestern district or transported local products such as rice, cotton, silk, and cocoons to the port city. Group after group, they passed in a continual stream from dawn till dusk. She and the neighbor women in charge of the booths, both married and unmarried, all wore freshly laundered and starched coats and trousers of glazed cotton and had aprons of patterned cloth tied around their waists. With flushed cheeks, beads of perspiration covering their noses, they carried the water kettle or the rice bowls, busy as butterflies in springtime, darting from booth to stove, from this table to that, and all the time smiling pleasantly and chatting with their customers.

After being attentively served by her or the other booth keepers, those travelers would stamp dust off their feet, blow their noses, and put on smiles indicative of their present contentment and temporary relief from their fatigue. And once on the road, they would again hear the sound of singing in the fields from near and far. Her husband and the neighbor menfolk were singing airily in the "Flower Drum" style as they worked in the fields.

After the fall harvest or during the first month of the year when there was no work to be done in the fields, these men would customarily set up a simple stage in the grain-drying area behind the huts, and with a few simple costumes plus gongs provided by this house and drums by that, and the clothes, jewelry, and cosmetics of their mothers and wives, they would for a number of nights give expert performances of such familiar pieces as *The Seventh Celestial Maid Descends to Earth*, *Ts'ai Miao-feng Leaves the Inn*, *A Gift of Fragrant Tea*, and *Chu Ying-t'ai*. The families and relatives of these actors, people from nearby villages, including the very old and the very young, as well as travelers staying overnight at the booths, all watched intently. In amusing moments they would guffaw and in sad moments they would draw up a corner of their clothing to wipe their tears. When it came time for group singing, they would sing in unison from before, behind, and even atop the stage. . . .

"Hsien-tzu." A short figure waddled down the road from the north, a fat old woman of over fifty. In one hand she held a stick which she used as a cane and over her shoulder she carried another stick with a large bundle of clothes at the end of it.

When the young woman heard the voice, she was suddenly roused from her deep thoughts. She turned her head toward the northern stretch of the road and saw that it was her own mother. "Mother," Hsien-tzu said lazily, "what are you doing back home again?"

The old woman walked into the booth, pulled up a bench from the pile of straw, and placed her bundle on the ground. As soon as she sat down on the bench, she unfastened her headband [3] and fanned her fat, wrinkled face with it, saying somewhat pantingly, "What am I doing back home? I came home for support in my old age! *Niang* [4] is about to starve to death!"

"It will never be your turn to starve."

"You unfilial bitch, what do you think happened to *Niang?* The

[3] *Pao-t'ou.* Author's note: "A piece of black silk in several folds. A son would donate money to the Kshitigarbha convent and have this piece imprinted with a Buddhist seal. He would then give it to his mother to wear around the area where her hair touched the brow, and she would still wear it when she was laid in her coffin. This fillet has the supposed power of redeeming its wearer's sins and reducing her punishment in Hell. Most grandmothers in that part of the rural country, whether of the gentry or peasantry, wear it."

[4] "Mother." In some parts of China it is customary for a woman to refer to herself as *Niang* when talking to her children.

master was afraid of bandits. The whole family moved to Shanghai.
The bandits wrote to the county yamen demanding fifty thousand dollars in ten days, fifty thousand. . . . Aiya, still this hot in the eighth
month! Even the weather isn't right!"

As she spoke, she put the headband on the bench and lifted the corners of her jacket with both hands and flapped it. "Still no business
here? How about Kou-tzu? [5] How much paddy did he thresh?"

"Everybody is dead. Even the ghosts don't come around."

"And Kou-tzu? How much paddy did he thresh? Enough for the
rent?"

"How much did he thresh? Don't ask. Even if we were starving to
death, we wouldn't ask you for a copper. Don't worry!"

"You unfilial bitch. What do you take *Niang* for? You think I'm
loaded? How much money do you think I've got?"

"I don't care how much you've got."

Listening to her daughter's words, the mother had the sensation of
swallowing several cold stones. She looked at the cold, hard face and
felt that this was not the time to tell her own misery. She blew her
nose and said with a sigh, "Aren't you going to pour a bowl of tea for
me?"

"Wait a while. The water's got to boil," answered the daughter as
she went listlessly inside the hut.

Another figure approached on the northern stretch of the road, a
long skinny body wearing a full, long-collared frock. Her bound feet,
encased in round-toed shoes, looked like a pair of small breams and she
limped with each step she took. The dragon-headed cane in her hand
gave forth a series of crisp sounds as she kept tapping it against the
stone pavement. Her clean-shaven, round head swayed in the sunlight.

The old woman recognized Sister Lien, a nun from the Kshitigarbha
Convent at Mount Sunset. She stood up and waved, saying, "Sister
Lien, coming from the city?"

"From the city. . . . What a wonderful scent from the *kuei* blossoms!" She stood still, pinching her rosary with her left hand as she
spoke.

"Have you heard the news? The bandits wrote a letter to the

---

[5] Hsien-tzu's husband is called Kou-tzu (Dog). His mother and some others,
however, call him Hsiao-kou-tzu (Little Dog). To avoid confusing the reader
I have not used the latter form.

county yamen demanding fifty thousand in ten days, fifty thousand! . . . . This road is hard to walk on, though you are strong enough to manage. Rest a while."

"Are you still helping at Mr. Chao's at West Gate?[6] Come back to see your daughter?"

"That's right. Please have a seat, Sister Lien." As she spoke, she moved to let Sister Lien sit down on the same wobbly bench. "Altogether I've helped there for nine years. Now Mr. Chao's whole family has moved to Shanghai. Moved to Shanghai. Left yesterday. The master didn't want to part with me and I didn't want to leave him. *T'ai-t'ai* wanted to take me along to Shanghai. How could I go, with my large brood of big and small? Drag these old bones to a strange place? Make a lot of bother for Mr. Chao? I thought it over and decided not to go. The third master of the Yuan-k'ang-hsiang store at East Gate said he'd hire me. I went today to inquire, but they said they weren't hiring. Bandits, bandits. Every family has felt the pinch."

"You haven't done badly. It's time for you to return home and care for your old age."

"Sister Lien, what are you saying? Care for my old age? Do I have this kind of good luck? I care for the old age of my children and grandchildren instead. And yet I have a daughter who regularly vexes me with her red eyebrows and green eyes."

"How many sons? I should remember."

"Three useless hulks, eight small ones. The past few years our rice crops have been sold at a loss and there have been no buyers for our silk cocoons. The eldest went to the city to be a militiaman, thanks to Mr. Chao's kindness, his great, great kindness. The second and third worked in sundry goods stores in town; one by one they have lost their jobs and come home! This family of starving bedbugs, what can they do except suck blood from my old corpse? And still I have a daughter vexing me with her red eyebrows and green eyes!"

"Hsien *ku-niang*[7] has a rather bad temper," the nun spoke in a low-

[6] In the original, Mr. Chao's house is further identified as *Tsan-chih-ti* (an assistant military governor's residence). Presumably it is an old house rendered locally famous as the residence of such an official in times past. But *Tsan-chih-ti* could be the name of the street or lane in which Mr. Chao's house is located.

[7] "Hsien *ku-niang*" has the force of "Miss Hsien." In talking to her mother, the nun refers to Hsien-tzu as *ku-niang* to emphasize her status as a daughter.

ered voice. "The last time I ran into you here I noticed the expression on her face. It really wasn't the kind of expression to greet her mother. It was nasty, really nasty. But you gave her suck; no wonder you are so attached to her."

"It wasn't this way before." The answer came in a similar whisper. "Last year Kou-tzu, my son-in-law, couldn't pay the rent on his farm. The landlord called the district office to send a couple of fellows to dun him. They wanted to arrest him. Hsien-tzu came to the city to beg me, saying there hadn't been any business in the tea booth lately and they didn't have a cent. And she asked me to lend her the money for rent. See how simple she made it sound! I'm not a city magistrate —where would I get the money to lend her? The past few years there's been no demand for cocoons. Didn't everybody stop raising them when they saw which way the wind was blowing? But the two of them buried their brains in dung, still wanted to go on raising them. Said they were going to raise them precisely because the others weren't. Stupidly thought they'd make a lot of money. Raised no fewer than ten big trays. The few mulberry trees they had didn't supply enough leaves. When it came time for the third sleep and the silkworms were just about grown they ran out of leaves. Came calling on me again for money to buy leaves. If there's no business in your booth and you don't have the mulberry leaves or the money, how can you raise silkworms, Sister Lien?"

"Young people always do things heedlessly."

"I couldn't help that. You make a mess of things and you clean it up yourself. I didn't care—well, really it's not that I didn't care, but how could I? What about the rest of my family, more than ten, more than ten mouths to feed? Is my old corpse the only one that should die?"

"Hm, hm, isn't it so though." The nun pursed her wrinkled lips, continuously nodding her shaven head. "After all, the ones living with you demand more of your attention."

"She buried her brains in dung, said I had money to join credit unions but no money to lend her. Damn it, do I go around joining credit unions? How many credit unions have I joined? It just happened that some years ago Mrs. Chang's husband [8] died and she didn't have

---

[8] Almost certainly Mrs. Chang (Chang Sao-tzu) was a fellow servant in the employ of Mr. Chao.

money to bury him. I had to heed *T'ai-t'ai* and so I joined Mrs. Chang's five-dollar-a-share ten-member union. We throw dice twice a year to determine who'll get the money each time. Once in the third month and once in the ninth. This is the fourth year. I've done nothing but pay so far; my turn hasn't come up yet. The way it looks, I'll be the last person in the group to get hold of the money. A few years back everybody had some money; that's when I joined. I wanted to sell out, I wanted to get a substitute. I begged people as if they were my grandfather and grandmother, but who's going to substitute for you? People were actually begging you to substitute for them, to join their groups! For two years I've been borrowing money to pay. It was last spring that I borrowed five dollars at your convent so I could pay. She saw the money and wanted me to turn over the loan to her to buy mulberry leaves. I've paid four long years into this thing, why shouldn't I continue? Should I just forfeit everything I've paid in? She hated me, took me for a rich person, took me for a millionaire, as if I had ingots of gold and silver hidden away and wouldn't get them out to help her. I've slaved till my hair is white—have I been a thief? Robbed people? Does money grow out of my skin? Well, things are dandy now! The master's gone. Gone! We're all the same now, all going to starve to death. She's seeing this happen with her own eyes!" As the old woman spoke, her feeble eyes filled with tears. So she placed a shaking hand inside her coat and fumbled for a while until finally she pulled out a handkerchief to wipe her eyes.

"Married-off daughters are like water poured outside the door. All a mother can do is to heave a long sigh. Where is she?"

"Inside making tea. Seeing how I've walked more than ten li and sweated buckets, she didn't even offer me a bowl of tea. I had to beg —beg for it myself."

"People's hearts have changed greatly. The Bodhitsattva Kuan-yin appeared to me in a dream; did you hear about it? It happened last month. The Bodhisattva had a steel whip in her hand and a furious look on her face, I've never seen her that furious before. When I saw the steel whip in her hand, I knew it augured something ill. She was carrying a steel whip in the year of the Republican Revolution, too. Amitabha, have mercy, have mercy!" The nun assumed a grave and frightened look, pursing her mouth in such a way that it was surrounded by wrinkles. At the same time she was telling her beads and sighing.

"Oh, what did the Bodhisattva say?"

"The Bodhisattva pointed her steel whip toward the northwest and didn't say anything for a long time. I was kneeling, not daring to raise my head. How would I dare to? After a long, long time she spoke. Her voice was like a brass gong—it's not like that usually. She said the end was coming:

> Of the white-haired half may be spared;
> Of the black-haired none shall be spared.

Only these two sentences; then nothing for a long, long time. I kept begging her to save the sinning souls." At this point she took in a deep breath and then exhaled.

Riveting her eyes on the shaven head, the old woman also straightened her back and sighed, asking, "What else did the Bodhisattva say?"

"As a matter of fact, three days after the vision, the bandits at the Five-Dragon Mountain started up. You've just asked if I knew the bandits wanted fifty thousand. Of course I knew! If I hadn't told Mr. Chao, you think he would have decided to move away? These man-made troubles, however, don't count for much. What even the Bodhisattva can't tolerate is that men's hearts have changed greatly. From the fourth of the tenth month the sky will darken for seven days."

"The Bodhisattva said so?"

"Say, who's there? Is that Sister Lien talking?" Hsien-tzu Sao, her eyes squinting, stuck her head out of the thatched hut and asked without any expression on her face.

"Sister Lien's telling about a dream in which the Bodhisattva warned her of the calamities to come. Hsien-tzu, come and listen."

"Rich people are afraid of the calamities. Not us. If the sky fell down, those taller than we, better off than we, would have to sustain the crash first. You two had better make plans." She went inside again.

"Listen to that."

"Oh, my." Sister Lien shook her head continuously, grunting her disapproval.

"Hsien-tzu, Hsien-tzu, still no tea?" the old woman called out in a loud voice.

Hsien-tzu Sao came out carrying an earthenware pot and two large bowls and plunked them on the ground. "Dying of thirst, eh?" she said sarcastically, rubbing her eyes. "Guzzle it down, guzzle your fill."

The old woman exhaled deeply, bent down, and picked up the bowls. First she poured a bowl for the nun and then one for herself. She drank one bowl and then a second.

"Sister Lien, a person like me drags on year by year, day by day. When you really think about it, you don't entertain any hope. People say, 'Raise children to provide for old age; store grain to guard against famine.' Me, right now, I'm, I'm . . ."

"What happened?" Hsien-tzu Sao waved toward the southern road and called aloud, "Still won't let us pay less rent?"

The man approaching was naked above the waist. A blue towel was thrown over his shoulder and his black cotton trousers were rolled above his calves. Although his build was muscular, his sensitive and good-looking triangular face indicated someone who could play female leads in Flower Drum operas.

"Is it Kou-tzu?" The old woman, who had just dashed the remains of her tea onto the floor, asked, an empty bowl in hand, "What's he been up to?"

Saying nothing, Kou-tzu came closer step by step. His sweat-covered face was stiff as a piece of carved wood.

"Kou-tzu," the old woman said, "Mother's just dandy now! Mr. Chao has gone, his whole family moved to Shanghai. We're all going to starve now, all going to starve. The bandits demanded fifty thousand. They wrote to the county yamen."

Still making no reply, Kou-tzu wiped his sweaty face with the blue towel and removed the hempen sweat-blotter from his forehead and squeezed it with both hands. As the sweat dropped on his bare feet, he stamped them a couple of times so that a small cloud of dust flew up. Then he turned and walked into the hut.

"Still won't let us pay less rent? Did you find a rice dealer?" Hsien-tzu Sao stood close behind him and asked.

"Rice dealers, rice dealers! They're all cannibals!" Kou-tzu yelled inside the house.

"A dollar sixty? Still just a dollar sixty? The same price as the miller in the city offered?"

"Still wanting to get rich, aren't you? A dollar sixty! Dream on!"

The nun stared vacantly for a long while, then grasped her cane and stood up. "The sun is setting. Still three li of mountain road to go. Men's hearts have changed greatly. Amitabha, have mercy, have mercy."

"You're leaving?" the old woman asked.

The nun staggered slightly as she took her first step. Using her cane to steady herself, she turned her head and said, "You rest here and take your time. I'm slower than you." She then hobbled out of the booth.

For a while the old woman stared blankly into the pitch-black hut. Finally she bent her back, groped inside her bundle on the floor and pulled out a few red candles and a cake of soap, and slowly made her way into the house.

The house was low-ceilinged and very dark. Only the small round window in the east wall let in a ray of dim light. When she first entered, a green haze seemed to float before her eyes and she couldn't tell where anyone was. Then she gradually made things out. Kou-tzu was squatting on the doorsill dividing the kitchen from the bedroom, holding his head in his hands, while Hsien-tzu was standing by the stove, using a gourd ladle to pour water into a wooden tub.

"Hsien-tzu, Hsien-tzu. I asked for a few of Mr. Chao's altar candles. They're going to melt. Put them in a cool place." She walked over to the large water jar and placed them in a corner by its side. "This cake of Sunlight Brand soap has been dried in the air. *T'ai-t'ai* gave it to me."

"Keep it for yourself."

"I've got some. . . . Now really, what's eating you, Kou-tzu? Still not enough to pay the rent this year?"

Silence.

"Still not enough, Hsien-tzu?"

"Our six and four fifth mou have yielded twenty-five piculs of rice. Several days ago he asked the miller, who would only give him a dollar sixty for a picul. Today he asked a rice dealer, who wouldn't even pay a dollar sixty. Just paying back what the miller has advanced us in foodstuffs will take thirty dollars. We might as well pay the landlord with our lives. He's hard as iron and won't let go half a penny that's his due. If we harvest one grain, he wants that one grain. Three stewards kept a watch on the threshing. All our rice is being held at the mill."

"Which one?"

"What do you ask that for? Fu-feng-t'ai, is it one of your Mr. Chao's concerns, too? Every one of the heartless lot is a Yama! In spring they measure the rice out and sell it to us for two fifty or two sixty. Now when we want to pay our debts, they'll only allow one sixty. Not even one sixty! They kill us without seeing any blood!" At this point she carried the tub into the bedroom, saying, "Take your bath."

"No use tilling the fields any more, Kou-tzu," advised the old woman. "Better quit—right now."

"Mother's! [9] Your father [10] wants to kill people! He'll start at Fu-feng-t'ai!" shouted Kou-tzu as he stood up and walked to the back room to take his bath.

"It's true. Farming is impossible. How many in this village of yours are still farming?"

"If we don't farm, what will we do? What will we eat?" Hsien-tzu gave a cold smile. "Such nice comforting words! We're not like your old ladyship. We—"

"Quit farming and turn bandit! I've heard Ch'en Pien-tan [11] say that Lao-ssu and Lao-san next door and the wheelbarrow pushers Hsiao-san-hua and Ta-mao-tzu have all gone to the Five-Dragon Mountain. Your father will go there, too. If you don't kill people, they will kill you. That's what it comes to!" The voice came from the back room.

"Watch what you are saying!" Hsien-tzu eyed her mother.

The old woman stood stiffly for a moment and sighed once again. As she walked outside, she said, "I'm going. Everything's dandy now! We're all going to starve to death."

II

Under a darkened sky the hills all around the village were wrapped in fog. A drizzle of oxhair-like rain floated everywhere. As a gust of cold

---

9 "Mother's," "his mother's" (ta-ma-ti), and "grandmother's" are expletives of obscenity commonly heard in China.

10 Meaning the speaker himself. In many parts of China a man may call himself "your father" (lao-tzu) in front of others when he is angry.

11 Pien-tan, meaning "a carrying pole," is a nickname.

wind blew in their direction, the trees around the thatched huts all rustled. The withered *kuei* flowers, now drenched with rain, scattered to the ground through holes in the thatched roofs of the tea booths.

Inside one booth huddled beggars in unbelievable tatters, sitting or lying about on the straw. They were refugees from famine. Some of the women, bare-breasted, sat with their legs crossed in the straw. They were trying to straighten the filthy rags piled around their feet while allowing their children to crawl from the ground to their breasts and suck at them. Others held chipped clay jars filled with grains which had been left in the fields after the harvest and stuffed them into their mouths by handfuls. They wrinkled their eyebrows in distaste as they licked or chewed the grains. Some of the men sat on the ground piling sticky mud onto pieces of broken pottery while others used molds to cast crude human figures in mud, drying them in rows at the foot of the wall. Still others, holding by one hand a bamboo stick with a bundle of straw tied to its end, were inserting into the straw human and animal figures made of coarse red and green paper. Those children who were not around their mothers were either stretching their ugly, dirty faces in loud howls, crawling about in the wet dirt, or picking up fallen *kuei* flowers and stuffing them one by one into their mud-covered mouths.

A woman pushed out of her hut a beggar with a baby fastened with straw ropes to her back and holding in both hands a broken pottery bowl filled with muddy grain.

"You want to steal?" said the woman as she closed the door of her hut.

The beggar gave a bitter smile and then spoke sullenly in a strange dialect, "Your grandmother's! The straw won't burn, so what's wrong in my using your stove for a while?" Following the complaint, she bent her head into the bowl, licked up a few grains with her tongue, and started chewing them slowly.

From afar came bugle notes that were sadly out of tune: "Di di di daa-daa daa-de-da."

After some time a column of men came winding down the mountain slope on the southern road. They approached slowly, their discordant footfalls reverberating through the surrounding countryside. These men, about forty or fifty of them, all wore ill-fitting gray cotton uniforms. Their leggings were carelessly done and their straw sandals and ankle socks were all encased in mud. Each carried a gun awkwardly on his shoulder: either a rifle, a locally made hunter's shotgun, or a "mountain-crossing dragon," which was over ten feet long.[12] Behind them rode a bespectacled officer of around forty in a neat Sun Yat-sen uniform properly decorated with a cartridge belt in front. He sported the kind of mustache that distinguished the man on a package of Jintan pills [13] and held an open umbrella in one of his white-gloved hands. His chest stuck out and, as he rode, the saber on his right clinked against his leather boot and iron stirrup. He looked very imposing, as if he were a great general.

A standard-bearer preceded the troops. Since the flagpole was heavy and long, he rested its lower end against his belly to help him propel it. But the work was obviously too strenuous for him and he perpetually grimaced, revealing one side of his teeth. The flag was soaked through with rain, but when an occasional gust of wind forced its folds to open slightly, one could still read several black characters against their white background: Third Detachment of the People's Militia, X X County.

"Halt! At ease!" The officer gave a shrill command as he approached the tea booths.

Several haggard women came out of the huts and stood in their doorways staring. The beggars in the particular tea booth described earlier all stopped what they were doing and looked with frightened eyes at the troops.

When the officer reached that booth, he closed his umbrella and dismounted. He stood facing the beggars, his right hand on the saber at his waist and his countenance stern. After a few moments, he raised his left hand to gesticulate, and spoke out in poor Mandarin:

"You, listen well. You, all have homes. You, all have. Now we, in this area, things are very difficult. Very, unpeaceful. You, should, all have been informed. You, must, within three days, leave, this area. Three days, three days. Understand? In three days, leave, this area.

[12] *Ku-shan-lung*, a Chinese-made gun normally requiring two men to carry. A Chinese foot is about fourteen inches long.

[13] Jintan, a Japanese-made nostrum, was highly popular in China until the middle thirties. On its package appeared a man's face distinguished by heavy mustache with pointed ends which curved upward.

Other groups, we have told also. No exceptions, all have to leave. Outside people, we, cannot allow, to stay."

He turned and looked at the village women watching the scene. Changing to local dialect, he asked, "Any men in your houses?"

"They aren't home," the women answered.

"Any guests staying in the booths?"

"No guests. Where would there be any guests? These past two years . . ."

"All right. Listen carefully. If you should have any customers who look the least bit suspicious, you must report to our office immediately. The area is not peaceful. We've already made plans. Just go about your work, don't get alarmed."

Everybody was silent.

Outside the tea booth a short militiaman emerged from the column of troops braving the rain "at ease." He held in his hand a "mountain-crossing dragon," which was almost thrice his own height. Walking hesitantly to the door of a hut, he put a forced smile on his face and called in a low voice, "Hsien-tzu!"

Hsien-tzu Sao was at first startled by the comic distress of the man who called her, but when she realized it was her elder brother, she laughed. "Congratulations! What a nice job you've got!"

"I don't drill good. I just can't. We've been on patrol since yesterday afternoon. We left the city at East Gate. . . . What about Kou-tzu? Heard he had trouble. . . ."

"Fall in!" the officer howled.

"Di di di di di," the tuneless bugle began blowing on cue. The short man raised his "mountain-crossing dragon" and tiptoed away like a deer.

When the ranks were formed, the stern officer again shouted an order, opened his umbrella, and mounted his horse to close up the rear. The troops now straggled off toward the north.

There was an outcry among the beggars. Some yelled, "His mother's!"

"Aren't you going to move out?" the woman in the doorway of the hut asked.

"Move his mother's!"

But Hsien-tzu Sao had no heart for conversation with the beggars.

Her brother's cryptic message had frightened her like a clap of thunder, causing her to stream with sweat. Full of misgivings, she closed the door and walked into her house.

But no sooner had she crossed the threshold of her bedroom than she ran out of her hut in three big steps as if she were insane. She dashed through the booth and pantingly yelled in the direction of the northern road, "Brother, brother!"

"Di di di daa-daa daa-de-da!"

Those tuneless bugle notes were already far away: the straggling troops had almost approached the mountain slope.

Hsien-tzu Sao stared for a long time at the troops, her haggard face gradually turning ashy. She felt as if her heart were scurrying inside her chest like a little mouse and her feet trampling on cotton.

She rubbed her sore eyes a couple of times to compose herself. After a while she returned to her house, closed the door, and sat down on the doorsill of the back room. Resting her right elbow on her knee, she placed her right palm on the temple covered with a headache plaster. Her head was swimming as if it had received a sudden blow. Slowly she recalled the events of a few days ago.

That day at dusk a big, rough-looking fellow with long hair walked into her hut. He held a reed torch, and its bright flame revealed a ferocious, drunken face.

"Aiya, isn't it Old Pien-tan?" asked she, startled.

"Where's Kou-tzu?"

"Gone to the city, will be back any time now."

"What, hasn't had his supper yet?"

"Maybe he'll return after having supper in town."

"Did you know I have a date with him? We've got business."

"He didn't say anything. What business?"

"Tell you later."

Before long her husband pushed open the door and walked in. Both men took handfuls of soot off the bottom of a cooking pot and smeared their faces with it.

"What are you two planning to do?" Her teeth were chattering.

"None of your business."

"Kou-tzu, you mustn't do that. You—"

"I've got to try this," her husband replied calmly.

"You mustn't. I won't let you go." She grabbed at his belt.

Her husband gave her a push, and the two men pulled the door open and rushed out.

That night she didn't sleep at all.

Around midnight she heard a tapping at the door. She opened it, and there stood her husband: on his blackened face his lips were dyed purplish-red with blood from his gums. Violently shaken, he staggered into the back room.

"Thought it was going to be a big haul. His mother's!" He ejaculated the words with his trembling red lips, panting hard. At the same time he fumbled in the money belt at his waist until he had pulled out eight silver dollars, two bank notes, and a gold bracelet. These he threw on the table.

"My God! Whose house?"

"At Mount Sunset. . . . What sharp eyes! She recognized me as soon as she saw me. Then she yelled and grabbed me."

"Recognized you, eh?" she cried, opening her eyes wide.

"Hush! Old Ch'en landed a blow right on her chest and threw her over on the front steps. To make sure she was dead, he seized a bronze incense burner and hit her on the head like crazy."

"My God!" she couldn't help uttering another cry.

"Hush! I said, 'You're asking for your own funeral, really asking for it!' "

Outside someone pushed the door open and walked in.

"Anybody home?"

Suddenly wakened from her confused train of thought, Hsien-tzu Sao raised her head and got up from the doorsill.

"Who is it?"

"It's me, ma'am."

The person came closer, beaming with a smile that revealed two gold teeth. He wore an old lined jacket of silk and held an umbrella upside down. The rubber galoshes on his feet glistened. His lean face was a long rectangle and the top of his head was flat. When Hsien-tzu Sao realized that it was the assistant deputy from the county yamen, her heart instantly jumped to her throat.

"Wang Ch'i-yeh." [14]

"Yes."

"What is it, Ch'i-yeh?" Hsien-tzu Sao asked casually, forcibly controlling herself.

"Nothing—I must attend to a small matter at Fen-chieh Ferry. The road is bad. Came in for a bowl of tea."

"You haven't been out here for a long time."

"Not so long, really. Last time I passed by, I was delivering a summons to a tenant farmer. It was getting late, and so I didn't stop here for tea."

"It's really embarrassing. I haven't yet brewed the tea. No business, Ch'i-yeh."

"I'm in no hurry. Just take your time."

"All right. What was the tenant's trouble?" As she spoke, she walked over to the stove to boil water.

"Same old thing. Right now everybody is hard up, and farmers suffer even worse. The harvest wasn't good, the price for rice in the husk is getting lower and lower."

"You're so right."

"The farmers' lot is hard, but the landlords have a difficult time, too. Taxes are too heavy. The price for rice in the husk goes down, but the land and other taxes stay high. It's hard for both sides."

"That's right. How did the case finally end?"

"The usual way. The tenant owed two years' rent—naturally, it wasn't that he wouldn't pay, but he just couldn't. He was lucky in having a large family, but there were too many mouths to feed. And the landlord couldn't let him go. You don't pay one year, you don't pay the second year—why should the landlord own the land? Isn't that so?"

"Right."

"The magistrate is a good-hearted man, easygoing about everything. Only had him beaten a few strokes and locked up in the Third Ward.[15] I saw how pitiful he was, getting on in years. He was an old man, that tenant."

"Yes."

"I'm no good working in the yamen. Heaven didn't cut me out for

[14] Meaning "Your honor, Mr. Wang VII."   [15] The misdemeanor ward.

the job, I'm too soft-hearted. In most routine cases, if I can help a man, I do. What are we born for? I have no choice but to work in the yamen, but I'm not good at it. I always want to help the poor."

"Ch'i-yeh, you are a good man."

"You say so, but other people are different. They curse me behind my back. So it's hard to be a good man, too. I told his family to bring a bit of money to thank the fellows at the jail. The fellows all heeded my words, and when it was possible for them to do so, they released him. The rent was an easy matter. I told him to pay it back little by little. But he had to pay it."

"You're certainly right."

"Isn't Kou-tzu home? This year's harvest wasn't too bad?"

"He's gone to the city. He went day before yesterday. Didn't you see him, Ch'i-yeh?" As she spoke, she felt as if her insides had been scalded with boiling water. She tried to throw some tea leaves into the tea bowl, but they scattered all over the stove.

"If the harvest is good, that's all that matters." The deputy seemed not to have heard her, following his own train of thought. "If business is a little slow in the booth, it doesn't matter. The bowl may be empty, but there's something in the pot. That's all you need."

"What do you mean, Ch'i-yeh? We till about six and a half mou and last year we had to borrow to pay the rent. This year—"

"You didn't have to borrow?"

"Didn't have to borrow!" Hsien-tzu Sao's heartbeat quickened and her eyes widened as she spoke. But she calmed down right away, saying, "Yes, all in all it was a little better than last year."

"Kou-tzu is very capable. I really like him for that."

"That's kind of you, Ch'i-yeh."

"Not so. I really liked him best in *The Seventh Celestial Maid Descends to Earth*. That, that singing of his and that acting were all outstanding. And that figure of his—ma'am, when he disguised himself, he carried it off better than you could have. I'm not being partial. And he hasn't sung for some years now."

"How true."

"That year in the first month I heard you people were going to stage an opera and I came especially to see it. It turned out to be *The Seventh Celestial Maid Descends to Earth*. Lao San next door played

Tung Yung. When he sold himself to bury his father, his filial heart moved Heaven itself. And Kou-tzu as the Seventh Maiden. . . .[16] Ma'am, I tell you it's no wonder you two are so much in love. I love him, too. Ha, ha, ha!"

"Ch'i-yeh is joking."

"No, I'm not. I would really love to see it again."

"This once-busy Fan Village is now deserted, Ch'i-yeh. All we can do is have him give a performance for you to watch by yourself."

"That's why I was saying all this in a joking way. If the singers were all here, the play still couldn't be put on. The whole area is in a state of emergency. The past two days the rumors have really been flying, ma'am."

"That's right. I hear that the Five-Dragon Mountain has sent another letter to the county yamen."

"Surely not just the Five-Dragon Mountain? Even in the southwestern district there have been several robberies lately."

"Really?" Hsien-tzu Sao, just getting calmer, was once again jolted. Steam rose to her face as she lowered her head to pour boiling water into the tea bowl. She placed it before the deputy, saying, "Your tea, Ch'i-yeh."

"Much obliged." The deputy threw away his cigarette butt and blew on the tea leaves floating in the bowl.

Hsien-tzu Sao again sat down on the doorsill, watching the deputy's embarrassment with a fixed stare.

"Several robberies, and then there's a murder."

"Murder?"

"So recent and you have heard of it already? The county yamen has just learned about it. They plan to examine the corpse tomorrow."

"Who said I knew? Nobody told me anything about it."

"I'm sure you know the accused. He's the peddler Ch'en Pien-tan. Long hair, big fellow—that one. The loads he carries are always over a hundred catties. Remember the man?"

On a sudden, uncontrollable impulse Hsien-tzu Sao got up without

---

[16] The story of Tung Yung and the celestial maiden has enjoyed immense popularity in the regionally diversified theater of traditional China. One ballad version of the story appears in Arthur Waley, tr., *Ballads and Stories from Tunhuang* (New York, 1960), pp. 155–61.

knowing what she was doing, and then she sat down again. She wanted to say something, her lips trembled, but no words came out.

"I never thought that man would do something like this." The deputy went on speaking slowly, his eyes following her. "Hard to blame him, though, the times are so bad. Who would set his mind on doing wrong? You just can't help it. This time we've got the stolen goods and the criminal. Caught him day before yesterday. Day before yesterday."

Seeing that Hsien-tzu Sao had buried her face in her hands, he drank some tea, heaved a deliberate sigh, and continued:

"He was too hasty and overbold, didn't know how to take proper precautions. He took a gold pin—actually it wasn't gold, just gold-plated—and wanted to get some money for it in the city. It was dark and the militiaman at the city gate wouldn't let him pass. He thought it was like any other day and therefore it wouldn't matter if he started an argument with the militiaman. But that militiaman was a guard from the yamen, an old hand at catching criminals. This was bound to be unfortunate. If it had been a local militiaman, the matter would have ended there. The old hand wanted to search him. One was afraid of being found out and wouldn't submit, while the other thought, 'You won't let me search you. Then I must.' So Ch'en Pien-tan was taken to the station. The search was made and the pin was found. There were five one-dollar Shanghai bank notes, too." He took another sip of tea. "They asked him, 'Where did you get this gold pin and the money?' The fellow is a numskull. He can carry a hundred-catty load, strong as an ox, really a Li K'uei,[17] completely straightforward and not a trick in his head. The first question stumped him. He couldn't answer. They held him at the station. The next day—that was yesterday—they sent him to the yamen. At first he wouldn't talk. Didn't talk even when they pressed his thighs between rods. But when they brought out the red-hot chains, he had to talk."

Hsien-tzu Sao had said nothing for a long time. Suddenly she put her hands to her face and wailed.

"What's this, what's this, ma'am? I understand! He made a false accusation. I understand, I understand, ma'am." The deputy feigned a serious expression as he spoke. He walked over to comfort her. Hsien-tzu

[17] A strong-bodied, simple-minded hero in the novel *The Water Margin*.

Sao paid no attention. Like a small child, she bobbed back and forth, slapping her knees and howling.

"Aiya, this is my fault."

Hsien-tzu Sao wailed for a while, then suddenly stopped. She picked up a corner of her jacket and dabbed her eyes. Sucking air through her mouth, she tried to stifle her sobs. "Ch'i-yeh, Ch'i-yeh," she cried out twice, and then resumed her grievous sobbing.

"I understand, I understand. He was scared stiff and so falsely accused your Kou-tzu."

"Ch'i-yeh, Ch'i-yeh, I just have to beg you to get us out of this." As she sobbed these words, her lower jaw moving up and down, she went over and knelt before the deputy.

"What's this, what's this, ma'am? You are going to cut my life short. Get up now, get up. I want to live a couple more years." As he spoke, he pulled Hsien-tzu Sao up by both arms and guided her back to the doorsill. "Ma'am, would I want you to beg me? We have known each other for years, Kou-tzu is my friend. If I wanted you to beg, I wouldn't have come in person to your house today."

Hsien-tzu Sao, still shaking with sobs, kept blowing her nose.

"Kou-tzu was most wrongly accused, that I know. Let me finish so you people won't have to suffer a false charge without knowing the whole story. That Ch'en Pien-tan told the truth, saying that the things were from the Kshitigarbha Convent at Mount Sunset. His Honor brought the gavel down with a bang and said, 'Rubbish! A gold pin and bank notes in a convent?' His Honor is a good man. How could he know that the convents around here all own some land and have some money on hand? This Sister Lien was really capable. Saved incense money and loaned it out at big compound interest. Don't laugh at me, ma'am, for telling you this, but the year before last when I needed money to tide me over the New Year I took two of my daughter-in-law's rings and pledged them for seven dollars at her place, and it was only this past spring that I got them back. Ch'en Pien-tan told about Sister Lien of the convent, told everything, everything. They asked him who was his helper. That was when he involved your Kou-tzu. And as luck would have it, Kou-tzu was settling his account at Fu-feng-t'ai and he had no way of knowing that a false charge would come flying down on his head without warning. Don't worry, ma'am,

just don't worry at all. They didn't open the inquiry yesterday. He's
in the, the. . . ."

"Where is he?" she asked anxiously. She had stopped crying.

"There's some difficulty here. If he were in the Third Ward, I'd
take care of everything and there'd be no problem."

"The First Ward?" [18]

"Murder. Robbery. Of course, he's in the First Ward. That's why I
am not exactly in the know. Tough, really tough. The whole thing is
in the hands of the keeper of the First Ward. He is a Shantung man,
very stern and strict. It's because it doesn't do you any good to have a
helpless friend like me that I came here to talk it over with you. We've
got to think of a plan."

Hsien-tzu Sao held her face in her hands and began wailing again.
Stumbling over, she knelt at the deputy's feet and sobbed, "Ch'i-yeh,
Ch'i-yeh, please think of something for me. I beg you, Ch'i-yeh, Ch'i-
yeh."

"Aiya, ma'am, what are you doing? Aiya, aiya! Get up quick, get
up now."

"Ch'i-yeh, Ch'i-yeh," she wailed, getting up unsteadily.

"Ma'am, this is no time for crying. Sit down, sit down. Let's take
our time and figure this out. We've got to think of something. Kou-tzu
and I are just like real brothers. I've got to help him; what need for
you to beg? I want to do everything I can myself. I'll tell you how
matters stand: Ch'en Pien-tan confessed, implicated, yes, implicated
Kou-tzu. His Honor issued a warrant on the spot. Two of my colleagues stupidly went right out into the street to search for him without even consulting me. They found him right at Fu-feng-t'ai. Found
him, didn't even tell me about it, and took him straight to the First
Ward. By the time I found out about the whole thing, the rice was
cooked already. I was worried, I thought, 'A murder charge is really serious. It will be too much of an ordeal for Kou-tzu. I've got to do the
best I can.' So I went to see the head of the First Ward. He knows I
like to meddle and help people. So he gave me a scolding and flung my
request three thousand eight hundred li! My face fell, too. I cared only
for righteousness, I had no ulterior motive, ma'am, and so I was not
afraid of him. I said, 'This man is a very close sworn brother of mine, a

[18] The felony ward.

very upright man. If you are really going to give him the works, then punish me first.' The warden was a good fellow after all. When he heard me talking like that, he calmed down, saying, 'If that's how things are, we're all friends and I'm willing to help.' So it looks as if we could cover up and keep this thing from being exposed. Looks as if we could do it. But although the warden was willing to help, those shrimps under him wouldn't go along. So I went and tried to soften them. I said, 'This man is my sworn brother, very close to me. Give me face and do it for my sake.' But being what they are, those fellows don't see very far. It was the same old thing: wanted me to pay them off. Mother's, yamen routine of this sort is always a big headache. I said, 'I can't do this! This sworn brother of mine is a peasant. The crops have been bad the past two years and there's no business in his wife's tea booth. You all know this. Where do you expect me to get money from? Aren't you deliberately pushing him to the wall?' "

"How much, Ch'i-yeh?" Hsien-tzu Sao asked impatiently.

"We can't just agree to what they want, ma'am. There are altogether fifteen or sixteen men under the warden. If you give each man ten dollars, you'll have to ask the God of Wealth to come down to help you. That can't be done! Right now, I can't agree to what they want. Kou-tzu, Kou-tzu—"

As the deputy spoke, he turned his head toward the round hole in the wall and looked at the sky. Suddenly he said, "Aiya, I'm going to be very late! How come it's getting dark already? Looks as if it will rain harder too. I've still to get to Fen-chieh Ferry, more than ten li of mountain road. I can't stay. Well, ma'am, you just borrow as you can and see how it turns out. Try your mother, she has ways and means. Whatever you get, let it go at that. Give it to me. I'll use my influence and try to reason with them. Years ago things were easy. In the past few years the fellows at the yamen have really been ducks stranded on a dry bank. It won't do not to give them something."

Toward the end of his speech the deputy got up, took his umbrella, and walked a couple of steps. Then he turned around again and said, "Don't worry, ma'am. I'll be there at the trial and do my best. He won't suffer bodily harm. And I'll think of a way to cover up for him, you can be sure of that. Be patient, don't worry and get upset."

Hsien-tzu Sao, gritting her teeth, stared at his receding back. After a long while she staggered to the back room and flopped on the bed. She covered her face with both hands and wailed convulsively.

III

The *kuei* blossoms had bloomed and fallen the third time. Leaves from the trees were falling now, too. It was already the middle of the ninth month.

The fields were redolent with the scents of wild flowers and grasses, and the wind blowing in one's face carried the promise of chill weather. The warm sun shone on the dingy, ramshackle huts of Fan Village, but the tea booths were now busier than usual.

Among the boards and benches lying about in the straw, those still serviceable had been pulled up and made to stand. Around one set of board and benches rested wayfarers of both sexes, forming two groups. They all had fair-complexioned, though worried-looking, faces. Sedan chairs and baggage were all crowded into the tea booths. Several booth keepers, their haggard faces now looking somewhat more cheerful, were once again busily running back and forth with their teakettles.

A short-haired girl in a blue cotton gown bent her head, stamped on the chestnut burs on a short broken branch, then picked them up and peeled them with her fine white hands. She smacked her lips as she ate the nuts and said to the worried-looking woman next to her, "Mom, these chestnuts are sweeter than the ones sold by venders near our house. Try them and see."

The woman forced a smile and said to another woman opposite her, "This daughter of ours doesn't know the first thing about life. Other people's hearts are in suspense with worry, but hers? She's not at all worried, she's very happy. All the way here she insisted on getting down from the sedan chair to pick those chestnuts."

"How old is she? Schoolgirls in the early teens or younger are all like that. And you can't blame them: in a world like this it's better to maintain good cheer. Getting worried and upset, what's the use? Now, can you believe it? We haven't brought along a thing. A big house left for a servant to look after. Can't bear to think of it, *T'ai-t'ai*, can't bear to think of it. If I had my way, I wouldn't leave. Even if I were to die, it would be better to die at home. One cannot escape fate."

"That's how I feel. Her father forced us to leave. I said, 'Why should I leave? If you want to, you take her and hide for a while. I'll watch the house. What am I afraid of, an old person like me? I'm not afraid. Bandits are also people.' "

"Where are you going?"

"Where is there to go? First, we thought we'd go to the port city. But we haven't got the money for that. The best thing we can do now is go to her nurse's home at the Water Bamboo Mountain. And you?"

"My cousin's home. As soon as the rumors got bad, she sent word for me to come. I—"

"Aiya, Mrs. Yü of the Episcopal Church is coming, too," the girl shouted and left off stamping chestnut burs under her feet to greet her.

Two sedan chairs approached from the north. A small American flag sticking out from the lintel of the first chair flapped in the wind. When the chair reached the tea booth, a woman in her early forties, with bobbed hair, and a small crucifix hanging on her chest, stepped down. A schoolteacher in her early twenties got down from the second chair. When the girl saw her, she skipped forward and called with warmth, "Aiya, Miss Liu!"

"Pao-chen!" the schoolteacher held her hand.

"How is it over there, Mrs. Yü?" a woman stood up and asked.

"Still camped at Green Maple Ferry, determined to stay on. Our minister told us just as we were leaving. *T'ai-t'ai*, this time the people of the northern district are in trouble."

"Isn't that so, though. If we'd known earlier they would stick to their word, we could have scraped up the money through small individual contributions and given them the fifty thousand to end it all. I wonder if our militiamen can cope with them. Isn't it dreadful!"

"You're right in leaving, *T'ai-t'ai*. Our minister said the militia here is no good. He phoned the yamen in the provincial capital and the yamen ignored him."

"If the worst comes to the worst . . ."

Another woman who had been silent so far began to weep, covering her eyes with a handkerchief and sniffling continuously. A young man next to her patted her back and urged her to have a drink of tea. Several other ladies became upset, too, and they sighed with reddening eyes.

"Mrs. Yü, where are you two going?" asked the girl.

Mrs. Yü was about to reply when a male servant with hair combed in the Western style came up to her with a vacant stare and whispered something in her ear. She changed color instantly and walked over to the schoolteacher.

Covering her nose and mouth with a handkerchief and squinting her eyes in disgust, the schoolteacher was surveying the piles of dirty straw and spitting one mouthful of saliva after another.

"The refugees made them so, really filthy," a booth keeper said apologetically. "The militia tried to drive them off many times, but with no success. During the day they all hide in the hills and find some wild stuff to eat. At night they come back here again to sleep."

"Miss Lui, I want to talk to you," Mrs. Yü called. She mumbled to the schoolteacher for a moment.

With a flustered look, the schoolteacher called to the booth keeper who had just taken the bowls to make tea, "No tea, please." Then she called to the chair-bearers, "Let's go. Hurry."

The manservant also joined in hastening the chair-bearers. The girl stood before the schoolteacher, nonplused. Looking up, she blinked her unbelieving eyes and asked, "Miss Liu, what is it?"

"Not too long ago," the schoolteacher said in a low voice, "not too long ago. . . . All of you'd better leave, too. Tell your mother to leave with us, don't stay here any longer."

Over there Mrs. Yü was whispering something to the weeping woman. Suddenly the woman jumped up from the bench, quickly grabbed the purse on the table, and said in alarm, "Really? Really? It happened here? Here?"

"Three li from here. The Kshitigarbha Convent on Mount Sunset."

Thus talking, all got up and started to leave. A woman who found her sedan chair at the rear of the procession called excitedly, "Mrs. Yü, please wait for me, wait for me. I need your protection."

Mrs. Yü was already seated in the chair, but she complied gladly and called her manservant to straighten the American flag at the front of her chair.

"Mrs. Yü, go on ahead, our chairs will follow yours," another lady called out.

"Sure, sure," replied Mrs. Yü.

In a while the sedan chairs and loads of baggage were all gone, and Fan Village was once again desolate.

Several booth keepers were clearing away the tea bowls and collecting the coins from the tables. One woman holding a small child in her arms looked toward the north and said to another, "This bandit trouble has brought us a little business."

"What business? There's just this much each morning. Once the sun passes that post, no one comes again. Yesterday was like that, too."

So talking, the booth keeper noticed a short, fat old woman entering the booth on the south side. She greeted her happily, "What's new, Auntie? She didn't come out to do business." She twisted her mouth in the direction of a closed door to her right.

"Now what am I supposed to do?" the old woman said, frowning. "At first Ch'i-yeh told her to collect a few dollars and that would cover it—nothing important. Day before yesterday, Hsien-tzu came to see me and said that because the situation in general was getting worse the yamen was going to try the case right away and be very strict about it, allowing no chance for bribery. Since there's no chance for bribery, well, one might as well just accept one's fate."

"I hear the First Ward wants a lump sum."

"Dream on! Where to get a large sum like that? Hsien-tzu still vexes me with her red eyebrows and green eyes, believing I'm loaded, a millionaire, no less. Damn it! Am I a magistrate? Does money grow out of my skin? Without fear of Heaven or law, they acted shamelessly and made this trouble. What am I supposed to think up now? Mr. Chao and his whole family left for Shanghai; otherwise I could go with her to beg Mr. Chao. What am I supposed to do now? You know what? Day before yesterday, Hsien-tzu came and served me notice. She put it eloquently: Kou-tzu's life is in my hands now. If I want him to die, he'll die; if I want him to live, then he'll live. What words were these, I ask you! Did I tell him to rob people? Did I tell him to kill? They make me so angry it will be the death of me."

"It can't be helped, Auntie. They really love each other too much."

"Love! A son-in-law like that has totally shamed me. It's not because I want to be hard-hearted that I say even if he got off scot-free I wouldn't have anything to do with him. Guilt by association, you know."

"Hm!" The booth keeper reddened and said with a sarcastic smile. "But that's how the world is today, there are lots of men like Kou-tzu."

Not knowing what to make of the remark, the old woman continued, "I kept telling Hsien-tzu, 'Listen to me, listen. You are not old yourself. A live tiger doesn't have to keep company with a stone lion.' "

The booth keeper turned her head and walked into her house with the tea bowls. The old woman made a wry face and refrained from further speech. Picking up her cane, she left the booth for the northern road.

"Auntie," called the booth keeper with a child in her arms. "Aren't you going inside to see her? She hasn't eaten for several days."

Upon hearing this, the old woman turned and said, "I'm not going in. I've still got a little business in town. I'll see her when I get back."

"The rumors from town are very bad. Since day before yesterday there've been several hundred people passing here to get away from the trouble. Today was the worst. Since daybreak group after group —altogether seventy or eighty of them—has passed through here. I hear they're only a little over thirty li from the city."

"Really?" The old woman's face looked distressed. After musing for a while, she quickened her steps and hobbled on, saying, "I'll hurry then, I'll hurry."

"Auntie, wouldn't it be better not to go?"

But the old woman was already out of earshot.

The booth keeper who had gone inside a while ago came out again and said with a sneer, "What are you calling her for? You're so worried about her—would she listen to you?"

"What could be so important that it kept her from paying a visit to her daughter in distress?"

"It's her turn to get the credit union money today. Isn't fifty silver dollars more important than her daughter and son-in-law?"

"Oh, today's the fifteenth of the ninth month. No wonder she's so anxious."

"You're so right!"

"But if she gets the money, I wonder if she'll be willing to lend it to Hsien-tzu?"

"Farts! Didn't you hear her talking just now? Said a son-in-law like that is better off dead. Said that even if he gets released she won't have anything to do with him. Said Hsien-tzu should remarry. Her son-in-law isn't even dead yet and she tells her daughter to remarry. A procuress for a mother!"

While the booth keeper was talking, a yellow leaf from the *kuei* tree whirled down through the roof of the booth and rested on her neck. She was startled at first, thinking it must be a caterpillar, and brushed at it quickly with her hand, but when she found it was a yellowed leaf she placed it between her lips and held it there. There were many things she badly wanted to tell Hsien-tzu Sao, and so she looked in through a crack in the closed door, pushed it open, and walked in.

The sun was about to set in the western hills. The *kuei* trees over the tea booths glowed yellow in the light of the setting sun. It seemed as though their half-bare branches had once again burst into blossom.

Along the northern road group after group came with agitated steps. Some carried cloth bundles on their backs, some held rattan baskets, and some led children by the hand. Still others shouldered two baskets, one at each end of a carrying pole. Of every such pair, one basket usually contained a child sitting among bundles and chewing on a piece of puffed rice candy or some such sweetmeat.

Group after group, they passed the tea booths without stopping, heading south in a state of agitation.

Among them an old woman supported by a cane walked into a booth and raised her head to look at the late sun hanging over the western hills. The sun had already turned pink, and the clouds around it appeared especially dazzling in their orange and crimson colors. Some blue birds flew serenely in the sky, calling out blithely once or twice and then disappearing among the mountain clouds.

The old woman paused for a while, panting. She adjusted her headband, walked over to a hut, pushed the door open, and walked in.

The room was so dark that she could not see her hand in front of her face.

"Hsien-tzu, Hsien-tzu!"

There was no answer.

"Hsien-tzu, Hsien-tzu!"

"Hm." The noise came from the back room.

"Mother has come to see you. Did Ch'i-yeh come?"

"*Heng!*" [19] was the reply.

"Have you eaten anything? I am worried and have come especially to see you." She groped her way into the back room.

"*Heng!* I suppose you came from the city?"

"That's right. I went to ask around. . . . ."

"*Heng!* Congratulations, Madame, on getting the credit union money!"

"Don't talk about that. I'm really worried sick."

"*Heng!*"

"Have you heard? It's bad: the militia retreated—retreated twenty li. The militia's not very brave, can't face real fighting. The city is deserted. Even the magistrate has left. How could I get that money? I put it out for nothing. *Niang* put the money out for nothing, Hsien-tzu."

A sneer could be heard from the bed.

"If the bandits really get into the city, you don't have to worry, Hsien-tzu. They usually break open the jail first. Our Kou-tzu will be saved then."

"*Heng!*"

"But I'm afraid, afraid—Hsien-tzu."

"Hm."

"Afraid—there's such a rumor—afraid that the militia will retreat to the city and hold it and the bandits won't get in for a while."

"Won't that be good, huh?"

"I'm afraid for your elder brother, your elder brother—" Sensing the inappropriateness of her thought, she heaved a long sigh. After a pause, she asked, "Where is the kerosene lamp?"

Getting no answer, the old woman sat quiet and sighed deeply several times. She then got up and groped around the stove until she reached the water jar and found the altar candles where she had placed them during an earlier visit. She took one and returned to the other room.

"Where are the matches? Under your pillow?"

The old woman went to the bedside, felt about the straw pillow dampened with tears until she found by its edge some matches. She

[19] A nasal sound expressing contempt.

struck a match and in the candlelight saw her daughter lying on her side on a wooden bed, her face to the wall. She put the matches back by the pillow.

"It's late. I'm going to sleep here tonight. Tomorrow I'll go and ask around for news." There was a long pause. "I'm really useless now. Just walk a few li and I'm all aches and pains. Where should *Niang* sleep, Hsien-tzu?"

As she spoke, she looked at the red altar candle in her hand: some wax was dripping from its tip onto her finger.

"Where are your candleholders, Hsien-tzu?" She wiped her finger against the edge of a bench. "In the clothes cabinet?"

She went over to search the cabinet standing next to the wall. There was none in the upper drawer. But she found in a corner of the lower drawer the pair of small pewter candleholders that had been a part of her daughter's dowry. She took out one and closed the cabinet door. She then removed the wax stub from the iron spike of the holder, stuck the candle on it, and placed the light on the table.

After sitting abstractedly for a while, she felt her headband once and again breathed out a weary sigh. She got up, opened the cabinet, and took out a quilt and bed pad from its upper drawer. These she lugged to a small bamboo cot, on which she arranged them. She then took off her clothes, blew out the candle, and lay down on the cot.

In a short while the fat old woman was fast asleep.

Hsien-tzu Sao lay on her bed listening to her mother's snoring, her own head aching with a dull pain. Half awake and half dreaming, she thought confusedly of several things. Right in front of her eyes she saw Kou-tzu's sensitive, good-looking face and his bare, strong upper body. Now he was in her own glazed cotton jacket, performing moving scenes from Flower Drum operas on a stage erected on the grain-drying area; in another second he was working in the fields with his back bent and humming a Flower Drum tune. His face appeared care-worn as he returned from the landlord's in the city, and then it appeared covered with soot, blood streaming down his teeth. She also visualized Wang Ch'i-yeh's embarrassment during his recent visit and remembered what the booth keeper next door had told her earlier in the day her mother had said. She saw her mother's cruel, fat face, saw Kou-tzu's corpse befouled with blood.

She tossed and turned for a long time and thought again of the things she had pondered innumerable times before.

Her mother's heavy snoring assailed her ears continuously, making her feel as if her heart were on fire. She turned over and looked through the window in the south wall at the brilliant white moonlight outside.

She sat up slowly. Her head was numb and heavy. She held it in her hands and closed her eyes to rest for a moment. Then she felt around for the matches near the pillow and lit the altar candle on the table.

Her mother slept on the bamboo cot, huddled up like a giant rabbit. Her exposed hands held the headband on her brow, while her face was buried under one arm.

A thought suddenly leapt into Hsien-tzu Sao's mind. With the eagerness of one delving into a mystery, exposing a dark secret, or baiting an offending animal, she picked up the candleholder and walked stealthily to her mother's side.

Her mother's clothes were thrown over the quilt. She felt in a pocket and pulled out a dirty handkerchief and a bunch of keys. Disappointed, she put them back in the pocket and turned her attention to the headband guarded by her mother's hands.

She lightly removed one of the hands, which made her mother stir a little. She then gently touched the headband and felt a stack of crisp bank notes under its several layers of pleated silk.

Her heart pounded, sending upward a rush of uncontrollable anger. Gritting her teeth, she pulled hard with her left hand at the headband. But before it could be pulled off, her mother awoke in a fright, desperately seized the hand with both hands, and cried out, "Oh! Oh! My headband, my headband! You're stealing my headband!" Thus screaming, she flopped about like a fish and pulled at the offending hand so frantically that the candleholder in Hsien-tzu's other hand was violently shaken. Molten wax spilled upon the old woman's face and body and the quilt, but she held on to her daughter with all her strength, determined not to release her grip. Hsien-tzu Sao pulled backward and the candle fell from the pewter holder to the floor.

Instantly the room turned dark, even though a sliver of moonlight coming through the window in the south wall illuminated the shaking candleholder in Hsien-tzu Sao's hand. She saw the sharp iron spike on the holder. In a flash she was holding it upside down and with savage strength she was repeatedly thrusting its point into her mother's head.

Her mother gave forth two shrill cries and then fell by the edge of the bed, silent and motionless.

Hsien-tzu Sao held the headband in her hands, stupefied for a moment. Then her whole body began to shake violently.

Though in a daze, she was vaguely aware of the still flickering candle at her feet. She picked it up and touched it to the straw mattress of her own wooden bed and to the quilt and pad. . . . Panting hard, she wrapped the headband tightly around her hand, opened the door, and ran out of the hut.

Outside it was bright as day. There were only piles of straw in the tea booth; all the beggars had rushed to the city. Like someone possessed of the devil, Hsien-tzu Sao ran swiftly along the road toward the north.

Just as she approached the mountain slope, she ran into a man with a clean-shaven head who grabbed her by the arm.

"Where are you going, Hsien-tzu?" The voice was very familiar.

Hsien-tzu Sao blinked her wild eyes, looking at the man's face—a handsome, familiar face. "You, you, you—ah, it's you! Has the city really . . ." She panted, thinking she was in a dream.

The frantic gong beats had started up in Fan Village. Tongues of fire, leaping out from the roof of the hut, were already licking that majestic *kuei* tree.

March 19, 1934

Eileen Chang

In *History* I have called Eileen Chang "the best and most important writer in Chinese today." This statement still holds true, since no Chinese author of recent years can as yet boast a body of short fiction as rich and brilliant as hers plus a novel of classic standing comparable to *The Rice-sprout Song* (*Yang-ko*). But partly thanks to her salutary influence, serious young writers of today like Shui Ching and Pai Hsien-yung of the present volume are turning out first-rate short stories distinguished by their conscious use of metaphorical language. On the whole, the fiction of the thirties lacked that metaphorical dimension.

Eileen Chang (Chang Ai-ling) comes from a distinguished family. Her grandmother's father was the statesman Li Hung-chang, and her grandfather was Chang P'ei-lun, the chief political casualty of the Sino-French War of 1884 but nonetheless an earnest official in his youth and a classical scholar. Her father, however, was a domestic tyrant, and Eileen Chang suffered greatly in her youth. She studied at the University of Hong Kong until Pearl Harbor and then returned to Shanghai to begin her literary career. Most of her short stories and essays date from the period 1942–45. In 1952 she left the mainland for Hong Kong, where two novels appeared: *The Rice-sprout Song* (1954; English version, 1955) and *Naked Earth* (*Ch'ih-ti chih lüan*, 1954; English version, 1956). She arrived in the United States in 1955 and has since lived a most secluded life. Recently she produced two versions of a novel based on her story "The Golden Cangue" (*Chin-so chi*, 1943)—*The Embittered Woman* (*Yuan-nü*, Taipei, 1968) and *The Rouge of the North* (London, 1967)—as well as the revision of a novel first serialized in the forties, newly titled *Half a Lifetime's Romance* (*Pan-sheng yuan*, Taipei, 1969).

I have maintained in *History* that "The Golden Cangue" is "the greatest novelette in the history of Chinese literature." Certainly, by its side, even the finest vernacular tales of comparative length and scope, such as "The Pearl-sewn Shirt" and "The Oil Peddler," appear victims of the storyteller's conventions in their occasional adulteration of moral and psychological reality, while none of Eileen Chang's successors have yet told an essential truth about Chinese civilization in a novelette of equal weight and terrifying power. In *History* I have commented on the story as follows:

Eileen Chang has evinced an unerring knowledge of the manners and mores of the decadent upper class throughout the story and has studied the heroine's life in terms of an unflinching psychological realism; but what elevates this perception and this realism into the realm of tragedy is the personal emotion behind the creation, the attitude of mingled fascination and horror with which the author habitually contemplates her own childhood environment. In *The Golden Cangue* Eileen Chang has found a perfect fable to serve as the dramatic correlative of her emotion, and the result is an overpowering tragedy embodying an acute moral vision, uniquely her own.

The reader who finds the story fascinating should by all means read *The Rouge of the North*.

Eileen Chang has translated three other stories of hers into English: "Stale Mates," *The Reporter*, XV, No. 4 (September, 1956); "Little Finger Up," in Lucian Wu, ed., *New Chinese Stories*; and "Shame, Amah!" in Nieh Hua-ling, ed., *Eight Stories by Chinese Women*. The last two are somewhat abridged versions of "Waiting" (*Teng*) and "Indian Summer: A-hsiao's Autumnal Lament" (*Kuei-hua-cheng A-hsiao pei-ch'iu*), collected along with "The Golden Cangue" in *The Short Stories of Eileen Chang* (*Chang Ai-ling tuan-p'ien hsiao-shuo chi*, Hong Kong, 1954; Taipei, 1968).

THE GOLDEN CANGUE

TRANSLATED BY *the author*

Shanghai thirty years ago on a moonlit night . . . maybe we did not get to see the moon of thirty years ago. To young people the moon of thirty years ago should be a reddish-yellow wet stain the size of a copper coin, like a teardrop on letter paper by To-yün Hsüan,[1] worn and blurred. In old people's memory the moon of thirty years ago was gay, larger, rounder, and whiter than the moon now. But looked back on after thirty years on a rough road, the best of moons is apt to be tinged with sadness.

The moonlight reached the side of Feng-hsiao's pillow. She was a slave girl brought by the bride, the new Third Mistress of the Chiangs. She opened her eyes to take a look and saw her own blue-white hand on the half-worn blanket faced with quilted Korean silk. "Is it moonlight?" she said to herself. She slept on a pallet on the floor under the window. The last couple of years had been busy with the changing of dynasties. The Chiangs coming to Shanghai as refugees did not have enough room, so the servants' quarters were criss-crossed with people sleeping.

[1] To-yün Hsüan (Solitary Cloud Studio) was famous for its fine red-striped letter paper, popular down to the thirties.

Feng-hsiao seemed to hear a rustle behind the big bed and guessed that somebody had got up to use the chamber pot. She turned over and, just as she thought, the cloth curtain was thrust aside and a black shadow emerged, shuffling in slippers trodden down in the back. It was probably Little Shuang, the personal maid of Second Mistress, and so she called out softly, "Little Sister Shuang."

Little Shuang came, smiling, and gave a kick to the pallet. "I woke you." She put both hands under her old lined jacket of dark violet silk, worn over bright oil-green trousers. Feng-hsiao put out a hand to feel the trouser leg and said, smiling: [2]

"Colorful clothes are not worn so much now. With the people down river,[3] the fashions are all for no color."

Little Shuang said, smiling, "You don't know, in this house we can't keep up with other people. Our Old Mistress is strict, even the young mistresses can't have their own way, not to say us slave girls. We wear what's given us—all dressed like peasants." She squatted down to sit on the pallet and picked up a little jacket at Feng-hsiao's feet. "Was this newly made for your lady's wedding?"

Feng-hsiao shook her head. "Of my wardrobe for the season, only the few pieces on view are new. The rest is just made up of discards."

"This wedding happened to run into the revolution, really hard on your lady."

Feng-hsiao sighed. "Don't go into that now. In times like this one should economize, but there was still a limit! That wedding really lacked style. That one of ours didn't say anything, but how could she not be angry?"

"I shouldn't wonder Third Mistress is still unhappy about it. On your side the trousseau was passable, but the wedding preparations we made were really too dismal. Even that year we took our Second Mistress it was better than this."

Feng-hsiao was taken aback. "How? Your Second Mistress . . ."

Little Shuang took off her shoes and stepped barefoot across Feng-hsiao to the window. "Get up and look at the moon," she said.

[2] *Editor's note:* The repetition of the phrase "said, smiling" (*hsiao tao*) may seem tiresome to the reader. However, this and similar phrases are routinely prefixed to reported speeches in traditional Chinese fiction, and Eileen Chang, a dedicated student of that fiction, has deliberately revived their use in her early stories. It is to be regretted that their English equivalents cannot be equally unobtrusive.

[3] On the lower Yangtze.

Feng-hsiao scrambled quickly to her feet. "I was going to ask you all along, your Second Mistress . . ."

Little Shuang bent down to pick up the little jacket and put it over her shoulders. "Be careful you don't catch cold."

Feng-hsiao said, smiling, as she buttoned it up, "No, you've got to tell me."

"My fault, I shouldn't have let it out," Little Shuang said, smiling.

"We are like sisters now. Why treat me like an outsider?"

"If I tell you, don't you tell your lady though. Our Second Mistress's family owns a sesame oil shop."

"Oh!" Feng-hsiao was surprised. "A sesame oil shop! How on earth could they stoop so low! Now your Eldest Mistress is from a titled family; ours can't compare with Eldest Mistress, but she also came from a respectable family."

"Of course there was a reason. You've seen our Second Master, he's crippled. What mandarin family would give him a daughter for wife? Old Mistress didn't know what to do, first was going to get him a concubine, and the matchmaker found this one of the Ts'ao family, called Ch'i-ch'iao [4] because she was born in the seventh month."

"Oh, a concubine," said Feng-hsiao.

"Was to be a concubine. Then Old Mistress thought, since Second Master was not going to take a wife, it wouldn't do either for the second branch to be without its proper mistress. Just as well to have her for a wife so she would faithfully look after Second Master."

Feng-hsiao leaned her hands on the window sill, musing. "No wonder. Although I'm new here, I've guessed some of it too."

"Dragons breed dragons, phoenixes breed phoenixes—as the saying goes. You haven't heard her conversation! Even in front of the unmarried young ladies she says anything she likes. Lucky that in our house not a word goes out from inside, nor comes in from outside, so the young ladies don't understand a thing. Even then they get so embarrassed they don't know where to hide."

Feng-hsiao tittered. "Really? Where could she have picked up this vulgar language? Even us slave girls—"

[4] The old phrase *ch'i-ch'iao*, clever seven, refers to the skill of the Weaving Maid, a star that is reunited with the Cowherd, another star, across the Milky Way every year on the seventh of the seventh moon.

Little Shuang said, holding her own elbows, "Why, she was the big attraction at the sesame oil shop, standing at the counter, and dealing with all kinds of customers. What have we got to compare with her?"

"Did you come with her when she was married?"

Little Shuang sneered. "How could she afford me! I used to wait on Old Mistress, but Second Master took medicine all day and had to be helped around all the time, and since they were short of hands, I was sent over there. Why, are you cold?" Feng-hsiao shook her head. "Look at you, the way you pulled in your neck, so cuddlesome!" She had hardly finished speaking when Feng-hsiao sneezed. Right away Little Shuang gave her a push. "Go to bed, go to bed. Warm yourself."

Feng-hsiao knelt down to take her jacket off. "It's not winter, you don't catch cold just like that."

"The window may be closed but the wind squeaks in through the crevices."

They both lay down. Feng-hsiao asked in a whisper, "Been married for four, five years now?"

"Who?"

"Who else?"

"Oh, she. That's right, it's been five years."

"Had children too, and gave people nothing to talk about?"

"As to that—! Plenty to talk about. The year before last Old Mistress took everybody in the house on a pilgrimage to Mount P'u-t'o. She didn't go because it was just after her lying-in, so she was left at home to look after the house. Master-in-law [5] called a bit too often and a batch of things was lost."

Feng-hsiao was startled. "And they never got to the bottom of it?"

"What would have come of that? It would have been embarrassing for everybody. Anyway, the jewelry would have gone to Eldest Master, Second Master, and Third Master one day. Eldest Master and Eldest Mistress couldn't very well say anything on account of Second Master. Third Master was in no position to, he himself was spending money like water and had borrowed a lot from the family accounts."

The two of them talked across ten feet. Despite their effort to lower their voices, a louder sentence or two woke up old Mrs. Chao on the

[5] *Chiu-yeh*, lit., Master Brother-in-law, in this case Ch'i-ch'iao's elder brother.

big bed. She called out, "Little Shuang." Little Shuang did not dare answer. Old Mrs. Chao said, "Little Shuang, if you talk more nonsense and let people hear you, be careful you don't get skinned tomorrow!" Little Shuang kept still. "Don't think you're still in the deep halls and big courtyards we lived in before, where you had room to talk crazy and act silly. Here it's cheek by jowl, nothing can be kept from other people. Better stop talking if you want to avoid a beating."

Immediately the room became silent. Old Mrs. Chao, who had inflamed eyes, had stuffed her pillow with chrysanthemum leaves, said to make eyes clear and cool. She now raised her head to press down the silver hairpin tucked across her bun and the chrysanthemum leaves rustled with the slight stir. She turned over, her whole frame pulled into motion, all her bones squeaking. She sighed, "You people—! What do you know?" Little Shuang and Feng-hsiao still dared not reply. For a long time nobody spoke, and one by one they drifted off to sleep.

It was almost dawn. The flat waning moon got lower, lower and larger, and by the time it sank, it was like a red gold basin. The sky was a cold bleak crab-shell blue. The houses were only a couple of stories high, pitch-dark under the sky, so it was possible to see far. At the horizon the morning colors were a layer of green, a layer of yellow, and a layer of red like a watermelon cut open—the sun was coming up. Gradually wheelbarrows and big pushcarts began rattling along the road, and horse carriages passed, hoofs tapping. The beancurd soup vender with the flat pole on his shoulder hawked his wares slowly, swingingly. Only the long-drawn last syllable carried, "Haw . . . O! Haw . . . O!" Farther off, it became "Aw . . . O! Aw . . . O!"

In the house the slave girls and amahs had also got up, in a flurry to open the room doors, fetch hot water, fold up bedding, hook up the bed-curtains, and do the hair. Feng-hsiao helped Third Mistress Lan-hsien get dressed. Lan-hsien leaned close to the mirror for a careful look, pulled out from under her armpit a pale green blossom-flecked handkerchief, rubbed some powder off the wings of her nose, and said with her back to Third Master on the bed, "I'd better go first to pay my respects to Old Mistress. I'd be late if I waited for you."

As she was speaking, Eldest Mistress Tai-chen came and stood on the doorstep, saying with a smile, "Third Sister, let's go together."

Lan-hsien hurried up to her. "I was just getting worried I'd be late

—so Eldest Sister-in-law hasn't gone up yet. What about Second Sister-in-law?"

"She'll still be a while."

"Getting Second Brother his medicine?"

Tai-chen looked around to make sure there was no one about before she said, smiling, "It's not so much taking medicine as—" She put her thumb to her lips, made a fist with the three middle fingers, sticking out the little finger, and shushed softly a couple of times.

Lan-hsien said, surprised, "They both smoke this?"

Tai-chen nodded. "With your Second Brother it's out in the open, with her it's kept from Old Mistress, which makes things difficult for us, caught in between—have to cover up for her. Actually Old Mistress knows very well. Purposely pretends she doesn't, orders her around and tortures her in little ways, just so that she can't smoke her fill. Actually, to think of it, a woman and so young, what great worries could she have, to need to smoke this to take her mind off things?"

Tai-chen and Lan-hsien went upstairs hand in hand, each followed by the slave girl closest to her, to the small anteroom next door to Old Mistress's bedroom. The slave girl Liu-hsi came out to them whispering, "Not awake yet."

Tai-chen glanced up at the grandfather clock and said, smiling, "Old Mistress is also late today."

"Said she didn't sleep well the last couple of days, too much noise on the street," Liu-hsi said. "Probably used to it now, making up for it today."

Beside the little round pedestal table of purple elm covered with a strip of scarlet felt sat Yün-tse, the second daughter of the house, cracking walnuts with a little nutcracker. She put it down and got up to greet them. Tai-chen laid a hand on her shoulder. "Sister Yün, you are really filial. Old Mistress happened to be in the mood yesterday to want some sugared walnuts made, and you remembered."

Lan-hsien and Tai-chen sat down around the table and helped to peel the walnut skin. Yün-tse's hands got tired and Lan-hsien took the nutcracker that she put down.

"Be careful of those nails of yours, as slender as scallions. It would be a pity to break them when you've grown them so long," said Tai-chen.

"Have somebody go and get your gold nail sheath," Yün-tse said.
"So much bother, we might as well have them shelled in the
kitchen," said Lan-hsien.

As they were talking and laughing in undertones, Liu-hsi raised the
curtain with a stick, announcing, "Second Mistress is here."

Lan-hsien and Yün-tse rose to ask her to sit down but Ts'ao Ch'i-
ch'iao would not be seated as yet. With one hand on the doorway and
the other on her waist, she first looked around. On her thin face were a
vermilion mouth, triangular eyes, and eyebrows curved like little hills.
She wore a pale pink blouse over narrow mauve trousers with a flickering blue scroll design and greenish-white incense-stick binding.[6] A lavender silk crepe handkerchief was half tucked around the wrist in one
narrow blouse sleeve. She smiled, showing her small fine teeth, and
said, "Everybody's here. I suppose I'm late again today. How can I
help it, doing my hair in the dark? Who gave me a window facing the
back yard? I'm the only one to get a room like that. That one of ours
is evidently not going to live long anyway, we're just waiting to be
widow and orphans—whom to bully, if not us?"

Tai-chen blandly said nothing. Lan-hsien said, smiling, "Second Sister-in-law is used to the houses in Peking, no wonder she finds it too
cramped here."

Yün-tse said, "Eldest Brother should have got a larger one when he
was house-hunting, but I'm afraid this counts as a bright and airy
house for Shanghai."

Lan-hsien said, "That is so. It's true it's a bit crowded, really, so
many people in the house—"

Ch'i-ch'iao rolled up her sleeve and tucked the handkerchief in her
green jade bracelet, glanced sideways at Lan-hsien, and said, smiling,
"So Third Sister feels there're too many people. If it's too crowded for
us, who have been married for years, naturally it's too crowded for
newlyweds like you."

Before Lan-hsien could say anything, Tai-chen blushed, saying,
"Jesting is jesting, but there's a limit. Third Sister has just come here,
what will she think of us?"

Ch'i-ch'iao pulled up a corner of her handkerchief to cover her
mouth. "I know you're all young ladies from respectable homes. Just

[6] So called because the binding is rounded and narrow.

try and change places with me, I'm afraid you couldn't put up with it for even one night."

Tai-chen made a spitting noise. "This is too much. The more you talk, the more impertinent you get."

At this Ch'i-ch'iao went up and took Tai-chen by her sleeve. "I can swear—I can swear for the last three years. Do you dare swear? You dare swear?"

Even Tai-chen could not help a titter, and then she muttered, "How is it that you even got two children?"

Ch'i-ch'iao said, "Really, even I don't know how the children got born. The more I think about it the more I can't understand."

Tai-chen held up her right hand and waved it from side to side. "Enough talk in this vein. Granted that you take Third Sister as one of our own, and feel free to say anything you like, still Sister Yün's here. If she tells Old Mistress later, you'll get more than you want."

Yün-tse had walked off long ago, and was standing on the veranda with her hands behind her back, whistling at the canary to make it sing. The Chiangs lived in a modern foreign-style house of an early period, tall arches supported by thick pillars of red brick with a floral capital, but the upstairs veranda had a wooden floor. Behind the railings of willow wood was a row of large baskets of bamboo splits, in which dried bamboo shoots were being aired. The worn sunlight pervaded the air like gold dust, slightly choking and dizzying when rubbed in the eyes. Far away in the street a peddler shook a rattle-drum whose sleepy beat, *bu lung dung . . . bu lung dung*, held the memory of many children now grown old. The private rickshas tinkled as they ran past and an occasional car horn went *ba ba*.

Because Ch'i-ch'iao knew that everybody in this house looked down on her, she was especially warm to the newcomer. Leaning on the back of Lan-hsien's chair, she asked her this and that and spoke admiringly of her fingernails after giving her hand a thorough inspection. Then she added, "I grew one on my little finger last year fully half an inch longer than this, and broke it picking flowers."

Lan-hsien had already seen through Ch'i-ch'iao and understood her position at the Chiangs'. She kept smiling but hardly answered. Ch'i-ch'iao felt the slight. Ambling over to the veranda, she picked up Yün-tse's pigtail and shook it, making conversation, "*Yo!* How come your hair is so thin? Only last year you had such a head of glossy black hair—must have lost a lot?"

Yün-tse turned aside to protect her pigtail, saying with a smile, "I can't even lose a few hairs without your permission?"

Ch'i-ch'iao went on scrutinizing her and called out, "Eldest Sister-in-law, come and take a look. Sister Yün has really grown much thinner. Could it be that the young lady has something on her mind?"

With marked annoyance Yün-tse slapped Ch'i-ch'iao's hand to get it off her person. "You've really gone crazy today. As if you're not enough of a nuisance ordinarily."

Ch'i-ch'iao tucked her hands in her sleeves. "What a temper the young lady has," she said, smiling.

Tai-chen put her head out, saying, "Sister Yün, Old Mistress is up."

Each of them straightened her blouse hastily, smoothed her hair in front of her ears, lifted the curtain to go into the next room, curtsied, and waited on Old Mistress at breakfast. The old women holding trays went in through the living room; the slave girls inside took the dishes from them and they returned to wait in the outer room. It was quiet inside, scarcely anybody saying anything; the only sound was the rustle of the thin silver chain aquiver at the top of a pair of silver chopsticks.

Old Mistress believed in Buddha and made it a rule to worship for two hours after breakfast. Coming out with the others, Yün-tse managed to ask Tai-chen without being overheard, "Isn't Second Sister-in-law in a hurry to go for her smoke? Why is she still hanging around inside?"

Tai-chen said, "I suppose she has a few words to say in private."

Yün-tse could not help laughing. "As if Old Mistress would listen to anything she had to say!"

Tai-chen laughed cynically. "That you can't tell. Old people are always changing their minds. When it's dinned into your ears all day long, it's just possible you'll believe one sentence out of ten."

As Lan-hsien sat cracking walnuts, Tai-chen and Yün-tse went to the veranda, though not purposely to eavesdrop on the conversation in the main chamber. Old Mistress, being of advanced age, was a little deaf, so her voice was especially loud. Intentionally or not, the people on the veranda heard much of the talk. Yün-tse turned white with anger; she first held her fists tight, then flicked her hands forcibly and ran toward the other end of the veranda. After a couple of running steps she stood still and bent forward with her face in her hands, sobbing.

Tai-chen hurried up to hold her. "Sister, don't be like this! Stop it quick. It's not worth your while to heed the likes of her. Who takes her words seriously?"

Yün-tse struggled free and ran straight to her own room. Tai-chen came back to the living room and clapped her hands once. "The damage is done."

Lan-hsien hastened to ask, "What happened?"

"Your Second Sister-in-law was just telling Old Mistress, 'A grown girl won't keep,' and Old Mistress is to write to the P'engs to come for the bride quick. Look, what kind of talk is this?"

Lan-hsien, also stunned, said, "Wouldn't it be slapping one's own face, for the girl's family to say a thing like this?"

"The Chiangs will only lose face temporarily, but not Sister Yün. How are they to respect her over there when she gets married? She still has her life to live."

"Old Mistress is understanding, she's not likely to share that person's views."

"Of course Old Mistress didn't like it at first, saying a daughter of our house would never have such ideas. So *she* said, '*Yo!* you don't know the girls nowadays. How can they compare with the girls when you were a girl? Times have changed, and people also change, otherwise why is there trouble all over the world?' You know, old people like to hear this sort of thing. Old Mistress is not so sure any more."

Lan-hsien sighed, saying, "How on earth did she have the gall to make up such stories?"

Tai-chen rested both elbows on the table and stroked an eyebrow with a little finger. After a moment of reflection she snickered, "She thinks she's being specially thoughtful toward Sister Yün! Spare me her thoughtfulness."

Lan-hsien grabbed hold of her. "Listen—that can't be Sister Yün?" There seemed to be loud weeping in a back room and the rattle of brass bedposts being kicked and a hubbub of voices trying to soothe and reason to no avail.

Tai-chen stood up. "I'll go and see. This young lady may be good-tempered, but she can fight back if cornered."

Tai-chen was gone when Third Master Chiang came in yawning. A robust youth, tending toward plumpness, Chiang Chi-tse sported down his neck a big shiny three-strand pigtail loosely plaited. He had the classic domed forehead and squarish lower face, chubby bright red cheeks, glistening dark eyebrows, and moist black eyes where some impatience always showed through. Over a narrow-sleeved gown of bamboo-root green he wore a little sleeveless jacket the color of sesame-dotted, purplish-brown soy paste, buttoned across with pearls from shoulder to shoulder. He asked Lan-hsien, "Who's talking away to Old Mistress inside there?"

"Second Sister-in-law."

Chi-tse pressed his lips tight and shook his head.

"You've had enough of her, too?" Lan-hsien said, smiling.

Chi-tse said nothing, just pulled a chair over, pushed its back against the table, threw the hem of his gown up high and sat down astride the chair, his chin on the chair back, and picked up and ate one piece of walnut after another.

Lan-hsien gave him a look from the corners of her eyes. "People peeling them the whole morning, was it all for your sake?"

Just then Ch'i-ch'iao lifted the curtain and came out. The minute she saw Chi-tse she involuntarily circled over to the back of Lan-hsien's chair, put both hands around Lan-hsien's neck and bent her head down, saying with a smirk, "What a ravishing bride! Third Brother, you haven't thanked me yet. If I hadn't hurried them to get this done for you early, you might have had to wait eight or ten years for the war to be over. You'd have died of impatience."

Lan-hsien's greatest regret was that her wedding had happened in a period of national emergency and lacked pomp and style. As soon as she heard these jarring words, her narrow little face fell to its full length like a scroll. Chi-tse glanced at her and said, smiling, "Second Sister-in-law, a good heart does not get rewards, as of old. Nobody feels obliged to you."

"That's all right with me, I'm used to it," said Ch'i-ch'iao. "Ever since I stepped inside the Chiang house, just nursing your Second Brother all these years, watching over the sickbed day and night, just for that alone you'd think I've done some good and nothing wrong, but who's ever grateful to me? Who ever did me half a good turn?"

Chi-tse said, smiling, "You're full of grievances the minute you open your mouth."

With a long-drawn-out groan she kept fingering the gold triad [7] and key chain buttoned on Lan-hsien's lapel. After a long pause she suddenly said, "At least you haven't fooled around outside for a month or so. Thanks to the bride, she made you stay home. Anybody else could beg you on bent knees and you wouldn't."

"Is that so? Sister-in-law never asked me, how do you know I won't?" he said, smiling, and signaled Lan-hsien with his eyes.

Ch'i-ch'iao doubled up laughing. "Why don't you do something about him, Third Sister? The little monkey, I saw him grow up, and now he's joking at my expense!"

While talking and laughing she felt bothered; her restless hands squeezed and kneaded Lan-hsien, beating and knocking lightly with a fist as if she wished to squash her out of shape. No matter how patient Lan-hsien was, she could not help getting annoyed. With her temper rising, she applied more strength than she should using the nutcracker, and broke the two-inch fingernail clean off at the quick.

"*Yo!*" Ch'i-ch'iao cried. "Quick, get scissors and trim it. I remember there was a pair of little scissors in this room. Little Shuang!" she called out. "Liu-hsi! Come, somebody!"

Lan-hsien rose. "Never mind, Second Sister-in-law, I'll go and cut it in my room." She went.

Ch'i-ch'iao sat down in Lan-hsien's chair. Leaning her cheek on her hand and lifting her eyebrows, she gazed sideways at Chi-tse. "Is she angry with me?"

"Why should she be?" he said, smiling.

"I was just going to ask that. Could I have said anything wrong? What's wrong with keeping you at home? She'd rather have you go out?"

He said, smiling, "The whole family from Eldest Brother and Eldest Sister-in-law down, all want to discipline me, just for fear that I'll spend the money in the general accounts."

"By Buddha, I can't vouch for the others but I don't think like that. Even if you get into debt and mortgage houses and sell land, if I so

[7] A toothpick, tweezers, and ear-spoon.

much as frown I'm not your Second Sister-in-law. Aren't we the closest kin? I just want you to take care of your health."

He could not suppress a titter. "Why are you so worried about my health?"

Her voice trembled. "Health is the most important thing for anybody. Look at your Second Brother, the way he gets, is he still a person? Can you still treat him as one?"

Chi-tse looked serious. "Second Brother is not like me, he was born like this. It's not that he ruined his health. He's a pitiful man, it's up to Second Sister-in-law to take care of him."

Ch'i-ch'iao stood up stiffly, holding on to the table with both hands, her eyelids down and the lower half of her face quivering as if she held scalding hot melted candlewax in her mouth. She forced out two sentences in a small high voice, "Go sit next to your Second Brother. Go sit next to your Second Brother." She tried to sit beside Chi-tse and only got onto a corner of his chair and put her hand on his leg. "Have you touched his flesh? It's soft and heavy, feels like your feet when they get numb . . ."

Chi-tse had changed color too. Still he gave a frivolous little laugh and bent down to pinch her foot. "Let's see if they are numb."

"Heavens, you've never touched him, you don't know how good it is not to be sick . . . how good . . ." She slid down from the chair and squatted on the floor, weeping inaudibly with her face pillowed on her sleeve; the diamond on her hairpin flashed as it jerked back and forth. Against the diamond's flame shone the solid knot of pink silk thread binding a little bunch of hair at the heart of the bun. Her back convulsed as it sank lower and lower. She seemed to be not so much weeping as vomiting, churning and pumping out her bowels.

A little stunned at first, Chi-tse got up. "I'm going, if that's all right with you. If you're not afraid of being seen, I am. Have to save some face for Second Brother."

Holding onto the chair to get up, she said, sobbing, "I'll leave." She pulled out a handkerchief from her sleeve to dab at her face and suddenly smiled slightly. "You're so protective of your Second Brother."

Chi-tse laughed. "If I don't protect him, who will?"

Ch'i-ch'iao said, walking toward the door, "You're a good one to talk. Don't try to act the hypocrite in front of me. Why, just in these rooms alone . . . nothing escapes my eyes—not to mention how wild you are once outside the house. You probably wouldn't even mind having your wet nurse, let alone a sister-in-law."

"I've always been easygoing about things. How am I supposed to defend myself if you pick on me?" he said, smiling.

On her way out she again leaned her back against the door, whispering, "What I don't get is in what way I'm not as good as the others. What is it about me that's no good?"

"My good sister-in-law, you're all good."

She said with a laugh, "Could it be that staying with a cripple, I smell crippled too, and it will rub off on you?" She stared straight ahead, the small, solid gold pendants of her earrings like two brass nails nailing her to the door, a butterfly specimen in a glass box, bright-colored and desolate.

Looking at her, Chi-tse also wondered. But that would not do. He loved to play around but had made up his mind long ago not to flirt with members of the family. When the mood had passed one could neither avoid them nor kick them aside, they would be a burden all the time. Besides, Ch'i-ch'iao was so outspoken and hot-tempered, how could the thing be kept secret? And she was so unpopular, who would cover up for her, high or low? Perhaps she no longer cared and would not even mind if it got known. But why should a young man like him take the risk? He spoke up: "Second Sister-in-law, young as I am, I'm not one who'd do just anything."

There seemed to be footsteps. With a flip of his gown he ducked into Old Mistress' room, grabbing a handful of shelled walnuts by the way. She had not quite come to her senses, but when she heard someone pushing the door she roused herself, managing the best she could and hiding behind the door. When she saw Tai-chen walk in, she came out and slapped her on the back.

Tai-chen forced a smile. "You're in better spirits than ever." She looked at the table. "My, so many walnuts, practically all eaten up. It couldn't be anybody but Third Brother."

Ch'i-ch'iao leaned against the table, facing the veranda and saying nothing.

"People had to shell them all morning, and he came along to enjoy himself." Tai-chen grumbled as she took a seat.

Ch'i-ch'iao scraped the red table cover with a piece of sharp walnut shell, one hard stroke after another until the felt turned hairy and was about to tear. She said between clenched teeth, "Isn't it the same with money? We're always told to save, save it so others can take it out by the handfuls to spend. That's what I can't get over."

Tai-chen glanced at her and said coldly, "That can't be helped. When there're too many people, if it doesn't go in the open it will go in the dark. Control this one and you can't control that one."

Ch'i-ch'iao felt the sting and was just about to reply in kind when Little Shuang came in furtively and walked up to her, mumbling, "Mistress, Master-in-law is here."

"Master-in-law's coming here is nothing to hide. You've got a growth in your throat or what?" Ch'i-ch'iao cursed. "You sound like a mosquito humming."

Little Shuang backed off a step and dared not speak.

Tai-chen said, "So your brother has come to Shanghai too. It seems all our relatives are here."

Ch'i-ch'iao started out of the room. "He's not to come to Shanghai? With war inland, poor people want to stay alive too." She stopped at the doorstep and asked Little Shuang, "Have you told Old Mistress?"

"Not yet," said Little Shuang.

Ch'i-ch'iao thought for a moment and went downstairs quietly because she didn't have the courage after all to go in and tell Old Mistress of her brother's arrival.

Tai-chen asked Little Shuang, "Master-in-law came alone?"

"With Mistress-in-law, carrying food in a two-decked set of round wooden boxes."

Tai-chen chuckled, "They went to all that expense."

Little Shuang said, "Eldest Mistress needn't feel sorry for them. What comes in full will go out full too. To them even remnants are good, for making slippers and waistbands, not to mention round or flat pieces of gold and silver."

"Don't be so unkind. You'd better go down," Tai-chen said, smiling. "Her family seldom comes here. Not enough service and there'd be trouble again."

Little Shuang hurried out. Ch'i-ch'iao was just cross-questioning

Liu-hsi at the top of the stairs to see if Old Mistress knew. Liu-hsi replied, "Old Mistress was at her prayers, Third Master was leaning against the window looking out, and he said there were guests coming in the front gate. Old Mistress asked who it was. Third Master looked hard and said he was not sure that it wasn't Master-in-law Ts'ao, and Old Mistress left it at that."

Fire leaped up inside Ch'i-ch'iao as she heard this. She stamped her feet and muttered on her way downstairs, "So—just going to pretend you don't know. If you are going to be so snobbish, why did you bother to carry me here in a sedan chair, complete with three matchmakers and six wedding gifts? Ties of kinship not even a sharp knife can sever. Even if you're not just feigning death today but are really dead, he will have to come to your funeral and kowtow three times and you will have to take it."

Her room was screened off by a stack of gold-lacquered trunks right inside the door, leaving just a few feet of space. As she lifted the curtain, all she saw was her brother's wife bent over the box set to remove the top section containing little pies so as to see if the dishes underneath had spilled. Her brother Ts'ao Ta-nien bowed down to look, hands behind his back. Ch'i-ch'iao felt a wave of acid pain rising in her heart and could not restrain a shower of tears as she leaned against the trunks, her face pressed against their padded covers of sandy blue cloth. Her sister-in-law straightened up hastily and rushed up to hold her hand in both of hers, calling her Miss over and over again. Ts'ao Ta-nien also had to rub his eyes with a raised sleeve. Ch'i-ch'iao unbuttoned the frogs on the trunk jackets with her free hand, only to button them up again, unable to say anything all the while.

Her sister-in-law turned to give her brother a look. "Say something! Talking about Sister all the time, now that you see her you're again like the gourd with its mouth sawed off." [8]

Ch'i-ch'iao said in a quavering voice, "No wonder he has nothing to say—how could he face me?" and turning to her brother, "I thought you would never want to come here! You have ruined me well and good. You walked away just like that, but I couldn't leave. You don't care if I live or die."

[8] An idiomatic expression in Chinese.

Ts'ao Ta-nien said, "What are you saying? It's one thing for other people to talk like this, but you too! If you don't cover up for me you won't look so good either."

"Even if I say nothing, I can't keep other people from talking. Just because of you I've got all kinds of illnesses from anger. After all this, you still try to gag me with these words!"

Her sister-in-law interposed quickly, "It was his fault, his fault! Miss has been put upon. However, Miss has not suffered just on that account alone—be patient anyway, there will be happiness in the end." The words "However, Miss has not suffered just on that account alone" struck Ch'i-ch'iao as so true that she began to weep. It made her sister-in-law so nervous she kept shaking a raised hand from side to side, saying, "Be careful you don't wake up *Ku-yeh*." [9] The net curtains hung still on the big dark bed of purple cedar over on the other side of the room. "Is *Ku-yeh* asleep? He'd be angry if we disturbed him."

Ch'i-ch'iao called out loudly, "If he can react like a human being, it won't be so bad."

Her sister-in-law was so frightened she covered Ch'i-ch'iao's mouth. "Don't, *Ku-nai-nai!* [10] Sick people feel bad to hear such talk."

"He feels bad and how do I feel?"

Her sister-in-law said, "Is *Ku-yeh* still suffering from the soft bone illness?"

"Isn't that enough to bear, without further complications? Here the whole family avoids mentioning the word tuberculosis, actually it's just tuberculosis of the bones."

"Does he sit up for a while sometimes?"

Ch'i-ch'iao started to chuckle. "Huh huh! Sit up and the spine slides down, not even as tall as my three-year-old, to look at."

Her sister-in-law ran out of comforting words for the moment and all three were speechless. Ch'i-ch'iao suddenly stamped her feet, saying, "Go, go, you people. Every time you come I have to review once more in my mind how everything has led to this, I can't stand the agitation. Go away quick."

Ts'ao Ta-nien said, "Listen to a word from me, Sister. Having your

[9] Honorific for the son-in-law of the family.

[10] Honorific for the married daughter of the house.

own family around makes it a little better anyhow, and not just now when you're unhappy. Even when your day of independence comes, the Chiangs are a big clan, the elders keep browbeating people with high-sounding words, and those of your generation and the next are like wolves and tigers, every one of them, not a single one easy to deal with. You need help too for your own sake. There will be times aplenty when you could use your brother and nephews."

Ch'i-ch'iao made a spitting noise. "I'd be out of luck indeed if I had to rely on your help. I saw through you long ago—if you could fight them, the more credit to you and you'd come to me for money; if you're no match for them you'd just topple over to their side. The sight of mandarins scares you out of your wits anyway: you'll just pull in your neck and leave me to my fate."

Ta-nien flushed and laughed sardonically. "Wait till the money is in your hands. It will not be too late then to keep your brother from getting a share."

"Then why bother me when you know it's not yet in my hands?"

"So we're wrong to come all this distance to see you!" he said. "Come on, let's go. To be perfectly frank though, even if I use a bit of your money it's only fair. If I'd been greedy for wedding gifts and asked for another several hundred taels of silver from the Chiangs and sold you for a concubine, you'd have been sold."

"Isn't a wife better than a concubine? Kites go farther on a longer string, you have big hopes yet."

Ta-nien was just going to retort when his wife cut in, "Now hold your tongue. You'll still meet in days to come. One day when *Ku-nai-nai* thinks of you she'll know she only has this one brother."

Ta-nien hustled her into tidying the box set, picked it up, and started out.

"What do I care?" Ch'i-ch'iao said. "When I have money I won't have to worry about your not coming, only how to get rid of you." Despite her harsh words she could not hold back the sobs that got louder and louder. This quarrel had made it possible for her to release the frustrations pent up all morning long.

Her sister-in-law, seeing that she was evidently clinging to them a little, succeeded by cajoling and lecturing in pacifying her brother, and at the same time, with her arm around her, led her to the carved pearwood couch, set her down, and patiently reasoned with her, until she gradually dried her tears. The three now talked about everyday affairs. It was more or less peaceful in the north, with business as usual at the Ts'aos' sesame oil shop. Their present trip to Shanghai had to do with their future son-in-law, a bookkeeper who happened to be in Hupeh when the revolution started. He had left the place with his employer and finally come to Shanghai. So Ta-nien had brought his daughter here to be married, visiting his sister on the side. Ta-nien asked after all the Chiangs of the house and wanted to pay his respects to Old Mistress.

"Just as well that you don't see her," said Ch'i-ch'iao. "I was just being mad at her."

Ta-nien and his wife were both startled.

"How can I help myself?" Ch'i-ch'iao said. "The whole family treading me down, if I'd been easy to bully I'd have been trampled to death long ago. As it is, I'm full of aches and pains from anger."

"Do you still smoke, Miss?" her sister-in-law said. "Opium is still better than any other medicine for soothing the liver and composing the nerves. Be sure that you take good care of yourself, Miss, we're not around, who else is there to look after you?"

Ch'i-ch'iao went through her trunks to take out lengths of silks of new designs to give to her sister-in-law and also a pair of gold bracelets weighing four taels, a pair of carnelian hairpins the shape of lotus pods, and a quilting of silk fluff. She had for each niece a gold earspoon and each nephew a miniature gold ingot or a sable hat, and handed her brother an enameled gold watch shaped like a cicada. Her brother and sister-in-law hastened to thank her.

"You didn't come at the right moment," Ch'i-ch'iao said. "When we were just about to leave Peking, what we couldn't take was all given to the amahs and slave girls, several trunkfuls they got for nothing."

They looked embarrassed at this. Taking their leave, her sister-in-law said, "When we've got our daughter off our hands, we'll come and see *Ku-nai-nai* again."

"Just as well if you don't," Ch'i-ch'iao said, smiling. "I can't afford it."

When they got out of the Chiangs' house her sister-in-law said, "How is it this *ku-nai-nai* of ours has changed so? Before she was married she may have been a bit proud and talked a little too much. Even later, when we went to see her, she had more of a temper but there was still a limit. She was not silly as she is now, sane enough one minute and the next minute off again, and altogether disagreeable."

Ch'i-ch'iao stood in the room holding her elbows and watched the two slave girls, Little Shuang and Ch'iang-yün, carrying the trunks between them and stacking them back one by one. The things of the past came back again: the sesame oil shop over the cobbled street, the blackened greasy counter, the wooden spoons standing in the buckets of sesame butter and iron spoons of all sizes strung up above the oil jars. Insert the funnel in the customer's bottle. One big spoon plus two small spoons just make a bottle—one and a half catties. Counts as one catty and four ounces if it's somebody she knows. Sometimes she went marketing too, in a blouse and pants of blue linen trimmed with mirror-bright black silk. Across the thick row of brass hooks from which pork dangled she saw Ch'ao-lu of the butcher shop. Ch'ao-lu was always after her, calling her Miss Ts'ao, and on rare occasions Little Miss Ch'iao,[11] and she would give the rack of hooks a slap that sent all the empty hooks swinging across to poke him in the eye. Ch'ao-lu plucked a piece of raw fat a foot wide off the hook and threw it down hard on the block, a warm odor rushing to her face, the smell of sticky dead flesh . . . she frowned. On the bed lay her husband, that lifeless body. . . .

A gust of wind came in the window and blew against the long mirror in the scrollwork lacquered frame until it rattled against the wall. Ch'i-ch'iao pressed the mirror down with both hands. The green bamboo curtain and a green and gold landscape scroll reflected in the mirror went on swinging back and forth in the wind—one could get dizzy watching it for long. When she looked again the green bamboo curtain had faded, the green and gold landscape was replaced by a photograph of her deceased husband, and the woman in the mirror was also ten years older.

Last year she wore mourning for her husband and this year her mother-in-law had passed away. Now her husband's uncle, Ninth Old Master, was formally invited to come and divide the property among the survivors. Today was the focal point of all her imaginings since she had married into the house of Chiang. All these years she had worn the

[11] A familiar form of address, as to a child of the family.

golden cangue but never even got to gnaw at the edge of the gold. It would be different from now on. In her white lacquered silk blouse and black skirt she looked rouged, from the eyes rubbed red to the feverish cheekbones. She lifted her hand to touch her face. It was flushed but the rest of her body was so cold she was actually trembling. She told Ch'iang-yün to pour her a cup of tea. (Little Shuang had been married long ago; Ch'iang-yün was also mated with a page.) The tea she drank flowed heavily into her chest cavity and her heart jumped, thumping in the hot tea. She sat down with her back to the mirror and asked Ch'iang-yün, "All this time Ninth Old Master has been here this afternoon, he's just been going over the accounts with Secretary Ma?"

Ch'iang-yün answered yes.

"Eldest Master and Eldest Mistress, Third Master and Third Mistress, none of them is around?"

Ch'iang-yün again answered yes.

"Who else did he go to see?"

"Just took a turn in the schoolroom," said Ch'iang-yün.

"At least our Master Pai's studies could bear checking into. . . . The trouble with the child this year is what happened to his father and grandmother, one after the other. If he still feels like studying, he's born of beasts." She finished her tea and told Ch'iang-yün to go down and see if the people of the eldest and third branches were all in the parlor, so she would not be too early and be laughed at for seeming eager. It happened that the eldest branch had also sent a slave girl to find out, who came face to face with Ch'iang-yün.

Ch'i-ch'iao finally came downstairs slowly, gracefully. A foreign-style dining table of ebony polished like a mirror was set up in the parlor for the occasion. Ninth Old Master occupied one side by himself, the account books with blue cloth covers and plum-red labels heaped before him along with a melon-ribbed teacup. Around him besides Secretary Ma were the specially invited *kung ch'in*, relatives no closer to one than to the other, serving more or less in the capacity of assistant judges. Eldest Master and Third Master represented their respective branches, but Second Master having died, his branch was represented by Second Mistress. Chi-tse, who knew very well that this day of reckoning bode no good for him, arrived last. But once there he never showed any anxiety or depression: that same plump red smile was still on his cheeks and in his eyes still that bit of dashing impatience.

Ninth Old Master gave a cough and made a brief report on the Chiangs' finances. Leafing through the account books, he read out the main holdings of land and houses and the annual incomes from these. Ch'i-ch'iao leaned forward with hands locked tight over her stomach, trying hard to explain to herself every sentence he uttered and match it with the results of her past investigations. The houses in Tsingtao, the houses in Tientsin, the land in the hometown, the land outside Peking, the houses in Shanghai. . . . Third Master had borrowed too much from the general accounts and for too long. Apart from his share, now canceled out, he still owed sixty thousand dollars, but the eldest and second branches had to let it go at that since he had nothing. The only house he owned, a foreign-style building with a garden bought for a concubine, was already mortgaged. Then there was just the jewelry that Old Mistress had brought with her as a bride to be divided evenly among the three brothers. Chi-tse's share could not very well be confiscated, being mementos left by his mother.

Ch'i-ch'iao suddenly cried out, "Ninth Old Master, this is too hard on us."

The parlor had been dead quiet before, now the silence became a sandy rustle that sawed straight into the ears like the damaged sound track of a movie grating rustily on. Ninth Old Master opened his eyes wide to look at her. "What? You wouldn't even let him have the bit of jewelry his mother left?"

" 'Even brothers settle their accounts openly,' " Ch'i-ch'iao quoted. "Eldest Brother and Sister-in-law say nothing, but I have to toughen my skin and speak out this once. I can't compare with Eldest Brother and Sister-in-law. If the one we lost were able to go out and be a mandarin for a couple of terms and save some money, I'd be glad to be generous, too—what if we cancel all the old accounts? Only that one of ours was pitiful, ailing and groaning all his life, never earned a copper coin. Left us widow and orphans who're counting on just this small fixed sum to live on. I'm a crab without legs and Ch'ang-pai is not yet fourteen, with plenty of hard days ahead." Her tears came down as she spoke.

"What do you want then if you may have your way?" said Ninth Old Master.

"It's not for me to decide," she said, sobbing. "I'm only begging Ninth Old Master to settle it for me."

Chi-tse, cold-faced, said nothing. The whole roomful of people felt it was not for them to speak. Ninth Old Master, unable to keep down a bellyful of fire, snorted, "I'd make a suggestion, only I'm afraid you won't like it. The second branch has land and nobody to look after it, the third branch has a man but no land. I'd have Third Master look after it for you for a consideration, whatever you see fit, only you may not want him."

Ch'i-ch'iao laughed sardonically. "I'd have it your way, only I'm afraid the dead one will not. Come, somebody! Ch'iang-yün, go and get Master Pai for me. Ch'ang-pai, what a hard life your father had! Born with ailments all over, went through life like a wretch, and for what? Never even had a single comfortable day. In the end he left you, all there is of his bone and blood, and people still won't let you be, there're a thousand designs on your property. Ch'ang-pai, it's your father's fault that he dragged himself around with all his illnesses, bullied when he was alive, to have his widow and orphan bullied when he's dead. I don't matter, how many more scores of years can I live? At worst I'd go and explain this before Old Mistress's spirit tablet and kill myself in protest. But Ch'ang-pai, you're so young, you still have your life to live even if there's nothing to eat or drink except the northwest wind!"

Ninth Old Master was so angry he slapped the table. "I wash my hands of this! It was you people who begged and kowtowed to make me come. Do you think I like to go looking for trouble?" He stood up, kicked the chair over and, without waiting to be helped out of the room, strode out of sight in a gust of wind.

The others looked one another in the face and slipped out one by one. Only Secretary Ma was left behind busy tidying up the account books. He thought that, with everybody gone and Second Mistress sitting there alone beating her breast and wailing, it would be embarrassing if he just walked off, and so he went up to her, bowing repeatedly, holding his own hands and moving them up and down in obeisance, and calling, "Second Mistress! Second Mistress! . . . Second Mistress!"

Ch'i-ch'iao just covered her face with a sleeve. Secretary Ma could not very well pull her hand away. Perspiring in despair, he took off his black satin skullcap to fan himself.

The awkward situation lasted for a few days, then the property was divided quietly according to the original plans. The widow and orphans were still taken advantage of.

Ch'i-ch'iao took her son Ch'ang-pai and daughter Ch'ang-an and rented another house to live in, and seldom saw the Chiangs' other branches. Several months later Chiang Chi-tse suddenly came. When the amah announced the visit upstairs, Ch'i-ch'iao was secretly worried that she had offended him that day at the family conference over the division of property and wondered what he was going to do about it. But "an army comes and generals fend it off," so why should she be afraid of him? She tied on a black skirt of iron-thread gauze under the Buddha-blue solid gauze jacket she was wearing and came downstairs. When Chi-tse got up all smiles to give his best regards to Second Sister-in-law, and asked if Master Pai was in the schoolroom and if Little Miss An's ringworm was all cured, Ch'i-ch'iao suspected he was here to borrow money. Doubly on guard, she sat down and said, smiling, "You've gained weight again lately, Third Brother."

"I seem like a man without a thing on his mind," Chi-tse said, smiling.

"Well, 'A blessed man need never be busy.' You're never one to worry," she said, smiling.

"I'd have fewer worries than ever after I'd sold my landed property," he said, smiling.

"You mean the house you mortgaged? You want to sell it?"

"Quite a lot of thought went into it when it was built and I loved some of the fixtures; of course I wouldn't want to part with it. But later, as you know, land got expensive over there, so the year before last I tore it down and built in its place a row of houses. But it was really too much bother collecting rent from house to house, dealing with those tenants; so I thought I'd get rid of the property just for the sake of peace and quiet."

Ch'i-ch'iao said to herself, "How grand we sound! Still acting the rich young master in front of me when I know all about you!"

Although he was not complaining of poverty to her, any mention of money transactions seemed to lead them onto dangerous ground, and so she changed the subject. "How is Third Sister? Her kidneys haven't been bothering her lately?"

"I haven't seen her for some time, either," Chi-tse said, smiling.

"What is this? Have you quarreled?"

"We haven't quarreled either all this time," he said, smiling. "Exchange a few words when we have to but that's also rare. No time to quarrel and no mood for it."

"You're exaggerating. I for one don't believe it."

He rested his elbows on the arms of the rattan chair, locking his fingers to shade his eyes, and sighed deeply.

"Unless it's because you play around too much outside. You're in the wrong and still sighing away as if you were wronged. There's not one good man among you Chiangs!" she said, smiling, and lifted her round white fan as if to strike him. He moved his interlocked fingers downward with both thumbs pressed on his lips and the forefingers slowly stroking the bridge of his nose, and his eyes appeared all the brighter. The irises were the black pebbles at the bottom of a bowl of narcissus, covered with cold water and expressionless. It was impossible to tell what he was thinking. "I must beat you," she said.

A bubble of mirth came up in his eyes. "Go ahead, beat me."

She was about to hit him, snatched back her hand, and then again mustered her strength, saying, "I'd really beat you!" She swung her arm downward, but the descending fan remained in mid air as she started to giggle.

He raised a shoulder toward her, smiling. "You'd better hit me just once. As it is, my bones are itching for punishment."

She hid the fan behind her, chuckling.

Chi-tse moved his chair around and sat facing the wall, leaning back heavily with both hands over his eyes, and heaved another sigh.

Ch'i-ch'iao chewed on her fan handle and looked at him from the corners of her eyes. "What's the matter with you today? Can't stand the heat?"

"You wouldn't know." After a long pause he said in a low voice, enunciating each word distinctly. "You know why I can't get on with the one at home, why I played so hard outside and squandered all my money. Whom do you think it's all for?"

Ch'i-ch'iao was a bit frightened. She walked a long way off and leaned on the mantelpiece, the expression on her face slowly changing. Chi-tse followed her. Her head was bent and her right elbow rested on the mantelpiece. In her right hand was her fan whose apricot-yellow tassel trailed down over her forehead. He stood before her and whispered, "Second Sister-in-law! . . . Ch'i-ch'iao!"

Ch'i-ch'iao turned her face away and smiled blandly. "As if I'd believe you!"

So he also walked away. "That's right. How could you believe me? Ever since you came to our house I couldn't stay there a minute, only wanted to get out. I was never so wild before you came; later it was to avoid you that I stayed out. After I was married to Lan-hsien, I played harder than ever because aside from avoiding you I had to avoid her too. When I did see you, scarcely two sentences were exchanged before I lost my temper—how could you know the pain in my heart? When you were good to me, I felt still worse—I had to control myself—I couldn't ruin you just like that. So many people at home, all watching us. If people should know, it wouldn't matter too much for me, I was a man, but what was going to happen to you?"

Ch'i-ch'iao's hands trembled until the yellow tassel on the fan handle rustled against her forehead.

"Whether you believe it or not makes little difference," he said. "What if you believe it? Half our lives are over anyway, it's no use talking about it. I'm just asking you to understand the way I felt, then it wouldn't be unfair that I suffered so much on your account."

Ch'i-ch'iao bowed her head, basking in glory, in the soft music of his voice and the delicate pleasure of this occasion. So many years now, she had been playing hide-and-seek with him and never could get close, and there had still been a day like this in store for her. True, half a lifetime had gone by—the flower-years of her youth. Life is so devious and unreasonable. Why had she married into the Chiang family? For money? No, for meeting Chi-tse, because it was fated that she should be in love with him. She lifted her face slightly. He was standing in front of her with flat hands closed on her fan and his cheek pressed against it. He was also ten years older, but he was after all the same person. Could he be lying to her? He wanted her money—the money she had sold her life for? The very idea enraged her. Even if she had him wrong there, could he have suffered as much for her as she did for him? Now that she had finally given up all thoughts of love he was here again to provoke her. She hated him. He was still looking at her. His eyes—after ten years he was still the same person. Even if he was lying to her, wouldn't it be better to find out a little later? Even if she knew very well it was lies, he was such a good actor, wouldn't it be almost real?

No, she could not give this rascal any hold on her. The Chiangs were very shrewd; she might not be able to keep her money. She had to prove first whether he really meant it. She took a grip on herself, looked outside the door, gasped under her breath, "Somebody there!", and rushed out. She went to the amahs' quarters to tell P'an Ma to get the tea things for Third Master.

Coming back to the room, she frowned, saying, "So hateful— amah peering outside the door, turned and ran the minute she saw me. I went after her and stopped her. Who knows what stories they'd make up if we'd talked, however briefly, with the door shut. No peace even living by yourself."

P'an Ma brought the tea things and chilled sour plum juice. Ch'i-ch'iao used her chopsticks to pick the shredded roses and green plums off the top of the honey layer cake for Chi-tse. "I remember you don't like the red and green shreds," she said.

He just smiled, unable to say anything with people around.

Ch'i-ch'iao seemed to be making conversation. "How are you getting on with the houses you were going to sell?"

Chi-tse answered as he ate, "Some people offered eighty-five thousand; I haven't decided yet."

Ch'i-ch'iao paused to reflect. "The district is good."

"Everybody is against my getting rid of the property, says the price is still going up."

Ch'i-ch'iao asked for more particulars, then said, "A pity I haven't got that much cash at hand, otherwise I'd like to buy it."

"Actually there's no hurry about my property, it's your land in our part of the country that should be gotten rid of before long. Ever since we became a republic it's been one war after another, never missed a single year. The area is so messed up and with all the squeeze—the collectors and bookkeepers and the local powers—how much do we get when it comes to our turn, even in a year of good harvest? Not to say these last few years when it's either flood or drought."

Ch'i-ch'iao pondered. "I've done some calculating and kept putting it off. If only I'd sold it, then I wouldn't be caught short just when I want to buy your houses."

"If you want to sell that land it had better be now. I heard Hopeh and Shantung are going to be at war again."

"Who am I to sell it to in such a hurry?"

He said after a moment of hesitation, "All right, I'll see if I can find out for you."

Ch'i-ch'iao lifted her eyebrows and said, smiling, "Go on! You and that pack of foxes and dogs you run with, who is there that's halfway reliable?"

Chi-tse dipped a dumpling that he had bitten open into the little dish of vinegar, taking his time, and mentioned a couple of reliable names. Ch'i-ch'iao then seriously questioned him in detail and he set his answers out tidily, evidently well prepared.

Ch'i-ch'iao continued to smile but her mouth felt dry, her upper lip stuck on her gum and would not come down. She raised the lidded teacup to suck a mouthful of tea, licked her lips, and suddenly jumped up with a set face and threw her fan at his head. The round fan went wheeling through the air, knocked his shoulder as he ducked slightly to the left, and upset his glass. The sour plum juice spilled all over him.

"You want me to sell land to buy your houses? You want me to sell land? Once the money goes through your hands what can I count on? You'd cheat me—you'd cheat me with such talk—you take me for a fool—" She leaned across the table to hit him, but P'an Ma held her in a desperate embrace and started to yell. Ch'iang-yün and the others came running, pressed her down between them, pleaded noisily. Ch'i-ch'iao struggled and barked orders at the same time, but with a sinking heart she quite realized she was being foolish, too foolish, she was making a spectacle of herself.

Chi-tse took off his drenched white lacquered silk gown. P'an Ma brought a hot towel to wipe it for him. He paid her no attention but, before sauntering out the door with his gown on his arm, he said to Ch'iang-yün, "When Master Pai finishes his lesson for the day, tell him to get a doctor for his mother." Ch'iang-yün, who was too frightened by the proceedings not to say yes, received a resounding slap on the face from Ch'i-ch'iao. Chi-tse was gone. The slave girls and amahs also hurriedly left her after being scolded. Drop by drop, the sour plum juice trickled down the table, keeping time like a water clock at night —one drip, another drip—the first watch of the night, the second watch—one year, a hundred years. So long, this silent moment. Ch'i-ch'iao stood there, supporting her head with a hand. In another second she had turned around and was hurrying upstairs. Lifting her skirt, she half climbed and half stumbled her way up, continually bumping against the dingy wall of green plaster. Her Buddha-blue jacket was smudged with patches of pale chalk. She wanted another glimpse of him from the upstairs window. No matter what, she had loved him before. Her love had given her endless pain. Just this alone should make him worthy of her continuing regard. How many times had she strained to suppress herself until all her muscles and bones and gums ached with sharp pain. Today it all had been her fault. It wasn't as if she did not know he was no good. If she wanted him she had to pretend ignorance and put up with his badness. Why had she exposed him? Isn't life just like this and no more than this? In the end what is real and what is false?

She reached the window and pulled aside the dark green foreign-style curtains fringed with little velvet balls. Chi-tse was just going out the alley, his gown slung over his arm. Like a flock of white pigeons, the wind on that sunny day fluttered inside his white silk blouse and trousers. It penetrated everywhere, flapping its wings.

A curtain of ice-cold pearls seemed to hang in front of Ch'i-ch'iao's eyes. A hot wind would press the curtain tight on her face, and after being sucked back by the wind for a moment, it would muffle all her head and face before she could draw her breath. In such alternately hot and cold waves her tears flowed.

The tiny shrunken image of a policeman reflected faintly in the top corner of the window glass ambled by swinging his arms. A ricksha quietly ran over the policeman. A little boy with his long gown tucked up into his trouser waist ran kicking a ball out of the edge of the glass. The postman in green riding a bicycle superimposed his image on the policeman as he streaked by. All ghosts, ghosts of many years ago or the unborn of many years hence. . . . What is real and what is false?

The autumn passed, then the winter. Ch'i-ch'iao was out of touch with reality, feeling a little lost despite the usual flares of temper which prompted her to beat slave girls and change cooks. Her brother and his wife came to Shanghai to see her twice and stayed each time not longer than ten days, because in the end they could not stand her nagging, even though she would give them parting presents. Her nephew Ts'ao Ch'un-hsi came to town to look for work and stayed at her house. Though none too bright, this youth knew his place. Ch'i-ch'iao's son Ch'ang-pai was now fourteen, and her daughter Ch'ang-an about a year younger, but they looked only about seven or eight, being small and thin. During the New Year holidays the boy wore a bright blue padded gown of heavy silk and the girl a bright green brocade padded gown, both so thickly wadded that their arms stuck out straight. Standing side by side, both looked like paper dolls, with their flat thin white faces. One day after lunch Ch'i-ch'iao was not up yet. Ts'ao Ch'un-hsi kept the brother and sister company throwing dice. Ch'ang-an had lost all her New Year money gifts and still would not stop playing. Ch'ang-pai swept all the copper coins on the table toward himself and said, smiling, "I won't play with you any more."

"We'll play with candied lotus seeds," Ch'ang-an said.

"The sugar will stain your clothes if you keep them in your pocket," Ch'un-hsi said.

"Watermelon seeds will do, there's a can of them on top of the wardrobe," said Ch'ang-an. So she moved a small tea table over and stepped on a chair to get on it and reach up.

Ch'un-hsi was so nervous he called out, "Don't you fall down, Little Miss An, I can't shoulder the blame." The words were scarcely out of his mouth when Ch'ang-an suddenly tipped backwards and would have toppled down if he had not caught her. Ch'ang-pai clapped his hands, laughing, while Ch'un-hsi, though he muttered curses, also could not help laughing. All three of them dissolved in mirth. Lifting her down, Ch'un-hsi suddenly saw in the mirror of the rosewood wardrobe Ch'i-ch'iao standing in the doorway with her arms akimbo, her hair not yet done. Somewhat taken aback, he quickly set Ch'ang-an down and turned around to greet her, "Aunt is up."

Ch'i-ch'iao rushed over and pushed Ch'ang-an behind her. Ch'ang-an lost her balance and fell down but Ch'i-ch'iao continued shielding her with her own body while she cried harshly to Ch'un-hsi, "You wolf-hearted, dog-lunged creature, I'll fix you! I treat you to three teas and six meals, you wolf-hearted, dog-lunged thing, in what way have I not done right by you, and yet you'd take advantage of my daughter? You think I can't make out what's in your wolf's heart and dog's lungs? Don't you go around thinking if you teach my daughter bad things I'll have to hold my nose and marry her to you, so you can take over our property. A fool like you doesn't look to me as if he'd think of such a trick, it must be your parents who taught you, guiding you by the hand. Those two wolf-hearted, dog-lunged, ungrateful, old addled eggs, they are determined to get my money. When one scheme fails another comes up."

Ch'un-hsi, staring white-eyed in his anger, was just about to defend himself when Ch'i-ch'iao said, "Aren't you ashamed? You'd still answer back? Get out of my sight right away, don't wait for my men to drive you out with rods." So saying, she pushed her son and daughter out and then left the room herself, supported by a slave girl. Being a quick-tempered youth, Ch'un-hsi rolled up his bedding and left the Chiang house forthwith.

Ch'i-ch'iao returned to the living room and lay down on the opium couch. With the velvet curtains drawn it was dark in the room. Only when the wind came in through the crevices and moved the curtains was a bit of sky hazily visible under their hems fringed with green velvet balls. There was just the opium lamp and the dim light of the stove burning red. Having had a fright, Ch'ang-an sat stunned on a little stool by the stove.

"Come over here," Ch'i-ch'iao said.

Ch'ang-an didn't go over right away, thinking her mother would hit her. She fiddled with the laundry hung on the tin screen around the stove and turned over a cotton undershirt with little pink checks, saying, "It's almost burned." The shirt gave out a hot smell of cloth fuzz.

But Ch'i-ch'iao, not quite in the mood to beat or scold her, merely went over everything and added, "You'll be thirteen this year after the New Year, you should have more sense. Although Cousin is no outsider, men are all rotten without exception. You should know how to take care of yourself. Who's not after your money?" A gust of wind passed, showing the cold white sky between the velvet balls on the curtains, puncturing with a row of little holes the warm darkness in the room. The flame of the opium lamp ducked and the shadows on Ch'i-ch'iao's face seemed a shade deeper. She suddenly sat up to whisper, "Men . . . leave them alone! Who's not after your money? Your mother's bit of money didn't come easy nor is it easy to keep. When it comes to you two, I can't look on and see you get cheated. I'm telling you to be more on guard from now on, you hear?"

"I heard," Ch'ang-an said with her head down.

One of Ch'i-ch'iao's feet was going to sleep, and she reached over to pinch it. Just for a moment a gentle memory stirred in her eyes. She remembered a man who was after her money.

Her bound feet had been padded with cotton wool to simulate the reformed feet, half let out. As she looked at them, something occurred to her and she said with a cynical laugh, "You may say yes, but how do I know if you're sensible or silly at heart? You're this big already, and with a pair of big feet, where can't you go? Even if I could control you, I wouldn't have the energy to watch you all day long. Actually at thirteen it's already too late for foot-binding, it is my fault not to have seen to it earlier. We'll start right now, there's still time."

Ch'ang-an was momentarily at a loss for an answer, but the amahs standing around said, smiling, "Small feet are not fashionable any more. To have her feet bound will perhaps mean trouble when the time comes for Little Miss to get engaged."

"What nonsense! I'm not worried about my daughter having no takers; you people needn't bother to worry for me. If nobody really wants her and she has to be kept all her life, I can afford it too."

She actually started to bind her daughter's feet, and Ch'ang-an howled with great pain. By then even women in conservative families like the Chiangs were letting out their bound feet, to say nothing of girls whose feet had never been bound. Everybody talked about Ch'ang-an's feet as a great joke. After binding them for a year or so, Ch'i-ch'iao's momentary enthusiasm had waned and relatives persuaded her to let them loose, but Ch'ang-an's feet would never be entirely the same again.

All the children of the Chiangs' eldest and third branches went to foreign-style schools. Ch'i-ch'iao, always purposely competing with them, also wanted to enroll Ch'ang-pai in one. Aside from playing mahjong for small stakes, Ch'ang-pai liked only to go to amateur Peking opera clubs. He was working hard day and night training his singing voice, and was afraid that school would interfere with his lessons, so he refused to go. In desperation Ch'i-ch'iao sent Ch'ang-an instead to the Hu Fan Middle School for girls and through connections got her into one of the higher classes. Ch'ang-an changed into a uniform of rough blue "patriotic cloth" and in less than six months her complexion turned ruddy and her wrists and ankles grew thicker. The boarders were supposed to have their clothes washed by a laundry concession. Ch'ang-an could not remember her own numbers and often lost pillowcases, handkerchiefs, and other little items, and Ch'i-ch'iao insisted on going to speak to the principal about it. One day when she was home for holidays, in going over her things Ch'i-ch'ao found a sheet was missing. She fell into a thunderous rage and threatened to go to the school herself the next day to demand satisfaction. Ch'ang-an in dismay tried just once to stop her and Ch'i-ch'iao scolded, "You good-for-nothing wastrel. Your mother's money is not money to you. Did your mother's money come easy? What dowry will I have to give you when you get married? Whatever I give you will be given in vain."

Ch'ang-an dared not say anything in reply and cried all night. She could not bear to lose face like this in front of her schoolmates. To a fourteen-year-old that seems of the greatest importance. How was she to face people from now on if her mother went and made a scene? She would rather die than go to school again. Her friends, the music teacher she liked, they would soon forget there was such a girl who had come for half a year and left quietly for no reason. A clean break —she felt this sacrifice was a beautiful desolate gesture.

At midnight she crawled out of bed and put a hand outside the window. Pitch-dark, was it raining? No raindrops. She took a harmonica from the side of her pillow and half squatted, half sat on the floor, blowing it stealthily. Hesitantly the little tune of "Long, Long Ago" twirled and spread out in the huge night. People must not hear. Held down strictly, the thin, wailing music of the harmonica kept trailing off and on like a baby sobbing. Short of breath, she stopped for a while. Through the window the moon had come out of the clouds. A dark gray sky dotted sparsely with stars and a blurred chip of a moon, like a lithographed picture. White clouds steaming up underneath and a faint halo over the street lamp showing among the top branches of a tree. Ch'ang-an started her harmonica again. "Tell me the tales that to me were so dear, long, long ago, long, long ago . . ."

The next day she summoned up enough courage to tell her mother, "I don't feel like going back to school, Mother."

Ch'i-ch'iao opened her eyes wide. "Why?"

"I can't keep up with the lessons, and the food is too bad, I can't get used to it."

Ch'i-ch'iao took off a slipper and slapped her with its sole just by the way, saying bitterly, "Your father was not as good as other people, you're also not as good? You weren't born a freak, you're just being perverse so as to disappoint me."

Looking down, Ch'ang-an stood with her hands behind her back and would not speak. So the amahs intervened, "Little Miss is grown up now, and it's a bit inconvenient for her to go to school where there're all sorts of people. Actually, it's just as well for her not to go."

Ch'i-ch'iao paused to reflect. "At least we have to get the tuition back. Why give it to them for nothing?" She wanted Ch'ang-an to go with her to collect it. Ch'ang-an would have fought to the death rather than go. Ch'i-ch'iao took two amahs with her. The way she told it when she returned, although she did not get the money back, she had thoroughly humiliated the principal. Afterwards, when Ch'ang-an met any of her schoolmates on the street, she reddened and paled alternately. Earth had no room for her. She could only pretend not to see and walk past them hastily. When friends wrote her, she dared not even open the letters and just sent them back. Thus her school life came to an end.

Sometimes she felt the sacrifice was not worth it and was secretly sorry, but it was too late. She gradually gave up all thought of self-improvement and kept to her place. She learned to make trouble, play little tricks, and interfere with the running of the house. She often fell out with her mother, but she looked and sounded more and more like her. Every time she wore a pair of unlined trousers and sat with her legs apart and the palms of both hands on the stool in front of her, her head tilted to one side, her chin on her chest, looking dismally but intently at the woman opposite and telling her, "Every family has its own troubles, Cousin-in-law—every family has its own troubles!", she appeared Ch'i-ch'iao's spit and image. She wore a pigtail and her eyes and eyebrows had a taut expressiveness about them reminiscent of Ch'i-ch'iao in her prime, but her small mouth was a bit too sunken, which made her look older. Even when she was younger, she did not seem fresh, but was like a tender bunch of vegetables that had been salted.

Some people tried to make matches for her. If the other side was not well off, Ch'i-ch'iao would always suspect it wanted their money. If the other side had wealth and influence, it would show little enthusiasm. Ch'ang-an had only average good looks, and since her mother was not only lowborn but also known for her shrewishness, she probably would not have much upbringing. So the high were out of reach and the low Ch'i-ch'iao would not stoop to—Ch'ang-an stayed home year after year. But Ch'ang-pai's marriage could not be delayed. When he gambled outside and showed enough personal interest in certain Peking opera actresses to attend their performances regularly, Ch'i-ch'iao still had nothing to say; she got alarmed only when he started to go to brothels with his Third Uncle Chiang Chi-tse. In great haste she betrothed and married him to a Miss Yuan, called Chih-shou as a child.

The wedding ceremony was half modern, and the bride, without the customary red kerchief over her head and face, wore blue eyeglasses and a pink wedding veil instead, and a pink blouse and skirt with multicolored embroidery. The glasses were removed after she entered the bridal chamber and sat with bowed head under the turquoise-colored bed curtains. The guests gathered for the "riot in the bridal chamber" surrounded her, making jokes. Ch'i-ch'iao came out after taking a look. Ch'ang-an overtook her at the door and whispered, "Fair-skinned, only the lips are a bit too thick."

Ch'i-ch'iao leaned a hand on the doorway, took a gold ear-spoon from her bun to scratch her head with, and laughed sardonically, "Don't start on that now. Your new sister-in-law's lips, chop them up and they'll make a heaping dish!"

"Well, it's said that people with thick lips have warm feelings," said a lady beside her.

Ch'i-ch'iao snorted; pointing her gold ear-spoon at the woman;

she lifted an eyebrow and said with a crooked little smile, "It isn't so nice to have warm feelings. I can't say much in front of young ladies —just hope our Master Pai won't die in her hands." Ch'i-ch'iao was born with a high clear voice, which had grown less shrill as she grew older, but it was still cutting, or rather rasping, like a razor blade. Her last remark could not be called loud, nor was it exactly soft. Could the bride, surrounded by a crowd as she was, possibly have registered a quiver on her severely flat face and chest? Probably it was just a reflection of the flames leaping on the tall pair of dragon-and-phoenix candles.

After the Third Day Ch'i-ch'iao found the bride stupid and unsatisfactory in various things and often complained to relatives. Some said placatingly, "The bride is young. Second Sister-in-law will just have to take the trouble to teach her. It just happens that the child is naïve."

Ch'i-ch'iao made a spitting noise. "Our new young mistress may look innocent—but as soon as she sees Master Pai she has to go and sit on the nightstool. Really! It sounds unbelievable, doesn't it?"

When the talk reached Chih-shou's ears, she wanted to kill herself. This was before the end of the first month, when Ch'i-ch'iao still kept up appearances. Later she would even say such things in front of Chih-shou, who could neither cry nor laugh with impunity. And if she merely looked wooden, pretending not to listen, Ch'i-ch'iao would slap the table and sigh, "It's really not easy, to eat a mouthful of rice in the house of your son and daughter-in-law! People pull a long face at you at the drop of a hat."

One night Ch'i-ch'iao was lying on the opium couch smoking while Ch'ang-pai crouched on a nearby upholstered chair cracking watermelon seeds. The radio was broadcasting a little-known Peking opera. He followed it in a book, humming the lyrics word by word, and as he got into the mood, swung a leg up over the back of the chair rocking it back and forth to mark the rhythm.

Ch'i-ch'iao reached out a foot to give him a kick. "Come Master Pai, fill the pipe for me a couple of times."

"With an opium lamp right there why put me to work? I have honey on my fingers or something?" Ch'ang-pai stretched himself while replying and slowly moved over to the little stool in front of the opium lamp and rolled up his sleeves.

"Unfilial slave, what kind of answer is that! Putting you to work is an honor." She looked at him through slitted smiling eyes. All these years he had been the only man in her life. Only with him there was no danger of his being after her money—it was his anyway. But being her son, he amounted to less than half a man. And even the half she could not keep, now that he was married. He was a slight, pale young man, a bit hunched, with gold-rimmed glasses and fine features meticulously drawn, often smiling vacantly, his mouth hanging open and something shining inside, either too much saliva or a gold tooth. The collar of his gown was open, showing its pearly lamb lining and a white pajama shirt. Ch'i-ch'iao put a foot on his shoulder and kept giving him light kicks on the neck, whispering, "Unfilial slave, I'll fix you! When do you get so unfilial?"

Ch'ang-pai quoted with a smile, " 'Take a wife and the mother is forgotten.' "

"Don't talk nonsense, our Master Pai is not that kind of person, nor could I have had a son like that either," said Ch'i-ch'iao. Ch'ang-pai just smiled. She looked fixedly at him from the corners of her eyes. "If you're still my Master Pai as before, cook opium for me all night tonight."

"That's no problem," he said, smiling.

"If you doze off, see if I don't hammer you with my fists."

The living room curtains had been sent to be washed. Outside the windows the moon was barely visible behind dark clouds, a dab of black, a dab of white like a ferocious theatrical mask. Bit by bit it came out of the clouds and a ray of light shone disconcertingly from under a black strip of cloud, an eye under the mask. The sky was the dark blue of the bottomless pit. It was long past midnight, and Ch'ang-an had gone to bed long ago. As Ch'ang-pai started to nod while rolling the opium pills, Ch'i-ch'iao poured him a cup of strong tea. The two of them ate honeyed preserves and discussed neighbors' secrets. Ch'i-ch'iao suddenly said, smiling, "Tell me, Master Pai, is your wife nice?"

"What is there to say about it?" Ch'ang-pai said, smiling.

"Must be nice if there is nothing to criticize," said Ch'i ch'iao.

"Who said she's nice?"

"Not nice? In what way? Tell Mother."

Ch'ang-pai was vague at first but under cross-examination he had to reveal a thing or two. The amahs handing them tea turned aside to chuckle and the slave girls covered their mouths trying not to laugh and slipped out of the room. Ch'i-ch'iao gritted her teeth and laughed and muttered curses, removed the pipe bowl to knock out the ashes with all her strength, banging loudly. Once started, Ch'ang-pai found it hard to stop and talked all night.

The next morning Ch'i-ch'iao told the amahs to bring a couple of blankets to let the young master sleep on the couch. Chih-shou was up already and came to pay her respects. Ch'i-ch'iao had not slept all night but was more energetic than ever and asked relatives over to play mahjong, women of different families including her daughter-in-law's mother. Over the mahjong table she told in detail all her daughter-in-law's secrets as confessed by her son, adding some touches of her own that made the story still more vivid. Everybody tried to change the subject, but the small talk no sooner started than Ch'i-ch'iao would smilingly switch it back to her daughter-in-law. Chih-shou's mother turned purple. Too ashamed to see her daughter, she just put down her mahjong tiles and went home in her private ricksha.

Ch'i-ch'iao made Ch'ang-pai cook opium for her for two nights running. Chih-shou lay stiffly in bed with both hands on her ribs curled upward like a dead chicken's claws. She knew her mother-in-law was questioning her husband again, although heaven knew how he could have anything fresh to say. Tomorrow he would again come to her with a drooling, mock-pleading look. Perhaps he had guessed that she would center all her hatred on him. Even if she could not fight savagely with tooth and nail, she would at least upbraid him and make a scene. Very likely he would steal her thunder by coming in half drunk, to pick on her and smash something. She knew his ways. In the end he would sit down on the bed, raise his shoulders, reach inside his white silk pajama shirt to scratch himself, and smile unexpectedly. A little light would tremble on his gold-rimmed spectacles and twinkle in his mouth, spit or gold tooth. He would take off his glasses. . . . Chih-shou suddenly sat up and parted the bed curtains with the sound of a bucket of water crashing down. This was an insane world, a husband not like a husband, a mother-in-law not like a mother-in-law. Either they were mad or she was. The moon tonight was better than ever, high and full like a white sun in a pitch-black sky, not a cloud within ten thousand li. Blue shadows all over the floor and blue shadows on the canopy overhead. Her feet, too, were in the deathly still blue shadows.

Thinking to hook up the bed curtains, Chih-shou reached out groping for the hook. With one hand holding on to the brass hook and her face snuggled against her shoulder, she could not keep the sobs from starting. The curtain dropped by itself. There was nobody but her inside the dark bed, still she hastened to hook the curtains up in a panic. Outside the windows there was still that abnormal moon that made one's body hairs stand on end all over—small white sun brilliant in the black sky. Inside the room she could clearly see the embroidered rosy-purple chair covers and table cloths, the gold-embroidered scarlet screen with five phoenixes flying in a row, the pink satin scrolls embroidered with seal-script characters embellished with flowers. On the dressing table the silver powder jar, silver mouth-rinsing mug, and silver vase were each caught in a red and green net and filled with wedding candies. Along the silk panel across the lintel of the bed hung balls of flowers, toy flower pots, *ju-yi*,[12] and rice dumplings, all made of multicolored gilded velvet, and dangling underneath them glass balls the size of finger tips and mauvish pink tassels a foot long. In such a big room crammed full of trunks, spare bedding, and furnishings, surely she could find a sash to hang herself with. She fell back on the bed. In the moonlight her feet had no color of life at all—bluish, greenish, purplish, the tints of a corpse gone cold. She wanted to die, she wanted to die. She was afraid of the moonlight but dared not turn on the light. Tomorrow her mother-in-law would say, "Master Pai fixed me a couple more pipes and our poor young mistress couldn't sleep the whole night, kept her light on to all hours waiting for him to come back—can't do without him." Chih-shou's tears flowed along the pillow. She did not wipe her eyes with a handkerchief; rubbing would get them swollen and her mother-in-law would again say, "Master Pai didn't sleep in his room for just one night and Young Mistress cried until her eyes were like peaches!"

Although Ch'i-ch'iao pictured her son and daughter-in-law as a passionate couple, Ch'ang-pai was not very pleased with Chih-shou and Chih-shou on her part hated him so much her teeth itched to bite. Since the two did not get along, Ch'ang-pai again went strolling in

[12] Literally, "as you wish." An odd-shaped ornamental piece, usually of jade.

"the streets of flowers and the lanes of willows." Ch'i-ch'iao gave him a slave girl called Chüan-erh for a concubine and still could not hold him. She also tried in various ways to get him to smoke opium. Ch'ang-pai had always liked a couple of puffs for fun but he had never got into the habit. Now that he smoked more he quieted down and no longer went out much, just stayed with his mother and his new concubine.

His sister Ch'ang-an got dysentery when she was twenty-four. Instead of getting a doctor, Ch'i-ch'iao persuaded her to smoke a little opium and it did ease the pain. After she recovered she also got into the habit. An unmarried girl without any other distractions, Ch'ang-an went at it singlemindedly and smoked even more than her brother. Some tried to dissuade her. Ch'i-ch'iao said, "What is there to be afraid of? For one thing we Chiangs can still afford it, and even if I sold two hundred *mou* of land today so the brother and sister could smoke, who is there who'd dare let out half a fart? When the girl gets married she'll have her dowry, she'll be eating and drinking out of her own pocket, so even if *Ku-yeh* stints on it he can only look on."

All the same Ch'ang-an's prospects were affected. The matchmakers, who had never come running to begin with, now disappeared altogether. When Ch'ang-an was nearly thirty, Ch'i-ch'iao changed her tune, seeing that her daughter was fated to be an old maid. "Not married off because she's not good-looking, and yet blames her mother for putting it off, spoiling her chances. Pulls a long face all day as if I owed her two hundred copper coins. It's certainly not to make myself miserable that I've kept her at home, feeding her free tea and rice!"

On the twentieth birthday of Chiang Chi-tse's daughter Ch'ang-hsing, Ch'ang-an went to give her cousin her best wishes. Chiang Chi-tse was poor now but fortunately his wide social contacts kept him more or less solvent. Ch'ang-hsing said to her mother in secret, "Mother, try to introduce a friend to Sister An, she seems so pitiful. Her eyes reddened with tears at the very mention of conditions at home."

Lan-hsien hastily held up her palm, shaking it from side to side. "No, no! This match I dare not make. Stir up your Second Aunt with her temper?"

But Ch'ang-hsing, young and meddlesome, paid her no heed. After

some time she by chance mentioned Ch'ang-an's case to her schoolmates, and it happened that one of them had an uncle newly returned
from Germany, a northerner, too, even distantly related to the
Chiangs, as it turned out when they really investigated his background.
The man was called T'ung Shih-fang, and was several years older than
Ch'ang-an. And Ch'ang-hsing took matters into her own hands and arranged everything. Her schoolmate's mother would play hostess. On
Ch'ang-an's side her family was kept as much in the dark as if sealed in
an iron barrel.

Ch'i-ch'iao had always had a strong constitution but ever since
Chih-shou had got tuberculosis Ch'i-ch'iao thought her daughter-in-
law disgustingly affected, making much of herself, eating this and that,
unable to stand the least fatigue and seemingly having a better time
than usual, so she, too, got sick out of spite. At first it was just weak
breath and thin blood, but even then it sent the entire household into a
spin, so that they had no time for Chih-shou. Later Ch'i-ch'iao got seriously ill and took to her bed and there was more fuss than ever.
Ch'ang-an slipped out in the confusion and called a tailor to her Third
Uncle's house, where Ch'ang-hsing designed a new costume for her.
On the day of the dinner Ch'ang-hsing accompanied her in the late afternoon to see the hairdresser, who waved her hair with hot tongs and
plastered close-set little kiss-curls from the temple to the ears. Upon returning home, Ch'ang-hsing made her cousin wear "glassy-green"
jadeite [13] earrings with pagoda-shaped pendants two inches long and
change into an apple-green georgette gown with a high collar, ruffled
sleeves, and fine pleats below the waist, half Western style. As a young
maid squatted on the floor buttoning her up, Ch'ang-an scrutinized
herself in the wardrobe mirror and could not help stretching out both
arms and kicking out the skirt in a posture from "The Grape Fairy." [14]
Twisting her head around, she started to laugh, saying, "Really dolled
up to look like the celestial maiden scattering flowers!" [15]

[13] The most valued kind of jadeite, translucent and dark green in color.

[14] A short musical by Li Ching-hui, a most popular choice for school productions
during the twenties and thirties.

[15] *T'ien-nü san-hua* (The celestial maiden scatters flowers) is the title of a Peking
opera made popular by Mei Lan-fang. It is based on an episode from the Vimala-
kirti Sutra.

Ch'ang-hsing signaled the maid in the mirror with her eyes and they both laughed. After Ch'ang-an had finished dressing, she sat down straight-backed on a high chair.

"I'll go and telephone for a taxi," Ch'ang-hsing said.

"It's early yet," said Ch'ang-an.

Ch'ang-hsing looked at her watch. "We're supposed to be there at eight. It's now five past."

"It probably wouldn't matter if we were half an hour late."

Ch'ang-hsing thought it both infuriating and laughable for her cousin to want to put on airs. She opened her woven silver handbag to examine its contents. On the pretext that she had forgotten her compact, she went to her mother's room and told her all about it, adding, "T'ung is not the host today, so for whom is she putting on airs? I won't bother to talk her out of it, let her dawdle till tomorrow morning, it's none of my business."

Lan-hsien said, "Look how silly you are! You made the appointment, you're making the match, how can you not be responsible? I've told you so many times you should have known better, Little Miss An is just as petty as her mother and not used to company. She'll make a spectacle of herself and she's your cousin after all. If you lose face you deserve it—who told you to get into this? Gone crazy from having nothing to do?"

Ch'ang-hsing sat pouting in her mother's room for a long while.

"It looks as if your cousin is waiting to be pressed," Lan-hsien said, smiling.

"I'm not going to press her."

"Silly girl, what's the use of your pressing? She's waiting for the other side to telephone."

Ch'ang-hsing broke out laughing. "She's not a bride, to be urged three, four times and forced into the sedan chair."

"Ring up the restaurant anyway and be done with it—tell them to call. It's almost nine. If you wait any longer it's really off."

Ch'ang-hsing had to do as she was told and finally set out with her cousin.

Ch'ang-an was still in good spirits in the car, talking and laughing away. But once in the restaurant, she suddenly became reserved, stealing into the room behind Ch'ang-hsing, timidly removed her apple-green ostrich cape and sat down with bowed head, took an almond and bit off a tenth of it every two minutes, chewing slowly. She had come to be looked at. She felt that her costume was impeccable and could stand scrutiny but her body was altogether superfluous and could as well be shrunk in size and put away if she knew how to do this. She kept silent throughout the meal. While waiting for the dessert, Ch'ang-hsing pulled her to the window to watch the street scene and walked off on some pretext, and T'ung Shih-fang ambled over to the window.

"Has Miss Chiang been here before?" he said.

"No," Ch'ang-an said in a small voice.

"The first time for me too. The food is not bad, but I'm not quite used to it yet."

"Not used to it?"

"Yes, foreign food is more bland, Chinese food is more greasy. When I had just come back friends and relatives made me eat out for several days running and I easily got an upset stomach."

Ch'ang-an looked at her fingers back and front as if intent on counting how many of the whorls were "snails" and how many "shovels."

Out of nowhere a little neon light sign in the shape of a flower bloomed on the windowpane, reflected from the shop opposite, red petals with a green heart. It was the lotus of the Nile set before the gods and also the lily emblem of French royalty. . . .

Shih-fang, who had not seen any girls of his homeland for many years, was struck by Ch'ang-an's pathetic charm and rather liked it. He had been engaged long before he went abroad, but having fallen in love with a schoolmate he violently opposed the match. After endless long-distance negotiations he almost broke with his parents who for a time stopped sending money, causing him much hardship. They finally gave in, however, and put an end to his engagement. Unfortunately his schoolmate fell in love with somebody else. In his disappointment he dug in and studied for seven, eight years. His conviction that old-fashioned wives were best was also a rebound.

After this meeting with Ch'ang-an, they were both interested. Ch'ang-hsing thought she should finish her good deed but, however enthusiastic, she was not qualified to speak to Ch'ang-an's mother. She had to beg Lan-hsien, who refused adamantly, saying, "You know very well your father and your Second Aunt are like enemies, never see each other. Although I've never quarreled with her there's no love lost. Why ask to be cold-shouldered?"

Ch'ang-an said nothing when she saw Lan-hsien, merely shed tears. Lan-hsien had to promise to go just once. The sisters-in-law met and after the amenities Lan-hsien explained the purpose of her visit. Ch'i-ch'iao was glad enough when she first heard of it.

"Then I'll leave it to Third Sister," she said. "I haven't been at all well, I can't cope with it, will just have to trouble Third Sister. This girl has been a dead weight on my hands. As a mother I can't be said to have not done right by her. When old-fashioned rules were in force I bound her feet, when new-fangled rules were in force I sent her to school—what else is there? A girl I dug out my heart and liver to train, as it were, she shouldn't have no takers as long as she's not scarred or pock-marked or blind. But this girl was born an Ah-tou [16] that can't be propped up. I get so angry I keep yelling: 'Oh, for the day that I shut my eyes and am gone!'—her marriage will then be in the hands of heaven and left to fate."

So it was agreed that Lan-hsien would ask both sides to dinner so they could take a look at each other. Ch'ang-an and T'ung Shih-fang met again as if for the first time. Ch'i-ch'iao, sick in bed, did not appear, so Ch'ang-an got engaged in peace. At the dinner table Lan-hsien and Ch'ang-hsing forcibly took Ch'ang-an's hand and placed it in T'ung Shih-fang's. Shih-fang put the ring on her finger in public. And the girl's family gave gifts in return, not the traditional stationery but a pen set in a velvet-lined box plus a wrist watch.

After the engagement Ch'ang-an furtively went out alone with T'ung Shih-fang several times. The two of them walked side by side in the park in the autumn sun, talking very little, each content with a partial view of the other's clothes and moving feet. The fragrance of her face powder and his tobacco smell served as invisible railings that separated them from the crowd. On the open green lawn where so many people ran and laughed and talked, they alone walked an enchanted porch that wound on endlessly in silence. Ch'ang-an did not feel there was anything amiss in not talking. She thought this was all there was

16 The inept heir of Liu Pei, founder of the Shu Han kingdom during the Three Kingdoms period.

to social contact between modern men and women. As to T'ung Shih-fang, from painful experience in the past he was dubious anyway of the exchange of thought. He was satisfied that someone was beside him. Formerly he had been disgusted by the character in fiction who would say, when asking a woman to live with him, "Please give me solace." Solace is purely spiritual but it is used here as a euphemism for sex. But now he knew the line between the spiritual and the physical could not be drawn so clearly. Words are no use after all. Holding hands for a long time is a more apt consolation, because not many people talk well and still fewer really have anything to say.

Sometimes it rained in the park. Ch'ang-an would open her umbrella and Shih-fang would hold it for her. Upon the translucent blue silk umbrella myriad raindrops twinkled like a skyful of stars that would follow them about later on the taxi's glistening front window of crushed silver and, as the car ran through red and green lights, a nestful of red stars would fly humming outside the window and a nestful of green stars.

Ch'ang-an brought back some of the stray dreams under the starlight and became unusually silent, often smiling. Ch'i-ch'iao saw the change and could not help getting angry and sarcastic. "These many years we haven't been very attentive to Miss, no wonder Miss seldom smiled. Now you've got your wish and are going to spring out of the Chiangs' door. But no matter how happy you are, don't show it on your face so much—it's simply sickening."

In former days Ch'ang-an would have answered back, but now that she appeared a transformed person she let it go and concentrated on curing herself of the opium habit. Ch'i-ch'iao could do nothing with her.

Eldest Mistress Tai-chen, who had not been present when Ch'ang-an got engaged, came to the house to congratulate her sometime afterward. Ch'i-ch'iao whispered, "Eldest Sister-in-law, it seems to me we still have to ask around a bit. This is not a matter to blunder into. The other day I seemed to have heard something about a wife in the country and another across the seas."

"The one in the country was sent back before marriage," said Tai-chen. "The same with the one overseas. It's said that they were friends for several years; nobody knew why nothing came of it."

"What's so strange about that? Men's hearts change faster than you can say change. He didn't even acknowledge the one who came with the three matchmakers and six gifts, not to say the hussy that's neither fish nor flesh. Who knows whether he has anybody else across the seas? I have only this one daughter, I can't muddle along and ruin her whole life. I myself have suffered in matchmakers' hands."

Ch'ang-an sat to one side pressing her fingernails into her palm until the palm reddened and the nails turned white from the strain. Ch'i-ch'iao looked up and saw her. "Shameless girl, pricking up your ears to listen! Is this anything that you should hear? When we were girls we couldn't get out of the way fast enough at the very mention of marriage. You Chiangs had generations of book learning in vain, you may have to go and learn some manners from your mother's family with their sesame oil shop."

Ch'ang-an ran out crying. Ch'i-ch'iao pounded her pillow and sighed. "Miss couldn't wait to marry, so what can I do? She'd drag home any old smelly stinking thing. It's supposed to be her Third Aunt that found him for her—actually she's just using her Third Aunt for a blind. Probably the rice was already cooked before they asked Third Aunt to be matchmaker. Everybody ganged up to fool me—and just as well. If the truth came out, where should the mother and brother look?"

Another day Ch'ang-an slipped out on some excuse. When she got back she was going to report every place she had been before Ch'i-ch'iao had even asked.

"All right, all right, save your words," Ch'i-ch'iao barked. "What's the use of lying to me? Let me catch you red-handed one day— humph! don't you think that because you're grown up and engaged I can't beat you any more!"

"I went to give Cousin Hsing those slipper patterns, what's wrong in that?" Ch'ang-an was upset. "If Mother doesn't believe me, she can ask Third Aunt."

"Your Third Aunt found you a man and she's the father and mother of your rebirth! Never seen anybody as cheap as you . . . Disappears in the twinkling of an eye. Your family kept you and honored you all these years—short of buying a page to serve you, where have we been remiss, that you can't even stay home for a moment?"

Ch'ang-an blushed, tears falling straight down.

Ch'i-ch'iao paused for breath. "So many good ones were turned down before and now you go and marry a ne'er-do-well, the leftover of the lot, isn't that slapping one's own face? If he's a man, how did he live to be thirty-something, cross oceans and seas over a hundred thousand li, and never get himself a wife?"

But Ch'ang-an remained obdurate. Both parties being none too young, several months after the engagement Lan-hsien came to Ch'i-ch'iao as Shih-fang's deputy and asked her to set a date for the wedding.

Ch'i-ch'iao pointed at Ch'ang-an. "Won't marry early, won't marry late, has to choose this year when there's no money at hand. If we have a better harvest next year, the trousseau would be more complete."

"Modern-style weddings don't go in for these things. Might as well do it the new way and save a little," Lan-hsien said.

"New ways, old ways, what's the difference? The old ways are more for show, the new ways more practical—the girl's family is the loser anyway."

"Just do whatever you see fit, Second Sister-in-law, Little Miss An is not going to argue about getting too little, is she?" At this everybody in the room laughed; even Ch'ang-an could not help a little smile.

Ch'i-ch'iao burst out, "Shameless! You have something in your belly that won't keep or what? Can't wait to get over there, as if your eyebrows were on fire. Will even do without the trousseau—you're willing, others may not be. You're so sure he's after your person? What vanity! Have you got a presentable spot on you? Stop lying to yourself. This man T'ung has his eyes on the Chiangs' name and prestige, that's all. Your family sounds so grand with its titles and its eminent generals and ministers, actually it's not so at all. It's been strong outside and shriveled up inside long since, and for these last few years couldn't even keep up appearances. Moreover, each generation of your family is worse than the one before, no regard for heaven and earth and king and parent any more. The young masters know nothing whatsoever and all the young ladies know is to grab money and want men—worse than pigs and dogs. My own family was a thousand times and ten thousand times to blame in making this match—ruined my whole life. I'm going to tell this man T'ung not to make the same mistake before it's too late."

After this quarrel Lan-hsien washed her hands of the match. Ch'i-ch'iao, convalescing, could get out of bed a bit and would sit astride the doorway and call out toward Ch'ang-an's room day after day, "You want strange men, go look for them, just don't bring them home to greet me as mother-in-law and make me die of anger. Out of sight, out of mind, that's all I ask. I'd be grateful if Miss will let me live a couple of years longer." She had just these few sentences arranged in different orders, shouted out so that the whole street could hear. Of course the talk spread among relatives, boiling and steaming.

Ch'i-ch'iao then called Ch'ang-an to her, suddenly in tears. "My child, you know people outside are saying this and that about you, have smirched you till you're not worth a copper coin. Ever since your mother married into the Chiang family, from top to bottom there's not one that's not a snob. Man stands low in dogs' eyes. I took so much from them in the open and in the dark. Even your father, did he ever do me a good turn that I'd want to stay his widow? I stayed and suffered endless hardships these twenty years, just hoping that you two children would grow up and win back some face for me. I never knew it'd come to this." And she wept.

Ch'ang-an was thunderstruck. Never mind if her mother made her out to be less than human or if outsiders said the same; let them. Only T'ung Shih-fang—he—what would he think? Did he still want her? Was there any change in his manner last time she saw him? Hard to say. . . . She was too happy, she wouldn't notice little differences. . . . Between the discomfort of taking the cure and these repeated provocations Ch'ang-an was already having a hard time but, forcing herself to bear up, she had endured. Now she suddenly felt as though all her bones were out of joint. Explain to him? Unlike her brother, he was not her mother's offspring and could never thoroughly understand her mother. It would have been all right if he never had to meet her mother but sooner or later he would make her acquaintance. Marriage is a lifelong affair; you can be a thief all your life but you can't always be on guard against thieves. Who knew what her mother would resort to? Sooner or later there would be trouble, sooner or later there would be a break. This was the most beautiful episode of her life, better finish it herself before other people could add a disgusting ending to it. A beautiful, desolate gesture. . . . She knew she would be sorry, she knew she would, but unconcernedly she lifted her eyebrows and said, "Since Mother is not willing to make this match I'll just go and tell them no."

Ch'i-ch'iao held still for a moment before she went on sobbing.

Ch'ang-an paused to collect herself and went to telephone T'ung Shih-fang. Shih-fang did not have time that day, and arranged to meet her the next afternoon. What she dreaded most was the night in between, and it finally passed, each minute and every chime of the quarter hour sinking its teeth into her heart. The next day, at the old place in the park he came up smiling without greeting her; to him this was an expression of intimacy. He seemed to take special notice of her today, kept looking into her face as they walked shoulder to shoulder. With the sun shining brightly she was all the more conscious of her swollen eyelids and could hardly lift her eyes. Better say it while he was not looking at her. Hoarse from weeping, she whispered, "Mr. T'ung." He did not hear her. Then she'd better say it while he was looking at her. Surprised that she was still smiling slightly, she said in a small voice, "Mr. T'ung, I think—about us—perhaps we'd better —better leave it for now. I'm very sorry." She took off her ring and pushed it into his hand—cold gritty ring, cold gritty fingers. She quickened her pace walking away. After a stunned moment he caught up with her.

"Why? Not satisfied with me in some way?"

Ch'ang-an shook her head, looking straight ahead.

"Then why?"

"My mother . . ."

"Your mother has never seen me."

"I told you, it's not because of you, nothing to do with you. My mother . . ."

Shih-fang stood still. In China must her kind of reasoning be taken as fully adequate? As he hesitated, she was already some distance away.

The park had basked in the late autumn sun for a morning and an afternoon, and its air was now heavy with fragrance, like rotten-ripe fruit on a tree. Ch'ang-an heard, coming faintly in slow swings, the sound of a harmonica clumsily picking out "Long, Long Ago"—

"Tell me the tales that to me were so dear, long, long ago, long, long ago. . . ." This was *now*, but in the twinkling of an eye it would have become long, long ago and everything would be over. As if under a spell Ch'ang-an went looking for the person blowing the harmonica —looking for herself. Walking with her face to the sunlight, she came under a *wu-t'ung* tree with a boy in khaki shorts astride one of its forked branches. He was rocking himself and blowing his harmonica, but the tune was different, one she had never heard before. The tree was not big, and its sparse leaves shook in the sun like golden bells. Looking up, Ch'ang-an saw black as a shower of tears fell over her face. It was then that Shih-fang found her, and he stood quietly beside her for a while before he said, "I respect your opinion." She lifted her handbag to ward off the sun from her face.

They continued to see each other for a time. Shih-fang wanted to show that modern men do not make friends with women just to find a mate, and so although the engagement was broken he still asked her out often. As to Ch'ang-an, in what contradictory hopes she went out with him she herself did not know and would not have admitted if she had known. When they had been engaged and openly going out to-gether she still had had to guard her movements. Now her rendezvous were more secret than ever. Shih-fang's attitude remained straightfor-ward. Of course she had hurt his self-respect a little, and he also thought it a pity more or less, but as the saying goes, "a worthy man needn't worry about not having a wife." A man's highest compliment to a woman is a proposal. Shih-fang had pledged himself to relinquish his freedom. Although Ch'ang-an had declined his valuable offer, he had done her a service at no cost to himself.

No matter how subtle and awkward their relations were, they ac-tually became friends. They even talked. Ch'ang-an's naïveté often made Shih-fang laugh and say, "You're a funny one." Ch'ang-an also began to discover that she was an amusing person. Where matters could go from here might surprise Shih-fang himself.

But rumors reached Ch'i-ch'iao. Behind Ch'ang-an's back she or-dered Ch'ang-pai to send T'ung Shih-fang a written invitation to an informal dinner at home. Shih-fang guessed that the Chiangs might want to warn him not to persist in a friendship with their daughter after the break. But while he was talking with Ch'ang-pai over two

cups of wine about the weather, current politics, and local news in the
somber and high-ceilinged dining room, he noticed that nothing was
mentioned of Ch'ang-an. Then the cold dishes were removed. Ch'ang-
pai suddenly leaned his hands against the table and stood up. Shih-fang
looked over his shoulder and saw a small old lady standing at the doorway with her back to the light so that he could not see her face distinctly. She wore a blue-gray gown of palace brocade embroidered
with a round dragon design, and clasped with both hands a scarlet
hot-water bag; two big tall amahs stood close against her. Outside the
door the setting sun was smoky yellow, and the staircase covered with
turquoise plaid linoleum led up step after step to a place where there
was no light. Shih-fang instinctively felt this was a mad person. For no
reason there was a chill in all his hairs and bones.

"This is my mother," Ch'ang-pai introduced her.

Shih-fang moved his chair to stand up and bow. Ch'i-ch'iao walked
in with measured grace, resting a hand on an amah's arm, and after a
few civilities sat down to offer him wine and food.

"Where's Sister?" Ch'ang-pai asked. "Doesn't even come and help
when we have company."

"She's coming down after smoking a couple of pipes more," Ch'i-
ch'iao said.

Shih-fang was greatly shocked and stared intently at her.

Ch'i-ch'iao hurriedly explained, "It's such a pity this child didn't
have proper prenatal care. I had to puff smoke at her as soon as she
was born. Later, after bouts of illness, she acquired this habit of smoking. How very inconvenient for a young lady! It isn't that she hasn't
tried to break it, but her health is so very delicate and she has had her
way in everything for so long it's easier said than done. Off and on, it's
been ten years now."

Shih-fang could not help changing color. Ch'i-ch'iao had the caution
and quick wits of the insane. She knew if she was not careful people
would cut her short with a mocking incredulous glance; she was used
to the pain by now. Afraid that he would see through her if she talked
too much, she stopped in time and busied herself with filling wine cups
and distributing food. When Ch'ang-an was mentioned again she just
repeated these words lightly once more, her flat sharp voice cutting all
around like a razor blade.

Ch'ang-an came downstairs quietly, her embroidered black slippers and white silk stockings pausing in the dim yellow sunlight on the stairs. After stopping a while she went up again, one step after another, to where there was no light.

Ch'i-ch'iao said, "Ch'ang-pai, you drink a few more cups with Mr. T'ung. I'm going up."

The servants brought the soup called *i-p'in-kuo*, the "highest ranking pot," and changed the wine to Bamboo Leaf Green, newly heated. A nervous slave girl stood in the doorway and signaled the page waiting at the table to come out. After some whispering the boy came back to say a few words into Ch'ang-pai's ear. Ch'ang-pai got up flustered and apologized repeatedly to Shih-fang, "Have to leave you alone for a while, be right back," and also went upstairs, taking several steps in one.

Shih-fang was left to drink alone. Even the page felt apologetic. "Our Miss Chüan is about to give birth," he whispered to him.

"Who's Miss Chüan?" Shih-fang asked.

"Young Master's concubine."

Shih-fang asked for rice and made himself eat some of it. He could not leave the minute he set his bowl down, so he waited, sitting on the carved pearwood couch. Flushed from the wine, his ears hot, he suddenly felt exhausted and lay down. The scrollwork couch, with its ice-cold yellow rattan mat, the wintry fragrance of pomelos . . . the concubine having a baby. This was the ancient China he had been homesick for. . . . His quiet and demure well-born Chinese girl was an opium smoker! He sat up, his head in his hands, feeling unbearably lonely and estranged.

He took his hat and went out, telling the page, "Later please inform your master that I'll thank him in person another day."

He crossed the brick-paved courtyard where a tree grew in the center, its bare branches printed high in the sky like the lines in crackle china. Ch'ang-an quietly followed behind, watching him out. There were light yellow daisies on her navy blue long-sleeved gown. Her hands were clasped and she had a gentle look seldom seen on her face.

Shih-fang turned around to say, "Miss Chiang . . ."

She stood still a long way off and just bent her head. Shih-fang bowed slightly, turned, and left. Ch'ang-an felt as though she were viewing this sunlit courtyard from some distance away, looking down from a tall building. The scene was clear, she herself was involved but powerless to intervene. The court, the tree, two people trailing bleak shadows, wordless—not much of a memory, but still to be put in a crystal bottle and held in both hands to be looked at some day, her first and last love.

Chih-shou lay stiffly in bed, her two hands placed palms up on her ribs like the claws of a slaughtered chicken. The bed curtains were half up. Night or day she would not have them let down; she was afraid.

Word came that Miss Chüan had given birth to a son. The slave girl tending the steaming pot of herb medicine for Chih-shou ran out to share the excitement. A wind blew in through the open door and rattled the curtain hooks. The curtains slid shut of their own accord but Chih-shou did not protest any more. With a jerk to the right, her head rolled off the pillow. She did not die then, but dragged on for another fortnight.

Miss Chüan was made a wife and became Chih-shou's substitute. In less than a year she swallowed raw opium and killed herself. Ch'ang-pai dared not marry again, just went to brothels now and then. Ch'ang-an of course had long since given up all thoughts of marriage.

Ch'i-ch'iao lay half asleep on the opium couch. For thirty years now she had worn a golden cangue. She had used its heavy edges to chop down several people; those that did not die were half killed. She knew that her son and daughter hated her to the death, that the relatives on her husband's side hated her, and that her own kinsfolk also hated her. She groped for the green jade bracelet on her wrist and slowly pushed it up her bony arm as thin as firewood until it reached the armpit. She herself could not believe she'd had round arms when she was young. Even after she had been married several years the bracelet only left room enough for her to tuck in a handkerchief of imported crepe. As a girl of eighteen or nineteen, she would roll up the lavishly laced sleeves of her blue linen blouse, revealing a pair of snow-white wrists, and go to the market. Among those that liked her were Ch'ao-lu of the butcher shop; her brother's sworn brothers, Ting Yü-ken and Chang Shao-ch'üan, and also the son of Tailor Shen. To say that they liked her perhaps only means that they liked to fool around with her; but if she had chosen one of these, it was very likely that her man would have shown some real love as years went by and children were born. She moved the ruffled little foreign-styled pillow under her head and rubbed her face against it. On her other cheek a teardrop stayed until it dried by itself: she was too languid to brush it away.

After Ch'i-ch'iao passed away, Ch'ang-an got her share of property from Ch'ang-pai and moved out of the house. Ch'i-ch'iao's daughter would have no difficulty settling her own problems. Rumor had it that she was seen with a man on the street stopping in front of a stall where he bought her a pair of garters. Perhaps with her own money but out of the man's pocket anyway. Of course it was only a rumor.

The moon of thirty years ago has gone down long since and the people of thirty years ago are dead but the story of thirty years ago is not yet ended—can have no ending.

Nieh Hua-ling

A native of Yingshan, Hupeh, Nieh Hua-ling (1926–   ) belongs to the generation of Chinese who received their middle school and college education during the unsettled years of the Sino-Japanese War and its aftermath. She was only ten when her father, an army officer, fell in a battle against the Communist forces. Two years later she fled the Japanese to attend middle school in Chungking, and soon after her graduation from the Western Languages Department of National Central University in 1948, she again had to flee the Communists to begin her literary career in Taipei. Her short stories immediately attracted notice, and for almost eleven years she served as the literary editor of the outspoken journal of democratic opinion, *The Free China Fortnightly* (*Tzu-yu Chung-kuo*).

Nieh Hua-ling is among the few serious writers of her generation who brightened the literary scene in Taiwan at a time when little was being produced besides anti-Communist propaganda and escapist writing. Her short stories, collected in *The Green-jade Cat* (*Fei-ts'ui mao*, 1959) and *A Little White Flower* (*l-to hsiao-pai-hua*, 1963), are mostly ironic studies of the quiet desperation of middle-class men and women under all their surface gaiety and apparent satisfaction with their domestic and social routine. In 1961 Nieh Hua-ling published her first novel, *The Lost Golden Bell* (*Shih-ch'ü-ti chin-ling-tzu*; revised edition, 1964), drawing upon her memories of the war years. The "golden bell" in question is a species of tiny cricket prized by the Chinese for its melodious chirp, and it serves in the novel as a symbol of happiness or fulfillment. Despite is more mature craftsmanship, in its didactic tendency and its concern with the blighted lives of young women under the feudal family system the novel curiously reminds one of Pa Chin's overrated prewar novel *Family* (*Chia*).

Nieh Hua-ling has translated three of her four stories gathered in

The Purse (Taipei, Heritage Press, 1962) and included another story, "Camellia," in a volume edited by herself, *Eight Stories by Chinese Women*. Since coming to the United States in 1964, she has earned the degree of Master of Fine Arts at the University of Iowa and now serves as associate director of the International Writing Program there.

"The Several Blessings of Wang Ta-nien" (first published in *The Atlantic Monthly*, December, 1966, under the title "The Several Blessings of Ta-nien Wang") is a condensed adaptation of "Dinner" (*Wants'an*), included in *The Purse*. The two stories are radically different in intent, however. Whereas "Dinner," a typical story of Miss Nieh's Taipei period, gives a full, vivid account of two old classmates at a meal, mixing reminiscences with half-serious plans for financial independence, "Blessings" has eliminated much of the banter and reminiscence to concentrate on the hero's plan of breeding fish. He becomes at once more serious and pathetic, and quite intentionally all the descriptive and symbolic details are chosen to make him stand for Taiwan with its militant preparedness, its grandiose dreams for the future, and its actual helplessness (the rickety chair finally collapses under him). The story marks a new departure for the author and merits praise as a rare instance of Chinese political satire which blends ridicule with compassion. In revising the story, I have consulted its Chinese version entitled *Wang Ta-nien ti chi-chien hsi-shih*, which appeared in *The Crown Magazine* (*Huang-kuan Tsa-chih*), XXVII, No. 2 (Taipei, 1967).

THE SEVERAL
BLESSINGS OF
WANG TA-NIEN

Having served under three "emperors"—his own name for the principals—Wang Ta-nien became privileged to occupy a small house shaded by two palm trees, one in a series of three rows situated behind the school. He had lived with his wife and two sons in a single room as cramped as a chicken coop. Now they had a kitchen and a somewhat larger all-purpose room, though the furniture in the latter remained the same: two double beds made of bamboo, a table and four rattan chairs with legs bound with wire, a desk badly in need of a coat of paint, and a bookcase made by Ta-nien himself out of wooden crates.

There was also a mirror on the wall, and taped to its lower edge was a schedule. It now hung loosely, since a piece of tape had got unstuck. Every morning Ta-nien stood opposite the mirror studying his directions for the day's work, his head cocked and his teeth clenched with determination. The tape, however, remained unstuck, and every day the schedule dangled worse.

THE SCHEDULE OF TA-NIEN

Morning

6:30   I do fifty push-ups. I do deep breathing.

7:00   I listen to English lessons on the radio with an English-Chinese dictionary.

7:30   I read the *Speeches of Chiang Kai-shek.*

Evening

8:00   I read the *Speeches of Richard Nixon.*

10:00   I listen to English lessons on the radio with an English-Chinese dictionary.

11:00   I do fifty push-ups before going to bed.

Soon after the unexpected award of a house, Ta-nien's emperor bestowed upon him two further blessings: a bonus and a certificate of meritorious teaching:

This is to certify to the outstanding service rendered the First High School, Taipei, Taiwan, during the period from September 1961 to August 1965. . . .

"Wen-ch'in," Ta-nien cried triumphantly, holding the certificate which he had already recited to his wife a dozen times. "Wen-ch'in, our luck has turned at last! Who knows what good fortune awaits us tomorrow? Let's prepare something special for the Sage [1] this Sunday."

Little Oak, his four-year-old son in a G. I. cap, began goosestepping proudly. He sensed his father's triumphant mood.

The windows of Ta-nien's house were steamed with the fumes of pork being fried, with cigarette smoke and vapors from a boiling kettle. There were also baby odors compounded of urine and soap.

These odors and fumes swirled between ceiling and floor and found

[1] Ta-nien calls his friend by the affectionate but patronizing nickname *Fu-tzu* (learned teacher, master, sage). Confucius is known in Chinese as K'ung Fu-tzu (Master K'ung).

no outlet while the rain, fitfully furious, tried to get in through the tightly shut windows.

"Sage," Ta-nien tried to cheer up his old friend, "why so downcast? Good times are with us once again! Why, the way things are booming here and the way they're going to hell in a handcar over *there*, we'll be back on the mainland by this time next year!"

The Sage shook his head slightly: all his movements were cautious and unobtrusive. Inurement to the routine of a small provincial school had given him a vacant facial expression, a monotonous voice, and a smile that apologized to everyone all day long.

"We can never get those good years back," murmured the Sage to himself while casting a dull look at Wen-ch'in. He had long entertained the hope of inviting Ta-nien and Wen-ch'in to a restaurant for Peking duck. Every Sunday, as he dined here, this hope had returned. Yet even now as he was about to extend his invitation, he saw, in raising his wine cup, how frayed his sleeves had become. So all he said was, "To you, Wen-ch'in."

And as he drank, his eyes still upon her, he was once again reminded how time had marred her face: years ago, it was as bright as the moon on a night when the sky is clear. Now crow's-feet had frayed her eyes as poverty his sleeves, and her belly was swollen again.

He remembered her youthful figure moving along a bridge poised between two clusters of willows. One cluster would shine in the morning, and the other at sunset. That particular late afternoon she was walking toward him and toward the sunlit willows in a vermilion sweater and a white silk scarf. Later, they strolled together down Lovers' Lane.

"Stop staring at my wife, Sage," Ta-chien admonished his friend good-naturedly. "You had your chance and missed it."

"I never deserved her," acknowledged the Sage. "The better man won."

"I can't say that between you two I had a wide choice," Wen-ch'in interposed. She was chronically angry with her husband but did not find his presence bothersome; she could never get angry with the Sage but everything he did irked her.

"I'm eating you out of house and home," the Sage apologized as he apologized every Sunday.

"There is always a place for you here," Ta-nien reassured him as he did every Sunday. "Now—I wish to speak seriously: I have a plan which will make us both independent."

The Sage stroked his chin and stopped eating out of respect for his host.

"But it is strictly confidential," Ta-nien warned his friend.

"What else?" Wen-ch'in put in quickly. "Wasn't the prep school confidential? Wasn't the chain of correspondence courses confidential? Wasn't the plan for a farm confidential? Perhaps this time you'd better advertise."

Ta-nien ignored his wife with studied scorn. He straightway crossed his legs in the fashion of a Buddhist monk and sat up in his rattan chair with a show of self-importance.

"This time we've got to be resolute," he declared.

"Very resolute," the Sage promptly agreed without the faintest notion of his part in the latest plan. "I'm ready for The Plan," he assured Ta-nien.

"Breed fish!" Ta-nien announced his plan to the waiting world.

"Breed fish?" echoed the Sage as though it had just occurred to him that fish reproduced.

"Fish?" Wen-ch'in cut in. "Are all fish the same? What kind of fish? Eels? Mackerel? Bream? Carp?"

"Why"—Ta-nien grinned sheepishly; it had apparently not occurred to him that there was more than one kind—"why, carp, of course," he added quickly.

"The ducks will get the small fry," Wen-ch'in gave her verdict on the plan. "Hoodlums will electrify the pond to kill off what the ducks don't get. Or else they will die for lack of fresh water. Your fish will starve. So will your family."

"Now for the second step," Ta-nien went on, as if his wife hadn't said a word.

"What was the first?" she demanded.

"First, we clean out the pond. Second, we fertilize it. Third, we put in the fry. And finally, our Sage here guards our investment day and night, protecting us from ducks, hoodlums, and all disasters."

The Sage gave a start and turned pale. "I would have to leave the school," he reminded Ta-nien upon regaining his composure. "If it didn't work, I'd be jobless. You're asking me to take a great risk, Ta-nien."

"What? Are you going to go about with frayed sleeves all your life?"

"But, Ta-nien, I don't know how to breed fish," the Sage pleaded weakly.

"This is the age of specialization, old friend," Ta-nien assured him firmly. "Breeding fish will be my responsibility. Guarding them will be yours. Nothing ventured, nothing gained. Right?"

Wen-ch'in furtively shook her head at the Sage. She did so sadly and slowly as if to warn him not to keep up the game.

"I'll have to have a week to think it over," the Sage finally said.

"One week—but no more. We're now operating on a tight schedule, Sage," Ta-nien said. "A week is all we can let you have."

The Sage wondered who the "we" could be, but did not press the question for fear of embarrassing his host.

"Fry cost about seven cents each," Ta-nien went on. "Let's buy, say, twenty thousand. A grown carp sells for about nineteen dollars [2] in the market. But we'll sell wholesale at about ten. Now, tell me, Sage, how many dollars shall we take in by selling twenty thousand carp?"

The Sage blinked his eyes with the effort of calculation. "Two hundred thousand?"

"Two hundred thousand exactly!" Ta-nien slapped him on the shoulder in his state of imagined jubilation.

"How will you get the fish to the market?" Wen-ch'in asked.

Ta-nien poured himself a cup of wine and then answered without relinquishing the bottle, "One problem at a time, Madame."

"I'll join you in the venture," the Sage said with some enthusiasm. "But if we fail, I'll be jobless."

"When Daddy gets money, I want a whole sackful of chewing gum," Little Oak put in.

"And a dancing monkey as well," Wen-ch'in said. "You can count on your daddy. 'I do fifty push-ups,'" she mimicked him, "'I read the Speeches of Richard Nixon.'"

"Shut the window, woman!" Ta-nien got up from his seat and shouted.

[2] NT $40 (Taiwan currency) equals one U.S. dollar.

"It's not open," Wen-ch'in replied.

"Ta-nien." The Sage made him sit down in the creaking rattan chair and patted him on the shoulder. "Don't shout at her. You're a lucky dog. A wonderful wife, two lovely kids."

A whimpering came from the bed. Wen-ch'in dropped her chopsticks and rushed to the baby. "The little devil! Soil your diaper and stink up the room just when we're having dinner."

"She doesn't appreciate me," Ta-nien complained to the Sage.

"He means he cares for nobody but himself," Wen-ch'in said.

"If only there were more people in the world like you," the Sage paid Wen-ch'in a compliment as if he really meant it.

"Little Oak!" Ta-nien had now regained his good mood. "Hup, two, three, four! Hup, two, three, four!"

The boy promptly slid off his chair. Twisting his head to the right, straightening his shoulders, and holding his neck stiff, he began goose-stepping past Ta-nien.

"He's reviewing his troops," explained Wen-ch'in. She was seated on the edge of the bed nursing the baby.

The Sage could not refrain from laughing and choked on the piece of pork he had just put in his mouth. Ta-nien, however, said abruptly, "Sage, I was thinking of our school days on the mainland. You were then really quite active."

"He *was* a poet," Wen-ch'in commented.

"I knew a little about everything, but now can't claim to be expert in anything," confessed the Sage.

"I didn't like your dandified ways," Ta-nien recalled.

"I thought you were too uppish."

"Mama," Little Oak said, "I'm going outside. If Daddy and Uncle come to blows, call me."

"I had a right to put on airs," Ta-nien said with self-assurance. "At one time three girls were after me. One was the daughter of a high-ranking official. She used to wait for me at the corner of Lovers' Lane, and I didn't even look at her."

"How could you know she was waiting for you if you didn't even cast her a single glance?" Wen-ch'in asked. "Talk on!"

"Look at her, Sage! She's jealous. Back then, I tell you, if I'd only shown a little interest, huh!" Ta-nien stopped and gave his head a vigorous nod.

"Little Oak, here's a piece of spare rib for you!" Wen-ch'in called after her son.

Rushing back, he grabbed it, took a bite, and put it down again. "Mama—too cold."

Wen-ch'in flung it into Ta-nien's rice bowl.

Ta-nien shook his head, putting on the look of an injured husband. "You see, in my wife's eyes I've become a bear in the zoo and she's my trainer."

Little Oak clapped his hands with delight and shouted: "Daddy's a bear in the zoo! Daddy's a bear in the zoo!"

Ta-nien bellowed with laughter at his own joke. Then he leaned back and the chair collapsed with a snap. All three around him dashed to his rescue, and the baby, aroused from his sleep, yelled. Ta-nien struggled to get up, but to no avail. Finally the Sage got his arms under his shoulders and raised him to his feet.

"Thank you, thank you," Ta-nien said, debating whether he should appear angry or pleased. Then he kicked at the wrecked chair. "Damn it, throw it out! I don't want to see it again!"

"I'd like to treat you to Peking duck next Sunday," the Sage announced suddenly.

"No, Sage," Wen-ch'in said, holding her crying baby and patting it on the back. "Save your money and buy yourself a new suit."

"You think so little of me! I, Ho Cheng . . ." He approached Wen-ch'in with a forefinger on his own nose. "I haven't taught all these years for nothing, have I? I at least know how to get an advance of a month's salary!"

"Aiya," Ta-nien complained, "I'm getting old. Just falling off a chair has given me a backache." Sitting on the edge of the bed, he tapped himself above the hips with his fists.

"What difference does it make?" The Sage waved his hand gallantly. "Let's sing while the wine lasts, for life is brief, like the morning dew."

The rain had not quite stopped when the Sage took his leave. Ta-nien and his wife saw him to the door. Under the dim street lights they watched him walk to the turn.

"Sage!" Wen-ch'in called after him.

The Sage turned and stood waiting with his hand cupped to his ear.

"Don't let the ducks eat the fish!" Wen-ch'in shouted into the wind, and then hurried back into the house, slamming the door hard behind her.

For a long while the two men stood looking at each other, too far apart to converse about life's problems. The wind in the palms above them whispered a warning, but neither seemed to catch its import. Finally the Sage turned off down the narrowing road. Ta-nien watched until he was out of sight.

The wind that had once blown through the bright willows now rose in the two palms around Ta-nien's house, casting a chill spell. But turning inside, he pretended to feel afraid of nothing in the whole wide windy world.

Shui Ching

Shui Ching (pen name of Yang Yi) is not so well-known among Chinese readers as some of the more prolific authors, since he has published so far only a collection of short stories, *The Green Grasshopper* (*Ch'ing-sê ti cha-meng*, 1967), and a volume mainly of essays, *Brickbats* (*P'ao-chuan chi*, 1969). But I have no reason to doubt that he is one of the most original and accomplished short story writers in Chinese today. If he continues to experiment in his deliberate, conscientious fashion and keeps up his ambition not to write anything unworthy of his talent, he should in time win general recognition as a major writer.

Shui Ching (1935–   ) is a native of Nantung, Kiangsu. Like so many other serious young writers of Taiwan, he is a graduate of the Foreign Languages Department of National Taiwan University where he profited from the instruction of my late brother Tsi-an Hsia. A prolific contributor to magazines and newspapers in his nonage, by 1961 he had turned into a serious writer, and every story written since, while it may not adequately realize his artistic intentions, bears evidence of his painstaking labor to enrich his style, to use myth and symbol, and to profit from his study of modern Western masters. He is also well read in classical Chinese poetry and prose and has publicly avowed himself a disciple of Eileen Chang.

The Green Grasshopper collects ten stories written between 1961 and 1966. The best known of these is "A Man without a Face" (*Mei-yu-lien-ti jen*), a deeply moving story embodying the most successful attempt by a Chinese to adopt the stream of consciousness method. Since the publication of that volume Shui Ching has published "The Bell" (*Chung*, 1968), a superb novella of what were presumably his own school experiences in Nanking. It is told in terms of a primitive ritual and fraught with deep meaning. A translation of either story would, I believe, easily impress the Western reader with Shui Ching's talent, but "Hi Lili Hi Li . . ." is no less striking even though it is debatable whether this story should be taken as a *tour de force* or genuine philosophic fiction of the most serious kind. But although few Chinese authors have gone beyond the Chinese setting to treat such a momentous theme as the ultimate relapse of civilization into barbarism, the story would seem to indicate that at least one contemporary short story writer has fallen spiritual heir to the despair and irrationalism of modern Western literature.

The story makes use of the author's personal experience in Brunei, Borneo, where he served for a few years as a teacher and broadcaster before resuming his studies at the University of British Columbia and the University of Iowa. Since the Chinese population in so many parts of Southeast Asia lives a precarious life without adequate legal protection, the hero's awakening one Monday morning into an unrecognizable world of violent change objectifies a fear rooted in everyday reality. During his nightmarish wandering, he desperately seeks human contact, and with each successive failure the jungle seems more and more to take over civilization, until he is finally ready to succumb to the spell of his former sweetheart emerging from the limitless stretch of primeval forest by the barren sea. The story ends on a note of unresolved irony—indicative of the author's ambivalence regarding both civilization and primitivism. "Hi Lili Hi Li . . . ," which makes sense in English, appears as a series of nonsensical syllables in Chinese.

HI LILI HI LI...

TRANSLATED BY *the author*
and C. T. Hsia

"One day our civilization, whether sublimations or frivolities,
will all become the past."—Eileen Chang, "Preface to the
Second Edition of *Romances*"

Upon waking, Y finds the tropical morning sun perching upon his
eyelids like a persistent mosquito. His pupils instantly contract like a
cat's, and his eyelids feel stiff and heavy. He hadn't slept well last
night. Tossing and turning just because someone had forgotten to turn
tightly the faucet in the washroom next door. He felt as if the monotonous trickle, like the endless dripping of a water clock, had drilled a
hole in his head and caused his old memories to spill. At this instant his
skull, scooped clean of its contents, could roll a long way with one
kick, like a dried coconut shell.

A stiff pain goes over Y's whole body—the symptom of an im-
pending illness that he cannot trifle with or, worse, the omen of a natural or political calamity? For a Chinese living in the South Sea Is-
lands, no place offers true security. Recently the celestial signs have
boded ill: all those meteors and solar eclipses can only bring about a
period of war and famine. No wonder cholera has broken out again
and is getting more menacing every day in the city. Some old supersti-
tions, however absurd, simply cannot be eliminated from one's subcon-

scious. So then, he asks himself, what prompted you to leave the island bastion of your own country for this overseas island, sun-baked and barren? Huge tropical flowers, girls wrapped in rich-colored sarongs, exotic, percussive music—things that set Gauguin's canvas aglow —can be found only in Tahiti. Here, you can see only stretches of primitive jungle or waves of the as yet uncharted sea beating against the coast.

Y looks at the picture of the Crucifixion on the wall, which he has been too lazy to remove. The former tenant must have been a Christian, and a devout one, too, he thinks. The emaciated Christ, a crown of thorns on his drooping head and a torn cloth around his loins, is hitched up on the cross. One of his legs is drawn upward, and blood oozes from his palms and soles.

Under the dying stare of Christ is Y's desk. A ray of sunlight rests upon the book which Y was reading last night: a new biography of Oscar Wilde. On its jacket appears the lust-ravaged face of Wilde which, pallid and swollen, offers a sharp contrast to the dolorous countenance of the crucified Christ.

Y walks to the washroom next door. The faucet is still dripping, leaving a rusty stain on the sink. The water must have changed color again. Thanks to the malfunctioning of the city government, the water supply frequently assumes the color of milk, occasionally that of urine. When Y turns on the faucet, as he has expected, a stream of yellow muddy water that faintly smells of urine gushes out. No shaving today, he tells himself, and get the washing done quick!

Toilet done, Y is walking back to his own room when he turns his head and notices on the cement floor the head of a rat. A few scattered blood stains right by it reinforce his belief that the debris must have been left by the Siamese cat making his regular prowl last night. The rat must have been of medium size, and although the head has been sawed off the body by the cat's teeth, it remains intact with its sparse whiskers, its protruding teeth, and its beady eyes staring at the world with a sort of fatuous twinkle. There is an American poet who, upon revisiting the site where a groundhog had lain dead three summers ago, could think

> Of China and of Greece,
> Of Alexander in his tent;

> Of Montaigne in his tower,
> Of Saint Theresa in her wild lament.[1]

Y bends down to examine the triangular face of the dead rat and feels a slight attack of nausea.

Y returns to his bedroom and switches on his transistor radio, hoping to receive some news from the outside world and iron out the ruffled feelings of a blue Monday morning. But there is only the plip-plop of static noise; neither the suave voice of Radio Australia's announcer nor the insistent, illogical message from the land of his ancestors can be heard.

"Must be due to the intervention of a sun-spot explosion," Y murmurs under his breath as he starts for the doorway.

A gray wall blocks his way, as if it marked the world's end, with no exit leading to any place, to any hope. Every morning, as he steps outside the door, he is seized by a sense of fear that he is being incarcerated in a prison, even though what he confronts is only a block of wall, a coarse ugly wall of plastered gray bricks.

Presently Y is pacing along the sidewalk of the asphalt main street. Bungalows remain exotic to him, perched as they are upon stilts, three feet above ground, to keep them from the malarial vapors rising from the earth. Roofs, walls, window lattices compose a somewhat unreal pattern of strange colors found only in fairy tales or in toyland.

The sun-baked earth sends forth spirals of steam. This is truly a miasmal land of barbarians—to hear the gurgling sound of streams meandering down the mountains, one has to go elsewhere! Hearing the tap-tap-tap of his footsteps, Y feels the rubble rapidly rolling away from his soles. The sun has melted his shirt into a gluey sheet of pressed bean curd, and it sticks to his back.

A clammy sense of dread now clings to him like his shirt. No, how can the whole street be so deserted at eight on a Monday morning? Not a person, a car to be seen? Intuitively, Y links the implacable calm of the present moment to the strange sensation he had when he woke

---

[1] These lines from "The Groundhog" are quoted from Richard Eberhart, *Collected Poems 1930–1960.* Copyright © 1960 by Richard Eberhart. Reprinted by permission of the author and Oxford University Press, Inc.

up this morning and asks himself: Could his uneasiness be traced to the unusual quiet around him?

He hastens his steps and feels the rubble rolling faster and faster from the sides of his shoes. The sense of fear now presses harder on him, as if he were passing through a graveyard at midnight. He turns around, and the main street, the bungalows, the coconut palms with their octopus-shaped heads of broad leaves, and the spirals of steam rising from the ground all look reassuringly the same as before. But where are the people? The people?

Heeding the premonition of a storm, Y examines the bungalows searchingly. The wooden windows are all tightly shut (glass windows are not common here) as if the occupants were still sound asleep, and the doors all bolted.

Y cannot imagine what could have happened overnight. In this changeable, often (to him) treacherous world, something untoward always happens just when he is completely off guard. Quick, he tells himself, be off to the broadcasting station where you work and find out.

The thought gives him some comfort. Hurrying, he arrives at the radio station.

The iron-wire fence still surrounds the station but the wicket, as if someone has forgotten to latch it, is swinging back and forth. Y slinks in and latches the wicket behind him. A glance at the sentry box shows that the dark brown guard, a member of the local royal armed forces customarily stationed there in his blue-black French cap and blue-black denim shorts, is missing. Y hesitates for a while, his eyes hurt by the brilliance of a cluster of rosebushes along the fence set afire by the sun. A black sparrow with red eyes—all the sparrows here are like that—hops for a while before flying off into the sky.

Full of apprehension, Y goes toward the station, but even inside the building not a soul can be seen and not a sound heard. And the day, he remembers only too well, is Monday, a workday. As he approaches the second floor, he is so petrified by what he sees on the wall facing the staircase that unwittingly he backs down one step.

All over the white wall are assorted bloody handprints, one upon another in total confusion. Among these handprints is a line of words in Islamic script, also written in blood. Y cannot decipher the meaning of this, but from the exclamation marks—there are, altogether, three of them, each bigger than the preceding one—he instantly senses the threatening weight the line carries.

Insurrection? A coup? Oh, heavens, now he knows why the whole street is deserted and why the windows and doors are all shut! In this part of the world a newly independent state, once it enjoys an excess of democracy and freedom, will behave like a pauper who has won the biggest lottery prize. It will spurn reason and turn mad!

What time is this, Y checks himself, to indulge in ineffectual moralizing? He holds tight to the railing, to steady himself. At the same time, his left palm is upon his brow, in an attempt to collect his thoughts. His soles are glued to one of the stairs for what seems a long while. In this eternal moment he doesn't know whether to retreat or advance. Retreat—who knows if the station is not already surrounded by rebels? Advance—what if his office has already been occupied by them?

The next moment Y finds the back of his head pressed against the tiled wall of the washroom because, he has convinced himself, this is the least important room in the building. Unless the rebels want to search the place, they would never bother to come here. But wait, what if they want to piss?

At this critical moment, he recalls with perverse futility a story he has read—was it by Sartre or Camus?—in which the anti-hero, a convict or fugitive, breaks jail and takes refuge in a washroom. Finally he surrenders because, with his cartridges all used up, he can no longer defy the law.

But I am innocent, he tells himself, why should I subject myself to this treatment? Why should I be in this sad but ridiculous quandary? What have I done?

At last Y summons enough courage to leave the washroom, hardly a place for a man to be captured in. He wants to preserve his dignity to the end. Moreover, even if he should be caught, he could always tell the rebels that he is but an alien resident. Maybe they would treat him not too badly, and perhaps do no worse than deport him. But—how could he account for his being an employee of the overthrown government?

While thus lost in thought, he has already stepped into the News Room—too late to back out now. Luckily there are no armed rebels in the room. He heaves a sigh of relief and smells the more keenly the stale air that has been confined in the room overnight. But the air is at the same time foul and rank as if it were newly released from a refrigerator stocked with meats and vegetables which has not functioned for days. He turns on the switch for the electric fan on the wall. But its four blades refuse to move—apparently, the power supply for the city must have failed. Y then sinks into his boss's high-backed swivel chair. For better security he turns its back so that it faces the window.

Keeping his eyes on the door, he begins to dial the telephone, trying to get in touch with police headquarters to find out what really has happened. Thank goodness, the line has not been cut, but the noise from the receiver—bleep, bleep, bleep—deafens his ear. He holds the receiver some distance from his ear, but the insistent noise continues and no one answers. He counts the bleeps and then has to hang up.

He tries several other places: the newspapers, the telecommunication bureau, the municipal building. But there is no answer—only the monotonous ringing at the other end of the telephone.

He tries in all seven places and then slams the receiver back onto the hook. Either the world has gone crazy or I have lost my senses, he murmurs to himself.

Then the telephone suddenly rings loud and clear as an alarm clock. Excited, he grabs the receiver. Once again the buzzing deafens him but now he eagerly presses the receiver against his ear as if afraid he might lose contact forever.

But a few moments later the receiver no longer transmits any sound. The telephone line must have been cut. The telephone that was alive in his hand a moment ago is now dead. Dejectedly he holds on to the receiver for a long time before replacing it.

Y can imagine that the party at the other end of the line must have also dejectedly replaced the telephone. He must have been as desperate as I, trying to get in touch with the radio station. Did he run into the same snag as I did? Why couldn't we make contact before the line snapped?

On the desk is a pile of teletype news from the Control Room. Y scans it and finds that the latest items of news had come in by 9:30 last evening. Since then this small town has been out of contact with the world. He checks the teletype again to see if there is any news about the coup or insurrection. Then he realizes that should there be any it would be sometime after 9:30 P.M.

What can Y do? The town is now in a state of ominous calm preceding the storm, and they, whoever they are, have just cut the telephone line. Very soon they will send out men to occupy strategical points, including the broadcasting station. He had better get out of here before the rebels swarm in.

Where to go? Will it be safe in the streets? If by chance he should be shot dead, it would have been better to remain in this room and wait for the worst. No, it would be better to be back at the dormitory. There he still has a few cans of food and can stave off hunger for a day or two. The tumult will sooner or later subside, whatever its outcome.

Then, distinctly, he hears someone starting a car. He is all ears, trying to tell from which direction the noise comes. It comes from across the fence and he hopes that the car will turn around to the front directly under his window so that he may have a clear view of who is behind the wheel. If it is not one of the rebels (they would presumably wear some kind of insignia), he will yell aloud to get the driver's attention and then he will be saved.

The humming of the starting motor gradually fills the room, and his hope rises with it. Then, to his dismay, the car apparently swerves to the back of the building. The driver seems in such a hurry that he jams the gear several times before he catches up with the speed. The wheels scraping the ground send off a screech. Eventually the driver seems to have made his way out. The deafening noise recedes.

The room is restored to calm, and the foul air assails his nose with renewed intensity.

It must be one of my friends, Y thinks, at least an acquaintance, who has left me in the lurch. Don't be too hard on him, though. How could he know I'm stranded here?

Very soon Y is plodding along once again under the sun, in the direction of his dormitory. He has chosen the side streets and back alleys, to avoid being a victim of stray bullets.

The white sun now radiates intenser heat so that Y feels like a pa-

tient dying of scarlet fever: dizzy, thirsty, talking incoherently to himself, and in the end almost fainting. Then he comes to, though his
cheeks are feverish and his eyes glazed. They stare at the world as if
reluctant to leave it.

For only a few days Y hasn't been to this street, but the grass on the
curbside has grown to the level of his eyes. He passes by the iron-wire
fence of a basketball field, along which the grass is even knottier and
more luxuriant. Walking in its shade, Y feels as if the sun has suddenly
darkened, even though the tallest blades of grass glisten skyward like
uplifted swords. Made uneasy by this incredible overgrowth, he continues walking, enveloped in the smell of verdure. Occasionally he
hears the rustle of wings among the leaves as the grasshoppers, disturbed by his approach, fly ahead for a more secure hiding-place.

He makes a turn, and right in the middle of the street a massive
black thing confronts him. It bears some resemblance to a car. Upon
closer inspection, it is indeed a car, but turned upside down like a bee-
tle lying on its back, unable to reverse its position. On what remains of
every broken windowpane are fine cracks like magnified crow's feet on
an old man's face. The exposed engine, burned black, is totally man-
gled. Someone must have wrecked the car before setting fire to it.

Riot . . . violence . . . Y hurriedly retraces his steps even though his
eyes continue to take in every sight like a camera. Blindly he makes
several turns, completely unaware that, in case of a riot, his aimless
dashing about can only court disaster.

Finally, after several such turns, his mechanical steps have carried
him to the end of a street. Ahead of him lies a wide expanse with no
buildings around it. It is paved all over with sharp, small fragments of
stone on top of which floats a layer of powder-white stone-dust. The
area directly beyond looks totally unfamiliar, and he is far more
numbed with fear than when he discovered the overturned car.
Quickly turning back, he sees a hospital with its front gate wide open.
He walks in unhesitatingly: his common sense tells him that the hospital is as much a sanctuary for refugees as is the church for penitent sin-
ners.

Gusts of cool breeze stroke his burning cheeks. He is now walking
under a Moslem-style dome along a corridor with white-plastered
walls. The sun floods exactly one half of the corridor while the other

half lies in darkness. The apparently deserted corridor is pervaded with a slight but unmistakable medicinal odor. Y can hear his own rhythmic footsteps, which sound hollow under the dome.

Now he has reached the door at the other end of the corridor. A victim of shock, he cautiously inclines his head to listen at the door. When he has made sure there are no movements inside, he gently pushes it open.

The door opens on an enormous sickroom, with a row of beds extending on either side. White sheets, white pillows lying neatly where the sheets are tucked in, the white paint on the iron frames and legs of the beds, the white in-patient cards hanging on pegs constitute a symmetrical pattern in white. There are twenty beds on one side, Y counts with his eyes, and there are twenty on the other.

Y walks ahead along the aisle, his steps again sounding hollow in the vault-like room. The beds on either side look like Egyptian mummies swathed in white cloth, a monotonous and dizzying pattern suggestive of Pop Art. Finally giddy, he trips and falls onto the last bed on the right row. His head against the soft pillow, he wants to take a nap: the happenings this morning have been too exhausting.

But he is immediately bothered by the sound of dripping which, upon first hearing, he takes to be that of his heartbeat. The noise, however, comes from the adjacent room, Ward No. 4. In desperation for a human companion, be he ever so sick, he gets up from bed and goes into the other room.

The medicinal odor is much stronger there. The ward is much smaller than the other, and also darker, because its blinds are tightly drawn. Each of the beds is screened from view by a white cloth curtain. Hung high on a hook outside the curtain of the second bed, however, is a bottle of saline solution. The drip-drop he has heard must have proceeded from this bottle because its mouth is no longer properly connected with the tube that injects the fluid into the patient's arm. It drips onto the floor. Looking downward, he sees an outstretched brown hand with its palm turned upward, though he cannot tell whether it belongs to a man or woman. As he rushes toward the extended hand, he stumbles upon a pail near the bed. A mop leaning against the pail hits the floor with a thud.

The pail soon regains its balance. Y peers inside and sees a layer of clammy, white fluid laced with streaks of blood and dotted with dark purple clots of what seem to be vomit. A fly hovers above the liquid before settling again on one of the clots.

Y realizes with the swiftness of lightning that he must have stumbled into a special ward for quarantined cholera patients. Hasn't there been an outbreak of cholera in this city? What lies at the bottom of the pail must be vomit. The outstretched hand under the bottle must belong to a cholera patient—maybe he is dead already?

Y wants to get out fast. In his hurry he brushes aside the white curtain and catches a glimpse of the patient in white smock and cap. He lies prone, his head over the side of the bed. His posture suggests that death caught him while he was making a last valiant attempt to empty all the contents of his stomach into the pail. The tube must have gotten loose from the bottle during his last struggle.

Suddenly a large amount of stomach acid gushes into Y's mouth. Covering it with his hand, he dashes out of the hospital through the enormous sickroom. Then he leans against a big tree outside the porch, and vomits mouthfuls of acid water because he hasn't had any breakfast this morning. But even though he throws up no food, the muscles in his throat feel sore after repeated contractions. Then, his vomiting done, he saunters to another big tree and sits upon its exposed roots. Heaving a sigh, he shuts his eyes to take a rest.

Y is now plodding along a seashore trail that leads to S town. He still cannot be quite sure what really happened in his own city. Coup? Riot? A severe epidemic of cholera? Perhaps all three concurrently? He must walk to S, a small town about twenty miles from where he lives, and get the news. Afraid that he might meet rebels if he took the main road, he has picked this trail, a pathway seldom trodden.

On his right lies the vast stretch of the South China Sea which has dozed under the sun, forlorn and forgotten, for thousands of years. Never have any sailboats or steamships emerged from its distant horizon. Even the pirates' ships do not stop here, because the island is too barren.

The sky is now gray, but the sea is grayer. The sun, however, shines on its surface and livens up its color. Heaps of cumulus clouds are piled up on the distant horizon.

Under his feet is a long stretch of sand whose silvery color indicates its high silicic content. The trail, therefore, looks as if it were paved with ashes—the kind of ashes poured from censers. The sand is dotted with pebbles, and here and there embedded among the pebbles are thistles flaunting their tiny, star-shaped white blossoms.

On his left, for mile after mile—maybe even hundreds of miles—lies the dark, primitive jungle.

A solitary pine emerges from the roadside, a noble specimen like those found in classical Chinese paintings. Leaning against its gnarled trunk, under its shade, Y steals a glance at his wrist watch.

It has stopped. Pressing its crystal against his ear, he is unable to hear its familiar tick-tock—surely it has stopped. Its hands point to 9:30: hard to tell whether it stopped last evening or this morning. He winds it up and lets it run its own course, since he doesn't know the correct time.

Then it occurs to him that he has become almost another Robinson Crusoe on a deserted island. Time has lost its importance for him; what difference does it make if he cannot tell the exact hour of the day?

But he cannot help wondering that, from the moment he rushed out of the Special Ward, vomiting and then leaning against the tree for a rest, until he started walking on the seaside trail, there could be no more than an hour's time altogether. Tilting back his head to watch the sun, he reckons that it must be between ten and ten thirty in the morning.

But suddenly the sun hides itself behind the clouds, and he feels somewhat chilly as a gust of wind rising from the sea blows against him. He no longer feels the heat of the sun even though it still shines on him. The sun behind the clouds looks to him as if it were screened by a sheet of dark-yellow translucent paper: it transmits only light, but no heat. His skin feels cold and clammy as if soaked in water. Could this be another eclipse? Three days ago as he left his office during the lunch hour, he remembers, the sun was in eclipse and transmitted only light and no heat, as it does now. The disgraced sun is no more potent than the moon. The sun in Dante's Inferno is probably like that. That noon, in proportion as the honking of cars and bicycles sounded muffled, the burden of terror in his heart increased until he felt as if doomsday were near. He knew, though, that the eclipse is but a natu-

ral phenomenon and cannot last more than half an hour, or an hour at
most.

That noon he was walking in a bustling street; now, alone in a
deserted spot under a vast sky, he feels even more helpless. He feels as
if something heavy and hideous like an incubus were pressing hard on
his chest. He wants to cry out, to dispel the nightmare, but he feels
limp and impotent.

He gets up, looking beseechingly around him.

To his great relief, he notices a human form emerging from the
primitive jungle and heading toward the seashore.

He cranes his neck for a better view. Whoever that person may be
—rebel or citizen, male or female, Chinese or foreigner—he is going
to greet him and make known to him his helpless condition.

The person advances, eventually becomes clearly visible.

It is a woman.

Her hair disheveled, her feet bare, her shabby clothes torn into rags
that can hardly cover her, the woman might have just stepped out of a
cave of our primordial past. Perhaps she might even be taken for the
Eve of Genesis.

Y stares at her with dazed eyes, but the woman, totally oblivious of
his presence, walks on unafraid and abstractedly. Shaking her bony
arms as she swings her hips, she advances as if she were dancing.

She is dancing, because Y can overhear her humming a tune.

The cold sunshine, a desolate seashore, a world which has lost its
sense of time, a crazy woman doing a step suggestive of the danse ma-
cabre. . . . Shivering, Y is ready to retreat and flee the scene, but then
he catches the tune the woman is humming: "Hi Lili, hi Li . . ." Yes,
"Hi Lili, hi Li . . ." Y remembers now. Hi Lili, hi Li . . . Leslie
Caron . . . an old film . . . puppet shows. The song R loved best to
hum, the doll-faced R that has occupied a permanent place in his
memory . . . could it be she?

It's she. It must be she. Y stares straight at the crazy woman advancing toward him. Those large, limpid eyes are now ashy dull . . . but
even if she has been reduced to ashes, I can still recognize her.

Suddenly a thousand mixed feelings surge up in his heart so that all
the words he would like to use are stuck in his throat. What has happened to him this morning is too absurd to account for in rational

terms. He feels himself falling apart, perhaps no less crazy than R. Looking into R's hazy eyes he sees the reflections of himself: huddled, small, and desperate. He slinks to her side and they're facing each other as if back in the good old days when they were locked in each other's arms, ready to join the other dancing couples for a "Put Down Your Little Feet."

R   (mechanically waves her bony arms): Hi Lili hi Li . . .
Y   (tiptoes around R. Then steals a glance at her for a second time): Oh, no.
R   (unperturbedly touches her rags): Hi Lili hi Li . . .
Y   (clutches his shirt collar. Summons up enough courage to talk): R, please wake up. Wake up. Do you know who I am?
R   (jumps up like a doe, kicking off a whirl of powdered dust): Hi Lili hi Li . . .
Y   (follows her, pleadingly): Are you still mad at me? After all these years, now that we've met again, why're you still mad at me?
R   Hi Lili hi Li . . .
Y   steps a little closer, wanting very much to touch her naked shoulder.
R   (totally unresponsive. Bends over to pluck a star-shaped white flower and sticks it among her disheveled hair. Then with a ringing voice louder than before): Hi Lili hi Li . . .
Y   (jumps up to grab R's shoulders with his tremulous hands. Raises his voice to a hoarse pitch): You must answer me, answer me! (Jolted, R stops her singing abruptly. With this also cease the natural sounds surrounding them made by the wind and the sea. Through the silence one hears Y's hysterical voice): Tell me, how did you come here? Tell me, why do we end in this mess? What have we done to deserve a fate like this? Tell me, can we escape? Do we still have any future at all? Why don't you speak? Why are you so cruel? Why do you mock and torture me like this? Speak up! Please speak up! (Reflected in R's opaque and lusterless pupils, Y sees his own face, which is a picture of pitiable helplessness, bewilderment, and desperation. He hates himself for that, and in no time two lines of tears course down his cheeks.)

R   (detaches herself from Y's grip, picks up the interrupted tune.
     More cheerfully): Hi Lili hi Li . . .
     (A roll of thunder on the distant horizon. The soft cumulus clouds
     now look like fierce, bulbous-eyed giants.)
Y   (disgruntled, wipes his tears with the back of his hand. Resumes
     the haughty manner of his former years): Hm, Hi Lili hi Li . . .
R   (excitedly faces the sea and raises her arms skyward as if invoking
     the rain god above for showers): Hi Lili hi Li . . .
Y   (attitude changed, side-glances at R in an appreciative manner):
     Hm, not bad. (Chants a classical quatrain):

> The witch pours the libation, clouds fill the sky,
> In the flaming coals of the jade brazier the fumes of incense throb.
> The God of the Sea and the Hill Nymph take their places,
> Votive papers rustle in the howling whirlwind.[2]

R   (spins her body like a top, the torn rags whirling. Sings even more
     shrilly): Hi Lili hi Li . . .
Y   (infected by her enthusiasm, or rather, caught in her spell, whirls
     around her): Hi Lili hi Li . . .
     (Black clouds lower, fraught with thunder and rain.)

R   and Y (gambol like a pair of innocent children playing hide-and-
     seek on the outskirts of a town, now chasing after each other,
     now holding or clapping each other's hands. They skip and hop as
     if inebriated with the brew of Dionysus. They continue to cross
     the expanse of the thistles, heading toward the impenetrable dark-
     ness of the tropical jungle, singing):
     Oh, hi Lili hi Li . . .
     Ah, hi Lili hi Li . . .
     (Again a roll of deafening thunder. The rain then falls like shoot-
     ing spears.)

[2] The opening quatrain of *Shen-hsien* ("Magic Strings") by the great T'ang poet
Li Ho, reprinted from A. C. Graham, tr., *Poems of the Late T'ang* (Baltimore,
1965), p. 94, by permission of Penguin Books Inc., Baltimore, Md.

Pai Hsien-yung

There can be little doubt that Pai Hsien-yung is the most important Chinese short story writer since Eileen Chang. His best stories have a supple, limpid style capable at times of sheer magnificence; a strong note of compassion rendered all the more poignant by the deliberate use of irony; and a comprehensive awareness of China from its past grandeur to its present helplessness. He has not yet produced a novel, and his further development as a major writer should be fascinating to watch.

A native of Kweilin, Kwangsi, Pai Hsien-yung (1937–   ) was the son of the prominent general Pai Ch'ung-hsi. After the war, he accompanied his family to Shanghai, Nanking, and Hong Kong before settling in 1952 in Taipei, where he completed high school and studied Western literature at National Taiwan University. His was the last class of literature majors to profit from Tsi-an Hsia's instruction and, like so many others, he published his first stories in my late brother's *Literary Review* (*Wen-hsüeh Tsa-chih*). Even before his graduation in 1961, Pai Hsien-yung had founded *Modern Literature* (*Hsien-tai Wen-hsüeh*), which over the years has featured his own stories as well as those of his classmates and friends, such as Wang Wen-hsing and Miss Hung Chih-hui. Pai arrived in the United States in 1963 and earned the degree of Master of Fine Arts from the Writers' Workshop at the University of Iowa. He now teaches Chinese language and literature on the Santa Barbara campus of the University of California.

Pai Hsien-yung's post-1963 stories have been confined to two categories: those about the people of Taipei (known collectively as *Taipei jen*) [1] and those about Chinese students and intellectuals in America.

[1] *Taipei jen* has been published by Ch'un-chung ch'u-pan-she (Taipei, 1971). It contains fourteen stories plus critiques by C. T. Hsia, Hung Chih-hui, Yen Yuan-shu, and Yü Li-hua.

There are several excellent stories in the second group, but the Taipei series is decidedly the greater achievement. As of March, 1970, that series includes ten stories which recount the latter-day careers of assorted mainlanders in Taipei—generals, businessmen, soldiers, movie actors, former professional singers and taxi dancers—with a poignancy and understanding unmatched in recent Taiwan fiction. It is because of the difficulties involved in recapturing the richer language of the best of these stories and in making understandable the subtle allusions contained therein that Pai Hsien-yung has decided against translating them in favor of "A Celestial in Mundane Exile" (*Tsê-hsien chi*)—here retitled "Li T'ung: A Chinese Girl in New York"—which is his best story in the American series.

"Li T'ung" is primarily a realistic story told by the sympathetic first-person narrator. It is only in the context of a private joke that the heroine is called "China"; but, while the comparison is never seriously intended, the author seems to suggest that, with all her beauty and pride, she does embody certain qualities of an aristocratic China that died with the sinking of the ship that carried her parents and all their portable wealth from the mainland on the eve of the Communist victory. But for this sudden, decisive break with her past, Li T'ung could never have become what she is: a Chinese girl stranded in New York who keeps up her pride as the only means of reconciling herself to a disinherited, purposeless existence. As the story progresses, she needs stronger and stronger stimulants to sustain her pride and keep herself amused. The author captures both her pride and her defeat in a number of memorable scenes, and the final scene depicting the hysterical reactions of her friends to the news of her suicide is one of the best in modern Chinese fiction for its firm, concrete realization of pathos unaccompanied by a trace of sentimentality.

Most of Pai Hsien-yung's stories are collected in *A Celestial in Mundane Exile* (Taipei, 1967) and *Transported to a Garden and Awakened from a Dream* (*Yu-yuan ching-meng*, Taipei, 1968). Nancy Chang Ing has translated two of his early stories—"The Elder Mrs. King" (*Chin ta-nai-nai*) and "Jade Love" (*Yü-ch'ing sao*)—respectively in *New Voices: Stories and Poems by Young Chinese Writers* and Lucian Wu, ed., *New Chinese Writing*. Pai's own translation of his story "Hong Kong 1960" appeared in *Literature East and West*, IX, No. 4 (December, 1965).

LI T'UNG: A CHINESE GIRL IN NEW YORK

TRANSLATED BY *the author*
and C. T. Hsia

Hui-fen was a Wellesley girl. Even years after our marriage she had not grown out of the habit of reminding me that, when she was a sophomore, each evening she would walk into the dining hall wearing her best Chinese silks. She said her wardrobe at that time, though a trifle smaller than Li T'ung's, was unquestionably superior to those of Chang Chia-hsing and Lei Chih-ling. The four of them had graduated in the same class at McTyiere's, an aristocratic girls' school in Shanghai. They all came from prominent families, but Li T'ung's was the richest since her father was a high-ranking minister in the government. When they had dancing parties, they had invariably gathered at Li's spacious, German-style villa on the fashionable Rainbow Bridge Road. There were two marble fountains in its garden, and when they danced outdoors the fountains illuminated by multicolored lights provided a rich and picturesque background. And since Li T'ung was an only daughter much pampered by her parents since her early childhood, her mother took great care in providing everything for her parties, including fancy foods laid out buffet-style in the garden.

Hui-fen said that in 1946, on the day when they left Shanghai for the States to study, the four of them had by coincidence all worn red Chinese gowns. Standing together in their flaming silks, they literally lit up the Lung-hua Airport, and as they looked at one another they bent double with laughter. Li T'ung claimed they were the Big Four of the postwar world—China, America, Great Britain, and Russia. She styled herself China, on the ground that her gown was the brightest. No one wanted to be Russia, however, because Russian women were of coarse skin and large build and a sizable number of them in Shanghai then were prostitutes. But Li T'ung quite arbitrarily appointed Chang Chia-hsing Russia, since she was the chubbiest of the four. Much peeved, Chang Chia-hsing was still bickering with Li T'ung after they had boarded the plane.

About a hundred relatives and friends came to see the four off. As they waved to the boarding girls, the whole airport was aflutter with handkerchiefs like a swarm of butterflies. The four were then only seventeen or eighteen, too excited to be properly solemn or sentimental at the moment of leavetaking. Her mother hugged Li T'ung and cried bitterly at the last minute and even her father was rubbing his eyes; but Li T'ung in her rakish sunglasses with upsweeping frames still had her mouth open in the form of a smile. Once on the plane, the four chatted interminably. Many foreign passengers looked at these four Chinese girls in red and nodded and smiled with approval or amusement. Hui-fen said that they were then truly elated, as if they were really the plenipotentiaries of the Big Four flying to New York to attend an international conference.

Right from the beginning they had become most popular at Wellesley. Hui-fen always loved to enumerate the large number of boys she had dated on weekends. Especially when I was not too attentive, she would rehearse how X had courted her and how Y had doted on her, thus reminding me of the power she had over boys in her prime. I didn't particularly care for these stories and was at times slightly jealous, but when I saw her soaking her white and delicate hands in the dishpan until they peeled I couldn't help loving and pitying her all the more. She is after all the daughter of an aristocratic family used to having her way, but ever since we were married, she has been doing all the household chores with a willing diligence which I can't help respecting.

Hui-fen said that, although all four had done well socially, Li T'ung far outshone the other three. She eclipsed even American girls from wealthy families. Wellesley was very style-conscious. She had brought over with her a fantastic wardrobe, and she certainly knew how to dress. Every day she walked around in something different, but equally eye-catching. Some American boys, seeing her in her shimmering silks, would teasingly ask her if she were a Chinese princess or something. Soon she had become a campus personality and she was elected May Queen.

The boys who dated her were too many to be enumerated. Counting on her beauty, Li T'ung was most haughty to them. Wang Chüeh, a Harvard Law School student highly regarded for his scholarship and character, was infatuated with her, but because Li T'ung appeared indifferent, he eventually became disappointed and stopped seeing her. Hui-fen told me that she knew Li T'ung liked him very much, but since she was used to putting on airs, she could not change her ways in time and thus lost her chance to be real friends with him. Hui-fen said that she could have bet that Li T'ung suffered a long time after that, but since she was very proud she would never admit it.

During their third year in the States, the civil war was getting worse in China. When Li T'ung's family tried to flee from Shanghai to Taiwan on the S. S. *Peace*, it was sunk on the way. Her whole family were killed in the accident and gone, too, were the valuables they had brought with them. When Li T'ung first learned the news, she was taken to the hospital and confined there for more than a month. She refused to eat anything and the doctors had to tie her up in bed and give her glucose and saline injections every day. After being released from the hospital she was very quiet and subdued. Her three friends, too, were no longer in the mood to compete for popularity since their families had also suffered reverses on account of the war, and all four of them now worked hard at their studies. When Hui-fen referred to her Wellesley period, she always began her recital with "When I was a sophomore." The junior and senior years she mentioned very seldom.

It was not until after her graduation that Li T'ung recovered her former gaiety. She went to New York and became a fashion designer at Originala, making a big salary, but her three friends all agreed, however, that there had been something disconcerting about Li T'ung ever since.

I met Li T'ung for the first time at my wedding. I had dated Hui-fen earlier in Boston; at that time I was a graduate student at M. I. T. and she came to Boston quite often to visit her relatives even though she was then working in New York. But Hui-fen insisted that we have our wedding in New York and make our permanent home there. She said that all her old friends were now working there and only in New York could she forget she was in a foreign country. Our reception was held in our new home on Long Island. Only our best friends were invited. After changing from her wedding gown, Hui-fen formally introduced me to Li T'ung, Chang Chia-hsing, and Lei Chih-ling. Actually I could spot them right away without these introductions since Hui-fen had described them from head to toe Heaven knows how many times. Chang was big, and Lei petite, rather true to Hui-fen's descriptions, both very self-assured and smart. But as for Li T'ung's looks, I must say Hui-fen's estimate was obviously too conservative. No, Li T'ung had not thought too highly of herself. Her beauty was devastating. She literally shone in the gathering and it hurt the eye to look straight at her, as at the blinding sun that has jumped out of the sea. She had finely chiseled features and a tall, graceful figure. Her eyes, dark and flashing, were spellbinding. A riot of shining black hair, two thirds of it combed across her forehead, tumbled down on her left shoulder. On the left temple just above her ear was a hairpin, a big glistening spider made of small diamonds, its claws digging into her hair, its fat, roundish body tilted upward. She wore that day a Chinese white satin gown of silvery sheen, with a red maple leaf design. The maple leaves were each the size of a palm and flamed like balls of fire. No woman is a reliable judge of another's beauty, and I couldn't help suspecting that Hui-fen's reluctance to praise Li T'ung's looks was a form of protest. After all, standing next to Li T'ung, my bride's extreme prettiness was unmercifully overshadowed by her dazzling beauty. That day I was especially happy not only over my own wedding but at meeting Hui-fen's attractive friends.

"So you're the one who broke up our mahjong team. Wait until I

get even with you." Upon being introduced, Li T'ung looked me all
over with a critical eye and said this with a laugh. She laughed in a
strange fashion, with her chin tilted, the left corner of her mouth
raised high, and her eyelids closing brusquely as if to obliterate everyone from her vision. Hui-fen had told me they used to live in a four-
room apartment on West End Avenue. After office hours the four of
them often got together to play mahjong and they called their apartment the Big Four Club. When Hui-fen moved out, the others also
split up.

"Then how about letting me join the Big Four Club and pay my
membership fee?" I said appeasingly, bowing slightly to Li T'ung and
her friends. I had learned to play mahjong and poker in America and
had become rather proficient since whenever Chinese friends met it
was customary for them to play a game.

"Welcome, welcome," the three girls all laughed at my reply. "You
should thank your lucky star that you know the game; otherwise we
might not let you marry Huang Hui-fen. We originally agreed that no
member of our club was permitted to marry a non-gambler."

"I have known about that for some time," I said. "I even know
which of you represents which power. Li T'ung is China, right?"

"Don't you dare mention it," Li T'ung cried. "This China of yours
has been beaten at every game, a catastrophic loser. You think I could
win playing against those content to win small games? You go and ask
Chang Chia-hsing: half of my paycheck each month goes into her
purse."

"You're a lousy player, don't just blame others," Chang Chia-hsing
put in.

"Come on, Li T'ung, be a good sport," Lei Chih-ling joined Chang.

"Ch'en Yin," Li T'ung drew close to me and said with her finger
pointing at the other girls, "you'd better heed my words: never try to
win big when playing with these people, including your beautiful
bride. They are the queens of the small game and the quick kill. I
build toward the best combination of tiles; if I can't make it, I would
rather lose."

The other girls all protested, attacking Li T'ung in unison. But she
held fast and wouldn't back down, her head raised high, smiling defiantly, the diamond spider glittering on her profuse black hair. I was

greatly intrigued by these smart-looking girls arguing among themselves.

"I too always aim big." I supported Li T'ung, sensing her isolation under the combined attack.

"Really? Really?" Li T'ung cried out in excitement and shook hands with me with evident warmth. "Then I have found my match. Let's have a contest real soon."

At our reception that day, Li T'ung darted here and there conspicuously, her body aflame with the brilliant red leaves on her gown. My bachelor friends were all visibly restless as if they had been scorched by these leaves. My former college roommate Chou Ta-ch'ing repeatedly asked me about Li T'ung that day.

After we returned to New York from our honeymoon, Chou Ta-ch'ing rang me up and asked us to have dinner at the Tavern-on-the-Green in Central Park. He wanted me to bring Li T'ung along. Chou had taken to several girls in college; nothing had worked out, however. He was a nice guy and rather good-looking, too, but somehow he didn't have luck with girls. Each time he fell in love, he was dead serious. I knew he had again lost his head, this time over Li T'ung. When I broke the news to Hui-fen, she said I'd better leave the girl alone since she was so very hard to please, but as I knew Chou Ta-ch'ing to be very honest and reliable, I eventually talked Hui-fen into arranging the meeting.

We picked up Li T'ung and headed for Central Park. She wore a pink organdy gown, very chic. But this time her diamond spider had slid down almost to the end of the flowing mane around her left shoulder, swaying there as if it were suspended from some invisible filament. It was altogether striking. Chou Ta-ch'ing had been waiting for us for some time at the Tavern-on-the-Green. He had just had his hair cut, and looked overly trim. He got up as soon as he saw us, with a stiff smile on his face, seemingly still as nervous as when, back in his college days, he had waited outside the girls' dormitory to take his date to a dance. After we were seated, Chou Ta-ch'ing removed the gold wrapping paper from a box with a transparent plastic lid and took therefrom a large purple orchid as a present for Li T'ung. She smiled, her eyelids drooping, and pinned the orchid to the sash around her waist.

Chou Ta-ch'ing ordered champagne for all of us, but Li T'ung asked the waiter to bring her a Manhattan.

"I detest champagne," Li T'ung said. "It tastes like water."

"A Manhattan is quite strong, isn't it?" Chou asked with evident concern as he saw Li T'ung emptying half of her glass in one gulp.

"It suits me beautifully." So saying, Li T'ung proceeded to drain her glass in no time, and picking up the cherry, she stuck it into her mouth. As a waiter passed by, she pointed to the empty glass with the cigarette between her fingers:

"Another Manhattan, please."

Thus drinking, Li T'ung began to talk with great gusto about her adventures at Yonkers. She said she had had no luck in horse racing either; she would win at the start but then lose. She asked me if I knew how to play poker; I said I was rather good at it. She stretched her arm across the table and gave me a firm handshake.

"Huang Hui-fen, your husband is so sweet!" Li T'ung turned to Hui-fen. "Better let me have him. He and I could run a prosperous casino in Chinatown."

We all broke out laughing. Chou Ta-ch'ing laughed uneasily: he knew nothing about gambling and Li T'ung had paid him scarcely any attention. A couple of times he had tried to change the topic of our conversation, but was brushed aside by Li T'ung.

"You may have him," Hui-fen answered Li T'ung laughingly and gave me a push. Li T'ung got up and slipped her arm into mine. We made for the dance floor in the open surrounded by lamps casting amber light. Li T'ung rested her head on my shoulder while dancing. The amber light shone radiantly on her hair and gown.

"Chou Ta-ch'ing is crazy about you," I whispered to her. Chou and Hui-fen had also stepped down to the dance floor.

"Oh?" Li T'ung tossed her head, smiling. "You should have told him to take lessons in gambling then."

"He's a very nice fellow."

"I'm not supposed to marry a non-gambler, you know that," she grinned, and rested her head on my shoulder again.

Li T'ung had five or six Manhattans before we finished our dinner. Each time she ordered a drink, Chou Ta-ch'ing looked at her with sheepish disapproval.

"Why look at me like that? Too stingy to buy me a drink or some-thing?" Li T'ung suddenly turned her head toward Chou Ta-ch'ing. She was laughing, her cheeks flushed crimson and the left corner of her mouth curved upward. Embarrassed, Chou Ta-ch'ing hastened to explain, "I was only afraid you have had too many."

"Tell you what, I'm not going to dance with you until I have an-other." Li T'ung flipped her fingers toward the waiter for another Manhattan. After finishing that, she got up to dance with Chou. The Latin American band was playing the La Tino Cha Cha with much spirit.

"I don't Cha Cha too well." Chou Ta-ch'ing got up after some hesi-tation.

"I'll coach you." Li T'ung stepped straight to the dance floor, Chou Ta-ch'ing following behind.

Instantly, Li T'ung attuned herself perfectly to the frenzied tempo of the Cha Cha. She danced very well, with ease and abandon. Chou Ta-ch'ing could hardly follow her. At first Li T'ung accommodated herself to Chou's clumsy steps, but soon she surrendered herself com-pletely to the ever-quickening pace. Her body surged up and down, whirling in wider and wider circles, her steps getting almost frantic. The Cha Cha rhythm became, as it were, a whirlwind of noise, blow-ing out her long rippling hair and the sash around her waist. The dia-mond spider was flung into the air, clinging tenaciously to her mane, but the purple orchid flew off the sash, swirled down to the floor, and was trodden to a pulp by her feet. She held up her head, her eyelids lowered, her brows closely knit, her long supple waist swaying ur-gently. She was like a cobra mesmerized by a magic flute, whirling agonizingly even to the point of allowing its body to disintegrate. The Latin musicians played in frenzy until at the climax of the tune they broke out in singing and yelling. The other dancers had stopped to watch Li T'ung even though Chou Ta-ch'ing still struggled to stay near her, and they applauded with the musicians when the tune stopped. Li T'ung waved to the musicians and came back to her seat. Sweat stood in beads all over her face and a big tuft of hair clung to her cheek. Chou Ta-ch'ing kept wiping his forehead with a handker-chief, his face flushed purple. The minute she sat down, Li T'ung waved to the waiter for another Manhattan.

"Li T'ung, you're going to get stoned," Hui-fen patted Li T'ung's hand, trying to stop her.

Li T'ung flung her arms around Hui-fen's neck and said laughing, "Huang Hui-fen, my dear Huang Hui-fen, don't stop me, not tonight. I'm so happy. I've never been so happy as this."

She pointed to her chest, her eyes burning darkly. Before she would let us lead her away, she had two more Manhattans. She staggered a little on her way out. As the Negro porter opened the door for us, Li T'ung suddenly pulled out a ten-dollar bill and unsteadily stuck it into his hand.

"Your Manhattans are the best in the world!" Li T'ung said, bending forward.

On reaching home, Hui-fen blamed me. "I told you to leave Li T'ung alone. She is so willful I really feel sorry for Chou Ta-ch'ing."

Our first two years in New York were as busy as the Lexington Avenue Express. Both of us worked on weekdays, but as soon as we got home, we would be asked by Hui-fen's friends to go out again. On weekends there were the inevitable dinner parties, very often planned weeks ahead. Both Chang Chia-hsing and Lei Chih-ling were then going steady, Chang with Dr. Wang, a physician, and Lei with an engineer named Chiang T'eng. Both Wang and Chiang loved to play mahjong and poker, and when we saw the two couples, we passed the time playing either one or the other game: you might say their courtship was carried out among cards and tiles. Li T'ung did not have a steady boy friend and changed her escorts often. Moreover, she had lost interest in mahjong, calling it a tepid game, and one Saturday she suggested horse racing. So off we went that afternoon, the eight of us, to the Yonkers racecourse. Li T'ung's escort was Teng Mao-ch'ang, a businessman from Hong Kong in his late thirties who ran a Chinese curio shop on Fifth Avenue. Li T'ung said that Teng was an expert on horse racing, winning nine out of ten times. It was a sunny and hot day and all four girls wore broad-rimmed straw hats. Li T'ung also wore magenta shorts and a white shirt. Its collar was turned back, exposing a rakish wisp of her lavender neckerchief.

The racecourse was already packed when we got there. Except for Teng Mao-ch'ang, we all knew little about horse racing, and he enthusiastically acted as our broker, running up and down in the crowd to gather information and then ordering us with authority to place bets. The first two rounds we each won thirty or fifty dollars and on the third race Teng urged us to throw in a big bet on Lucky.

"I don't want him," Li T'ung said. "I want to pick my own horse."

"Just listen to me once, will you?" Teng advised anxiously, his hand holding a bundle of bills we had given him. "I swear Lucky will hit the jack pot."

Checking over the program, Li T'ung pointed to a name and told Teng, "I want to bet on Bold Lad."

"Lucky's got to win," answered Teng.

"But Bold Lad, what a pretty name! I want to bet fifty bucks on that."

"But that's a lousy horse."

"Throw in a hundred for me then." Li T'ung fished out five twenty-dollar bills and stuck them into Teng's hands. While he was still trying to talk her out of it, Chang Chia-hsing cut in, "Why should you care if she loses? She makes over a thousand a month."

"Why are you so sure I'm going to lose?" Li T'ung turned to Chang with a sneer. "You people like to run after a sure thing. I don't."

Lucky dashed to the forefront as the race began and after two or three rounds of the track he had left the other horses far behind. Chang Chia-hsing, Lei Chih-ling, and Hui-fen, hugging each other, jumped with excitement. Bold Lad, however, had lagged behind from the very beginning. Li T'ung took off her hat and swung it in the air, shouting at the top of her voice:

"Come on, my boy! Come on!" [2]

Her face went red and her voice got hoarse but her Bold Lad failed her pitiably. In the end we all won big on Lucky except Li T'ung. In the next few rounds she got more and more erratic and made random bets on whichever horses took her fancy. The day over, Hui-fen and I turned out to have made the biggest pot, over five hundred dollars. Li T'ung, the sole loser, had thrown away over four hundred. In a happy mood Hui-fen took all our friends to a Chinese restaurant on Upper Broadway and ordered a sumptuous dinner. At the table Teng Mao-ch'ang began to recount his experiences at the Hong Kong races;

[2] English in the original.

much fascinated, Chang Chia-hsing and Lei Chih-ling showered him
with questions.

"*You* made me slip today," Li T'ung suddenly broke in on Teng.
"You are responsible for all my losses."

"You wouldn't have lost if you had listened to me," Teng said.

"Why should I have listened to *you?* Who gave you the right to
boss us around anyway?" Li T'ung flipped her chopsticks down on the
table and retorted, her eyes flashing.

"All right, all right, I'll try to keep quiet the next time we go to
Yonkers," Teng smiled appeasingly.

"What next time? Can't I go horse racing without you?"

Teng couldn't find anything to say to these cutting words; he
looked at Li T'ung with that helpless smile fixed on his face. We all
felt a little uneasy. It was an uncomfortable dinner.

During the third year of our stay in New York, Hui-fen came down
with a serious case of insomnia. The doctor blamed it on her taut
nerves, but I knew it must be those frantic parties that had impaired
her health. Without waiting for Hui-fen's consent, I asked for a transfer to the Buffalo branch of our company. Although Hui-fen didn't
make too much of a fuss about the move, I knew she must resent it.
When Chang Chia-hsing and Lei Chih-ling heard the news, they all
became indignant and accused me of kidnaping their Huang Hui-fen.

During the six years we lived in Buffalo, we came back to New
York only twice, once for Lei's wedding and the other time for
Chang's. We met Li T'ung on both occasions. In fact, she was Chang's
bridesmaid. She looked thinner, but her striking beauty still arrested attention. The reception was held in Dr. Wang's luxurious apartment on
Central Park West; with his wide connections, little wonder that he
had so many well-wishers gathered in the living room and dining
room. Pushing through the crowd, Li T'ung came near me and asked
me to take her out for a walk. She dragged me to Hui-fen's side, asking
with a smile, "Won't you lend me your husband for a moment?"

"Take him along. I don't want him any more," Hui-fen smiled.

"You'd better keep an eye on that girl," Lei Chih-ling teased. "She's
going to kidnap your husband."

"All the better," Hui-fen said, still smiling. "I won't have to go back to Buffalo then."

"There were too many people in there and I was suffocating," Li T'ung said to me when we were in Central Park. "To tell you the truth, Ch'en Yin, I want you to buy me a drink, too. It was all Chang Chia-hsing's brilliant idea: a champagne party. You know I loathe that stuff."

I walked Li T'ung to the Tavern-on-the-Green and ordered a Manhattan for her and a Scotch on the rocks for myself. She chatted gaily while drinking. She said she had changed her job. Originala had raised her pay to fifteen hundred a month, but she had quit because she had had a fight with her boss. Now she worked at Vogue where she got even higher pay as the second in command in the Design Department. Not happy with her new job, either, she shrugged her shoulders, since her new boss was an unbearable crank who had rheumatism all year round. I asked her if she still lived on Lexington Avenue. She laughed and said she had moved three times since I had last seen her. She had already gulped down three drinks during our talk and her face was beginning to turn red.

"Take it easy, Li T'ung," I said to her, "you don't want to get high as you did the last time here."

"So you still remember it," Li T'ung tossed her head and laughed. "I must have been terribly drunk that night. Did I scare your friend Chou Ta-ch'ing?"

"No, he wasn't scared, but he has been saying since that you're the best-looking girl he's ever met."

"No kidding," Li T'ung laughed. "Now I remember seeing him at Macy's four or five months ago. He was shopping with his wife. He gave me his address and asked me to visit him."

"He's a very nice guy."

"He must be," Li T'ung laughed again, "he keeps sending me a Christmas card each year with best wishes for my happiness. A very interesting fellow, but he doesn't gamble."

I asked Li T'ung if she still went to the races. She suddenly beamed, gulped down her drink, and gave me a slap on the hand.

"Tell you what, last Saturday I went to Yonkers, all by myself. I picked Gallant Knight—isn't that a cute name? Guess what, I won four hundred and fifty on that. *Four hundred and fifty* on a single bet! That was my greatest accomplishment in my whole damn life, Ch'en Yin. You remember Teng Mao-ch'ang, don't you, the self-appointed expert on horse racing. He went back to Hong Kong and married someone of Chinese and Portuguese blood. Well, anyway, I've suddenly become lucky on horses since he left. I've won every single bet for the last three months."

Li T'ung talked rapidly, shaking with laughter, and kept asking the bartender to fill it up for her. It was getting dark outside and Li T'ung got up abruptly, saying, "We'd better go; otherwise Huang Hui-fen might think I've really kidnaped her husband."

We had Lili during our second year in Buffalo. When the time came for her to go to kindergarten, Hui-fen gave me her ultimatum: if I persisted in staying in Buffalo, she would take Lili with her to New York and resume her work there. She said she wouldn't mind having insomnia again. I agreed that the methodical, dull life in Buffalo was not very healthful and so we moved back to New York and bought a new house on Long Island. Hui-fen decided that we should give a big party the first Saturday after we moved into the new house. On that day Chang Chia-hsing and Lei Chih-ling came with their husbands. Li T'ung, however, came unescorted. Some other friends came in Dr. Wang's car.

Hui-fen had spent three solid days preparing for the party, and came up with over a dozen Chinese dishes. After dinner we began to play poker and mahjong. Hui-fen asked Chang, Lei, and Li T'ung to join her at the same table to play mahjong so that they might talk about the good old days at the Big Four Club. After one round, however, Li T'ung got up to exchange places with someone at the men's poker table. She said she had not touched mahjong for ages and had forgotten practically all the rules. I wasn't playing that night, busy serving drinks to spare Hui-fen further work. After both tables had warmed to the games, I came to the poker table in the dining room but couldn't find Li T'ung there. The men said she had left the table a while ago for a short recess. After searching everywhere, I finally opened the door separating the living room from the porch and found her asleep in a rattan rocking chair.

The porch was dimly lit by a small yellow lamp hanging down from the ceiling. Li T'ung's head inclined to her right shoulder, her hands were on the armrests, her long slender fingers dangling limply. Her long dark red skirt almost touched the floor; in the dim light it appeared dingy, as if it were an old blanket of faded color. Her hair seemed to have grown much longer, covering the whole of her left cheek, flowing down to her chest. The diamond spider was still there, squatting on her left cheek, fierce, shimmering. I had never seen Li T'ung so haggard, so fatigued. No matter where I had seen her before, she had always looked defiantly gay and untamed, as if she would never agree to lie down for a rest. My footsteps woke her. With a start, she sat up, pushed back her hair, and said with a yawn, "Is that you, Ch'en Yin?"

"You were asleep, Li T'ung," I said.

"Oh? I felt a little tired at the table and so I quit. I thought I would just take a little rest here, but I passed out. Isn't that funny? Thank God, you're here. Get me a drink, will you?"

I fixed a bourbon on the rocks and took it to the porch. Li T'ung took a big gulp and heaved a sigh, "Jesus, that was good. I had bad luck tonight. Haven't had a darn hand the whole evening. It bored me to tears watching them playing. I'm getting more and more impatient, I guess. I can't even stand poker any longer."

In the living room Hui-fen, Chang Chia-hsing, and Lei Chih-ling were interminably talking and laughing. Chang had a loud voice, and every once in a while she would burst out laughing, drowning out other sounds. The poker players were also quite spirited: the chips kept knocking against the table.

"Probably Chang Chia-hsing has made another smashing combination of tiles," Li T'ung remarked, shaking her head in amusement. She looked even thinner than the last time I had seen her, her cheeks sunken a little, but her dark eyes flashed as brightly as before.

"Get me another one, will you?" She handed me the empty glass. I got her another bourbon. As we were chatting on the porch, my five-year-old daughter, Lili, popped in, bundled up in a white nightgown, a knot of hair tied with a blue ribbon sticking up on her head. She had a round chubby face, clear dark eyes. A real darling. She would never go to bed until I had kissed her good night. I bent down and she, standing on tiptoe, gave me a gentle kiss.

"Don't you want to give auntie a kiss, too?" Li T'ung said to Lili. Lili toddled to Li T'ung, bent down her neck with her encircling arms, and smacked her on the forehead. Li T'ung hugged her and put her on her lap.

"A perfect copy of Huang Hui-fen," Li T'ung said to me, "she'll turn out to be a real beauty, too."

"What's this, auntie?" asked Lili, toying with a big diamond ring on Li T'ung's finger.

"It's a stone."

"Let me have it," Lili said with her coaxing voice.

"Then it's yours." Li T'ung took the ring from her finger and slipped it on Lili's thumb. Lili raised her hand and swung it so that it glittered against the dim porch light.

"Don't let her play with such a valuable thing. It may get lost," I tried to intervene.

"It's Lili's now, I mean it." Li T'ung looked up to me, her face wearing a serious expression that came to her rarely. She bowed down and kissed Lili on her chubby face, saying, "Be a good girl. The ring is for your dowry. Get yourself a good husband in the future. Go along now and let Daddy keep it for you."

Lili handed the ring to me, laughing happily, and then left for bed.

"Mama gave it to me when I left Shanghai," Li T'ung pointed to the ring in my hand and said. "It was supposed to be part of my dowry."

"Since you like Lili so much, why can't you be her godmother?" I said.

"Oh, come on," Li T'ung got up abruptly, her strange smile again drawing up the left corner of her mouth. "Huang Hui-fen is a wonderful mother and what does Lili need me for? Look at me, am I the motherly type? Let's go in now. I've already lost a great deal. I'm going to win it back."

We didn't see much of Li T'ung after that evening, since she rarely attended our parties. One story had it that she was kept by an American millionaire from California on his Westchester estate, while another maintained that she was messily involved with a businessman from South America. On our way to downtown Manhattan one day, we were just entering the East River Freeway when a huge golden Continental convertible dashed past us and someone in it shouted at us in a shrill voice:

"Huang . . . Hui- . . . fen. . . ."

Hui-fen stuck out her head from the window and heaved a disapproving sigh. "She's given me a real scare!"

It was Li T'ung yelling from that open convertible. She was seated next to the driver, but she had turned around to face us, her arms flung wide apart and waving desperately, a huge bright red scarf on her head flapping in the air. The convertible shot forward like a golden dart and carried Li T'ung with it. The man driving the car was a big fellow; he looked Caucasian. That was the last time we saw Li T'ung.

Lei Chih-ling gave birth to a boy during the fourth year of her marriage. When the boy was one month old, the happy parents gave a party in their Riverdale apartment to celebrate. Chang Chia-hsing and her husband didn't show up for dinner that evening, which was rather unusual with them. We had already played a few rounds of poker when they finally arrived. A telegram in her right hand, Chang Chia-hsing waved to us and cried:

"Li T'ung is dead! Li T'ung is dead!"

"Which Li T'ung?" Lei Chih-ling walked quickly to meet her.

"What do you mean 'Which Li T'ung'?" Chang said impatiently.

"Nonsense," Lei cut her short, "Li T'ung left for Europe only two weeks ago."

"Look at this." Chang forced the telegram into Lei's hand. "I just got it from the Chinese Consulate in Italy. Li T'ung drowned herself in Venice. She didn't even leave a note and didn't have a single relative here. The police must have found my address in her purse and then asked the consulate to wire me. So I went with the police to open up her apartment on Fifth Avenue. Closets and bureaus full of clothes and shoes—I don't know what to do with them."

Chang Chia-hsing and Lei Chih-ling started arguing over why Li T'ung had killed herself. Why? Why? Suddenly both of them became indignant, as though Li T'ung had deceived them by committing suicide. Hui-fen took the telegram and read it in silence; she didn't say anything.

"How can one account for it? Why should she kill herself?" cried Chang Chia-hsing. "She earned more money than any of us here—how could she be so fed up with everything?"

"I told her many times to get married and settle down. But she was always mockingly evasive, never taking my words seriously," said Lei Chih-ling.

"So many men after her and she spurned them all. Whom to blame?" added Chang Chia-hsing.

Lei Chih-ling went to her bedroom and took out a picture to show us, saying, "I've forgotten to show you this. I received it only last week—who could have expected her suicide?"

It was a color picture. Li T'ung was standing there by herself in an unbuttoned black topcoat, her left arm akimbo, her right hand raised high as if she were waving to some people. Her chin tilted, her eyelids lowered, she had that strange arrogant smile on her face. In the background stood a leaning tower, seemingly about to topple on her. Hui-fen held the picture in her hand and looked at it intently. I went over to her side and found her reading the lines written at the back of the picture:

> Dear members of the Big Four:
> This is the Pisa Tower.
> China, December, 1960

Chang Chia-hsing and Lei Chih-ling continued to argue over the cause of Li T'ung's suicide, Chang saying that it was probably because that American had deserted her and Lei maintaining that she had been suffering from a bad case of nerves. But both agreed that Li T'ung shouldn't have died.

"I know," Chang Chia-hsing suddenly broke out, shaking her head as if something had dawned upon her. "Li T'ung shouldn't have gone to Europe by herself. A Chinese should never do that, running around in Europe by herself like the Americans. Her ghost will now be wandering there all alone. She ought to have stayed in New York; at least we could have kept her busy with cards or something. Then she wouldn't have had the time to die."

Lei Chih-ling seemed to agree with Chang Chia-hsing's conclusion and stopped arguing. A moment of silence fell. The two of them sat facing each other, lost in their thoughts. Hui-fen, her head lowered, kept turning the picture in her hand. The men at the card table were either fiddling with the chips or smoking quietly. When the silence was getting oppressive, a lusty cry from Lei's baby broke out in the bedroom. Lei jumped up with a start and said, "Come on, people, let's get back to our game. No use talking further."

She herded us back to the card table and poker was resumed. Somehow the game got wild and our bets grew bigger and bigger. Chang Chia-hsing was heard repeatedly shouting, "Show your hand! Show your hand!" She had her sleeves rolled back and bet a pile of chips for each hand. Lei Chih-ling followed suit, and even Hui-fen, usually a cautious poker player, seemed to have been infected with their frenzy and pushed heaps of her chips into the pool recklessly. Even with their better self-control, the men also played with abandon since the game had already got out of hand. Chips of all colors kept rolling back and forth from one player to another. Each time Chang Chia-hsing won, she threw her arms across the table and swept the chips to her side, shouting and laughing until she came to tears. Lei Chih-ling had a small voice, but she tried to vie with Chang by raising it to a pitiable screech. Round after round went on. We didn't realize it was already morning until Lei Chih-ling's husband went to draw aside the curtains and a flood of dazzling sunlight poured through the windows. We all averted our faces and narrowed our eyes. Chang Chia-hsing threw her cards on the table and covered her face with her hands. We stopped the game and Lei Chih-ling left for the kitchen to make coffee for us. It turned out that both Hui-fen and I were big losers.

When Hui-fen and I walked out of the apartment building, we found it had snowed during the night. There on the street patches of frozen mud partially covered with a thin layer of fluffy snow looked as if they had gotten moldy overnight. The apartment houses on this Riverdale street all looked the same: tall, old buildings a stale brown color. It was Sunday and there was nobody on the street. People were apparently still in bed since yellow curtains were drawn across their windows. From opposing sides of the street these windows stared at one another like huge vacant eyes with their pupils removed. The sun had risen above the buildings and lit up the whole street, but the air was still freezing.

Hui-fen walked in front of me, her overcoat huddled around her shoulders. Her head was bent in order better to watch her steps and avoid the muddy patches of snow. The hair that had been tied into a bun now fell over the collar of her coat in an unkempt fashion. I had forgotten to wear my gloves to the party; now my hands were thrust inside my overcoat pockets, still feeling stiff and cold. The chill morning air made my eyes smart, and since I had drunk too much coffee last night, my throat also felt very dry. Our car was frozen, too, and it was some time before I got it started. When we got to Broadway, Hui-fen opened the window on her side. The cold air blew in, making me very uncomfortable.

"Close the window, Hui-fen," I said.

"I want to get some fresh air," she said.

"Close the window, will you?" I said. My hands on the wheel were getting numb with cold. Hui-fen turned to the other side, her chin resting on the window ledge, without saying a word.

"Close the window, did you hear me?" I suddenly found myself shouting at her in a fit of annoyance. It was as if the cold wind had pumped up some suppressed irritation inside me, like stomach acid. Hui-fen turned around and closed the window quietly. When our car got near Times Square, I suddenly found that Hui-fen was weeping. She was sitting stiffly beside me, looking blankly in front of her. Tears kept rolling down her cheeks; she didn't even try to wipe them away and let them fall on her chest. I had never before seen Hui-fen so pale, so haggard. As a proud person, she rarely showed emotion before people. Even when she was alone with me, she would not show on her face that she was troubled or unhappy. But now I could feel a kind of profound and yet strangely hollow grief that came to me through her weeping. Sob followed convulsive sob, each as flat and as monotonous as the other. All of a sudden I felt I could fully understand her profound and yet hollow grief. I knew that no words could allay it and all she needed was privacy. I turned my head away and didn't look at her any more. When we got to Forty-second Street I speeded up. The neon lights on both sides of the street were still on but they looked dim and weak in the sunlight. There weren't many cars on the street and very few pedestrians. I had never suspected that one of the busiest streets in New York could be so empty and deserted on a Sunday morning.

Iowa City, 1965

TRANSLATIONS FROM THE ORIENTAL CLASSICS
PREPARED FOR THE COLUMBIA COLLEGE PROGRAM

WM. THEODORE DE BARY, EDITOR

Major Plays of Chikamatsu, tr. Donald Keene — 1961	*Essays in Idleness: The Tsurezuregusa of Kenkō*, tr. Donald Keene — 1967
Records of the Grand Historian of China, translated from the Shih chi of Ssu-ma Ch'ien, tr. Burton Watson 2 vols. — 1961	*The Pillow Book of Sei Shōnagon*, tr. Ivan Morris, 2 vols. — 1967
Instructions for Practical Living and Other Neo-Confucian Writings by Wang Yang-ming, tr. Wing-tsit Chan — 1963	*Two Plays of Ancient India: The Little Clay Cart and The Minister's Seal*, tr. J.A.B. van Buitenen — 1968
Chuang Tzu: Basic Writings, tr. Burton Watson, paperback ed. only — 1964	*The Complete Works of Chuang Tzu*, tr. Burton Watson — 1968
The Mahābhāratā, tr. Chakravarthi V. Narasimhan — 1965	*The Romance of the Western Chamber (Hsi Hsiang chi)*, tr. S.I. Hsiung — 1968
The Manyōshū, Nippon Gakujutsu Shinkōkai edition — 1965	*The Manyōshū*, Nippon Gakujutsu Shinkōkai edition. Paperback text edition. — 1969
Su Tung-p'o: Selections from a Sung Dynasty Poet, tr. Burton Watson — 1965	*Records of the Historian: Chapters from the Shih chi of Ssu-ma Ch'ien*. Paperback text edition, tr. Burton Watson — 1969
Bhartrihari: Poems, tr. Barbara Stoler Miller. Also in paperback ed. — 1967	*Cold Mountain: 100 Poems by the T'ang poet Han-shan*, tr. by Burton Watson. Also in paperback ed. — 1970
Basic Writings of Mo Tzu, Hsün Tzu, and Han Fei Tzu, tr. Burton Watson Also in separate paperback eds. — 1967	*Twenty Plays of the Nō Theatre*, ed. by Donald Keene. Also in paperback ed. — 1970
The Awakening of Faith, attributed to Aśvaghosha, tr. Yoshito S. Hakeda — 1967	*Chūshingura: The Treasury of Loyal Retainers*, tr. by Donald Keene — 1971
Reflections on Things at Hand: The Neo-Confucian Anthology, comp. Chu Hsi and Lü Tsu-ch'ien, tr. Wing-tsit Chan — 1967	*The Zen Master Hakuin: Selected Writings*, by P. B. Yampolsky — 1971
The Platform Sutra of the Sixth Patriarch, tr. Philip B. Yampolsky — 1967	*Chinese Rhyme-Prose: Poems in the Fu Form from the Han and Six Dynasties Periods*, by Burton Watson — 1971

COMPANIONS TO ASIAN STUDIES

Approaches to the Oriental Classics, ed. Wm. Theodore de Bary — 1959	*The Classic Chinese Novel: A Critical Introduction*, by C. T. Hsia — 1968
Early Chinese Literature, by Burton Watson — 1962	*A Syllabus of Chinese Civilization*, by J. Mason Gentzler — 1968
Approaches to Asian Civilizations, ed. Wm. Theodore de Bary and Ainslie T. Embree — 1964	*A Syllabus of Japanese Civilization*, by H. Paul Varley — 1968
A Guide to Oriental Classics, ed. Wm. Theodore de Bary and Ainslie T. Embree — 1964	*Chinese Lyricism; Shih Poetry from the Second to the Twelfth Century*, tr. by Burton Watson — 1970

INTRODUCTION TO ORIENTAL CIVILIZATIONS

WM. THEODORE DE BARY, EDITOR

Sources of Japanese Tradition	1958	Paperback ed., 2 vols.	1964
Sources of Indian Tradition	1958	Paperback ed., 2 vols.	1964
Sources of Chinese Tradition	1960	Paperback ed., 2 vols.	1964

COLUMBIA UNIVERSITY PRESS